Pages Book Emporium
1011 Baker St.
Cranbrook, BC V1C 1A6
250-489-3262

Also by Adam McOmber

This New & Poisonous Air: Stories

The
WHITE
FOREST

ADAM McOMBER

A TOUCHSTONE BOOK
PUBLISHED BY SIMON & SCHUSTER
NEW YORK   LONDON   TORONTO   SYDNEY   NEW DELHI

Touchstone
A Division of Simon & Schuster, Inc.
1230 Avenue of the Americas
New York, NY 10020

First Touchstone hardcover edition September 2012

TOUCHSTONE and colophon are registered trademarks of Simon & Schuster, Inc.

For information about special discounts for bulk purchases, please contact Simon & Schuster Special Sales at 1-866-506-1949 or business@simonandschuster.com.

The Simon & Schuster Speakers Bureau can bring authors to your live event. For more information or to book an event contact the Simon & Schuster Speakers Bureau at 1-866-248-3049 or visit our website at www.simonspeakers.com.

Designed by Akasha Archer

Manufactured in the United States of America

10 9 8 7 6 5 4 3 2 1

Library of Congress Cataloging-in-Publication Data

McOmber, Adam.
  The white forest / Adam McOmber.
      p. cm.
1. Upper class—England—Fiction. 2. Children of the rich—Fiction. 3. Triangles (Interpersonal relations)—Fiction. 4. Cults—Fiction. 5. Murder—Fiction. I. Title.
  PS3613.C58645W45 2012
  813'.6—dc23

                                                        2011048720

ISBN 978-1-4516-6425-6
ISBN 978-1-4516-6427-0 (ebook)

The
WHITE
FOREST

CHAPTER 1

———◄••●••►———

Hampstead Heath, 18—

When Nathan Ashe disappeared from the ruined streets of Southwark, I couldn't help but think the horror was, at least in part, my own design. I'd infected him, after all, filled him up with my so-called disease. The rank shadows and gaslight in the human warrens beyond Blackfriars Bridge did the rest. Madeline Lee, my dearest friend, would come to hate me for what I'd done. She said I ruined Nathan because of love, and that infecting him was my way of laying claim to his attentions. I couldn't make her understand how he begged for it, begged me to touch him until he was changed. It wasn't me—Jane Silverlake—he desired. He wanted the Empyrean, that improbable paradise, and I was its doorway. By the end, Nathan was no longer the boy we had adventures with on the Heath nor the young man who went to war in the Crimea. He grew to be half a human being and half some ancient and unnamed thing, and despite my warnings, we were all pulled into his hell, as if by the swift currents of an unseen river.

I can see the three of us there in the Roman ruin of my father's garden. It was a warm day in spring, two months before Nathan's disappearance, and looking back, I realize he was already beginning to lose himself. The ruin was a folly, meant to resemble the baths of Emperor Diocletian, and the broken gods of Rome stared down at us from their high pedestals—regal Apollo with hands and forearms missing and Venus with her face nearly worn away. Maddy and I sat together on the cool terrazzo near the sunken bath, our skirts pooled around us. We were the same age, not yet two and twenty. Maddy tended to be bold where I was circumspect, yet we shared a common affection for Nathan Ashe. He was a year older—aristocratic and lissome—and most importantly, he treated us as something more than girls. The three of us had been friends for years—taking restorative walks on the Heath and making our discussions in the garden. When Nathan began to change, everything was thrown off balance. We lost our careful orbits and began to fall.

In her lap, Maddy held a bouquet of purple comfrey she'd gathered from the outlying wilds. Her dress was a pale yellow with lovely white fox fur trim at the collar. Even her buttons were elegant—carved from ivory. I felt insubstantial beside her, wearing my fawn-colored linen gown and dark sash. A passing stranger might have mistaken me for Maddy's servant or perhaps even a chaperone, present only to ensure nothing untoward happened between the lady and the young man. It's difficult to even picture myself in those days—a mere girl in a plain dress, filled up with longings for things I could never have.

Nathan stood near the cracked bathing pool, which was littered with the remains of winter. Piles of decaying leaves and odd bits of bramble obscured the painted tiles. A lantern casing had fallen into the pool, and Nathan attempted to fish it out, using the tip of his cane. He'd only recently returned to us from the war in Crimea and still sported the red uniform and high jackboots of the Queen's Guard. I could not help but admire his lithe figure as he strained to reach the lantern. He looked every bit the noble son of Lord William Ashe, famed arbiter in parliament, though Nathan was set to prove he did not share his father's appreciation for power—at least not the traditional variety.

Crimea had clearly changed him, fraying some indispensable

part of his consciousness. Since his discharge, Nathan had become involved with what amounted to a cult in Southwark, a gathering of the wealthy sons of London's elite. These lost boys met in the chambers beneath a broken pleasure dome called the Temple of the Lamb, where they were instructed by their spiritual leader, Ariston Day. Day was a foreigner who'd recently appeared on the London scene with all manner of arcane philosophies in tow, and his Temple was our topic that afternoon in the garden.

Miss Anne, Father's servant, brought a steaming pot of Indian tea from the house, but none of us touched it. Maddy and I were too caught up in our concern, and Nathan was oblivious to simple refreshments. As he worked to rescue the stray lantern, he described to us, for the first time, how he wanted to live upon the *bedrock* of the earth—this being Ariston Day's own mantra. "Reaching a spiritual bedrock is the hidden enterprise," Nathan said, a faint breeze playing at his auburn hair. "It's the secret tract to all the world's religions."

Maddy lowered her head, running her fingers over her fox fur collar. Her rosy lips and large expressive eyes appeared less vibrant than usual. "I'm not sure I understand your sudden interest in these foolish ideas," she said.

"It's not meant for you to understand—not yet, at least," he replied. "And the ideas aren't foolish, Maddy. Living on the bedrock elicits a state like death—a perfect state, which is, in fact, eternal life. We can all attain such an existence if we find the right path."

"So you're looking for death?" Maddy asked. "Your adventures in Southwark have turned you morbid, Mr. Ashe."

"Not actual death," he said. "A state *like* death."

"Those are Ariston Day's words, not your own," she replied. "It's not a Temple he's created down there. It's—I don't even know what to call it—a pit where good people get lost."

Nathan finally succeeded in hooking the tip of his cane through the loop atop the brass casing of the lantern. He slowly pulled the rusted thing free from the bramble and deposited it neatly at his feet, looking proud, as though he'd accomplished something of merit. "Your father really should have this place cleaned up, Jane," he said.

"It's one thing to have a folly and quite another to make your guests feel as though all of Rome is going to come toppling down on their heads."

"Father is—distracted," I said. This was of course an understatement, as both Nathan and Maddy were well aware. My father had cut our family off from London's social line after the death of my mother, years before, and I'd been largely a recluse in our decaying house until my friends came into my life.

Forked shadows of oak branches creased the brows of the stone gods that surrounded us, mirroring the troubled look on Maddy's face. She said, "Why don't you return to telling us how you're going to avoid getting yourself murdered down there in wretched South-wark, Nathan?" I could see she wasn't going to give up on her inquisition of him, and though I took exception to her willful approach, I agreed with her intent. I wanted to know more about Nathan's experiences at the Temple as well. He'd always had an interest in spiritism, ethereal planes, and the like—such curiosity being provoked by his mother's frequent séances and my own unnatural abilities, which I'd shared with him. But joining Ariston Day and the other young men at the Temple of the Lamb revealed a far more serious commitment. I couldn't comprehend Nathan's talk about the spiritual bedrock any more than Maddy, but I knew from firsthand experience how easily our Nathan could be affected by the promise of transcendence.

"I wouldn't expect any response from you other than dismay, Maddy," Nathan said. "You're afraid of every little thing. If we're being honest, you're even afraid of Jane."

"I am *not*," she said. "Jane, you don't think I'm afraid of you, do you?"

I smiled at her, letting her know things were fine between us. "You have your moments, dear."

She laid the bouquet of wildflowers on the stone floor of the ruin and looked sternly at Nathan. "I think fear is an absolutely appropriate response to Ariston Day. Since you've been crossing Blackfriars Bridge you've changed, Nathan. And not for the better. Now comes all this talk of death."

"I merely know my purpose," Nathan said.

"What *is* your purpose?" Maddy asked. "Define it. Stop being so cryptic."

"You know I can't do that," he said, then looked to me. "Jane, why don't you speak up? Talk some sense into Maddy."

I found I couldn't respond. When the two of them argued, I became even more timid. Maddy said my quiet manner made me generally less attractive and was sometimes even off-putting. "Girls should be demure, Jane," she advised, "but there are times when I see you from across a room, and I think you might have turned to stone. I'm loath to sound conventional, but we must at least *sometimes* consider how we are perceived by prospective suitors."

Such concerns as my comportment had gone by the wayside when Nathan's involvement with the Temple came to our attention. Maddy and I were privy to precious few details about Ariston Day and his rituals, but as far as I could gather, Day was a charismatic who spouted half-formed theories about a return to the original Paradise—his so-called bedrock—that lay beneath the scrim of common reality. He promised his followers that if they continued to provide support, he would help them find the entrance to that Paradise. Day was a dangerous creature, the type of worm who worked his way into minds already weakened by boredom and alcohol, and I worried that his hold on Nathan was only growing stronger.

"Wouldn't it be better to simply live freely," I suggested to Nathan finally, "away from any sort of rocks?" I tended to side with Maddy in our discussions, as solidarity put her at ease.

Nathan came closer and took my hand. I found his touch all too hot, and he smelled of the awful glue factory near the Temple of the Lamb. "We *are* free," he said. "But with the help of Ariston Day, we could be so much more. We could find the bedrock and live together like this—the three of us—forever. Jane, I tell you, Day would be fascinated by all the things you can do, your secret talents. I believe he could even help us achieve the Empyrean."

I pulled my hand away. "I don't want to start talking about the Empyrean again."

"Please, let's not," Maddy said. There was fear in her voice, real fear. Nathan was right; my closest friend, more often than not, found me unnerving.

"That business is finished," I said. "It has to be."

"I'm only saying that Ariston Day might be able to help you, Jane," Nathan said. "He knows so many things."

"I'm sure I'll be fine without his help."

Nathan released my hand and walked toward the edge of the folly, pausing to look toward the southern woods. Afternoon was quickly slipping into evening, and the whole sky had turned the color of granite. I closed my eyes and listened to the wind stir the branches of the budding oaks, trying to calm myself. Beneath the blossoms of spring, I could still smell winter. Nathan would not be deterred. Soon he'd insist on experimenting with the Empyrean again, and I wondered if I'd let him.

We'd previously put our explorations aside after the terrible events that occurred before Nathan left for the Crimea—events that had changed us all. I certainly didn't want the likes of Ariston Day probing those memories, nor did I like it when Nathan talked about my *abilities* in the presence of Maddy. She was apt to start calling me a witch again. There'd been a time, shortly after I'd revealed my talent to them, when Maddy carried the *Malleus Maleficarum*, a hoary medieval text otherwise known as the "Hammer of Witches," that was meant to help inquisitors suss out and dispose of so-called unnaturals. When I told her I took offense, she replied that the book had nothing to do with me or my "afflictions." Rather, it was research for a series of historical daguerreotypes she intended to make. I wasn't certain about Maddy's explanation. For weeks after her initial experience with my talent, she'd adopted an air of mistrust in my presence. I didn't think she wanted to go as far as tying me to a stake, though the looks she gave me were, at times, as searing as any fire.

It was clear that both of my friends misunderstood me. I wasn't a witch meant for burning, nor was I precisely the doorway Nathan imagined. I had no lock that could be picked. If anything, I was the landscape behind the door, and even on that day in the ruin, I was still only beginning to comprehend my own flora and fauna.

"We should go for a walk on the Heath," I said quietly. "It might clear our heads."

"Jane's right," Maddy said. "Let's forget all this business about Ariston Day—at least for a while."

"I don't want to walk," Nathan said. He took a cigarette from the silver case he kept in his uniform jacket. "I'm sorry, girls. Maybe another time." He struck a match on Mercury's pedestal and lit the cigarette while gazing out across the unkempt garden. The more time Nathan spent at the Temple of the Lamb, the quicker he slipped into such bouts of melancholy. There was nothing Maddy or I could do to wrest him from these moods, so we fell silent there among the broken gods.

The Heath remained a memory of younger days when our friendship was still elegant—not yet fettered by jealousies or thoughts of unnatural forces. The three of us had forged our bond walking those houseless heights beneath the great marble skies, watching storm-dark clouds cast shadows on the tall grass. We passed through forests of hawthorn and birch that rose above purple bogs and walked fields lush with wild iris and lavender. Hampstead Heath was like a chapel, serene and godly, and I loved the feeling of the wind burning my cheeks as it swept down over the hills. When I walked there, I felt the poetry of Keats and Coleridge clinging to its winding paths. But such poetry was nothing compared to the presence of my friends. Our walks provided a sense of stability and comfort that I hadn't felt since before my mother died. When I was with Maddy and Nathan, I was no longer the lonesome girl lurking in shadows. Instead, I imagined I belonged. I could laugh and even felt that I might one day fall in love.

It was Maddy who'd rescued me from obscurity. Her family had been driven from central London, where they'd lived in the fashionable area of Mayfair, and they settled at the edge of Hampstead Heath not far from where I lived. She accompanied her father on his first visit to our home, called Stoke Morrow, as he sought legal advice from my own father. I remember watching Maddy from the dark recesses of the stairwell on that long-ago day. She was a petite girl in a honey-colored dress with an impressively complicated braid in her hair. To others, she appeared to be a displaced society girl, charming and quick with wit, but I would come to know her secret life. Her beauty was of her own invention. She drank a glass of vinegar mixed with honey once a week to banish the color from her skin and darkened her hair to a near black with silver nitrate from her father's daguerreotype studio. Her wish was to become the opposite of all the simple, sunny girls who'd rejected her after her father was ousted from the London Society of Art for a series of unsavory daguerreotypes. Perhaps this will toward difference was why she chose me as her friend. I was as far from a society girl as one could get.

She'd moved about our foyer slowly, studying Father's collection of oil paintings—all of them odd and varied depictions of the Holy Ghost. To me, she seemed impossibly fresh and alive, and I held my breath, not wanting to hear her scream if she mistook me for a spirit. But when her gaze finally fell upon me, Maddy did not seem taken aback. Her features softened, and rather than moving away, she stepped toward me. The smell of lilacs that wafted from her made me realize all the more how much I smelled like dust.

It was later, as we walked in the garden, that Maddy said something marvelous; she declared that we were going to be *companions*. "We're so clearly meant for that," she said. "Both of us are all alone out here in this wilderness. I had so many friends in the city, Jane, but out here, well, out here there's only you."

I wondered if I detected a slight bitterness in her voice, and I considered, for a moment, whether Madeline Lee might feel that she was "settling." In all honesty, I didn't care. I'd never had a proper friend before. I'd never even imagined that I *could* have one, and I wasn't going to lose my chance. Though we were only fifteen at the time, Maddy seemed a woman of the world, and I could think of nothing finer than remaining constantly in her presence.

Nathan Ashe joined our little group soon after, a graceful creature of myth who'd ventured out of the tangled woods. He was a wealthy boy with manners such as I had never seen who played equally at games of war and more mystical enterprises. It was Maddy who pulled him in. She was charming where I was not. She was the one who first invited Nathan to take a walk with us on the Heath, where he lived in a great Tudor mansion, called Ashe High House. To my astonishment, Nathan took a liking to *both* of us and even began visiting Stoke Morrow of his own accord. After our first charmed walk together, I never wanted to be lonely Jane Silverlake lost in her manor house again. I wanted to be always with my new friends. I imagined that the three of us might even make a little cottage of our own one day in the hills beyond the Heath. Nathan would hunt and Maddy and I would make a garden. We'd have everything we needed.

Such memories of my naïveté are painful even now.

Nathan left us there in the ruin that spring evening after our discussion of Ariston Day's Temple, cigarette smoke trailing behind him as he made his way toward the path that led through the southern woods. I followed him with my gaze for as long as I could, watching as his red uniform coat dimmed and finally disappeared in the shadows of the trees. The air was becoming cool as dew set in, and I felt my consciousness drifting, mingling with the old gods. I wondered about Nathan and the trouble he was involving himself in at the Temple of the Lamb. I wondered about Maddy too—what would become of her should anything happen to him?

"We have to do something, Jane," she said quietly behind me. There was a new desperation in her voice.

"What do you suggest?" I asked.

"Is tying him to a heavy piece of furniture out of the question?"

I closed my eyes, taking a deep breath of spring air. "I don't know, Maddy," I said finally. "Do you really think we could catch him?"

CHAPTER 2

In the weeks after Nathan disappeared from the Temple of the Lamb, Maddy fell into a depression, and I became lost in a state of strife unlike any I'd ever known. My uncanny talent, which had possessed me since my mother's death, was stirred into a frenzy. I experienced odd sensations at every turn, and no matter how much concentration I applied, I could not quell the clamoring. Maddy and I no longer took pleasure in walking the bright arcades at Regent Street, arms linked and skirts rustling. No longer did we enjoy the yellow warmth of shop windows or the shining surfaces of black carriages as they passed by on fog-damp streets. Everywhere, we heard the desperate nature of Nathan's case, and we wondered what we might have done to save him.

Maddy couldn't make it any farther than Shaftsbury one dark afternoon as we attempted a stroll through fashionable St. Giles. Cinders rained from a darkening sky, and newsboys, caked in brick-colored mud, chanted their terrible mass: *two weeks out and still no sign—Inspector Vidocq confounded—Is Nathan Ashe in the river?—Will it be murder in Southwark?* We were near the poulter's stalls, where plucked chickens were displayed on benches, smooth flesh glowing beneath flaring jets of gas. We'd intended to visit the shop called Indigo to see a line of afternoon dresses known as the New Tran-

scendent, a title that brought to mind shimmering gauze and a pro-
fusion of blossoms, which Maddy, at one time, wouldn't have dared
to miss. She leaned against the filthy wheel of a cart selling oranges
and pomegranates while the fruit monger, a man with boils, leered at
her. "Make the newsboys stop, Jane," she said. "I can't hear any more
about poor Nathan."

I glared at the nearest boy, a large child in a ruined hat from the
previous century. "You're making my friend sick," I said. It pleased
me to protect Maddy so. In the shadow of a passing hackney-coach,
the newsboy's face became a dark idol, impenetrable and streaked
with ages of dirt. His mouth opened, and though I couldn't hear
his reply over the clatter of the coach, I could *feel* its meaning. Two
weeks out and no sign: Nathan Ashe, our dearest friend, was likely
dead or worse.

Though Nathan had become a figure of questionable character
due to his affiliations with the Temple, the mystery of his disappearance was something of a local sensation because of his father's
prominence. Men discussed the case in such establishments as The
Unicorn, a weather-stained coffee house where Nathan himself had
once spent hours alone, smoking and pretending to contemplate the
pastorals of Barrett Browning. These idle men drank black Italian
coffee from bone china cups and sifted through discrepancies that
might prove to be clues. Why, for instance, hadn't Nathan taken a
pint at his regular spot, the Silver Horne, before going to the Temple
of the Lamb on the evening of his disappearance? And why was he
seen with a male nymph in Southwark—a petite and foreign-looking
youth?

Outside the coffee house, rent girls and other lowborn ephemera
regarded the details of Nathan's face inked on posters that fluttered
from black iron lampposts—his high pale cheekbones, architectural
brow, and eyes that seemed, even on paper, like holes that lead to a
system of tunnels in the earth. Nathan Ashe was becoming more
myth than man, and everyone in London was touching him, running
their fingers over the contours of his absent body. They knew his list
of qualities. He was the well-born son of Lord William Ashe. He'd

been a soldier in Lord Wellington's brigade in the Crimea and was adept at archery and fond of pistols. He possessed a kind of ethereal Saxon beauty, and when he entered a room, those present—no matter how they felt about him socially—paused to admire his stature. Nathan disliked the law and abhorred his father's House of Lords. He was a free spirit who read poetry and, on more than one occasion, was found curled on a doorstep after a drunken night at the Silver Horne. But none who could make such a list knew the true Nathan Ashe that Maddy and I came to know. He was filled with the sort of fret and despair that needed tending. At the same time, he acted as though we were his equals, taking us on adventures most would have considered too dangerous for young women. We were the ones who truly loved him, and yet we too were left without him.

After Maddy had composed herself at the fruit cart near Shaftsbury, we managed to continue our walk, passing dress shops and smoking salons in St. Giles with barely a glance as we attempted to avoid coming within earshot of another newsboy. We ducked into one of Maddy's favorite tea shops, the Queen's Host, a setting that normally provided quiet respite in the busy shopping district. The interior was decked in white Italian marble and gold trim. China cabinets lined the wall, displaying saucers and cups painted with scenes of waterfalls and gilded pine forests. Maddy had great appreciation for the linen-clothed tables that were placed at discreet distances, so one could keep conversations private.

Only a handful of customers were in the Queen's Host that day, and there, sitting near the window over an untouched cup of Darjeeling, was Pascal Paget, Maddy's French ward. Though younger by a few years, Pascal had become a kind of confidant for Nathan, Maddy, and me. She tensed at the sight of him now though, as recent events had altered her opinion of him. "Did you know *he* would be here, Jane?" she asked.

"Of course not," I said.

"I want to leave."

"You can't keep avoiding him," I said. "We'll go and say hello." I gave her a slight push to start her moving across the white marble floor.

The story of their friendship and Pascal's eventual dependence on Maddy for both room and board was straightforward enough. Maddy first made his acquaintance outside a small French-style café near Charing Cross. He'd been using a piece of charcoal to draw a picture of a street in the walled city of Nimes where white chickens wandered on cobblestone and irises made silent observance from tilted window boxes. She'd found his long artist's hair and wistful manner so picturesque she simply had to stop and speak with him.

One of Maddy's greatest gifts was that she could seemingly extract the heart and history of a common stranger using only a modicum of effort. People often lost their guard in the beguilement of her presence and spilled forth stories that they would have hesitated to tell even a boon companion. Pascal was no exception, and soon enough, Maddy was sitting next to him at his easel, and he was telling her how he'd lost his love in France and had come to London in order to find the boy again.

Maddy prided herself in being as progressive as her father, and she acted as if it didn't surprise her that Pascal's *interest d'amore* was a young man instead of a young woman. She elegantly crossed her legs at the ankle, took a sip of her demitasse, and told him in no uncertain terms that he must tell her *everything*.

Pascal had met his beloved friend, Alexander Hartford, at the *Musée du Vieux* in the French city of Nimes. Alexander was a student from America, son of a wealthy shipping magnate, who was making a study of medieval art as a way toward earning his degree. The boys struck up a conversation in front of a painting called *Sleep and Death* in which two dark-haired youths lay on a bed, entangled in each other's arms. Sheets were twisted into a hectic landscape, and the figures in the painting appeared as though they were not brothers, as stated in the myth, but lovers.

"Isn't it interesting that we supposed Christians are often drawn to pagan imagery?" Alexander said to Pascal. "It seems that a show-ing of a god—any god—will stimulate."

"What sort of stimulation should this produce?" Pascal asked, pointing toward the painting of *Sleep and Death.*

"That depends on your disposition, I suppose," Alexander said.

Pascal gave him a sheepish smile. "Sleep and Death appeal to me greatly."

"Which of them do you imagine yourself to be?" Alexander asked, trying for an academic tone and drawing closer to Pascal in the process.

The French boy took a moment to look at the two shirtless youths in their frenzy of bedclothes. "I'm not sure. They seem very much alike—nearly twins."

"You must be Sleep, then," Alexander said. "Sleep is, at times, in-decisive. Death, however, always knows his aim and purpose."

During the days that followed, the boys became fast friends, and a feeling rose between them, the sort of emotion that triumphs over dust. They walked arm in arm down the narrow streets of Nimes, drinking red wine in midnight cafés, and spending nights together in small, rented rooms, reenacting the scene of *Sleep and Death.* What came between them was Ariston Day himself. Alexander found a pamphlet, tucked into a street corner kiosk, promising en-lightenment. The pamphlet called for young men of intelligence and means to come to London and gather at a hall called the Temple of the Lamb, where a great man would provide means to experience what they'd only heard about in myth. "The winds of the cosmos will blow through your very soul," the pamphlet read. "And your heart will become the gateway to a new Paradise." As a student of theology, Alexander found he could not resist such a calling; he came to the Temple to see if true enlightenment could be achieved, and Pascal followed him there to London, hoping to rekindle what they'd once had. He was, in fact, the puckish nymph mentioned as being seen with Nathan in Southwark on the night of the disappearance.

*　　*　　*

After the formalities of greeting in the Queen's Host, Pascal ventured, once again, into the story of Nathan's final night. He seemed to believe that the very act of repeating the tale provided penance for his imagined sins. I tried to signal him with my eyes that it was an inopportune moment to tell the story, with Maddy in such a fragile state, but Pascal was too agitated to pay me any mind.

"How do I explain it in English?" he said, searching the room, never looking at us directly. "I feel I am *en purgatoire*, going over that night in my mind, wondering what I might have done differently." He adjusted the cuff of his plum-colored suit—a brazen garment brought from France where, he assured us, everyone believed meringue and alabaster were colors of a hopeful future. Pascal had a lovely face, so delicate and soft that I found myself often wanting to touch his cheek and offer kindness.

"Master Nathan was behaving so strangely," Pascal continued. "He was complaining that his hand had gone numb and then his leg, so I decided to remain at his side. But just before whatever theatrical event they had planned for the evening was about to commence, I was escorted out of the Temple by two rough boys—two savages— who said it had been decreed that I didn't have what it took to be a Fetch. I was no longer welcome."

"Fetches," Maddy said, the flesh around her eyes red from her tears. "I don't think I can hear another word about them."

Fetches were what the followers of Ariston Day called themselves, a name that I gathered alluded to a double-self or doppelgänger. Nathan had been a Fetch since his return from the Crimean War.

Pascal said, "It doesn't matter what you call them, mademoiselle. It's all a foolish game. I tried to get the attention of Alexander as I was being dragged out, but he wouldn't come to my aid. He's become so brutish, like all the rest of them. And then I looked for Nathan, and he was nowhere to be found. Soon enough I was on the street, staring up at the plume of yellow smoke rising from the awful Southwark glue factory and wondering how I would get home to Hampstead."

Pascal seemed so small and helpless there in the busy tea shop.

He had the dark appearance of the French, black hair and shadowed eyes, and he smelled of the wilting chrysanthemum he wore in his lapel. His hands, clasped and resting on the table, looked as though they were made of fragile porcelain.

"Nathan has a way of escaping when he wants to," I said, attempting comfort. "It isn't your fault, Pascal dear."

"Don't defend him, Jane," Maddy snapped. Her face was drawn, and her dark hair was wound tightly in a braided bun, a glittering pin stabbed through its center. "If Pascal and his beloved Alexander hadn't dragged Nathan down to Southwark in the first place—if they hadn't indoctrinated him into that unholy theater, that cult—then we'd all be here, safe."

Pascal nearly crumbled at her words. As for a rebuttal, he could only muster, "Alexander is not my beloved. He will no longer even speak to me. He says if I cannot be a Fetch with him, he has no use for me."

I was particularly sensitive when it came to Alexander Hartford, as I knew how much Pascal cared for him. "Alexander will come around," I said. "And Nathan is his own man. These were all his choices. We shall simply have to wait for news."

My calm was a facade that I feared would crack at the slightest jarring. I was, perhaps, more worried about Nathan than anyone else because I knew the extent to which our experiments with my abilities had exposed him to unnatural forces, making him susceptible to their influences. I felt nearly as culpable as Ariston Day for leading him astray. And then there was also the last terrible evening Nathan spent with Maddy and me. So much had happened there in the southern woods on that final night. I only half-remembered most of those events, and I wasn't ready to consider my own actions. Not yet.

I ordered a cup of Chinese tea for Maddy and me, to soothe our nerves. When the host returned, she brought not only the tea but also a newspaper neatly folded on a tray. Pascal had apparently requested the paper before our arrival. It seemed even in the Queen's Host, Maddy and I couldn't escape the tangle of London ink. At least the paper was the *Herald*, which primarily printed the truth about Nathan's case. The *Magnet* and the *Athenaeum*, two lesser rags, claimed to provide interviews with so called intimates, though most such interviews proved to be creative pieces of fiction. Nathan had very few intimates, after all. His disposition prevented such things. The *Herald* came closest to fact, describing fragmentary reports of the events leading up to Nathan's disappearance.

Night workers from the Southwark glue factory gave testimony as to having seen Nathan Ashe enter the Temple of the Lamb on the evening of June 16, but none could likewise attest to seeing him leave. The Temple, as the *Herald* reported, was a defunct pleasure dome on the docks of the Thames and home to a sprawling, disreputable tavern as well as a recently born sect known as the Theater of Provocation. Little was understood about this "theater" other than that it was open only to select members, and its proprietor, Ariston Day, was fond of pulling the rebellious sons of wealthy and prominent families into his fold. It was there that Day showed them what one of the youths described as "new geometries with which to measure the earth."

These young men, like Nathan, wanted to dissolve their bond to tradition and the confines of rational human experience. Mr. Day reportedly had interests in dream theory as well as what was being called "immersive reality," in which a subject's mind was manipulated in a false environment for the possibility of reaching an ecstatic state, an opening of the soul.

Before Nathan was fully indoctrinated into the theater and began refusing to divulge information about its secret rituals, he told us some of Day's theories. "Mr. Day says the soul of London is diseased like a body can become diseased, and one day we Fetches will be the ones to heal it."

"That sounds rather ominous," Maddy said.

"Not at all," Nathan replied. "It's a pure thought—maybe the only pure thought in the whole city."

"How does one go about *curing* a city?" I asked.

Nathan smiled the big rakish smile I was accustomed to, but there was something different this time, as if an edge had broken off of it.

"The only way to cure a city," he said, "is to make it *stop* being a city."

"And what do you expect that to look like?" Maddy asked.

"A garden," Nathan said, "untouched by human hands."

Beyond descriptions of Nathan's final evening, the *Herald* also reported the details of the search through the slums of Southwark conducted by the aging Inspector Vidocq, cofounder of Scotland Yard and famed model for the rational detective in the stories of the American writer Edgar Allan Poe. Vidocq, a dominating presence and an old friend of Nathan's father, Lord William Ashe, had come out of retirement to pursue the case. Before leaving his home in Paris, he was said to have gone to the nave of Saint-Denys du Saint-Sacrement and prayed to St. Simeon, patron of detectives, for strength and wisdom. But when he'd arrived in London he found himself shaken by our Babylon. Our city proved a language untranslatable.

Reporters documented Vidocq's comings and goings across the city as he questioned owners of pubs and shops. He was said to be surprisingly broad shouldered for one so old and wore a black coat and a dark hat, not adhering to the frivolous styles of France that Pascal described. His face was graven and white, and he had nearly colorless eyes. His air was of one who gazed at life through a lens of death, and Maddy told me we needed to take care, lest he discover the secret compartments in Nathan's character. She was adamant that only she and I should know the true Nathan. As always, it seemed she wanted to keep our boy's heart in a treasury box, untouched and free from harm.

We were halfway through tea at the Queen's Host when Maddy announced abruptly that she needed to leave. She seemed panicked, almost knocking her cup from its saucer as she stood. I glanced around the room, hoping to discover what had disturbed her but found nothing out of the ordinary.

"What is it, Maddy?" I asked in a low voice.

She could barely look at me. "It's difficult to explain. I can't keep my memories in check. The past has come untethered from its moorings and floats into view at unpredictable moments. I suddenly remembered sitting here at this very table with you and Nathan. We'd been to the Zoological Garden in Regent's Park to see the new hippopotamus on display. Do you recall that day, Jane?"

"Of course," I said.

"We watched the zookeeper feed porridge to the hippo with a tiny spoon. Nathan adored the hippo. He was going to ask if he might be permitted to feed it himself on our next visit, and I made some joke at his expense and—" There were tears in her eyes. "Can you ride back to the Heath with your father, Jane?" she asked. "He's still at his offices, isn't he? I'm afraid—I'm afraid I need to be alone."

"Of course," I said. "I'll see you tomorrow. I'll help you write a few correspondences."

Pascal stood as she left, making a polite half-bow. When she was gone, he resumed his seat and took a quiet sip of tea. "Mademoiselle hates me," he said. "She thinks all of this is my fault."

"Rest assured it's not," I said.

"Then who is to blame? What possibly could have happened to Master Nathan?"

I shook my head and looked at the wilted black tea leaves at the bottom of my bone-colored cup, as if they might provide an answer.

"There's something I need to tell you, Jane," Pascal said. "Something I've remembered in my sifting through that evening's events. I didn't want to say anything in front of Madeline because I thought it might disturb her."

"Then why tell *me*?"

"Because you don't shy away from strange things," he said. "One might even say they are part of your nature."

I sighed. Though Pascal was unaware of my particular abilities, the boy knew me well enough. "Go ahead, then."

He pushed his tea aside, leaned close, and said, "On the night he disappeared, Nathan told me that Ariston Day had helped him come to some new understanding about a place called the Empyrean."

"Ariston Day?" I said.

"That's right. You've turned pale, Jane. Is everything all right?"

I assured Pascal I was fine, though I felt anything but. Nathan had told Ariston Day about the Empyrean, even though I'd explicitly asked him not to. I did not want my secrets exposed. I felt hurt, but more than that I felt afraid—for reasons I didn't fully understand.

"Please continue," I said, trying to mask my emotions.

"I'd never heard him talk about it before," Pascal said, "but that night, Nathan said the word with such reverence—*Empyrean*—as if it was a holy place. When I asked him to tell me more, he became guarded. He said one day I would understand the importance of the Empyrean. We all would. That's what Ariston Day claimed, at least. And then he left me, following the other Fetches deeper into the chambers beneath the Temple. Do you know what he meant, Jane? It's a religious term, isn't it? Something from the Middle Ages? I know I've heard it before."

"Pascal, I—"

"The priest at my parents' church used to lecture about the old customs and beliefs. I think he might have mentioned that word."

I steadied myself, looking directly into Pascal's dark eyes. I could hear Nathan's voice in my head, solemnly listing the seven levels of the medieval Heaven as he attempted to explain my talent: "There's the Faerie, Ethereal, Olympian, Fiery, Firmament, Aqueous, and most importantly, the Empyrean, Jane. That's where the saints and the angels are said to live. A place of purity and stillness." I told him I didn't care for such cosmologies. They were nothing more than children's stories. But Nathan persisted. "You're hedging, Jane. You believe in all this more than you let on. You have to. You've seen it."

I pulled myself away from that memory and directed my attention again toward Pascal. "Nathan said so many odd things before he disappeared. I'm sure he was merely spouting more of Day's rubbish." I lied because telling the truth would make things worse for Pascal. Knowledge of the Empyrean spread through one's body like an infection. I didn't want that for him. In many ways, Pascal was like a child to us. We all did our best to take care of him because he was alone in London, and Alexander had broken his heart.

After Pascal's mention of the Empyrean, I found I couldn't continue to sit in the Queen's Host and act like everything was fine. I excused myself, saying I had to catch my father before he left his offices.

"You aren't angry with me too, are you, Jane?" he asked.

"Never, dear," I said.

By the time I opened the tea shop door to leave, I could barely breathe, wondering why on earth Nathan had been foolish enough to divulge our secrets to Day. Nathan was so unpredictable near the end. I wondered too who else he'd told. Perhaps it was due to my distracted state there on the doorstep of the Queen's Host that I did not shun the newsboy who approached me. He was small and filthy haired, and he rudely shoved an equally filthy newspaper into my hands. It was a copy of the *Illustrated Penny*, the worst of the rags, and rather than push back, I paid him and opened its pages.

The *Penny* was printed for illiterates and told the news entirely in pictures. In this particular issue, a series of images purported to show the last moments before Nathan's disappearance. Thick ink lines conjured the sullen streets of Southwark and the domed turrets at the Temple of the Lamb. In the first frame, Nathan bid farewell to a group of nefarious-looking young men, presumably the Fetches of Ariston Day. Hollow-cheeked and grim, the boys made knowing expressions as they watched Nathan stumble down the empty cobblestone. The smoke from the glue factory consumed him, turning him into a living shadow.

He passed through pools of gaslight, moving toward the Thames, which appeared as a black vein in the landscape. Nathan seemed drunk or otherwise of altered consciousness, leaning too heavily on his walking stick. He paused at a railing above the water to check his clock. In doing so, he lost his footing.

His expression as he fell toward the rushing current of the Thames was exaggerated—mouth a wide zero, eyes flat circles, and yet the artist captured enough of the actual sharp edges of Nathan Ashe to make my heart quicken.

Nathan's body was tossed along in the inky depths, sweeping past ancient debris long sunk in the river. The artifacts were nothing more than a scribble on the page, but I found my imagination presenting me with specific objects over which Nathan floated—the smooth head of a Roman god, a medieval cross burned in the great London fire, a carriage wheel, a coin box, an ax handle, and a rotted psalter with pages open and undulating. Soon, in my mind, the objects became fabled things lost beneath the waters: whole sunken Saxon villages, forests lying flat, a phalanx of dead Roman soldiers still in armor. There were even the bones of a monster. Nathan floated gently through its rib cage, and shadows of bone caressed him.

The next image was sun-washed and showed Nathan limp and soaking on a wooded shore. He was nowhere near London. The Thames had carried him to some outer environ, but this was not Dartford or even Gravesend. This was a place of fernlike trees and massive erect stones.

Faces hovered among the tree trunks—not precisely human, as their eyes were too large and their mouths were lipless and cruel. The creatures regarded him with desire. It was clear he could not escape them. There was nowhere to go. And so Nathan crouched on the beach, waiting as the creatures disgorged themselves from their hiding places.

I closed the newspaper but could not force the image from my mind—beautiful Nathan in his French-cut suit, set upon by beasts. What they wanted from him, I didn't know. But certainly they would take him.

I touched my own face, felt the coolness of my cheek. I'd shed no tears, standing there at the entrance to the Queen's Host. Instead, my expression had hardened with worry. The fantasy in the *Penny* was not beyond my imagining. I was concerned, in fact, that such a scene might be closer to the truth than the illustrators could possibly know.

Only Nathan and Maddy knew my secret. I was familiar with realms of the unnatural, for I myself was an unnatural. Not a monster in appearance; I looked like other young women, though perhaps not as primped and manicured. But I wasn't the same as other girls. My friends believed I was sick or gifted. Either way, I was unfortunate. Something entirely new upon the earth.

CHAPTER 3

I should take a moment to explain myself and the beginnings of what Nathan called my "talent" and others, my "disease." I must start with my mother, as her death was the measure of my loss and the origin of my strangeness. I was only six when the earth took her on the Heath near Parliament Hill. On that day, she'd been walking along an outcropping of shale that had deep fissures in the stone. Her dogs had wandered there to hunt for voles and snakes, and she followed, pulling her cloak against the chill of the morning, careful to avoid stepping in the black fissures. The sky was a pall of white, and beyond the shale, grass shifted, as if moved by some unseen body. Mother told me she'd attempted to distract herself from the eerie scene by making lists of flowers she'd seen on the Heath: maiden pink and feverfew, harebell and yarrow. She'd made a list of guests she wanted to invite to the festival of St. Dunstan's Day and imagined ink drawings of their likenesses decorating the invitations. Soon each guest had a flower for a face. Her cousin was a marigold; her aunt, a death lily; and my father was the red bloom of the pomegranate tree.

She was pulled from these reveries by a sound rising from the fissures in the earth, an old voice trying to sing, and there was a smell that she later described as the cloyingly sweet scent of another world. The sweetness made her feel heavy, as if she were sinking into the stone, and when the dogs grew weak, Mother knew she had to gather herself. She carried the vizsla back to Stoke Morrow with the spitz lagging behind, and eventually she fell to her knees in the foyer, putting her face on the cool flagstone, calling for Father.

I stood in the entryway and watched as he took her into his arms, as if her body had no weight. He brought her to the sofa in the Clock Parlor, where his collection of some twenty clocks kept time. I followed, hovering near Father's side as he covered Mother with a quilt, watching as her skin turned a terrible shade of cornflower. When she began raving, she told us the fissures in the earth had stony teeth. These deep holes had been looking to devour her, she said.

The expression on Father's face went from confusion to alarm as he realized his wife had lost her sense. Before he could take me to the maids, Mother grabbed my wrist so tightly it hurt.

"Jane," she said. "Come close now." She drew me forward until my face was nearly touching her own. This gesture was as much a surprise as anything, because Mother was known for keeping herself at some remove. In many ways, she was a mystery, rarely showing emotion and never coming close.

There in the parlor, I could smell the earthiness of her breath as she told me that a part of her remained in the stomach of the stone out in the field of shale. There was a world down there that wasn't anything like ours, and she was damned for seeing that place.

I kissed her cold hand and held back tears. I wanted to beg her to stop talking, but she was my mother, and I knew I had to listen. I let myself weep beside her as she repeated over and over again that I must never be swallowed and that there were *two* worlds. I must be vigilant to ensure I remained in this one. Going to the other world would be the end of me.

I made no sense of her warning. I knew only that a woman could leave the house her normal self and then return a few hours later a lunatic. The earth must have been a cold king to do a thing like that.

Mother resumed an expression of clarity shortly before I was led away. She looked into my eyes and said, "Has the Lady of Flowers come for me, Jane? Do you see her at the door?"

I turned toward the parlor door and saw no one. "Who is the Lady of Flowers?" I asked.

Mother barely had enough strength to answer. "She's there, blooming in the darkness, silent and waiting—"

Before I could ask Mother to explain further, the maids hurried me to my room and gave me a sip of laudanum tea to help me sleep. They tucked me into my feather bed, and I dreamed Mother's body bloomed with mouths that drifted across the surface of her skin, moving to the vasculations of her heart. I found a garden deep inside her, a second Earth, hoary and white, with trees made of tusk and unmoving streams of bleached paper pulp. Moonlike blossoms glowed in the underbrush. All that whiteness terrified me, as it was the color of absence, the color of abandonment. Even in the dream I knew Mother was leaving me, and I sensed there were creatures waiting among the trees, creatures I could not see. I dreamed of the white forest and the invisible creatures night after night, though I was never able to explore that place, only to look, as if it was a picture painted on the walls of my mind.

A comet appeared in the sky above Stoke Morrow shortly after my mother's death, and Father took me into the garden to see it. He said the spray of its tail made it look like an Egyptian eye staring down on us, and he told me bitterly that the Egyptians had been correct about their gods. "Gods are animals, Jane. A jackal, a hawk, a common house cat, and like animals, they hunt and sleep and kill, never conscious of their own cruelty."

And in that moment, I was taken again by a vision of the white forest from my dream. I had a sense that the creatures that waited for me behind the trees were animal in nature, and Father's statements made me wonder if somehow they might also be gods. I continued to dwell on the image, and though it was clear enough in my mind, I did not know what any of it might mean.

It was my grief and my vision of the pale forest that opened me to what Nathan would later call my "talent." After the death of my mother, I was changed. I no longer cared for girlish things—my glass house filled with velvet moths or my family of Austrian puppets with amber-colored eyes. I didn't cry when my father loaded our carriage with both his trunks, intending to leave me in the care of the maids as he embarked on a curative tour of the walled city of Bath. By then, he was already absent, barely acknowledging me when he passed me in the hall. Mother's death had driven him into a state of willed unconsciousness. The expression on his face said that the universe was not a mystery worth solving. Life was without plot. Better to forget. Better to fall asleep.

As he boarded his carriage for Bath, I stood watching, with my hands folded in front of me like some penitent anchoress, and I was aware that something was happening inside my body. Mother's death might have driven Father to sleep, but it had the opposite effect on me. For the first time, I felt that I was truly *awake*. It was as though her passing had torn open the very cells of my body, causing an ache like I'd never known. These cells were now pouring forth some strange material, giving birth to a new Jane Silverlake who I did not yet fully comprehend.

In the days of isolation that followed Father's departure, I became preoccupied with the changes that were overtaking me. I often felt a subtle pressure building in my chest and caught glimpses of shadows moving at the corners of my vision, but when I turned to look, nothing was there. At the same time that these experiences were occurring, I was thinking a great deal about Mother's Lady of Flowers, wondering at her identity. I paid special attention to the flowers in Father's gardens, watching through the rippled window glass of the library to see if the Lady might appear among the roses and daffodils. But no such figure came, and soon enough I grew tired of waiting.

I went to Mother's dressing room, hoping to find answers there. It was a quiet place with damask drapes drawn to keep the shadows in. I was forbidden to go into the dressing room, not only because Father wanted to preserve it but also because the maids believed the room to be haunted. Miss Herron-Cross herself attested to having seen my dead mother sitting at her mirror glass in a funeral shroud, carefully brushing grave dirt from her black hair. I'd overheard her frightening Miss Anne with the story: "There she sat, our Evelyn, and her eyes were white as bleached stone, and she dragged that brush through her hair that was more like a thicket of crabgrass. The dirt fell on the vanity in bits, making an awful mess. And our lady paid the mess no mind. She went on brushing as though she'd never stop."

Even at my young age, I understood what a foolish story that was; Mother was gone from Stoke Morrow. She no longer watched over me. I could sit at her vanity for an entire day and not expect to feel the touch of her hand. I could lie in her bed and never dream of her lying next to me. There were no ghosts in our house. Stoke Morrow was empty but for memories and Father's peculiar, growing collections, a bitter irony for a house with such a name. *Stoke* from the old English meaning "place," and Morrow, a family name, which could be taken to mean future. *In the morrow, life will be different.*

I sat before the dressing room's mirror glass, gazing at the painted robins on the frame. I put my finger absently on the handle of Mother's silver brush, and the moment my skin touched the metal, a color passed across my field of vision—a pinkish fleshy tone, and along with the color came a high ringing, like someone was sounding a dinner bell from the garden beneath the window. I drew my hand back, frightened, wanting to run from the room but forcing myself to remain. In the dim light, I leaned forward, examining Mother's brush without touching it. The black bristles and silver backing looked innocent enough. I'd certainly touched the brush before when Mother was alive, and I'd had no such preternatural experience.

When I finally gathered enough courage to touch the handle again, I heard the ringing once more, louder this time, and saw the pink color flash before my eyes. I was no longer frightened of the sensation. It seemed, rather, that the object was extending itself toward me, showing me something that others could not see. I continued to touch the objects on the vanity. The perfume atomizer caused a hazy blue to steal across my vision. The powder box made a chuffing noise, producing no color but rather a feeling of density. I grew heavier by the simple act of touching it.

I considered the fact that I might be taking ill like Mother. She'd brought a sickness home from the Heath and infected me. My perceptions were now addled, as happens with a high fever. But upon further experiment, I came to realize my ability was something quite different—not a dissolution of the rational mind, but a force that allowed me to see *beyond* the rational entirely. Mother's dressing room was not actually a static space, as it appeared to the normal eye. The room was alive. The surfaces of objects were nothing more than a fragile veneer. My newfound ability allowed me to see past those surfaces into another reality—a universe of animate space concealed within the inanimate. I began to imagine I'd found a way to see the objects' very souls, and I felt as though this was the *correct* way of seeing the world. Everything up until that point had been a misunderstanding.

As I was pondering my new ability in the dressing room I heard another sound—an elegant sort of sighing that seemed somehow more significant than the rest of the sensations. I decided to investigate and climbed off the vanity seat, walking around the room until the sighing was at its loudest. The sound came from some object inside Mother's sturdy oak wardrobe. I touched the brass door handle and paused, momentarily overcome by the maids' superstitions. I imagined that if I opened the wardrobe, I'd see Mother inside, glaring down at me, eyes white as marbles, dirt falling from her hair.

The other objects in the room were still murmuring around me, and they seemed to grow agitated when I hesitated at the wardrobe. They chittered and vibrated, as if urging me to open it. Finally, I steeled myself and threw open the door. Inside, I found Mother's dresses and corsets, still all hanging in a row, and looking at them made my eyes burn and my throat feel tight. I wanted to gather the dresses and press them against my mouth and nose, to breathe her into me. But I forced myself to continue the search, as it was clear that the sighing sound was coming from behind the dresses. I pushed the clothing aside, and there at the back of the wardrobe was an object that stole my breath.

It was a large oval portrait in a gilded frame that had been hidden away, likely by Mother herself. The canvas was covered in dark, almost grotesque flowers that had been created using a technique of layered oils. Emerging from that rank flora was a black-eyed woman who seemed to be pulling herself up out of the flowers and into the light. It looked as though she was trying to disgorge herself from the painting, and I found it difficult to tell where her body began and the foliage ended. Thick vines were tangled in her hair, and the swollen blossoms of the boggy flowers were indistinguishable from the folds of her dark dress. She was a woman born of plant matter. Even her flesh had the iridescent look of a petal. The most striking aspect of the painting, the aspect that would make me return to it again and again, was the woman's face—for it seemed to be my mother's own. I say "seemed" because I already found it difficult to remember the specifics of Mother's features. She was dissolving from my memory, faster by the day. But this woman, looking down at me from her bed of engorged flowers, gave me the *feeling* of Mother. She had the same countenance, and like my mother, there was something superior in her, something almost otherworldly, as if she surveyed me from some precipice.

I realized this was most certainly the Lady of Flowers Mother had been asking for. *She's there, blooming in the darkness, silent and waiting.* Why the Lady wore my mother's face, I did not know. Yet I was sure the painting had called out to me, willing me to find it, using my new talent as a kind of guide. I wondered what meaning this Lady might have, and though my curiosity was strong, I believed the answer would come if I remained patient.

In the meantime, I began to fancy myself a new breed of detective, piecing together a world that no one else could see. I made my way around Stoke Morrow, allowing the house to open itself to me. The fainting couch in the Clock Parlor made a noise like rushing water when I put my ear against its cushion. The marble table in the foyer emitted a dazzling shade of azure light from its surface. Every room was breathing and alive, and I was an explorer in this alien world.

Father had once told me that primitives believed everything to be ensouled. There were souls of nature that were quiet and gentle because they'd been created by a deity, and then there were the souls of man-made objects, which were tormented because their maker was imperfect. I believed that I'd become a primitive dressed in the guise of a nineteenth-century girl. I even allowed myself to think that one day I might learn to use my talent to control the world.

Father began growing his Byzantine collections in earnest when he returned from Bath, and the Lady of Flowers became a kind of psychic anchor for me in that sea of objects. His was a *horror vacui*— a fear of empty spaces. Animals carved from jade, medieval Italian serving plates, arabesque sculptures of songbirds appeared in the black halls along with a hundred other oddities. Even the gardens turned queer. Father continued to enhance the ruin—a Roman folly that to me looked no different from the statued graves of Highgate. It was as if he believed that filling the house and grounds with curiosities might edge the sickness from his heart. My newfound senses were jangled by the appearance of so many objects. I heard their mutterings, saw their colors, felt their tingling vibrations. When I needed respite from all of this, I went to the secret portrait, sometimes going as far as curling my body inside the wardrobe to be closer to the Lady. I listened to her high and whispered song, and she kept me strong in the chaos. I said nothing to Father, as I believed it was likely that he'd never seen the oval portrait. It was so well hidden in the wardrobe after all, and keeping it so made me feel connected to Mother, as if she and I both shared some secret life.

*   *   *

The more I experimented with my talent, the more intense the sensations became until I was moving down the long halls of Stoke Morrow in a field entirely awash in sound and color, listening to the murmurings of teacups and observing a bright halo above the newel post. It seemed there was an aura extending from me, and as long as the objects were in the field of my aura, I could experience their essences. At times, their babbling was so loud, I could barely hear the maids when they called for me. Stoke Morrow was no longer a house at all. It had become a body, mysterious and alive.

In the years that followed, I learned that I could momentarily infect others with my ability through touch. I overheard the maids, one afternoon, reporting this phenomenon to each other, in ridiculous and breathless whispers. When Miss Anne washed me, putting her hands on my skin, she said she heard a high moan coming from the silver tub. When Miss Herron-Cross undressed me before bed, she claimed the painted walls of my bedroom momentarily glowed a deep shade of red. "The very color of Hell," she intoned. "I felt that if I turned around, I might see a devil leering at me." The maids were briefly experiencing what I experienced, and instead of finding such heightened perception fascinating, they feared it.

They brought the local cleric to the house one day when father was away at his law offices. Miss Herron-Cross believed that my grief over the death of my mother had made me vulnerable to demons.

"You think our Jane is possessed?" Miss Anne asked.

"I'm quite certain of it," Miss Herron-Cross said. "Even the child's face seems to be changing. She grows stonier by the day. I don't like her looking at me with those cold little eyes of hers."

The cleric was an old man with loose and hanging skin. He raised a crucifix before my face for several minutes then asked who it was I saw on the cross. When I answered Jesus Christ, the cleric asked if I understood the terms of my salvation. I said I did, all the while listening to the terrible, creaking sound the wooden cross made, wondering if Christ himself had heard such sounds while hanging there.

Then the cleric laid his hands on me in an attempt to drive out the unholy presence. In the next moment, he drew back, as if burned, and a look of fear spread across his face.

"What was the meaning of that?" he asked, sharply.

I fixed my dark gaze on him and provided no answer.

"The room seemed full of life," he said, his voice quavering. "There was color and pagan song. How did you conjure such illusion, child?"

The truth of the matter was that I didn't know how I'd done it. The transference was still very much a mystery to me. And even if I did understand, I didn't think I'd tell him. He was such a pompous man, and I liked the fact that I'd disturbed him. I folded my hands and watched.

The cleric looked to Miss Herron-Cross. "Did you say you have reason to believe the mother was a witch?"

Miss Herron-Cross put a silencing finger to her thin lips.

"Not a *witch*," blurted Miss Anne. "She was—"

I turned to look at her, wondering what she might reveal. "Evelyn Silverlake was good to us," Miss Anne said finally. "She was as good to us as she had the strength to be."

The cleric began collecting his instruments of exorcism. "This girl is attempting an enchantment," he said. "She wishes to ensnare all of us in some manner. If I were the two of you, I'd relinquish my position and flee."

"You cannot help her, then?" Miss Anne asked.

"There are some things in the world that are beyond Christian *aid*. I suggest again that both of you take your leave of this house. Before this child puts some mark on you that cannot be erased."

Only Miss Herron-Cross heeded his warning. When she gave notice of her departure to Father, she also told him he should promptly send me to a hospital or an asylum—Bethlehem Royal, perhaps.

"There's nothing wrong with Jane," Father said. "She's lost her mother, and she keeps to herself. That's all."

"Her shyness is nothing more than a disguise," countered Miss Herron-Cross. "She's secretly willful, and on top of that, I believe she might be ill. And she makes everyone around her ill. Even Stoke

Morrow is susceptible to her disease. I have heard and seen terrible things in this house when she is near."

"Now it's you who sound mad," Father said. "I think it's best if you just go."

"You've experienced these things yourself," Miss Herron-Cross said. "And you can't deny that even Jane's mother manifested certain unnatural qualities."

"I won't have you talking about my wife in that manner," Father said. "Gather your things, and be on your way."

I continued to wonder what Miss Herron-Cross meant about my mother's unnatural qualities. What had she told the cleric that led him to believe Mother was a witch? And how much did Father understand about my skills? There were instances when he wore a haunted expression, and he eyed his collections suspiciously, as though he could hear their chatter. If I asked him what was wrong he would make some remark about digestive problems. One night, when he was particularly tired, he asked if I believed in ghosts.

"Ghosts?" I said.

"Shadows seen from the corner of the eye. Sounds heard only in some deep and secret chamber of the ear."

When I didn't respond, he gave me a sad smile. The years of troubled sleep after Mother's death had taken their toll on him. His face was no longer the face I remembered from childhood. It looked as if some wax worker had made a mask and forgotten to fix its shape. "Never mind, Jane. I'm turning into such an old fool. Your mother certainly wouldn't have approved of such talk."

I acted as though I found his self-deprecation endearing, yet all the while I felt terribly guilty, wondering if I was driving my own father mad with my transference.

After the departure of Miss Herron-Cross, Miss Anne became my primary caretaker. She was bound to Stoke Morrow, it seemed, as she was less experienced and had fewer options for employment. It was clear she feared me. I was soon labeled by her a variety of evil on par with, if not higher than, Satan. There were days when she made me say prayers nearly every hour, but instead of asking anything of God, I would get on my knees and listen to the sounds the house made. I imagined that I was the god of the objects, and they were making prayers to me in their alien tongues.

I decided that rather than complaining to Father about Miss Anne's treatment of me, I would become her personal devil. That's what she wanted, after all. So I began tormenting her—touching her hands and arms at odd times and letting her experience the house as I experienced it. She feared me and therefore did not retaliate. I was so cruel to her. She couldn't have committed nearly as many sins as I punished her for.

I realized if I could frighten Miss Anne in this way, I could control her. I was building my strength and no longer needed to feel cowed by anyone. But this feeling of superiority was also the start of my undoing. By the time I met Maddy and Nathan, I thought I understood myself and my talent. I thought I could control it enough to make a friendship with them. But experience proved me quite wrong.

CHAPTER 4

———————

After the disappearance of Nathan Ashe, the objects began to exhibit a heightened agitation reminiscent of the episode when I discovered the oval portrait in Mother's wardrobe. Yet this agitation seemed to come on an even grander scale. Colors pulsed in garish hues—bizarre shades of silvery pink and hot, phosphorescent purple. Sounds grew loud enough to startle me from sleep. At first, I thought the amplified sensations might be due to my own distress. Perhaps the crude images of Nathan set upon by beasts in the *Illustrated Penny* had upset me more than I realized, and I was projecting my own troubled thoughts onto the objects. Certainly the drawings in the *Penny* were nothing more than the product of some opium-addled artist, but I found I couldn't write them off entirely. I'd learned from Nathan himself not to dismiss *anything* as too fantastical.

As the disturbances increased in frequency and variety, it became clear that my own nerves were not the cause. Some unseen force, concealed within Stoke Morrow, had irritated the objects. Writing desks, oil lamps, cigar boxes, and all the rest started acting out in my presence, soon producing near blinding flashes of light and terrible explosions of sound. Father asked me on more than one occasion if I was quite all right. "You look so pale, Jane," he said. "And your eyes—it's as though you're staring at something in the far distance. Something that troubles you."

"It's nothing," I said. "A headache."

"Your mother used to get such headaches," Father said. "Oftentimes lying down in a dark room would help."

"I'll be fine, Father."

The more I attempted to ignore the new sensations, the more insistent the objects became. I began isolating myself, spending time in the garden away from the aggressive house. Elements of nature—anything that was not man-made—soothed my senses and could sometimes even quiet them completely. I stopped talking to Father and then even to my dearest Maddy. I wanted nothing more than to meditate in the garden and to dampen my senses enough so as not to feel as if I was losing my grip on reality entirely. I sat among the yellow daffodils that were just beginning to burst their fragile sheaths and wondered what Nathan himself would have made of this new agitation of the objects. After he experienced the transference for the first time, he believed he could come to some understanding of it. He made a careful research project out of me. Though together we'd only fallen deeper into mystery, and then he was gone, leaving me with more questions than answers.

I lay down on the stone bench in the garden, gazing at Stoke Morrow. The old manor was fortified like a castle. Its high stony walls were encased in vines, and its fingerlike chimneys were black and reaching. From my perspective, it was difficult to see the roof, as the tiles were obscured by a scrim of crenellated parapets decorated with skyward-gazing stone sparrows whose mouths remained perpetually open. Rain mixed with London ash had blackened the birds and the whole of the house. Stoke Morrow might have once possessed an architecture of hope—perhaps its builders meant for it to look as though it was attempting an ascent into Heaven. But in later years, as the foundation settled and cracked, the skyward-reaching house reversed its trajectory and began sinking into the mossy earth that surrounded it.

I fell asleep there on the bench, and thankfully I did not dream. When I opened my eyes again, the afternoon sun had grown hotter and my senses were more than irritated—they throbbed, responding to a low rumbling that had developed in the distance. Perhaps it was that very rumbling that had drawn me from my sleep. The sound was coming from Stoke Morrow itself; the stone walls of my home were literally trembling. Then, as I watched, blue flamelike auras rose from the pediments of my own bedroom window. The flames curled and extended until they encased the entire vibrating manor in an eldritch glow. My childhood home was sealed in the cocoon of some cold enchantment, and to my chagrin, I realized I was once again its enchantress.

I knew I could not let these escalations go on any longer, as I feared I might start transferring them to Father. I made my way into the foyer, determined to learn the cause of the amplifications, and it was there, near the grand staircase, that I did something I'd never attempted before. I *spoke* directly to the objects. "What do you want me to see?" I asked, in as bold a tone as I could muster. "What exactly has disturbed you?"

I don't know what I expected would happen. Certainly I didn't believe the objects would start speaking to me, but before any kind of response could come, I heard a familiar voice from the kitchen, a sort of avian warble. "Did you ask for something just now, Jane?" Miss Anne said. She appeared in the shadow of the doorway, twining a rag nervously between her fingers.

"I didn't," I replied.

She must have noticed the odd expression on my face, for she paused a moment. Perhaps she wondered if I was about to sprout horns and finally assume my rightful place in the underworld.

"Leave me, Anne," I said. "I'm occupied."

She moved off, muttering something about how I didn't look like I was *occupied* by anything of merit.

The tremulations of the house did not abate upon Miss Anne's departure but rather continued to intensify. Blue flames slithered up and down the foyer walls. I was still aware of some unseen force causing the disturbance. It was as if I could sense the stone that had been dropped into the pond to create a ripple.

I focused my senses, giving myself over to the objects entirely and allowing the sensations to act as my guide. It was then that I heard a kind of ringing in the distance, like an alarm bell, and I ascended the grand staircase, following. The alarm was coming from my own bedroom—from the cedar hope chest at the end of my bed. Father had the chest built for me when I was a newborn, assuming, I suppose, that my life would have a different trajectory than it did.

I kept few items in the chest. Once when Maddy looked inside, she said it appeared as though I didn't have any hope at all. This was meant as a bit of humor, of course, but I felt the sting of tears when she said it. For a long time, I hadn't had much hope, though when she and Nathan came into my life, I believed that could change.

The ringing was clearly coming from somewhere near the bottom of the chest. I pushed aside a box of silver cutlery and a childhood doll, and finally my fingers came into contact with an envelope.

I knew what object was inside the envelope well enough, though I hadn't thought of it for a long time. It was a loose button that had fallen off Nathan's jacket one evening when he'd been visiting Maddy and me. I told him I would mend the jacket for him if he liked. Maddy, not unkindly, reminded me I didn't know how to sew. "You're not exactly domestic, Jane," she said. "In fact, I'd expect to see you spreading cobwebs and dust to suit your Gothic sensibilities rather than tidying." I merely glared at her. It was true; I had very few qualities that might be desirable in a wife. But I promised Nathan I would learn, and soon I'd mend his jacket. He was amused by my conviction, and I kept the button on my dresser for a long time, picking it up often to examine it. The little button had fallen off the breast of his suit, from a place near his heart. I imagined I could conjure Nathan's entire warm and sturdy body just by touching this totem. I envisioned him putting his hands on my flesh, feeling the transference and remaining unafraid. He would be bold enough to kiss my neck and then my mouth. I could almost feel his lips and his smooth cheek. He'd speak to me as no one ever had, telling me how much he loved me and that I wasn't so strange. He'd say he took pleasure in my difference; in fact, he desired me because of it.

Eventually I relinquished such fantasies, putting the button in the hope chest and forgetting about it, along with my will to sew. But the ringing alarm drew me back to the button again. I opened the envelope and found the little piece of Nathan was just as I remembered, dark and made of tarnished brass. The button had never been particularly problematic to my senses before, but it was indeed the object that was making the god-awful sound—the fly in the ointment at Stoke Morrow.

I turned the envelope over and let the button drop into the palm of my hand. As soon as it touched my skin, I experienced the flash of an image that was quite distinct and unlike anything I'd ever perceived from an object before. What I saw appeared to be a stage set populated by painted trees, and above the trees was a black sky decorated with odd bits of glass that were meant to look like stars. The entire false forest was contained within some type of stone chamber, reminiscent of a catacomb. It was so dark there that I could barely see, and the acrid smell of paint that had been used to create the illusion of trees filled my lungs. I had a sense that what I was seeing was an actual place, somewhere in London. Then I heard the distant sound of a trumpet, the sort of horn that signaled the opening of a hunt.

Fear churned in my stomach—not my own but a fear that I was experiencing empathically. The emotion belonged to something in the forest. I watched as a lean, four-legged shadow darted among the thick trunks. The beast was in grave danger and was stumbling from time to time, as if wounded. I wanted to call out to it but found I could not, so I silently watched the dark form move haphazardly along. It was an elegant creature, nothing that deserved such torment. I willed the beast to come to me, and just as it seemed to take notice of my presence, my hand went limp and the button fell to the floor. The image of the stage set faded and was gone.

I stood looking down at Nathan's now silent button, utterly confused. I hadn't seen a play since I was a child. Father had taken me to a very poor production of *Macbeth*. I'd enjoyed the performance of the witches but had forgotten much of the rest. And as I was thinking this, I realized there was now a smell in my bedroom, cigarettes and tonic—the smell of Nathan Ashe.

"Nathan?" I said. "Are you here somewhere?"

The room rippled around me, but no answer came.

If I'd learned anything from Nathan, it was the importance of experiment. When something new occurred, I was to examine that occurrence carefully. Before I had time to think, I'd pulled my shawl over my shoulders and left Stoke Morrow. I nearly ran down Hampstead Road, making my way toward the house where Maddy lived with her mother, an Italianate cottage called La Dometa. My heart beat quickly, and I felt as though I was being pursued by those invisible hunters myself. I could almost again hear the sound of their horn, and the smell of Nathan lingered around me too. I could not help but wonder if he'd found some way to send me a vision and, if so, what message did he mean to communicate?

I must have knocked too vigorously on the door of La Dometa because when Maddy answered, she looked tired and irritated. Her mother, Eusapia Lee, had recently dismissed their help for some reason that was logical only to her. Eusapia was in the throws of a degenerative nervous illness that caused her mind to wander and confabulate. She often forgot people and even whole episodes of her life.

Maddy wore a charcoal-colored dress—a mourning gown, if I'd ever seen one. A bit of black lace was tied around her neck. "Jane, what is it?" she asked. "You're a mess."

I raised my hand to feel the perspiration on my brow and then attempted to smooth my hair back into its bun. "Something's happened," I said.

"Is there news about Nathan?" she asked, looking momentarily hopeful.

"No, not precisely," I said. "But I need to speak to you. I saw something strange, Maddy."

She stepped aside without a word. I followed her into the quaint powder-blue foyer, which was filled with music—a flute, if I was not mistaken.

"Are you having a recital?" I asked.

"It's Mother," Maddy said, disdainfully. "She's hired some awful man from a music hall to come and play for her. She read a pamphlet recently about symphonic therapy. Apparently, if music is played once a day in the home, it has the effect of organizing the mind. Daily treatments are supposed to improve memory and even calm the nerves, if we're to believe the pamphlet writer. I told Mother no amount of flute playing would cure her brazen senility, so she might as well give it up."

"You're terrible, Maddy," I said. I tended to enjoy Eusapia's milder eccentricities, but then again, I didn't have to live with them.

Maddy shook her head. "I want to take up rooms in the city, Jane. I want so very much to get away." I'd heard her express this sort of desire before. Maddy was the sort of "New Woman" who thought a girl living alone in London would be liberating rather than debasing.

"Where's Pascal?" I asked, taking off my shawl, looking to change the subject.

She waved her hand, as if shooing an insect. "I don't keep track of him any longer."

"None of this is his fault," I said. "You know—"

"Jane, you arrived at my door for some purpose, and I don't believe it was to lecture me about my French ward."

I took a breath. Discussing aspects of my talent with Maddy was generally unpleasant, but in this case, I felt it was necessary. "I took a nap this afternoon and when I awoke, all of the objects in my house were terribly agitated."

She became visibly tense. "Jane, I'm not really interested in hearing about your occult experiences right now. Not when we should be thinking about Nathan."

"But I believe this might somehow pertain to Nathan."

She sighed. "Let's go sit in the parlor then. I can't stand to hear mother's music a moment longer."

We retired to the front parlor of La Dometa, and Maddy closed the large sliding doors, muting the sound of the flute to a degree. The Lee parlor was a gaudy place, decorated by Eusapia's late husband, Adolphus. He'd ascribed to the Pre-Raphaelite philosophy that, when making art or home furnishings, one should hold to the rule of nature: *reject nothing, select nothing, and scorn nothing.* The parlor walls were covered in vined tapestry and the furniture was painted a floral pattern. The pale nudes that had led to his downfall glowered from their leaded frames. On the desk, an ivory clock showed a scene in which the allegorical figure of Chastity bound Cupid with ropes of ivy. Vases of orange marigolds populated the room. I was glad for the flowers because they had the effect of numbing my senses enough so that I could concentrate on this conversation with Maddy.

She sat in a chair across from mine, curling her legs comfortably under her body.

"Do you still have the necklace Nathan gave you?" I asked. "The one with his spoon on it?" Nathan had given Maddy the necklace as a gift one Christmas. He'd drilled a hole into a small silver spoon that he'd used as a child and hung it from a chain. The note he attached to it read, "Mother me?" I suppose the gift was meant as one of his jokes, but Maddy loved the necklace. She wore it every day for nearly a year.

Her face hardened when she heard my question. "Do I still *have* it?"

"Yes, I'd like to—"

"Of course I have it, Jane," she said. "Do you think I just tossed it away?"

"Well, may I see it?"

She leaned back in her chair and studied me from beneath half-lidded eyes. Though she was my dearest friend, she could be very queenly at times. "It's locked in a box in my room," she said finally. "I'm not sure I remember where the key is at the moment."

"Could you go and get the necklace for me, please? I need to perform an experiment." As soon as I spoke, I realized I'd used the wrong word. Maddy hadn't liked the experiments between Nathan and me one bit.

"I don't think I want you handling my necklace. It's the only piece of Nathan I have left, and allowing you to use your so-called talents on it seems like sacrilege."

I reminded myself that Maddy was under a great deal of strain. "I'm not going to harm it. I merely want to see if it reacts in the same way as—"

She held up a hand to silence me. "Your experiences are personal, Jane. You know very well what happened to Nathan when you started sharing too much. In fact, I doubt we'd be in this trouble if—"

"Maddy, don't you dare level accusations at me," I said, surprised at my own boldness. "Whatever happened isn't *my* fault. Nathan wanted to experience my talent. All of the choices were his."

I knew that I protested too much. Images of the final night we'd spent with him—the night he disappeared—rose in my mind. I saw myself lying in the field of shale on Hampstead Heath, weeping and whispering into the deep fissures of the rock. The purple dusk was above me, and the black rock was below. I was full of fear and sorrow, and I was aware that something had come up and taken hold of me, stretching me beyond my own boundaries. The rest of that night, I remembered only fragments—shards that I could not reassemble to form a whole.

Maddy cleared her throat to draw my attention. She regarded me carefully, and I knew I needed to focus on the conversation at hand, lest she begin to question me.

"I'm glad you're here at any rate, Jane," she said. "We have an actual problem to discuss."

"What problem is that?" I asked.

"Vidocq," she said, accentuating the hard *k* sound at the end of his name.

"The French inspector?"

"The very same. Has he interviewed you?"

"No," I said. "I wasn't aware he planned to. Has he spoken with you?"

"I'm sorry to say he has," Maddy replied, "and I've realized all my fears are coming true. He's out to tarnish Nathan's name."

"How do you mean?"

"He's digging up all sorts of facts, prying into everything. Then he's reporting it all to Lord Ashe."

"Oh God," I said. Nathan's father was one of the staunchest members of the House of Lords, superior in upbringing and rigid in his systems of rules and philosophies. If he learned even half of what his son had been up to since Nathan returned from the Crimea, it wouldn't matter if we found our friend or not. Nathan would be disowned—stripped of his inheritance and left to live on the street.

"You must be prepared, when the time comes, to speak appropriately to Inspector Vidocq," Maddy said. "You're easily intimidated, and I don't want you telling him too much."

"I haven't even been called upon," I said, the idea of being questioned by the inspector already making me nervous. "I doubt that I matter much to him."

"Not so," she replied. "Vidocq seems quite interested in you—in both of us, actually. The nature of our relationship with Nathan has come under some scrutiny. The inspector seems to think the friendship unnatural."

"Well, it is unnatural in some respects," I said. It felt good to be honest about this.

"I'm only asking that you watch yourself, Jane."

"Of course," I said.

"And don't *touch* the inspector. Don't offer your hand. We wouldn't want his tie pin to start singing lullabies to him."

"That isn't funny," I said.

"It wasn't meant to be."

As I was leaving La Dometa, Maddy said, "When I find the key to my treasure box, Jane, I promise I'll show you the necklace. I'm sorry if I seemed abrupt earlier. I'm just—well, I'm beside myself. It's been weeks, and we've heard nothing."

"I'm sure we'll have some information soon, dear."

"Do you think so?"

"I do."

I did not kiss her cheek in parting. I knew Maddy wouldn't appreciate my skin against her own at that moment. Even a brief transference would be too much for her.

CHAPTER 5

As I walked slowly back to Stoke Morrow, I focused on the silence of Hampstead Road. There were no carriages or merchants' carts, and I found myself alone on the isolated lane where tall willow trees provided shade. The cool of the air felt good against my skin, and I stroked the white feverfew gathered at my wrist. I'd learned once from a physician friend of the Lees that this medicinal flower, when consumed, was known to reduce the size of blood vessels in the human brain. It muted the symptoms of headaches, and it seemed to have a similar effect on my talent. Yet even feverfew could not quell my thoughts of Nathan Ashe. He'd known how to upset me, and thinking about our experiments together made a flush rise in my cheeks. I'd worked against losing control with him, yet in the end, I'd lost that battle. The image of the creature making its way through the painted trees lingered in my thoughts, and I wished, yet again, I had some further possession of Nathan's to experiment with.

When Stoke Morrow, black and crumbling, appeared on the horizon, I did not want to return to it. The house looked, for all the world, like a prison. As a child, I sometimes fantasized about simply slipping away and walking forever on the open Heath where no man-made object could trouble me. These fantasies became more pronounced when I reached my teenage years. A series of tutors came and went, never able to completely explain the reason for their departures. Some said I was not teachable. Others said I had a disease of the mind, and I was attempting to infect them. I wanted to punish those tutors as I punished Miss Anne, but I knew they were too intelligent to stand for it. The best I could do was hide myself in the darkest corners of Stoke Morrow and wait for them to go.

Father had finally given up on hiring tutors, saying I could educate myself in the library as I saw fit. "People aren't reliable these days, Jane," he said. "Learning to do for yourself is a better lesson than any those so-called teachers could provide."

Instead of reading in the library as Father suggested, I wandered the long halls of our ancestral home. The objects murmured softly, often seeming more alive than the people in my life. I immersed myself in color and sound, readily intoxicated. I loved my father, yes, but even he was beginning to pale in comparison to the clamoring souls of these objects. I do not know when precisely I surrendered myself to the talent entirely, but I remember how I began to feel that I was no longer a girl. I was a wraith. I thought that if I continued to let myself go, I might be absorbed by the energy of the house, and if that happened, I wondered if anyone would think to look for me.

I must have looked like some ragged wastrel on the day that I first met Maddy and she drew me out of my dark corner on the stairs. I remember gazing into her violet-colored eyes and thinking I'd found my savior. If anyone could free me from the solipsistic prison I'd built, it was this lively child of the age.

I remember she attempted humor after she'd examined my dark and threadbare dress, asking if Stoke Morrow was perhaps some cloister. When I looked embarrassed, she softened and asked me to take the gray cap off my head.

I did as she wished, and she helped me unfasten my long hair from the tangle Miss Anne called a bun, then further surprised me by arranging my tresses. The maid only touched me when she had to, and it was strange to feel someone paying such loving attention to my body. Unlike the maids or my tutors, Maddy didn't say I frightened her. She didn't claim to see evil in me. I felt that if I stayed close to her for long enough, I would become something new—a girl, normal in almost every respect.

"Your hair is a lovely color," Maddy said. "Like burnished oak. We should brush it, don't you think?"

And so we did, sitting at the vanity in my bedroom. I had no idea that we would sit just that way for years to come.

Maddy went through my wardrobe, searching for anything of color. She resorted to taking a red table covering from beneath the vase of flowers in the hall and fashioning a sort of wrap, which she put around my shoulders. She turned me toward the mirror. "I'm fond of paleness as much as the next girl, Jane," she said. "It provides an air of dignity and interest, but I simply think you've taken it too far. You don't look like a lily as much as like some phosphorescent plant growing in the gardens of the underworld."

It was true; my skin was nearly translucent. Even my lips had only the faintest pigment. "I rarely go walking," I admitted as I admired the wrap. The color red suited me, and I wondered how many different types of table coverings were in the house and what sort of clothes my new friend could make from them.

"My old friends in Mayfair and I would play at dressing up," Maddy said. "They no longer speak to me, though."

"Why is that?" I asked, wondering again what mystery this girl held.

"Because I suppose they weren't really my friends to begin with," she said. "You and I could be so much more for each other. We'll assist one another in becoming women. I'm sure you have certain knowledge that would help even me."

I didn't think I knew anything that would help Madeline Lee, and yet I agreed. There was a moment, some bit of fun on her part, when she grabbed my hand, and I braced for her reaction to the transference. I thought she'd spring back and call me a devil when the house started singing around her, but Maddy reacted only with a moment of blankness. She seemed to be no longer focusing on my dressing room but looking at some distant shape. Then she composed herself. "I had quite a spell," she said, laughing. "I get a bit foggy sometimes, Jane."

"It was—" I started. I was ready to reveal my true nature because I already felt close to her.

"A terrible spell," she said. Was there a tone of warning in her voice?

We slipped from Stoke Morrow into my father's garden, a place where we would spend much of our time, as it was so isolated from the main house and any vigilant eye. The cold gods of Rome presided from their pedestals. Dionysus in a pair of stone antlers studied the two of us with interest as Maddy instructed me (the first of many instructions) on the components of an eighteenth-century "perfect garden."

"There must be an orangerie, which you have," she said, approvingly, pointing to the greenhouse on our property where black branches of lemon trees pressed at steamed glass panes. "They are everywhere in France, you know. Beautiful glass houses where the citrus trees are kept. The smell is dazzling in midwinter. I've always thought I'd like to live in an orangerie and sit among the citrus groves in the sunlight all day."

"That's lovely," I said, still feeling shy.

"And then of course there must be a *menagerie*," she said. "I've been begging my father to purchase a few animals that I could tend. Imagine feeding a miniature Chinese deer from one's own hand. Wouldn't that be darling, Jane?"

"I suppose it would."

"They have such tiny, gentle mouths. I've heard one can even teach them to kneel in one's presence, as if they are at worship. I would feel like the goddess of the deer, you know."

We both laughed. It had been a long time since I'd felt such levity, and this was the moment I decided I should never let go of Madeline Lee. She acted as though she didn't notice my admiration. Instead she went on with her lecture. "And then, of course, you need a folly—and though yours is lovely, there is more to life than Rome. Have you ever thought of including a ruined abbey or perhaps even a Tartar tent?"

"I have no control over the folly," I said. "It belongs to my father."

"Fathers," she said. "They do have their follies." She paused here, weighing a thought in her mind. "I might as well tell you, Jane. I don't think you're going to shun me like those other girls. You don't seem the type. My father's folly is that he makes pictures using a daguerreotype machine, or at least he did before he took ill. In Mayfair last year, he made pictures of nude women."

"Nude?" I asked.

She nodded, solemnly. "Prostitutes, mostly. He took hundreds of such images. Perhaps he was too naive to know what would happen, but then again maybe in some way he wanted this. He always said that Mayfair and even the London Society of Art was full of arrogant philistines. And he was right, of course, the philistines judged him for his pictures. Father isn't well, and he couldn't properly defend himself against those fools. There was gossip that he'd caught his sickness from those lowborn women—that it's some disease of the liver. I don't believe that, but I suppose it doesn't matter what I think. Here I am, and here is not such a bad place, is it, Jane? Tell me it's not."

"The Heath?" I said, looking toward the southern woods. "I rarely venture out of my house. Father thinks it's dangerous." I didn't tell Maddy of the black shale with the fissures that led into the earth where my mother had been poisoned. That was perhaps too singular a bit of information for such a sunny day.

"Oh, but we must go walking!" she said. "That's the whole point of the Heath, isn't it? To take a lovely walk. Perhaps I can find us an appropriate escort to take us adventuring."

"Yes," I said, wondering what kind of escort she could provide.

Maddy nearly took my hand again but then seemed to think better of it. "It's good to find a friend like you, Jane Silverlake, even in these wilds."

We stood at the tree line. Two girls, peering into the darkness together.

The arrival of our guide, Nathan Ashe, left me in a state of shock. I had not met anyone of his status before. Though my father did have some connection to society, he hadn't made use of such connection for some time and tended to shy away from worldliness. Therefore, the son of a lord was barely within the range of my imagining—particularly a specimen such as Nathan, a pale and sinewy god in his own right with his rake of hair and his strong-looking neck. When he arrived in the Roman ruin, all of seventeen, emerging from the shadows of the southern woods, I felt oddly light in the head. It was as though one of Father's statues had come to life. Nathan carried his father's brass headed cane and wore a youthful suit. His manner was light and pleasant, and when Maddy said, "Jane Silverlake, meet Nathan Ashe," and he kissed my gloved hand, I was worried less about blushing than fainting dead away.

It occurred to me that he would never have come if it weren't for Maddy. This knowledge stuck in my heart like a splinter—a constant irritation that would grow infected over time.

Unlike Maddy, Nathan had been born in Hampstead Town, though I'd never before had the opportunity to meet him. I wasn't quite certain how she had lured the young Mr. Ashe. Perhaps it was something as simple as her physical beauty, though I doubted it. Nathan's river ran deeper. More likely it was her father's scandalous reputation and her mother's forays into occult phenomena, which she promised to discuss with him.

I remember him speaking to me alone on the second or third walk when Madeline went off to pick wildflowers. I felt warm in his presence. He seemed to radiate heat, and though my father warned me that Lord Ashe's son was another goat in the wilderness—a Pan looking for trouble—Nathan struck me as earnest. His eyes were kind and thoughtful, and there was intelligence in his face.

"You and Maddy are of different natures," he said, leaning on his cane.

I knew silence would make me look foolish, so I forced myself to agree.

"However did you find each other?" he asked. "Not at some cotillion, I'm guessing."

"Maddy found me," I said. "She's been working on my transformation."

He grinned, running his fingers through his hair. "Don't let her change you too much, Jane. Your difference makes you intriguing. You seem like, well, someone promising."

I thought about my talent and wished that he knew my secret.

Even then, I wished he knew.

Upon returning to Stoke Morrow from my trip to La Dometa, I noticed the objects in Father's collections had quieted to some degree. The button was no longer buzzing in my bedroom. There was still an insistence in the objects' murmurings, though. I was still irritated with Maddy for not giving me the necklace, yet on some level, I understood her motive. The necklace was like the button—a private piece of Nathan Ashe that one would not part with easily.

I went to the library, dropped my shawl on one of the wingback chairs, and rang the handbell that Father kept near his blotter. Miss Anne appeared promptly in her white apron and a steam-pressed blouse. Her frowsy gray hair was held back from her face with pins.

"Do you know any servants from Ashe High House?" I asked.

She wasn't accustomed to personal questions, especially from me, and she paused for a moment, trying to come up with an appropriate answer. "No, miss. Domestics on the Heath don't fraternize. It's frowned upon."

I folded my hands and regarded her. "I'm well aware of the protocol, Anne. I'm asking whether you *actually* know anyone there."

Her eyelids fluttered nervously. "There was my mother's sister. But she's passed."

"Is there no one else?" I asked.

"Honestly, there isn't. Are you looking for information about Master Nathan?"

"I want one of his possessions," I said, "for something I am attempting. I'd like a domestic to bring one to Stoke Morrow for me."

A familiar look came over Miss Anne's face—the look that

said she considered me poorly raised despite her best efforts. "You wouldn't ask someone to steal from Ashe High House, would you?"

I glanced away. If she was going to be of no help, there was no point continuing the conversation.

"If you're simply wanting for one of Master Nathan's possessions, I have something that will fit the bill."

I was startled by this bit of information. "How could you have something belonging to him?"

"He gave it to me," Miss Anne said. "Not too long ago. I'll go and get it."

When she reappeared in the library, she was carrying a black leather Bible with a gold cross on the front. I recognized it as Nathan's. The cover was brittle and one corner had broken off. The Bible made a low whistling sound, like a kettle beginning to boil.

"He *gave* that to you?" I asked.

"That's right," Miss Anne said. "It was the oddest thing. Happened not more than a month ago. You girls were upstairs getting ready, and Master Nathan was waiting in the parlor. He simply handed me the Bible and said he had no use for it anymore. I tried to argue, saying everyone had want of a Bible. But he said that wasn't true for him. He thought I'd find some better use. And so I took it, but the fact that he gave it away left me worried. I've always liked Master Nathan—he's so awfully regal and well appointed."

"Put the Bible on the desk, Anne," I said, uninterested in hearing her opinions about Nathan.

She put it down and slid it toward me, as if I was some hungry animal that might bite her hand.

"That's all," I said. "You can go."

"May I have it back when you're finished with it?" she said. "I feel so terrible about what's happened. I've been praying for him, you know. Praying each and every day."

"I'm sure wherever he is, Nathan appreciates your prayers. Now close the door behind you."

Miss Anne did as I asked, and I sat for a moment, listening to the spitting and whistling of the Bible in front of me. I had no love for holy books after having been labeled a devil for most of my child-hood, and I particularly feared what this one might reveal to me.

Finally, I took the book into my hands, and in the next moment, I was once again in the dark of the painted forest. The scene unfurled before me—skeletal trees and a sky full of glittering glass stars. It was the same carefully decorated chamber I'd seen when I touched the button, and once again I heard the distant note of the hunter's horn. Then a shadow shifted behind the false trees. It was the crea-ture, terribly frightened and stumbling. I could feel its uncertainty as I willed the animal to come forward.

Finally, the beast stepped into the light of the clearing, revealing itself in full. It was a great stag—muscular with powerful and woody antlers. I was in awe of its strength, and there was such intelligence in the stag's eyes that I felt it might open its mouth and speak. The stag's pelt was matted with blood about its neck and shoulders. I thought the hunters must have already harmed it.

The animal looked as though it wanted my help, even though I sensed the hunters were far away. It took me a moment to realize there was someone else in the painted forest, someone who did not emerge from the tree line but who remained hidden and watched the stag. I strained to make out the figure, and finally I saw it was a woman.

I could discern the outline of her long robe in the darkness, and her skin was moon-colored—so pale I thought she might be a dead thing. She swayed as she stared at the stag, utterly transfixed. Her eyes were like twin black skies, gleaming in the woods. And then she opened her mouth and made a high, eerie whistling sound, like wind blowing through a crack in a windowpane.

At the sound, the stag bounded away, and the woman, if she could rightly be called a woman, gave chase. As she came close to the clearing, I saw her mantle was dark and red.

I dropped the Bible from my hands, and the smell of Nathan Ashe was once again everywhere around me, so thick and cloying I found it hard to breathe. The book had fallen open to a specific page because the spine was broken, and I leaned down and saw that

Nathan himself had scrawled over the Bible's verses there in ink. I recognized his handwriting but not the message. He wrote: *In the beginning was not the Word. In the beginning was* She, *Red Goddess, the Unnamed. Here before the world was made. Here after it is laid to ruin.*

I wondered if it was the Red Goddess who pursued the stag through the woods, and if so, what did she want from the poor, suffering beast?

CHAPTER 6

By week's end, Maddy's prediction had come true, and I'd received a summons to meet with Inspector Vidocq at his makeshift office, set up in the second-floor parlor at Ashe High House. It was on the very morning of the interview, while I was still in my dressing room, donning my gloves and steeling myself for the encounter, that something unexpected and unwanted occurred. It was an event which shook me enough that I wondered if I'd be able to navigate the upcoming interview at all. A knock came at my dressing room door, and when I answered it, I found Miss Anne standing in the hall looking rather flummoxed. "A messenger brought this for you, Jane," she said, holding out an envelope that had been sealed with dark wax. "He says he'll wait for your reply. I didn't let him in the house. He's . . . well, a rather ragged-looking fellow, and I was afraid he'd track dirt or something worse inside."

"Who would send me a message?" I said, more to myself than to Miss Anne. The fact was, I didn't really have any acquaintances other than Maddy and Nathan. Even Father's relations rarely spoke to me anymore.

"I wouldn't know," Miss Anne replied. "But if the master is anything like his messenger, I doubt very much this could be anything good."

I broke the wax seal and found the letter within written in a florid script—a hand that I did not recognize.

My Dear Miss Silverlake,

Please accept my apology for not introducing myself at an earlier date. Now that I finally take up my pen, we are both involved in such desperate affairs that you will likely think me some opportunist. But I assure you, I have been making my way toward an audience with you for longer than you can know. In all honesty, I've been working toward this meeting for most of my life—though I did not know your name or even if you existed.

You are aware of my group in Southwark, I assume, and our failed attempts at reaching what religious men call transcendence. I assure you, this failure is not the product of a misguided philosophy as some would argue. We have failed, quite simply, because we lack the necessary means to achieve the outcome we seek.

I believe all of that is about to change, Miss Silverlake, because of you. Before his disappearance, young Nathan Ashe told me a great deal about your nature and led me to believe that you may, in fact, be the key to my lifelong quest. I must admit I am somewhat concerned about the veracity of his claims, especially in light of recent events. Nathan Ashe was not precisely what any of us believed him to be. But I would very much like to meet with you and come to some deeper understanding of your situation.

Please do not think I'm being mysterious here. I know I have a reputation for such a manner, but I assure you that I come to you in a spirit of sharing what I know. If what Nathan says is true, we may be able to help one another greatly. In fact, together we may be able to help the entire world. Send word with my boy as to when you would be willing to come and speak with me at the Temple of the Lamb in Southwark.

In Earnestness,
Ariston Day

I lowered the letter to my side, all too aware that Miss Anne was watching me, waiting for me to speak. Sweat had broken out across my brow and the morning sun streaming through the bedroom window seemed all too bright. Ariston Day was writing to me about my *nature*, which meant that Nathan had not only spoken to him about the Empyrean but revealed my talent to him as well. I realized the hand I held the letter with was trembling, and I willed it to stop before Miss Anne noticed.

"What response should I give the boy waiting in the courtyard?" she asked.

I cleared my throat. "I don't know," I said, honestly. Day was a charlatan and a false prophet. He couldn't possibly understand anything about me that I myself did not already know. Yet I couldn't deny there was a hope buried deep in my consciousness that said I should go to him. That he might actually hold some sort of key.

"Tell the boy to go back to where he came from," I said finally. "I need time to think."

She nodded curtly. "As you wish." She turned to leave and then looked back at me. "Jane, are you involved in something your father should know about?"

"There's no need for questions, Anne. I can take care of myself."

"Yes," she said. "I suppose you can at that."

After she'd closed the door, I went to my dressing room window, which overlooked the courtyard. I waited for a moment as Miss Anne spoke to the messenger, and I felt a chill as the boy stalked off down the stone drive. He was tall and threatening-looking, no more than eighteen, with a hard thin mouth and dark circles under his eyes. His black hair stuck up in whorls and spikes, making him look like something that had been dredged from the bottom of the Thames. This was surely one of Ariston Day's Fetches, for he wore the required red coat, a mockery of the Queen's Guard. Just before he passed behind the hedge at the end of the drive, he turned to look back at Stoke Morrow and caught me spying on him. His shining black eyes were so cruel, and before I could close the curtain, I saw the flash of an awful grin on his face. It was a grin that said he knew I'd come around. Sooner or later, I'd fall in line.

On my walk across the Heath to my interview at Ashe High House, I felt a new instability in my world. Nathan was gone, Maddy was overcome, and now a veritable monster was sending his minion to knock at the door of my home. I was exposed and too weak for any of it. I thought again about the final night Maddy and I had spent with Nathan. I remembered the grief I'd suffered, running through the woods, finally falling in the field of shale where Mother had perished. It was a place of death, and there was a part of me that wanted to die. I wept there, pounding my hand on the rock and finally putting my mouth against the fissures in the earth that had poisoned my mother. That night I'd whispered prayers into those fissures— prayers to the dead.

I attempted to put these memories out of my head and prepare myself for the interview. Vidocq's questions would require my utmost attention, not because I wanted to answer truthfully but because I needed to decide which details to reveal and which to obfuscate, as Maddy had instructed. My goal was to keep Nathan's reputation as clean as possible, even though he himself had endeavored to put a number of stains on it since his return from the war. Being at Ashe High House would also put me in close proximity to Nathan's belongings, and if I remained focused, I might be able to find time to make another experiment.

Nathan's family home rose dramatically on Parliament Hill. It was not a decrepit Gothic manor like Stoke Morrow or so many other of the shambling wrecks at the edge of the Heath. Nor was it Italianate cottagery, like Maddy's own whimsical La Dometa. Instead, Ashe High House was a full-fledged Tudor mansion, lofty and majestic. The Tudor had no fewer than sixty-seven rooms, including drawing rooms, bedchambers, a chapel, a china room, a servants' waiting hall, two dining rooms (one for summer and one for winter), three libraries, and even a postal office for Lord Ashe's mailings. There was a tree-lined inner courtyard accessible through the house's sunroom. The courtyard included a lake big enough for two rowboats to give each other chase. Being at the mansion generally made me feel I was in a small and bustling city, though with Nathan gone, the city had grown solemn. And on the day of my interview, it felt nearly abandoned.

I was escorted to the upper parlor by one of Vidocq's dark-suited assistants. Lady Ashe had a predilection for Egyptian decor, precipitated by Napoleon's conquering of the Africas, known in London as "Egyptomania." An onyx bust of the jackal-headed god Anubis glowered from one corner of the room—and the god's association with guiding lost souls to the underworld disturbed me. After Nathan's disappearance, I did not want to think too deeply of souls that were "lost."

The curtains were drawn, and Vidocq himself sat at a desk in near darkness, smoking a finely rolled black cigarette. I was unaccustomed to the acridity of his tobacco, so my first impressions of the detective were through a veil of tears. His image wavered and pulsed as he studied me with colorless eyes. His high collar seemed to support his head by bracing his neck, and he kept his large, square hands above the desk, glancing at my own hands from time to time. I'd read that Vidocq spent his younger years as a petty thief (an occupation that later helped him understand the minds of the criminals he sought), and I wondered if this checking of hands was a remnant of a thief's paranoia.

To the left of the desk stood a bronze ashtray with a carved hunting dog poised at the center of the bowl. When Vidocq balanced his cigarette on the tray, the dog seemed on point, and the cigarette, a felled pheasant.

"I have been told you have some knowledge of my history, Mademoiselle Silverlake," Vidocq said, tapping ash into the tray. His voice was terribly deep, though his accent still made it mellifluous.

"How could one not?" I replied, glad my nerves were somewhat intact. "I've read the stories by the American writer. 'The Purloined

Letter,' 'The Mystery of Marie Rogêt,' and, of course, his 'Murders in the Rue Morgue.' They are based on your exploits, I gather."

"Ridiculous embellishment," he said. "If there was any truth to them, it was altered by Mr. Poe's opiates. My actual cases tend to be mundane—misguided and angry young men doing harm to one another. No ghouls and certainly no *orangutans*."

"Reality," I said, attempting humor.

"Nathan Ashe wasn't much a proponent of reality, was he, Miss Silverlake?"

"How do you mean?" I asked, trying for an innocent tone.

"He was experimenting in the *unreal* before he disappeared, with the help of one Ariston Day."

"I know very little about Nathan's private affairs, especially those which coincide with Mr. Day's."

Vidocq raised his cigarette again, and I could tell from the look in his eyes that he didn't entirely believe me. "I met Mr. Poe a few years ago when he was traveling in France. Did you know that, Miss Silverlake?"

"I did not."

"At the time, I was still head of Napoleon's police, and we met in my office on the Rue de Terre. I'd heard from a literary friend that Poe wanted to find out if I was anything like the detective he invented—Auguste Dupin. He'd only read about me, you know."

"And were you like Dupin?" I asked.

Vidocq attempted a smile, though his thin lips weren't good at making one. "I suppose not. Nor was Edgar Allan much like the writer I'd envisioned. He was quiet, well spoken, a bit hollow around the eyes. The meeting was little more than small talk. I expected him to produce a raven or a bloodred mask at any moment, but Mr. Poe was simply an educated man, interested in hearing about the new cases I was pursuing."

"As models for stories?" I asked.

"He was beyond mysteries then, I believe. He was working on his novel about seafaring. Near the end of our conversation, he spoke of some scientific principles he'd been contemplating—a cosmology I could not much understand, other than that he thought that the universe went through cycles of expansion and contraction, and that we are currently in an age of contraction. All matter wishes to be unified as it was before creation divided it."

"Creation undone?" I asked, feeling my skin prickle. Such topics were a favorite of Nathan's and, so I'd heard, of Ariston Day's.

"Quite so. Speaking of this was the only moment where I believed I was in the presence of Edgar Allan Poe, but I did nothing to make him feel he was in the presence of Vidocq. My point here is that the actual body, the physical form, is not anywhere as interesting as the mind. There is no *real* in the human mind, is there, Miss Silverlake? There are only a variety of shifting phantasms. In order to rediscover the physical Nathan Ashe, I must come to understand something of his phantoms. Do you take my meaning?"

"Of course," I said.

"So what do you know of his phantoms, Miss Silverlake?"

I was taken off guard, and when I couldn't answer promptly, Vidocq offered a semblance of a laugh. "Mr. Poe had one thing right in his stories of Dupin. Deduction plays out exactly as it sounds—it's a system of subtraction. We remove this and remove that until all that is left is the truth or as close to the truth as we can come."

"I can assure you I know very little."

"And that's why I'm merely working to *remove* you."

I felt relieved at this and attempted a bit of flattery. "Lord Ashe assures us that if anyone can find Nathan, it's you, Inspector."

The tip of his cigarette crackled as he inhaled. "Lord Ashe puts a great deal of stock in an old man," he said. "Perhaps he would do better to name you as his detective, Miss Silverlake. I think men might answer your questions and forget guile entirely."

"I wouldn't know where to begin."

"One could simply ask: Did you abduct or aid in the abduction of Nathan Ashe?"

I glanced at the onyx statue of Anubis, studying his long jackal's muzzle and the staff he held at an angle against his chest. I wondered if the god used his staff to herd the dead, like sheep.

"Would you mind answering that question, Mademoiselle?"

"I would never want to see Nathan harmed. I care for him as I care for my own father."

Vidocq nodded. "And where were you on the evening in question—the evening of Nathan Ashe's disappearance?" The question was difficult to answer. How could I tell him that I'd spent the evening praying for everything to end, praying for all of it to be taken away. I'd lost myself that night, torn to pieces, and the stars came shining through.

I willed myself not to show any hint of this to Vidocq. I'd known, after all, that the inspector was going to ask about Nathan's final evening, and I'd prepared my answer carefully. "I spent a good part of the day in the company of Nathan and Madeline," I said. "The three of us were in the garden at Stoke Morrow, talking as we often did. Then a conflict arose."

"A conflict?" asked Vidocq.

"Maddy didn't like the idea of Nathan going to the Temple that night, and they argued. She said it was dangerous, but he wouldn't listen to reason. After we parted, I went for a long walk on Hampstead Heath to ease my nerves."

"Alone?"

"Yes."

"Why didn't Madeline Lee accompany you?"

"She was—distraught."

"So no one can account for your whereabouts that evening?"

I studied the flowers at my wrist. "Our maid at Stoke Morrow," I said. "When I returned from my walk it was late, and I was exhausted. She served me a soothing tea in our Clock Parlor. I fell asleep on the sofa, and she came to wake me near eleven o'clock."

"Very good," Vidocq said, making a note on the sheaf of paper in front of him. "Lady Ashe tells me that Nathan came home and ate a light supper before taking his regular carriage to Southwark. This must have been after he left you and Madeline Lee in the garden."

I paused. "I suppose that's correct."

"You did not see Nathan Ashe again after he left you?"

"I did not," I said.

"And before his disappearance, was Mr. Ashe courting you, Miss Silverlake?"

I hesitated, surprised at how the inspector drove ahead. "No."

"Then he was courting Miss Lee—daughter of the, how should I say, less than tasteful daguerreotypist?"

"We are friends," I said, "all of us together."

Vidocq cleared his throat, resting his cigarette in the bronze ash tray. "In France, it is not the custom for people of your age and of opposite sex to carry on as *friends*."

"Yes, well, it was irregular. We are irregular."

"What form does this irregularity take?" Vidocq asked.

I remembered to breathe, focusing on the feverfew to silence the tremor of objects in the parlor. "We spend time together and talk to one another about a great variety of things that men and women should not talk about according to convention. We are utterly open."

Vidocq nodded. Over the course of our conversation, a certain haziness had developed in his eyes, making me wonder if there was something other than tobacco in his cigarette. His sleepy look revealed his age and that he was perhaps no match for this case. "*Open* is an interesting word," he said. "Do you know, Miss Silverlake, that Nathan Ashe referred to you as 'the Doorway'?"

For a moment, I couldn't believe he'd spoken that name. Of course I knew Nathan called me the Doorway. He and I had many talks about my talent and what he believed the result of the talent might be if pushed, but how was it possible that Inspector Vidocq knew this as well? "He had pet names for all of us," I said, "as part of his playful nature."

"Calling someone a doorway is a curious endearment," Vidocq observed. "Any idea where he thought you might lead?"

"No," I said, lying and hearing Nathan's voice in my head: *the Empyrean, Jane. That's what the old mystics called it.* "Inspector, could you tell me where you heard about the name Nathan called me?" I asked.

He glanced up with faint interest. "Your friend and confidante Madeline Lee. Is there a problem?"

"It only made my heart heavy to hear Nathan's words," I said, trying not to show my shock at hearing of Maddy's revelation.

"Yes, well, you were both a great deal closer to the boy than any of his family, I gather," Vidocq said. "Especially after the war. His mother tells me he would go weeks without speaking to her. She only saw him from a distance. But he continued to speak to you and Miss Lee in confidence. Could you tell me about Mr. Ashe's comportment since his return from the Crimea?"

"He was *changed* by his experience in the war," I said, "as one would expect. Men are changed by war, are they not?"

Vidocq raised his brow but did not answer. Cigarette smoke churned in the air above his head. The room's shadows painted his sunken cheeks. "I was in a battle, Miss Silverlake—the First Coalition. A skirmish between France and Austria. You've probably never heard of it."

"I have not."

"No matter. I was a deserter and nearly arrested for it. One of my many crimes. I was nothing but a child then. Everyone around me was a child. I thought—why not leave this field of bloodied children? Why not walk away?"

I had no idea how to reply. Vidocq's haziness was causing him to reveal too much.

"Can you tell me anything about this *theater* in Southwark, Miss Silverlake?" he continued. "The Theater of Provocation beneath the Temple of the Lamb."

"Nathan did not share details of that place with me," I answered truthfully. "You'll have to ask Pascal Paget. He was involved with the Temple for a time."

"Monsieur Paget is reticent," he said. "It seems he's been cowed by the theater's proprietor."

"Ariston Day."

"Quite."

"Have you gathered any information on Mr. Day?" I asked.

Vidocq put out his cigarette, dropping the butt into the small pile of ash in the tray. "This and that," he said. "Nothing a young woman need bother herself with." He surveyed me. "Day is a dangerous man, Miss Silverlake. He has brought a great deal of harm to his followers in the past. I trust you'll steer clear of him."

"Of course," I said, thinking again of the letter I'd received that morning. "You might want to visit the Temple yourself. It's across Blackfriars Bridge in Southwark."

"I know where it is," Vidocq mumbled as he made more notes.

"We never imagined this would happen, Inspector," I said. "Of all the things we thought the future might—"

But I was cut off. A French agent in a charcoal suit and neckerchief appeared at the door and requested to speak to Vidocq immediately. The inspector stood, without excusing himself, and strode from the room, lighting another black cigarette on the way and leaving me alone. Perhaps it was his age or his altered state that caused him to leave his papers in such disarray on the desk. I leaned over, took the sheaf where he'd been making notes and read:

—*Jane Silverlake, friend to Nathan Ashe and Madeline Lee*
—*Known to Nathan as the Doorway*
—*Inconsequential, perhaps—not as pretty or exotic-looking as the Lee girl*
—*Appears calm, serene. Something beneath surface. Guilt? Anger?*
—*No: it's superiority. Isn't even looking at me. She's somewhere else, far away.*
—*Unlike anyone I've ever met. Certainly not as plain as she first appeared.*
—*Jane is hiding something*
—*Continually strokes the odd flowers at her wrist*
—*Difficult to look in her eyes . . . her quiet voice seems treacherous somehow.*

My face burned as I read this. How dare he write such things? I hadn't acted in a superior manner. I'd answered all his questions in turn. Treacherous, indeed. Emboldened by my anger, I looked toward the door to ensure that neither the inspector nor any of his

henchmen had reappeared, and then I sifted through the pile of papers on the desk until I found a sheaf marked "Ariston Day." I slipped
the papers into my dress pocket, took a final look at the statue of
Anubis, and made my way out of the room without bothering to wait
for Vidocq to dismiss me. It did not occur to me until much later that
I'd perhaps behaved exactly as the inspector intended.

CHAPTER 7

In my haste to leave Ashe High House, I forgot to look for another of Nathan's possessions. This missed opportunity troubled me, but even more troubling was the fact that Maddy had revealed my secret name to the inspector. To know that Vidocq was so close to understanding my true relationship with Nathan made me uneasy to say the least. I wondered what motive Maddy had for revealing such information. Was it possible my dearest friend did not trust me as much as she claimed?

For a moment, I wished I'd never shared my ability with either Maddy or Nathan. He had been nineteen and she and I, both a year younger. I'd been old enough to understand what damage my revelation could do, but at the time, I didn't care. The decision was fueled by my own vanity. I wanted them to think I was fascinating, especially Nathan, and I knew my talent would fix his gaze.

During my outing—as it were—the three of us held hands around a bottle of Tyndall's popular brand ink while standing in Heath's southern woods, not far from the outcropping of shale where my mother had succumbed. Oak leaves shone red and orange above us like fire, and the tree trunks looked like ancient pillars. The Heath was a temple that evening, and I was to be its priestess.

I'd chosen the ink bottle to demonstrate the transference because,

as an object, it was banal. I could have produced an extravagance
from Father's collection of curiosities—a Peruvian god-mask or a
mechanical bird designed by the medieval engineer Tommaso Fran-
cini. But there was no need. What I would show them would be extravagant enough.

I squeezed the cool slimness of Maddy's hand, and thrilled at the
sheer weight of Nathan's. I'd never touched him for such duration
before, and now that I had my chance, I cherished it. We huddled in
our small circle beneath the autumn sky, braced against the chill,
all staring down at the ink bottle nestled in the leaves. When nothing happened, Maddy, who was wearing one of her more dramatic
dresses, an emerald corseted gown with a dark silk flower in her
hair, said she was tired and would like to go home. "I don't know
what you mean to show us, Jane," she said. "But I'm not really in the
mood for a magic show."

Nathan hushed her. He was already interested in spiritism from
reading articles by William Crookes, head of the queen's Society
for Pyschical Research, and from his mother's own participation in
séances. My allusion to what I believed would happen with the ink
bottle pricked his interest further—another factor that contributed
to Madeline's state of perturbation.

I was experiencing some sort of anxiety over my performance and
felt as though I was pushing my consciousness against a batten of
wet cotton, trying to form some connection between the three of us.
Maddy made a kind of hiccupping sound, and then without warning,
the transference occurred. All the fine hair on my arms stood on end
and my teeth ached. I think even the leaves around us might have
rustled.

The three of us listened as the glass bottle of ink began to make
a high and wavering echo that was wordless, but later we all agreed
that listening to it allowed us each to feel something of what it was
to be the glass. There was a deeper sensation too—a greenish color
that made me think of old plant matter, great and sopping ferns blot-
ting out the sun. We were digging deeply into the bottle's ghosts,
glimpsing its most private layers. Nathan looked from the bottle to

my own face in shock, and Madeline began to giggle, as if someone had brushed a feather against the nape of her neck.

We broke hands, and for them, at least, the ink bottle grew silent.

"What in God's name, Jane?" Nathan asked, but I had no time to answer. Maddy was sinking toward the ground, still giggling, reaching her hand to a bed of leaves for support.

"Is the bottle haunted?" she asked. Maddy too was well apprised of séances. Nathan's mother had shared with us her investment in them, and Maddy's own mother, the venerable Eusapia Lee, became quite obsessed with summoning after the death of first her husband and then her son, Melchior.

"It's certainly not haunted," I said, picking the ink bottle out of the leaves and slipping it into the bag I'd brought. "I didn't think you believed in that kind of foolishness, Maddy."

"I don't," she said. "Of course, I don't. But, oh, it had a voice and it has been to strange places."

"It's not just the bottle. All objects emit sensation," I said. "It could have been anything: a pair of shears, a pocket watch, a mirror glass. Plants are soothing. That's why I wear flowers so often." I pointed at the feverfew tied at my wrist. "Flowers help me silence the objects."

Maddy's eyes became remarkably still, and I hated to see that I'd inspired fear in them. "Are you some kind of witch, Jane? I've been friends with a sorceress all this time?"

I sighed. "Oh, Maddy. Really."

Nathan helped her out of the leaves and to a bench some distance away. I followed, picking up her fringed wrap, which had fallen into the dirt.

"How fully have you experimented with this ability?" Nathan asked.

"Enough to know it isn't really much more than a parlor trick," I said. "There's beauty in it. A poetry of objects. But it doesn't go any further. I can't move them or alter them in any way. Sometimes if I let the experience go on too long, it gives me a splitting headache."

"But you have control over it?" Nathan asked. "You can make it stop and start?"

"A modicum of control, though there are times when it surprises me."

He was boyish about the whole endeavor, and I loved how he looked at me with fascination. My heart raced as he spoke. "Really, Jane, this is wonderful," he said. "I've seen mediums pull their tricks in parlors all over London, but that's all a bunch of wool. This, however, this is quite real."

I blushed. "I told you it would make for an interesting evening."

"Can you do it again?" he asked.

"No," Maddy nearly shouted from her bench. "Don't ever. That was the most frightening thing that's ever happened to me."

"I thought the most frightening thing was when you were thrown from your horse last summer," Nathan said.

"That wasn't *nearly* as bad as this," Madeline replied. "A horse, at least, is a rational creature."

"I don't want to repeat it," I said. "The transference makes me tired."

"Of course," he said. "But there are men who'd have an interest in this."

"If you're talking about William Crookes or any of the other pseudo-scientists setting up shop around London, I don't want to garner their interest. No one else should know about this. I'd rather not be studied, Nathan."

"Yes," he said, considering, as he handed Maddy a handkerchief. A fallen yellow leaf had attached itself to Nathan's lapel. He picked the leaf off carefully and turned to look at me, one sharp eyebrow cocked. Despite my fear of study, Nathan's new interest pleased me. I'd drawn his attention. I'd finally become a woman of significance.

After the tête-à-tête around the ink bottle, Nathan craved my touch. He wanted to experience the souls of objects everywhere and, at times, he seemed even to forget about Maddy.

"I don't know why you had to show yourself off like that, Jane,"

Maddy said one day in the privacy of my dressing room. "This whole affair has Nathan so out of sorts. He doesn't listen when I speak to him. He doesn't ask to go for walks."

I sat at the vanity, brushing my hair slowly and studying my face in the mirror—dark eyebrows and clear gray eyes. I wondered if it was possible that my face was growing slightly less plain as I matured. "I'm sorry, Maddy. It's just that—"

"What does it even mean," she asked, "your horrid little trick?"

I lay the brush on the vanity and turned to her, feeling for once I might have the upper hand. "When he looks at you, Maddy, he sees a beautiful girl. And now when he looks at me, he sees my talent. We both have something to offer, you see? My revelation will keep our little group strong."

When she next spoke, her tone was rueful. "You don't know the first thing about human nature, do you? It's because you were shut away for so long. You never learned how people really are."

When Nathan and I began our experiments, we would sit in the disorder of my father's study at Stoke Morrow with an object between us—a fire screen, a piece of embroidery, a picture frame, or even an image of the Holy Ghost pulled from the wall. Nathan would extend his hands, palms up on the table, and I would lay my hands on top of his—flesh against flesh. Touching him made a heat rise in my cheeks. Part of me wanted to open myself entirely to Nathan, to give him the shock of feeling everything inside me, yet I knew how dangerous that would be. My desire for Nathan was already doing more harm than good.

During our experiments, Nathan attempted to experience what I experienced, and all the while, I held back the greater part of my talent to protect him. The connection between us was so dampened that it did not always manifest, but there was still enough to excite him. A vein would appear on his temple, and his eyes would get a glassy look, as if he'd smoked opium. I should have known Nathan would try to force me to take the experience further. And, moreover, I should have realized where that furtherance would lead.

I can still hear his voice echoing in those darkened rooms: *Are you giving me everything, Jane? Is this all that you can hear and see?*

And my own response, a blatant lie: *Yes, Nathan, this is everything.*

Maddy wouldn't be kept away from these sessions. There were times she insisted on observing what she called our "dark rituals." I tried to persuade Nathan to simply cancel our work on those particular evenings, knowing how our apparent intimacy would provoke her, but he insisted on pushing ahead. I remember one particularly troubling evening. We were all together in my father's study, and the room was filled with dim flickering light from an oil lamp on the desk. Nathan held my hand, trying to see the golden bubbles that hovered around the lamp's glass chimney. I could see the bubbles clearly and could even hear them chirping faintly. He began rubbing my hand between his two hands, as if the friction might help produce the vision, and it was this rubbing that Maddy could not stand. She stood from the horsehair couch and said, "I don't want to look at the two of you fondling each other."

"We aren't expressing affection, Madeline," Nathan said, evenly. "As you know, I'm merely trying to experience what Jane experiences."

Hearing him provide such a frank explanation disturbed me, and I pulled away from him. I liked to imagine his touches meant something more. Suddenly, I felt like a creature, taken from its cage and handled. I was glad I hadn't shared everything with him. He didn't deserve the fullness of my talent.

"Here, then," Maddy said, standing over us, "take my hand, Nathan."

He grasped her extended hand, and then she waited. "So what do you *feel*?" she asked.

"Nothing," he said. "I feel nothing. Do you have some power you haven't told me about?"

I could see tears brimming in her eyes. "No," she said. "I clearly have no power whatsoever."

"Oh God, Madeline, don't make this into some *moment*," he said.

Without responding, she took her hand from his and ran from the room. I gathered my skirts to follow, but Maddy was too quick, already outside and halfway across the garden before I could reach the glass door in the conservatory. I watched her move through the Roman ruin and into the darkness of the southern woods.

"Leave her, Jane," Nathan said. "Maddy hasn't been in control of her emotions as of late, but she'll come around." His hand was on my shoulder, and I wondered if it was there to comfort me or once again merely to gain access to what was inside me.

"If she doesn't *come around*," I said, "we'll end all this experimenting. She's more significant than you know. I won't allow her to feel toyed with."

"Of course," he said.

I turned on him. "Don't think you can get away with some blithe 'of course,' Nathan. If this enterprise continues to disturb Maddy, we'll consider it finished."

"You don't take our experiments seriously, do you, Jane?"

"I take everything that concerns my affliction seriously," I said, attempting to control my emotions. I could feel anger rising from the pit of my stomach. I didn't want Nathan near me at that moment. I feared what might happen if my emotions got the best of me. "My father will be home soon. I need to rest before I speak to him. Please see yourself out."

After Nathan was gone, I went to my bed and lay facedown in my goose pillows, thinking of Maddy. She was as fierce a creature as I'd ever known, and I respected her greatly. She'd once said she and I were both outlaws—not unlike those famous villains of the American West that we read about from time to time in the *Herald*. "Society has abandoned us, Jane, and so we'll make our own society here on Hampstead Heath. We don't need the glittering fools of London or their parties." There was pain in her voice as she said this, and the paleness of her cheeks seemed authentic rather than a product of vinegar. We lay on my bed, staring up at the golden rings that held the bed curtains in place. Maddy was meant for those glittering parties—her fashionable clothes and refined manner spoke to that truth—but her father's art got her family cast out of such circles. Adolphus Lee's nude women on bicycles and in train cars ruined his daughter's chance at status, and God help me, I was thankful for his transgressions.

I could hear her whispering to me: "What forge was used to make your heart, Jane?"

"The very same that made yours," I said softly, though I wondered if that could possibly be true.

After Maddy's explosion in my father's study, life returned to nearly what it had been. I say "nearly" because there was a tincture of darkness that now appeared between the three of us, a shadow that expanded and contracted like a lung. The experiments ceased for the time being, and the following week, we all went walking on the Heath to clear our heads. I sat beneath a willow tree, legs curled comfortably, watching my friends play with Maddy's brass binoculars some distance away. Maddy wore an adorable cap and bicycle bloomers, and if I squinted, she looked every bit like some wayward boy from Saint Philip's Orphan Asylum. Her clothes, more often than not, came from her father's collection of costumes that he'd used for making his daguerreotypes. It seemed not to bother Maddy, or perhaps it pleased her, that these same outfits had been worn by the women who'd posed for Adolphus Lee in his various illicit images. "It wasn't Papa's photographs that were wrong," Maddy once said to me. "It was society's perception of them. You can see that, can't you, Jane?"

I demurred, as I'd seen Adolphus Lee's more risqué work, and I could not concede the problem lay entirely with society.

On the Heath that day, Maddy was bird-watching and Nathan leaned over her, perhaps attempting to help, but more likely trying to disrupt her efforts. Sunlight fell through the willow branches, turning the grass where I sat into a shifting sea of light and shadow.

I was afloat in the beautiful silence of the scene and the sweet fragrances of the Heath. I couldn't hear my friends' conversation—theirs was a secret moment. And I wondered if they talked about me, if they worried over what they should do with me in the long run. I tried to picture us together ten years in the future and then twenty but found I could not. No longer did I imagine we could all live together in some quaint little cottage. Life had grown complicated. We were all trapped in that lovely hour there on the Heath. But what did the future hold for any of us?

The answer to that question revealed itself in full a few days later during another walk. And when that revelation came, it shook us all. My talent was evolving, and not even I was sure what it might finally become. On that day, Maddy was using her brass binoculars again, trying to catch sight of the birds that filled the air with their song. We'd retreated to the Hampstead Hill where asphodels and blue cornflowers grew. "How can the birds make so much noise but apparently have no bodies?" Maddy asked, lowering the instrument.

"There's something sinister about invisible parakeets, isn't there?" Nathan replied, then pointing with his cane, "No, look. There's a kestrel on that low branch."

She swung around, trying to spot the bird but with no success because, of course, Nathan hadn't seen a bird at all.

"The only thing more sinister than invisible birds are birds of gross invention," I said, linking my arm gently through Maddy's and leading her in another direction.

When we realized Nathan wasn't following, we thought he was playing yet another boyish prank, but looking back, we found him in the shade of the oak tree where he'd claimed to have seen the bird. He was staring oddly down at his own hand.

Maddy called, "Come on then, Mr. Ashe. If we're out after dark we'll see more than kestrels. I've heard the dead crawl out Highgate at around half past six."

Nathan didn't respond.

"What is it?" I said. "Did you hurt yourself?"

He looked up, lips pulled back, so his teeth were showing. "I just had the strangest sensation—as if, well, as if my hand, my *own* hand, didn't belong to me."

"Who did it belong to?" Maddy asked, sounding concerned.

He blinked. "It belonged to Jane. For a moment, it felt as though my hand was her hand."

She glared at me. "What did you do to him, Jane?"

"Nothing," I said. "I did nothing."

"I knew those experiments would come to no good," she said, going to Nathan's side and looking at his hand. "It's all so bizarre, and now look—Nathan is paying for it. It's made him ill."

"It felt so *interesting*," he said, rubbing his hand against the leg of his linen trousers.

"It isn't interesting," Maddy continued. "If the two of you keep going like this, something awful is going to happen."

He disregarded her comment and looked instead at me. "You were inside me, Jane, unbidden."

"Perhaps you're inventing it because of your excitement," I countered.

He looked at me with something like longing. "Touch me again, Jane. Touch me so I can feel it again."

For a time after that day on the Heath, Maddy would not speak to me. Nathan wanted to continue our experiments, but I refused. During those lonely days without them, I spent my hours as I once had, wandering the halls of Stoke Morrow, and I was comforted mildly by sitting in the Tree Room, where Father gathered a wide variety of paintings and drawings with trees as their subjects. This room of trees reminded me of better times when Nathan and Madeline would jokingly ask me to tell the odd story of my birth as it was once related by my mother. They found the story amusing and said it made for a good explanation as to why I was so different. I both loved and hated the story, loved it because it was from my mother and hated it because, though fanciful, it reminded me of my difference.

When Mother told her stories, I felt close to her for once, as if she and I were a matched pair. I lay in my bed, with her standing over me, feeling as warm and comfortable as I would ever feel. As this happened before her death, I could not yet perceive the souls of objects. We were in the nursery, a room of quiet colors with battens of gauze fastened near the ceiling like clouds. Mother looked weathered and slightly frail. Only her dark, lush hair had the appearance of health.

There was a tree, Mother told me in a quiet voice, *a good strong oak*. She said she would admire the tree during her walks through the southern woods. It was the sort of tree that made her forget the sky because its canopy was so vast. She said druids might have once worshiped at such a tree. Mother walked around and around the oak, trailing her fingers over its fine bark. On the oak was a knot that caught her attention because, over the course of months, the knot expanded until it was nearly as large as a serving bowl. She would often touch the round hard knot, feeling curious warmth that emanated from it and hoping the tree wasn't ill. She returned often to check on the well-being of the tree. One day she found the knot split open, and there, cradled in the roots of the tree (for the roots had grown together to form a kind of bed), was a baby with dark hair, dark eyes, and the smoothest skin—nothing like the old ruined bark of the tree. She gathered the child in her arms and took it home for fear that the tree could not protect it from the animals that crawled upon the Heath. "I gave my little tree child a name," she said, stroking my hair. "I called her Jane."

The story frightened me, though I understood my mother intended it as a fairy tale. "Mother, I'm not a tree child," I would say. "I look like you. I *am* like you."

"I've thought about that," she mused. "It's possible that the oak loved me as much as I loved it, and so made a child in my image."

"You're telling lies," I said.

She brushed hair from my face with her hand. "I always wonder what my little tree child knows. What secrets does she keep?"

"No secrets," I said.

"You don't have tree knowledge?" she asked, playfully.

"Mother, please stop."

"As you command, tree child. As you command."

CHAPTER 8

I wanted to speak with Maddy, to learn why she'd revealed something as personal as the Doorway to Inspector Vidocq. I therefore went directly to La Dometa after my interview with the inspector and asked if she'd take a walk in the southern woods. Maddy was agreeable and told me that she was glad I'd come. She, apparently, had a kind of proposition for me. I'd already decided not to tell her about the letter from Ariston Day, as I no longer entirely trusted her with such information. I was wary of what she might reveal to the inspector if pressed once again.

The southern woods were silent, sprawling around us like a tendrilous dream. I could barely see the white of the sky through the tree branches. Maddy wore a dramatic Spanish mantilla fashioned out of black lace—an uncommon choice for a walk in the woods, and as I walked behind her, an awful image crawled into my head. I pictured myself attacking her, twining her mantilla around her neck and using it like a garrote to close her airways. I'd silence her so she could never reveal another of my secrets. The image left me feeling ill. I'd never harm her, of course, and yet I still could not understand why she'd betrayed me.

I suffered her initial questions about the interview, forcing myself to behave as I normally would, subdued and compliant.

"I told Vidocq nothing," I said. "I assure you."

"You didn't say anything about Nathan's erratic behavior near the end?" she asked.

"I did just as you instructed. But I learned something very curious from the inspector."

"What's that?" she asked.

"He knew that Nathan was fond of calling me the Doorway, and when I asked him how he knew, he told me you had revealed that information to him. Why would you tell him that, Maddy?"

She paused, looking momentarily unsure of herself. "Vidocq was so direct," she said, "so intent on plying every bit of information from me. I couldn't help myself. It merely slipped out. I'm so sorry, but I promise you I said nothing about your abilities. I would never do that."

"But you told me yourself that revealing even the slightest detail of significance could be dangerous," I said. "We're trying not to sully Nathan's good name. I'm just wondering why you tried to sully mine."

"I didn't mean—"

"You trust me, don't you, Maddy?"

"As if you were my own sister," she said.

"I believe you," I replied, and in my heart, I truly wanted to.

Maddy put her hand to her forehead, like she was checking for fever. "So many strange things are happening. At times, I think this couldn't possibly be my life."

"Unfortunately it's both of our lives," I said. "What was it you wanted to propose?"

She clutched the edges of the mantilla, drawing the drape of it around her body. "Last night, I had a realization—an epiphany, if you will. You're going to think it's mad, but I need your help."

"An epiphany?" I said, dryly. "Did the angels come and visit you?"

She ignored my comment. "I think we should take the investigation in hand, Jane."

"Meaning what, precisely."

"I've discovered the location of the tavern that's frequented by

Day's Fetches—the one called the Silver Horne that Nathan often talked about. We'll go there and question the patrons. Who knows, maybe Vidocq was correct in saying a woman might get more information than a man from these fools. And at any rate, it will make me feel as though we're *doing* something."

I thought of the Fetch who'd brought Day's message to Stoke Morrow—his black eyes and awful grin. I certainly didn't want to be in a room with so many boys who were like him. "Traveling south of the river is dangerous for people like us," I replied.

"The tavern isn't in Southwark," she said. "It's near Hyde Park. We can't expect the children of money to take their pints in the slums, can we?"

"I don't know about this, Maddy."

She paused and widened her eyes to evoke pity. "You wouldn't let me go alone, would you?"

I gave her a hard look. "You're such a fiend. People say I'm possessed, but I know very well that all the wicked demons are hiding in your pretty head."

"You're the dearest friend a girl could ask for, Jane. And I, for one, don't think you're even a bit possessed."

"Thank you for that," I said. "Will Pascal come along at least?"

She seemed only mildly disgusted at the mention of his name, and I hoped that her reaction meant their friendship was on the mend. "He's afraid of seeing Alexander there. We can take Ferdinand for protection, if it makes you happy."

I sighed. Ferdinand was the Lees' excitable shepherd hound. "I suppose a dog will have to do, or I could dress as a man."

"Like you used to?" Maddy asked.

I merely shook my head, amused at the notion. Before the world went wrong, she and I played a game where I pretended to be Nathan Ashe. This effect was garnered by my wearing one of Father's suit coats and placing a carnation in the lapel. I didn't mind playacting, as it pleased Maddy so.

We would sit in my bedroom at Stoke Morrow where the silk wallpaper was painted with blue forget-me-nots and white rosebuds.

After having instructed me never to *actually* kiss her, she would then try to persuade me to do just that. And in this way we could keep the game going. She would sweep about my chair, sometimes dipping nearly into my lap, sometimes hovering at my shoulder and whispering in my ear.

"Maddy, I hardly think behaving like a fly is the way to get Nathan to kiss you," I said.

"Jane, stop it," she said. "You *are* Nathan Ashe. He doesn't speak in the third person."

Assuredly, my characterization was far from perfect, as I had little notion of how to pose as our beloved. Maddy and I talked of Nathan like he was some figure from a romance novel. We'd layered him with so many conventions that we could barely be sure there was a human being beneath.

As Maddy swept about, I was to say things she thought Nathan might say—*are you quite ill, Madeline? Are we nearly done with this tomfoolery?* And as I sat there, I focused on my right hand, imagining that Nathan was touching me. I ran my hand gently down my cheek to my neck, not daring to dip lower.

"Whatever are you doing that for, Jane?" Maddy asked. "Nathan doesn't go about caressing himself, does he?"

"Sorry," I said. "I was drifting."

"Well, please apply some focus to your role."

And so I did. I focused every thought and devotion on Nathan Ashe. Even if I could not have his hand or Maddy's, I could certainly have my own.

"Jane, are you quite all right?" Maddy asked, pausing at her entreaties.

"Of course," I said.

"For a moment, you actually *looked* like him. I didn't like it at all."

I touched the sleeve of her dress, avoiding her skin. "I'm sorry, dear. I won't do it again."

*   *   *

Remembering our playacting was like coming upon some lost civilization. None of us knew the sort of lines that could be drawn among people who loved one another. And they did love me, Nathan and Madeline. There'd been times during our friendship when dark emotions from my solitary childhood resurfaced, and in those moments of doubt, I worried that they only *tolerated* my presence, that they were waiting for me to leave so they could be alone. I invented sidelong glances between the two of them. The combs in Maddy's hair chirped like petulant birds, the brass head of Nathan's cane spat sparks, and I imagined these objects were doing their masters' bidding, trying to frighten me away. Most often though, I believed my friends found me a necessary piece.

For a long while, we triangulated, and there was energy in that. I sometimes felt myself to be the center of our group, a project for both of them. It wasn't until Nathan discovered the Empyrean itself that everything truly got out of hand. The triangle was broken by that strange vision, and it was then that we began our free fall.

CHAPTER 9

The three of us were at Highgate Cemetery when Nathan made his discovery and first called me the Doorway. This was soon after Maddy started speaking to me again, having gotten over the fact that Nathan said I'd mysteriously possessed his hand. It was a warm afternoon in June, and we'd all paused near the entrance to the necropolis that bordered the Heath to the north. Nathan claimed he wanted to smoke. I preferred not to stop near the cemetery gates for the same reason I preferred not to travel to the interior of London. Being surrounded by so many manufactured objects agitated me, as the pollen of flowers agitates some. New objects were especially bad, and Highgate was largely new construction.

But Nathan insisted, taking a seat in the tall grass and resting his back against the stone wall. His auburn hair fell in a fine arc across his forehead, and the rest of his face was a picture of wistful elegance. The tombs rose behind him like windowless houses. The avenues of Highgate were cobbled and manicured in such a way one might believe the dead made actual use of them. How could it be that the cemetery was so freshly mortared, while London itself was breaking into ruin?

The air smelled of brake ferns and earth, as the parkland roused itself from winter, but I could take no pleasure in any of it. My

thoughts were with the carved stones, which each sounded like distant steam engines, beginning their approach.

I'd recently begun experiencing something new from the objects,
but I hadn't shared it with my friends. This new sensation was the
most dramatic turn my talent had taken since its inception. In fact, I
believed it might be my talent's final evolution—what my power was
meant for all along.

It was as if every object had become a curtain, and behind that
curtain lay a new realm. The realm was not of simple color and
sound—it was an actual place. Had I read any of the burgeoning literature of scientific fiction, I might have called the place a "parallel
dimension," but I had no word for what I saw. It was a landscape—a
white forest, pale as paper, clearly a vision of some alien landscape. In
the forest was a stream of milk-white water that did not flow but remained still, as if frozen. There were flowers in the undergrowth—
blossoms that appeared to be lit from within, like Chinese lanterns.
I recognized the place. As a child, I'd seen it in dreams inside the
mouths that opened in Mother's flesh. *Don't be swallowed, Jane. You
must never be.* This was the place where the old animal gods lived.
Where they waited for me. And I knew instinctively this forest was
meant to be a secret, like the oval painting in Mother's wardrobe.
The secret was not to be shared, even with my friends.

"If there was a God, I think he'd make his house on the Hampstead Heath," Nathan was saying, drawing a cigarette from its case.
Maddy had brought the cigarettes—case and all—from her travels
in France with her mother that winter. Nathan put the cigarette
between his thin lips and barely inhaled. Though there were times
when he said he "needed" to smoke, I suspected he was only making
a show for Maddy, as it seemed he didn't actually know how.

"Being on the Heath doesn't make me think of God," Maddy said.
"It makes me feel even more that we're alone. Time comes unhinged.
We're drifting into days that occurred before the Saxons or the Ro-
mans." She'd learned her atheism and her sense of poetry early on
from her father, Adolphus. "I can almost see a great, bony creature
there," she said, pointing to a far patch of grass that moved restlessly

in the wind, "raising its vulgar head to peer in our direction. It's something from the fossil record—come to life."

We looked out across the Heath but saw nothing. Nathan had read to us recently from an article on archaeological digs in North America where scientists were uncovering the bones of massive creatures from the past. He was fascinated by the idea that this history of the world was packed away beneath our feet. He said that one day we'd know everything that ever happened in the past and in what order.

"Will this creature devour us?" Nathan asked lightly, smoke curling from his open mouth.

"It only watches," she replied. "And wonders about us."

"It suffers from ennui," Nathan said, "like you, Jane."

I let his comment pass, focusing on the cemetery behind him. The stones were emitting the new frequency, smooth and low—and the frequency was organizing itself into an image of the pale forest with the white stream running through it. I must have shown these thoughts on my face because before I knew what was occurring, Nathan was beside me, saying, "Jane, what's the matter," and he put his hand on my hand. I didn't have time to dampen my experience and hide it from him. His expression changed from concern to dismay. He took a small step back, nearly stumbling over a loose rock. Maddy was there to steady him, and Nathan put one finger to his ear, as if to stop a ringing, all the while continuing to stare at me.

"What was that?" he asked.

I acted as though I didn't know what he meant.

"When I touched you," he said. "There was something new. My head was full of not a color or a sound, but a *place.*"

"Perhaps you should sit, Nathan," Maddy said. "Sit here." She helped him to a large rock. Nathan sat but barely acknowledged her help. His gaze was so fixed on me. "Jane, are you experiencing something new? Something you haven't told us about? I saw white trees and a still stream that looked as though it was made of marble."

I avoided his glance. How could I talk about what I was experiencing—that the souls of the objects had reconfigured to make a kind of geography? What the gravestones were now communicating was a transcendent realm—not merely an intuited space, but a physical space. The fact that the objects were alive was not as significant as the fact that they concealed within themselves a silent kingdom. Father had once told me the Gnostics believed each human being concealed within himself a Heaven. I wondered if this was somehow the Heaven of the objects.

"Jane," Nathan was saying, "are you a doorway to that place? Can we go there?"

I found I could not answer. My gaze shifted from Nathan to Maddy, and I caught an expression on her face that disappeared in the next instant. I was sure I'd seen it though. It had looked, quite impossibly, like loathing.

"Jane, the Doorway," Nathan added softly. "I felt almost like I could open you."

It was after the discovery at Highgate that Nathan began his research in earnest. He brought stacks of bound manuscripts to Stoke Morrow, most of them from the Middle Ages. I had no idea where he procured such texts, and he would only tell me that his father's wealth had its benefits. Nathan eventually began to focus on a particular Italian writer known as Theodore de Baras, a monk who'd lived on the island of Malta in the thirteenth century. De Baras wrote extensively about the levels of the medieval Heaven, specifically the highest, known as the Empyrean. Nathan translated a passage from de Baras's bound codex:

> The Empyrean is not made of fire as some would have it; rather it is a cool place, still as a stone. I hold the belief that the Empyrean is neither the lost Garden of Eden nor even a part of God's own Heaven, but rather a remnant of that realm which existed before Creation. The Empyrean is a place of innocence and purity where there is no question of good or evil. There are no trees of tempta-

tion, no fear of expulsion. It is most akin to the Hindu Nirvana—
a place free of greed and delusion. It is my studied opinion that
the Empyrean is a remnant that I will henceforth call the Great
Unmade, and to enter it would be to gain freedom from suffering
brought on by Creation. Many think it impossible to make a pilgrimage to such a place, but I believe there is a way. I speak here of
the Roman girl and the fabled *music of the spheres.*

"Who is the Roman girl?" I asked, intrigued.

Nathan turned the worn manuscript page. "It doesn't say any
more about her. This is only a partial document, I think. There appear to be pages missing. But listen to this, Jane." He began reading
again:

The music of the spheres is the vibration that all matter emits. It
is said to be inaudible to the human ear. Only God and his angels
can perceive it. Yet I now believe there are those gifted few who apprehend these vibrations. And through the cracks, they can see even
the silent place—that which existed before the Word. I pause here
to relate historical instances. In particular, a woman spoken of on
the island of Malta, known only as the Lady of Flowers.

"Stop," I said. I could feel my heart beating quickly in my chest.
I'd never revealed the name my mother had spoken to me. Nathan
hadn't even paused when he'd read it in the manuscript. "Give me the
book, Nathan."

"What's wrong?" he asked.

I held out my hand. "Just give it to me."

He did as I asked, and the codex moaned when I touched it. A
faded woodcut on the yellowed page showed a woman in a long
and twining robe. Wrapped about her body were coarse vines that
bloomed with mouthlike flowers—gaping things. Horrid. The
woman's expression was disdainful. She stared out at me, knowing
more than I knew. I thought of the oval painting concealed in the
wardrobe at Stoke Morrow, and then I thought of my mother's own

words: *She's there, blooming in the darkness, silent and waiting.* How was it possible that Mother's Lady was here in this medieval text?

The parlor around us was spinning. Objects creaked. I continued to stare down at the picture, looking into the woman's hard, black eyes. She, in turn, stared back at me, concealing the answer to all the mysteries I longed to solve. The desk between Nathan and me wanted to split open and reveal the terrible white forest beneath.

I let the book fall from my hands.

At some great distance, Nathan was saying, "Jane, are you quite all right? Can you hear me, Jane?"

CHAPTER 10

I left Maddy in the southern woods, Vidocq's record of Ariston Day still hidden in the pocket of my dress. Despite the fact that Maddy wanted to begin an investigation, I still didn't think it was wise to share the stolen information with her. I arrived home and spread Vidocq's papers on my father's writing desk, reading his meticulous script. I learned that "Ariston Day" was not the man's actual name but one in a series of pseudonymous affectations. Day was born Archibald Douglas in County Sligo, Ireland, to a destitute farmer who'd taken his own life shortly after the birth of his son. Several other monikers were listed: "Aristotle Dorn" and "Agathon Demeter." Day alternately presented himself as being from Italy, Greece, and the Russian Empire. He had no perceptible Irish accent and was, Vidocq wrote, "largely a product of erasure."

What came next was more troubling. The Theater of Provocation was apparently not Day's first foray into cults. The first such gathering was short-lived, assembled from boys who were Day's peers in County Sligo. This was before Day made his pilgrimage to Rome—an event that Vidocq said transformed the Irish boy into a philosopher and a possible mystic. The Sligo group met in a disused sheep barn outside of Day's humble village. According to records of the local magistrate, the meetings were halted by order of law after one of the members—Sean Fellhorn—had been spiritually "violated." The specific act of violation was not named in the magistrate's documents, but according to hospital records, Fellhorn became so corrupt he could no longer be allowed in the proximity of women. The boy also refused to read from the Bible and would not speak his father's name. Vidocq wrote:

> As is often the case with the ridiculous court systems in out-of-the-way villages, the punishment for the corruption of young Fellhorn did not suit the actual crime. Ariston Day (then called Archibald Douglas) was to be hanged for leading the boy astray, but by some miraculous last-minute overturning of the magistrate's rule, he was set free. This precipitated Day's escape from County Sligo and his perpetual life in hiding.

The second cult, which was of a more extravagant and nefarious nature, came to fruition in Suffolk after Day returned from his stint in Rome. Day based the Suffolk cult on the Eleusinian Mysteries, a series of ancient initiation ceremonies that were meant to honor Demeter and her daughter, Persephone, the queen of Hades. In order to participate in the Eleusinian Mysteries, Greek boys who'd reached the age of puberty were sworn to a vow of secrecy and sent into a system of tunnels where they were terrorized by priests and hierophants who were dressed as primeval monsters. The terror was intended to purify the boys—to make them heroes. It also provided them with visions of enlightenment that they were sworn never to share with anyone.

Day gathered his Suffolk cult in Saint Rudolph's cave, a narrow shaft that opened onto a ballroomlike subterranean chamber, which he filled with burning tapers and the effigies of animals made from sticks and pelts. As with Day's Fetches, the Suffolk boys were sworn to secrecy. Little was known about the rituals performed in the cave, though they were later believed to have involved some form of blood rite, as many of the boys bore similar scarification on their necks and chests. The reign of Day's Suffolk cult ended when one of his young followers was found naked in the woods one winter morning, mumbling something about the opening of the Heavens and a procession of angels. The boy later died in a hospital room from what was deemed exposure, and though no injunctions were placed on Ariston Day, he was soon enough gone from Suffolk, only to reappear nearly a year later in London.

"Throughout all of this," wrote Vidocq,

Day's goal has remained consistent. He wishes to achieve a large-scale transcendence in which humankind will be returned to what he imagines an original "Paradise"—his so-called spiritual bedrock. It is this grand delusion, this wish to be the world's savior, which makes him so dangerous. He will do anything to reach his goal, and my fear is that Day has found his perfect match in Southwark. He has learned to avoid the vigilant eye of small communities. Southwark is a chaos where he can submerge himself and experiment with his Fetches to his heart's content. I should note that I have made a thorough investigation of the Temple of the Lamb but cannot find sign of either Day or his Theater of Provocation. The proprietors of the tavern claim to know nothing of him. My search continues.

The papers made no specific mention of Nathan's case, but the inferences were frightening indeed. Ariston Day was not to be trifled with, and he was certainly capable of doing harm in his search for grand transcendence. Day's letter indicated that he believed me to be the key to his endeavors. It was likely he thought I had some connection to the original Paradise, and I worried that he believed I could provide that connection through the Empyrean itself.

I folded the sheaf and lowered it into the fire, which Miss Anne had recently stoked, and though the papers burned, my thoughts of Ariston Day persisted.

*　　　*　　　*

Before I could further agree or disagree with Maddy's plan to cir-cumnavigate Vidocq and take the investigation of Nathan's disap-pearance upon ourselves, we were off in her black carriage, shuttling toward Hyde Park for our rendezvous with the Fetches at a tavern called the Silver Horne that bordered the park's silent pastures. With us was the Lees' shepherd dog, Ferdinand, a mangy sort of animal that had not been bathed in some time and made me wish I hadn't asked for protection.

"You'll promise me you aren't going to do anything foolish," I said. "The Fetches aren't your run-of-the-mill society boys—at least not anymore."

Maddy scratched Ferdinand on his awful head and replied, "Hon-estly, Jane, when have you ever known me to behave foolishly? And you know my feelings on this subject—once a society fop, always a society fop. My guess is we could strong-arm the whole lot of the Fetches if we so choose."

"You're worrying me, Maddy," I said. "More so every day." I sat back against the hard bench seat of the Lees' carriage and watched the narrow streets of London ripple by. Yellow London brick had an interesting effect on my talent. I could hear the bricks marching, as if they were an army, gathering to protect the city.

It was fortuitous that Pascal did not come with us, as his beloved Alexander Hartford was the first Fetch we encountered at the Silver Horne—an establishment of dark oak and cozy gas lamps that was tucked away in an alley off Oxford Street. The Horne was not visible from the street itself. Only the faint glow of firelight reflected on the damp alley bricks betrayed its presence, making it a better en-vironment for the cult of Fetches than a street-facing tavern like the Boar's Head or the Three Cranes. The Horne smelled of liquor, old cigars, and the brittle leather that upholstered its benches. At least three groups of Fetches were gathered at round tables within, all young men in red coats. The boys seemed restless, as if they hadn't had enough sleep, and when Maddy and I passed over the threshold (our entrance was a bit sopping and less than elegant due to the rain), they all looked up with doggish faces. I was glad to see the messenger who'd come to Stoke Morrow was not in their number.

"Ladies," Alexander said in his flat American accent. He was Boston born, his father a shipping magnate, and his presence was nothing like Pascal's. I would have never marked him for an invert. He was blond and brutish, taller than most of the boys in the room. He was the sort of young man who should have been cheerful. In fact, he *had* been cheerful not so long ago when I'd first encountered him. But his once silvery blue eyes had turned to lead, and there was a new weight around his jaw. Alexander had become a serious individual, perhaps even morose, and though he had a near-empty pint in his hand, he didn't seem a bit drunk. "I didn't think you were the kind of girls to come to a standard unaccompanied," he said.

"We're not," Maddy replied, pulling back on the leash of Ferdinand, who was, in turn, straining forward to sniff at Alexander's jackboots. "But we're hoping you men would be civil enough to help us find our friend."

"Competing with the French inspector, are we?" Alexander said, nudging the boy next to him to rouse him from his stupor. The other boy was of a thicker sort, with a low Dorchester brow. Alexander introduced his companion as Master Rafferty, and Rafferty mumbled some slurry greeting before tipping back his pint glass to take another drink.

"Our investigation has nothing to do with Vidocq," Maddy said. "All we want is to find Nathan. No legalities."

"We don't know anything more than we've already told the inspector," Alexander said. He seemed bored by our presence, but I had a feeling that his boredom was an act to cover restless nerves. "That's the God's honest truth, Maddy. We all liked Nathan Ashe. We want him found. He's one of us, after all, and we Fetches stick together."

I looked at Rafferty as Alexander spoke, and there was some wince of pain in his heavy face. Was it remorse? It passed too quickly for me to tell.

"So you won't mind explaining to us exactly what went on at the theater that night," Maddy said, "the details of the provocation or whatever it was called."

"You girls know the Fetches are sworn to secrecy," Alexander said. "What good is a secret society if you start telling every woman in London about it?"

"Forgive me if the rules of boys' clubs don't interest me," Maddy said.

"Probably better if you were on your way." Alexander gestured toward the door with his pint. "Place gets rowdy as evening wears on. The boys can get a little—restless."

"Please, Alexander," I said. "We're only looking for a bit of information."

"I *am* sorry," he replied, suddenly earnest. "It's just—there's nothing I can say."

I was surprised that Maddy backed down at that, suddenly ushering me toward the exit, jerking on Ferdinand's leash. I paused long enough to call back, "Pascal would like to talk to you, Alexander. *Sleep and Death*, remember? You owe him a final conversation, don't you?"

Rafferty laughed at this, clapping Alexander hard on the back. Alexander looked queasy, but I didn't care. I was, in fact, *glad* to trouble him. He'd left Pascal in an utter lurch, and a person like that deserved his share of public humiliation.

"Why didn't you press Alexander?" I asked Maddy when we'd cleared the door of the Silver Horne. "He surely would have at least spilled some bit of information."

"Because the other boy looked like he wanted to speak to us alone. Go slowly, Jane, and watch."

Maddy was correct. A few moments later, before we'd reached the carriage waiting for us in the alley, a drunken voice sounded behind us. Ferdinand issued a warning bark, and Maddy hushed him. Rafferty appeared, still carrying his pint glass as he half-jogged to catch up with us.

"You girls," he said.

"Yes, us girls," Maddy replied.

We all stood there for a moment looking awkwardly at one another, letting the rain drench us further.

"You want to know about the provocation on Nathan's last night?" Rafferty said finally. "I'll tell you about the provocation, but you got to do something for me in return."

"I can't wait to hear what," Maddy said.

"You have to promise that one day you'll both let me take you out—make an evening of it. I heard Nathan Ashe used to take you out, and well—I don't know. I'd like a chance to have an evening," he said.

There was something so humble about this request; I wanted to tell Maddy to tread carefully.

"You want to take us to dinner?" Maddy asked. "That's far more innocent than what I was expecting, Mr. Rafferty."

"You can call me Paul," he said, bracing himself with one hand against the stone wall of the alley.

"Why are you doing this?" she asked.

"Because I have no love for those boys in there," he said. "I'm not as much of a flaunter as they are. My family doesn't make money. I don't even know why Mr. Day invited me into the group. Some told me he took a liking to me—that he likes fatter boys sometimes—but that's disgusting to me."

"Likes them for what?" Maddy asked.

Paul Rafferty made a sour face. "For whatever he gets up to in the solar above the theater. It ain't the kind of thing you say to girls."

"An evening with both of us," Maddy said. "You'll have it, Paul."

I wasn't sure how I felt about her offering me without my consent, but I remained silent.

"I don't care about their bloody secrets," Rafferty said, as if convincing himself. "You want to know how the thing went off that night?"

"We very much do," Maddy said. "Let's find some shelter where it isn't quite so wet."

The three of us stepped beneath the awning of a nearby shop, and the rain continued to pound London as Rafferty told his tale.

"Here's how it went," he said, "the last night anybody saw Nathan Ashe. The provocation was called *The Royal Hunt*. Maybe you know that already. We Fetches built a forest in the rooms under the Temple of the Lamb. Hard work. Lots of lifting. Most of those boys can't do a thing like that. I ended up putting up most of the trees myself. And that night in our forest, we hunted a stag."

"An actual stag?" I said, thinking of the creature I'd seen in the painted forest when I touched Nathan's Bible.

Rafferty shook his head. "It was a bloke playing at a stag. The stag was Nathan Ashe."

I wondered, momentarily, if I had been granted a vision of Nathan's final night. And if I was seeing those moments, who but Nathan could communicate such images to me? What had he been trying to tell me?

"You *hunted* Nathan?" Maddy asked, incredulous.

"He wore a pair of ridiculous stag's horns," Rafferty said, "and a pelt around his shoulders. He tried to hide from us in the forest. It was dark as Hell in there. The only light came from our lanterns. And he was scared because Ariston Day told him that if we caught him, we were allowed to hurt him—just like in a real hunt. And a bunch of the boys wanted to hurt Nathan because he'd become a favorite of Mr. Day's. Don't believe what Hartford tells you about all of us being friends. The Fetches were jealous of Nathan. One of them stuck him with a phony spear. Nathan was bleeding. They would have done worse if they caught him, I'm sure."

"How did they plan to hurt him?" Maddy asked.

Rafferty shrugged. "The usual ways, I suppose."

"But did they *hurt* him, Paul?" There was a note of desperation in Maddy's voice.

"We didn't find him," Rafferty said. "That's what I'm trying to tell you. Something went wrong with the provocation. Nathan got sick. He was dragging his left leg, and his arm was limp. He'd told us early that evening they'd gone numb because of some experiment he'd been undertaking with you, Miss Silverlake. He said his body was not his own."

"He spoke of me to the Fetches?" I asked.

"Spoke of you often," Rafferty said, solemnly. "We thought he'd be an easy mark—the way a stag that's hurt is easy. Alexander Hartford, that buddy of yours in there who's no proper buddy at all, was the Huntsman General. He kept blowing on his stupid bleeding horn."

I heard the sound of the horn from my vision—a bright high note in the darkness. The recollection of it made me cold.

"The call of the horn echoed through the theater," Rafferty said, "and I thought it might bring the whole ceiling down on us. We thought we had him, you know? Nathan was just in front of us—we saw his shadow there with the stag horns and the fur at his shoulders. And Alexander even said something like—*he's ours, men. The stag is ours.* But once we got around the tree, old Nathan Ashe wasn't there. He'd—well— he'd disappeared. And there was this odd smell in the air. It reminded me of the time my mother took me down to see the Egyptian mummy at the British Museum. The smell was sweet, but somehow like death.

"Mr. Day told us to light all the lamps 'round the theater. We checked the whole of the forest for him, but Nathan wasn't there. And the entrance was locked, as it always was when we did a provocation. He couldn't have gotten out. It didn't make a bit of sense. And then something surprising happened—Mr. Day got worried. And he's never gotten worried before, no matter what kind of business we got up to. He said a strange thing to us—that we should all go home and dream Nathan back—as if we could do a thing like that."

"You're telling us Nathan disappeared from a locked room?" Maddy asked, too sharply. "That doesn't make sense, Paul."

"It's what happened though," Rafferty replied.

"Is it possible that Ariston Day did something to him when all of you were off playing the hunt?"

"Anything's possible," Rafferty said. "And that place isn't so *stable*, if you catch my drift. Things are changeable in the theater, sometimes even mad. But I swear that Nathan was behind that tree and then—he just wasn't."

"Were there any women in the theater that night?" I asked, thinking of the creature dressed in red who'd pursued the stag in my vision.

"Women?" Rafferty said. "God no. Never in the theater."

Rafferty walked us back to the carriage, and when he kissed
Maddy good-bye, it was a gentle kiss on the cheek, not drunken.
Then he kissed me just as lightly, and I wondered if he heard the
bricks moaning around us when he touched my skin. As I pulled
away, he caught hold of my arm and whispered, "You be careful, Jane
Silverlake. Be careful of all of them. Even her."

And this was as confusing a warning as anything Rafferty could
have said. Be careful of Maddy? I wondered again about her revelation to Vidocq. Was it possible that more of the same was on its way?

"What was it Rafferty said to you at the end of our talk?" Maddy
asked as we were shuttling back toward Hampstead in her coach.

I thought of telling her the truth but knew it would only serve to
make her feel on edge. I said, "He told me you were pretty."

"Drunken fool," she said. Ferdinand had climbed onto the bench
seat and put his paws on Maddy's dress. She angrily pushed the dog
away. "I don't believe for a moment Nathan disappeared into thin air
from a locked room. There has to be something more."

"Yes," I said quietly. "Certainly something more."

CHAPTER 11

I was haunted by Rafferty's description of the hunt and my own experience of the scene. I'd felt the pain and the fear of the stag, and the creature reached out to me, as if it wanted my help. If the creature was actually some astral version of Nathan Ashe, that made things all the worse. I was beginning to fear that the events that had occurred at the provocation were, in some way, connected to my prayers at the field of shale that night.

Again I wished I could remember more of what happened after I'd said my prayers. I closed my eyes and tried to remember. I saw only some sort of red fabric fluttering in the darkness, as if moved by a strong wind. I knew that if my actions had somehow brought harm to Nathan, it was my duty to help him now. It didn't matter what he and Maddy had done in the southern woods that evening. I'd make my atonement, but first I needed to learn more about what had actually occurred.

I couldn't let Maddy know any of this, of course. If she made a connection between me and *The Royal Hunt*, I had no idea what she'd do. I hoped, in fact, that she might cease her investigation after our experience at the Silver Horne. But Maddy was intrepid. She came to Stoke Morrow the following morning and didn't bother to dismount her carriage to summon me. Instead, the Lees' coachman, a tall gentleman with a beard who slouched when he drove the horses, came to the door and said that Miss Lee requested my presence for an outing. I wrapped a shawl around my shoulders and stepped into the wet spring air.

The carriage was parked beneath the flowering trees. Horses, dark and well groomed, observed my approach. I tapped on the carriage window and when Maddy lowered it, I feigned surprise. "I was expecting an audience with the queen," I said.

"There's no time for humor, Jane," she replied. "Get in."

"I'd like to know where I'm going first, if you don't mind."

She sighed. "I'm abducting you."

"In light of recent events, I don't think that's terribly funny, Madeline."

"All right, I've made arrangements for us to meet with the sister of a Fetch," she said. "Her name is Judith Ulster. An acquaintance of mine in Cheapside told me that Miss Ulster has actually been *inside* Day's Theater of Provocation—despite the rule against women. She knows how it works, and she'll tell us the whole truth about the place."

"You have acquaintances in Cheapside?"

"I keep in touch with some of the girls who posed for my father. They're fascinating women. Now will you get in this carriage, or do I have to go without you?"

I complied, of course, in spite of my reservations. I wouldn't let her go alone. It wasn't until I was sitting on the bench seat across from Maddy that I asked where we were to rendezvous with Miss Ulster.

"The archery gardens outside the Crystal Palace."

My heart sank, and Maddy must have seen the trouble on my face. "That's right, Jane. Every so often we have to be seen in public. We can't spend all our days wandering the Heath like sylphs. I'm sorry."

"You know I have an aversion to the Crystal Palace," I said. "Why would you choose it?"

"*I* didn't choose it. Judith Ulster is quite the sportswoman, and she's to be at the archery field practicing all afternoon. She said if we want to speak to her, we should meet her there. She was hesitant about even meeting at all—something to do with her brother, the Fetch. I couldn't very well say, 'Oh, I'm afraid the Crystal Palace would never do, Miss Ulster. You see, my friend Jane thinks blood will pour out of her eyes and ears if she ever sets foot inside that place.'"

"I never said anything about blood," I replied.

"You might as well have. The palace is an amusement. Nothing more. At any rate, we don't even have to go inside. The archery gardens are on the outskirts of the palace grounds."

"You're so glib about the whole thing, Maddy," I said, "as if you don't even remember the prophecy."

"Oh, I'm finished with you, Jane. The so-called prophecy was nothing more than a hoax perpetrated by a charlatan in Piccadilly. The whole of it was merely brought on by one of Nathan's whims."

"His whims are beginning to have far greater import than we previously believed," I said.

Maddy removed a slim leather-bound volume of poetry from her skirt pocket. "If you don't mind," she said, "I'll read until we arrive. No more talk of prophecies. We are looking for facts."

I understood her mistrust of the events in Piccadilly, which had occurred nearly a year prior, shortly before Nathan left for the war. It had been a brighter time for all of us, though the evening itself was markedly strange. The prophecy seemed absurd, yes, but Maddy hadn't seen what I saw. The machine in question that gave us the prophecy was the only object I'd ever encountered that had no soul.

A knock had come at my dressing room door that particular evening, and I answered, thinking it would be Miss Anne, asking what I'd like for dinner, but it was Maddy, looking splendid in a lapis-colored dress and a yellow scarf. I was so happy to see her, so in love with the idea of her, that I forgot dinner entirely.

"Nathan wants us to go into the city with him," she said, excitedly. "To Piccadilly Circus."

"We were just in the city last week," I said.

She was wearing silk gloves, so she was able to take my hand with no fear of transference. "Come on, you hermit. We're going. He has some invention to show us. He's terribly enthusiastic about it, and you know how Nathan is when he gets excited."

"I suppose there's nothing we can do." I took the feverfew from my vanity and placed it on my wrist.

"We should give Nathan what he wants in these last few months, Jane," she said. "Make him happy before he goes off to war."

"Of course," I said, knowing Maddy would do whatever she could to please Nathan, war or no war.

I'd been hoping the three of us would sing at the piano that evening and then go walking on the Heath, naming flowers that grew from the undergrowth (feverfew and maiden pink, harebell and yarrow). But there would be no changing Nathan's mind. Maddy was right about that. Though the city would be full of clamoring objects, I could not deny him.

Maddy and I descended to the Clock Parlor, where Father's timepieces ticked away the hours—my favorite, an ivory elephant with a clock in its chest, seemed to observe me as I entered the room.

We found Nathan there pacing. "I'll never know what the two of you get up to in that bedroom," he said.

"Jane and I had to make hasty love," Maddy replied. "We can't seem to get enough of one another."

Nathan grinned at this. "Yes, well, I hope you've satisfied yourselves. It's a long trip to Piccadilly."

"Why precisely are we going there?" I asked.

Nathan raised his sharp eyebrows. "Maddy didn't tell you? They've installed a psychic vending machine. It's the damnedest thing. I want you girls to see it."

We boarded Nathan's carriage beneath a sky of low, dark clouds. Maddy and Nathan chatted about something inconsequential while I sat silent. The clouds seemed to settle in my chest, their damp weight pressing down on me. The hinges in the carriage trilled like a shrill flock of magpies, and again I wished that we'd stayed at Stoke Morrow, safe and warm, taking a light supper that Miss Anne prepared.

But we were already on Hampstead Road, and Nathan's horses were terribly swift.

London seemed a series of tall shuttered houses that evening, all crowded along a single narrow street. The air was full of dust and the pungent smell of dense humanity. We came as close to Piccadilly as traffic permitted and then dismounted, using a series of passages to avoid getting mired in the congested streets. These "secret passages" were oddities of London, symptoms of a city that had been built and rebuilt—a city without order or plan. The poor made their home in these passages, and we walked through their makeshift parlors, brushing lightly through the darkness with Nathan as our leader. The elderly and the infirm observed us guardedly, and I wondered what they made of the three of us. Their watchful gaze told me we didn't look like angels but some more sinister breed of visitant.

Finally we arrived in the bright world of Piccadilly Circus, a raucous street of commerce. The word *circus* was used in the ancient Roman sense, meaning circle, and Piccadilly Circus was just that, a wide circular avenue connecting to Regent Street. The place was filled with every sort of shop one could imagine. Maddy said it reminded her of a Parisian boulevard, so unlike most of the narrow and wandering streets of London.

We entered the Grand Bazaar, an open-air market in the center of the Circus, and quickly found Nathan's psychic vending machine—a large silver box with a dispensing tray and a metal arm. The machine was carved with figures from London life—a soldier, a flower girl, a man of commerce. People passed by in the crowded market, leaving the three of us unnoticed. I looked at my two friends as they admired the odd vending machine, and I could not believe how delicate they both seemed in the crush of London, how much I wanted to protect them.

"The way this works, then," Nathan said, "is that you put a halfpenny here in the slot—" Nathan used the tip of his father's cane to indicate the slot beneath a carving of a particularly well-endowed barmaid. "Then you pull this lever here, and the machine will give you what it thinks you should have."

Maddy said, "What it *thinks* you should have?"

"That's right," Nathan said. "It's a mind-reading machine. See here—" He pointed his cane to the inscription on the machine, which read DR. LOT'S PSYCHOMATIC DISPENSARY. "There are claims that it can even make *prophecies* like the Sibyls of ancient Rome."

"A mechanical Sibyl," Maddy said. "How darling."

"Have you already made use of it, Nathan?" I asked.

"I have," he said.

"And what did it give you?"

"A cheaply produced crucifix," Nathan replied. "Jesus looked like a little monkey on his cross."

"So this magic machine thought you needed a monkey Christ?" Maddy asked.

"Not magic," Nathan corrected, "technologically evolved."

"The technologically evolved mechanical Sibyl thought you needed a poorly made idol from a several-thousand-year-old religion?" she said.

"Correct," Nathan replied.

"And what message do you take from that?" I asked. "Is it a prophecy?"

"Yet to figure that out, Jane, my girl. But I'd certainly like to see what it gives the two of you."

"I didn't bring any money," I said, feeling a chill from the machine. I mistrusted the idea of a mechanical Sibyl. And I liked the machine even less because there was, in fact, something different about its essence. I perceived a black and shifting hole at the center of this so-called Psychomatic Dispensary. It emitted neither color nor sound as other objects did. In effect, the machine had no apparent soul. I watched the hole widen and contract like a hungry mouth, waiting for our coins.

Nathan produced two halfpennies, holding them over his eyes like a dead man.

Maddy and I took them.

"You first, Maddy," I said. "I'd like to see your trinket before I decide whether or not to spend my halfpenny."

She approached the vending machine. Yellow light from the Grand Bazaar's gas lamps illuminated her lapis dress. She looked quite beautiful in that moment, and I caught Nathan admiring her too. Maddy put the coin in the slot beneath the carving of the barmaid and then pulled the lever with a bit of difficulty. A wheel spun within the machine, and I could see the void inside distend, as if trying to push something forth. Then there was the faint noise of an object landing below.

Nathan took a velvet bag from the dispensary tray. "Your prophecy, my lady," he said, bowing to Maddy.

"Oh, I do hope it's not a monkey Christ," she said. "That would offend Mother." Maddy unfastened the string tie and overturned the bag to spill its contents into her palm. At first, it appeared that the vending machine had given her another coin, perhaps a shilling, which would have been a good trade up from the halfpenny. But the coin wasn't the right color for a shilling. "A token?" Maddy asked, reading the inscription. "It's good for one entrance to the Crystal Palace in Hyde Park."

"The machine thinks you need a little holiday," Nathan said.

"But the palace hasn't even opened yet." Maddy sounded a bit disappointed. "That's not for another six months."

"Keep in mind the Psychomatic Dispensary traffics primarily in the future," Nathan said. He waved his fingers in front of her face with mock theatricality, as if mesmerizing her. "One day, Madeline Lee, you will go to the Crystal Palace. There you'll meet a dark stranger. He'll tell you awful secrets—things you never wanted to know."

Maddy slipped the token into her dress pocket. "Jolly," she said. "I've been searching for a dark stranger for years."

I approached the machine, and the black hole within it recoiled. The machine seemed to know me for what I was. I adjusted the feverfew at my wrist, and I put my coin delicately in the slot, then touched the handle. There was a shimmering across my field of vision and the sound of a hammer pinging against metal.

"You all right, Jane?" Nathan asked.

The experience of touching the machine made me feel dizzy, but I steeled myself and pulled the handle, feeling the gears turn as if they were also turning inside me—as if they were there among my own heart and liver.

A thud startled me. Something large, far larger than Maddy's token, had fallen into the tray.

Nathan, once again, reached down to fish the prophecy out.

We were all taken aback by what was presented. The object was not concealed in a discrete velvet bag. My prophecy was on view for everyone to see.

"My God," Nathan said.

"Apparently your needs are significantly different than ours, dear," Maddy added.

What had fallen into the drawer was not a trinket but a piece of the machine itself that had been dislodged—a cog, glistening with oil. I noticed the vending machine's arm had not returned to its original position but hung at an awkward angle. And it was then that I realized the black hole inside the machine had closed.

Nathan sighed. "It appears our Jane was too much for Dr. Lot's Psychomatic Dispensary. I should have known." He produced a handkerchief, wrapping the cog carefully. "I think you'd better keep it, Jane. It is, after all, what the machine believed you needed."

I took the cog gingerly, not knowing quite what to do with it.

"So what's the prophecy?" Maddy asked. "How do we interpret this?"

Nathan shrugged. "Jane's meant to eventually break the machine and end the show. She breaks the machine, the curtain closes."

CHAPTER 12

From a distance, the Crystal Palace in Hyde Park appeared quite *impossible*—as if the whole of its turreted glass structure was nothing more than a grand illusion. It seemed an endless and transparent mirage, drifting over the park's grassy field, blazing in the sun. It had opened its doors in May as a showplace for the stunning achievements of Victoria's empire, and though I hadn't dared to pay a visit as most of London had, I'd read numerous reports.

The palace was a marvel of human invention, composed entirely of glass—some three hundred thousand panes, suspended across a scant metal skeleton that encompassed a great expanse of the park. Many viewers attested that being inside the structure was initially disturbing. The structure produced a dizzying sensation, as sunlight was amplified by the glass panes, and some said they feared being "crushed" by all that dazzling light.

The queen herself visited the Crystal Palace, showing particular interest in the great aviary that was filled with fifteen hundred canaries. It was well known that Victoria was a lover of birds, and this particular display was said to provide a marvelous and disorienting rush of color and noise. Despite her enthusiasm for visiting the birds, Victoria reportedly was melancholy upon leaving. When asked privately about her change in mood, the queen attributed it to a fleeting vision caused by the canaries. "We realize we are little match for God's empire," she said. "That such a thing as birds can be frightening is a testament to God's supremacy over any kingdom of Man."

I did not fear the birds in the palace nor the supremacy of Victoria's God. I didn't even really fear the prophecy from Dr. Lot's Psychomatic Dispensary, though admittedly the memory of it still lingered. Instead, I feared the machines themselves inside the Crystal Palace.

In its various industrial courtyards, the palace was said to collect and display every manner of modern invention—most of which were being newly unveiled to the general public. The prospect of all these inventions gathered into one place disturbed me. I had no idea how my body would react to them. Would my heightened senses be affected adversely by these new machines, especially since some of them were powered neither by steam nor water, but by *electricity*?

I'd once attended a lecture with my father that demonstrated Luigi Galvani's work on "bioelectricity." Galvani posited that the human body was animated not by a spirit but by electrical currents running through its nerves. If the machines inside the palace were likewise electrified, did they not become more akin to living organisms? Inanimate would become animate, and I worried this could have the effect of amplifying the machines' souls, which I already perceived full well. I could be driven mad in the presence of these living objects. It was all vague conjecture, of course, but I didn't feel the need to experiment by visiting the palace myself. Thank God I'd never told Nathan about these concerns. Upon hearing them, he would have immediately taken me to the Crystal Palace, and if I protested, he would have likely tied me to the back of his coach and dragged me.

I'd read that the palace contained electric French sewing machines, a calculating machine, and an electric submarine that surfaced and dived in an internal lake. There was even a daydreamer's chair in which electrified magnets were affixed to the sitter's scalp, and it was said doctors could manipulate the dreams of the sitter to produce any variety of effect. If one man wanted to swim the Aegean, such an effect could be achieved. If another would rather walk on the red surface of Mars, so be it.

"Isn't it a wonderment, Jane?" Maddy said, looking down on the palace from the hill where we stood waiting for Judith Ulster.

"Yes," I said. "I suppose it is, but I don't—"

My thought was left unfinished, as we were interrupted by a female voice saying, "Is one of you lot Madeline Lee?"

The voice belonged to Judith Ulster. She was a few years younger than Maddy and me, and she was stronger looking than any woman I'd ever seen. Judith was carrying her archery bow and dressed in sporting clothes—a pair of plum-colored bloomers with a white blouse that she'd modified so her arms were bare up to her shoulders. It looked as though she was wearing a men's swimming vest. Another set of eyes might have found her appearance quite indecent, but I'd learned from Maddy to accept all manner of things.

The horsehair string of Judith Ulster's bow glistened in the sun, and I thought she looked every bit like the strong, hard goddess Diana from my father's folly.

Maddy was in the process of introducing us when Judith Ulster extended her hand as a man would do. Maddy shook the hand, and before I knew what was happening, Judith seized my own hand as well. For a moment, her expression became vaguely fogged.

"Now, what was that?" she asked, looking down at her bow.

"What, dear?" Maddy said. She'd learned to play naive when it came to others experiencing my power.

"The strangest thing," Judith replied. "I thought my bow was mumbling something to me."

Maddy laughed lightly. "That would be Jane's fault, Miss Ulster. She's pursued by vengeful spirits. The feeling will go away once you've left her presence, much like indigestion dissipates when the offending meal has been passed."

Judith enjoyed this bit of toilet humor made at my expense, enough to forget her temporarily haunted bow. "Call me Judith, and Jane doesn't look anything like a piece of meat gone bad."

"Looks can be deceiving, dear," Maddy said.

"I left my quiver of arrows at the archery field," Judith told us. "Will you both walk with me?"

"Jane and I *adore* walking," Maddy replied.

The archery field was part of the garden that sprawled beyond the confines of the palace proper. Brightly dressed men and women drew bows, training the feathered arrows on a variety of straw-filled targets. A marquee for the rental of bows and quivers also sold lemonade, and Judith bought the three of us drinks, which we then sipped as we walked. In the valley below the archery ground was a tree-lined lake, which acted as a reservoir for the palace's variety of animated fountains. Gunshots rang out in the distance from what Judith said was a men's shooting range.

"Clearly only men should learn to use pistols, right, girls?" Judith said.

"Despicable," Maddy replied.

I was slightly unnerved at the connection they were forming. I wasn't used to sharing Maddy with anyone other than Nathan.

"It's good to meet you both, but I really don't know why you've asked to speak with me," Judith said. She took a long sip of her lemonade, looking toward the glittering lake. "I sympathize with your troubles, Madeline, but they aren't so very different from my own troubles, which I have yet to solve."

"The similarity of our situations is *exactly* why we want to speak with you," Maddy said. "I was told by a mutual acquaintance that you've actually been inside the Theater of Provocation."

Judith burst into laughter at this. "Our mutual acquaintance must have been taking a nip," she said. "I've been as far as the front door."

"That's farther than we've gotten," Maddy replied. "We're gathering information to understand Nathan Ashe's experience prior to his disappearance. Telling us what you learned might help us."

Judith shrugged. "If Nathan's experience is anything like my brother Corydon's, your boy is lost, Madeline, and that's the truth. That theater isn't a theater at all. Ariston Day isn't a showman, he's a thief. Corydon hasn't been the same since being indoctrinated. He and I are twins, you know. Terribly close when we were younger; we did everything together. My hair was cut short when we were children, and people said they could hardly tell me from Corydon. I love him more than I love anyone, but that wasn't enough to wrestle him from Ariston Day."

"Yes," Maddy said. "Love isn't enough."

"Our father owns the Bainbridge store," Judith said. Bainbridge's was a well-known feature of London—a grand emporium that was being referred to popularly as a "department store." All manner of things could be purchased under one roof—from hats to stationery to riding gear. It was unlike anything else the city offered, and shoppers were drawn to it in droves. "Corydon hates commerce," Judith said. "Hates our father's business. That's what sent him to that *theater* in the first place. His friend Seamus Holt told him there were other boys down there who hated their fathers' enterprises, and that they'd all found something better than a father in Ariston Day—they'd found a leader. Corydon went to his first provocation as a lark. I couldn't go, of course, because I wasn't the right sex. It made me so angry, but Corydon assured me that nothing would come of his visit. Nothing *could* come of it because the only thing he hated more than commerce was the theater. I laughed at his joke, and he kissed my cheek." Judith put her hand gently on her cheek, as if remembering the feeling of him. She continued, "That night when he came home, he was already changed. There was a new light in his eyes, and after that he went once a week to the theater, sometimes spending the night in Southwark, doing God knows what. And so I did what any loving sister would do."

"What was that?" I asked.

Judith looked at us grimly. "I bought myself a red coat and a hat, the rounded sort the young men are wearing these days. Then I filthied them up, as if I didn't know how to do a proper wash, and I made my way to Southwark."

"You posed as a *Fetch*?" Maddy asked. "Judith, that was terribly bold."

"I wasn't afraid of Day," she said. "I wasn't afraid of anybody. But I know better now. I learned." She paused. "I thought I could pass for a Fetch. I thought a little dirt and the dark alleys of Southwark would be enough to transform me and fool even Ariston Day. My costume worked fine in the tavern above the theater—the tavern's known as the Temple of the Lamb, you know. The name reminds me of a sac-rifice—gives me shudders thinking about it." She paused again, as if reliving the memory. "Anyhow, I wasn't called out in the tavern. One old man even said, 'excuse me, sir,' when he bumped against me.

"As soon as I made my way down the stairs to the theater below, I knew something was wrong. There was an awful tension in the air, and the place smelled like a men's arena. There were so many Fetches streaming down the stairs around me, some fifteen or twenty laughing boys in filthy red regalia. I couldn't turn back. I thought I could make it through the open door. As soon as I was at its threshold, though, one of the guards, a tall Fetch with a rash of freckles across his cheeks, reached up and tipped off my hat. I looked at him, astonished, and saw that he was laughing at me, as was the other guard. They knew exactly what I was—an imposter in their midst, and worse yet, a woman. They'd watched me come down the stairs, all the while planning to apprehend me. 'Your hat, sir,' he said, handing the bowler to me. 'And my, don't you have pretty hair.'

"I turned to run, but they quickly grabbed me by the arms. When I struggled, one of them knocked me against a stone wall and made a good gash on my face. They led me to a room outside the theater. I didn't even get a glimpse of what was going on inside. Then they told me to sit down in a chair, and when I'd done so, one of them spit in my face.

"Normally, I would have reacted with violence, but I was afraid of those boys. They had an air of vacancy, as if they could have done anything to me in that room and not lost a wink of sleep over it. I sat there, looking up at the two Fetches. And then the door behind them opened, and a third Fetch led my brother into the room. Corydon was terrified, and when he saw me he shook his head, as if to indicate that I should do nothing and say nothing. The Fetch who'd spit on me said, 'You want to know what we do down here, Judith Ulster?' I wanted to ask him how he knew my name but thought better of it because of the expression on Corydon's face. Instead I whispered, 'Yes.' The boy said, 'Well, we make dreams. Do you want to feel like you're dreaming, Judith Ulster?'

"I couldn't speak. I only looked at him. He took a blade out of his pocket, a long thin blade, and while the other boy held Corydon in place, the spitting boy brought the blade to my brother's face and sliced into his cheek. He sliced his cheek so deeply that a flap of Corydon's skin fell back—like the cheek was nothing more than meat. And I could see the yellow of Corydon's teeth under that piece of flesh." Judith reported this calmly enough, but her hand was shaking as she reached up to brush a windblown piece of hair from her face.

"My God," said Maddy. "Oh, Judith, that's so terrible."

I thought it was far worse than that. Judith's story made me believe that Day and his Fetches were capable of anything.

"And then another boy took something from behind his back, maybe it was a pipe, and he hit me in the head until I was unconscious. I woke up in an alley in Southwark with a vagrant standing over me, probably trying to decide if I was a boy or a girl and whether or not I should be robbed or violated. I've seen my brother since that night, but only from a distance. He acts like he doesn't know me, and he travels with packs of Fetches. He had his face stitched up, but there's still a scar. So while he hasn't disappeared like your Nathan, he's already gone from our family, you see. He's one of them now."

"I'm so sorry," Maddy said.

"No, *I'm* sorry," Judith replied. "I wish to God I could help you more, but I don't think anyone can help the two of you. That's my honest belief."

Maddy and I were both shaken by Judith Ulster's tale of the theater, and as we took our leave of her and walked across the sunlit park, it seemed as though night was falling in the middle of the afternoon. Maddy said, "Jane, hold my hand."

"But the transference, Maddy."

"Please don't argue. Just do as I say," she replied.

CHAPTER 13

It was several days after our visit with Judith Ulster that we were invited to tea by Nathan's mother, Mary-Thomas Ashe. Lady Ashe extended such an invitation monthly and spent hours recounting for us her private adventures at various séances and ghost hunts. I remember being initially surprised at Mary-Thomas's apparent warmth and grace. After all, neither Maddy nor I seemed a suitable match for the son of a lord. We were both outcasts in our own right. The fact that we spent so many hours alone with Nathan could have produced a certain animosity in Lady Ashe. We might have been viewed as a threat to her lineage. But instead, Nathan's mother accepted us as unlikely confidantes. She was a good deal more eccentric than her practical husband, and she confessed to finding such topics as class and breeding a bore. I believe she also secretly thought Nathan would never dare choose one of us as his wife. Even if he did, Lord Ashe would put a stop to such a union. We likely seemed nothing more than playthings to her, and there was safety in that.

Our carriage ascended Parliament Hill, trundling toward Ashe High House, the bright manse that presided over the Heath from its aerie.

Seeing it again made my heart feel like a stone. I was surprised that Lady Ashe was keeping up her invitations at all, considering the turmoil that had been caused by her son's disappearance, and I wondered if she might have some ulterior motive in inviting us for tea now. I was glad for the chance to enter the house once more, though, as it might provide another opportunity to try an experiment on one of Nathan's personal possessions.

In the carriage, Maddy and I discussed the stories we'd heard from Paul Rafferty and Judith Ulster but came to few conclusions. "Our investigation doesn't provide answers," I said. "Rather, it's putting us in danger."

Maddy studied me, eyes half-lidded. "No answers, Jane? We are now certain where Nathan spent his final hour. We also know that the Fetches are capable of extreme violence."

"But what good is that?" I asked.

"It's a step toward a solution. Honestly, at times I feel as though you don't even want to find him."

"Don't be ridiculous."

"Then show some initiative, Jane. Vidocq is proving more useless by the day. I read recently in the *Athenaeum* that he's taken to drinking pints to while away his afternoons."

"Do we believe the newspapers now?" I asked.

"My point is that discovering what happened to Nathan is up to us."

"I wouldn't underestimate the inspector, Maddy. If he's beginning to seem clouded, perhaps that's because he wants us to perceive him so." I knew for a fact that Vidocq was quite perceptive and resourceful, as could be seen in the research that I'd stolen from him.

The carriage came to a halt, and the tall driver opened the door to help me out onto the stone drive. Nathan's house, surrounded by oaks and cedars, had the honor of being the only inhabitance on the hill, as some antiquated law permitted the ancestors of Lord Ashe to build on the hallowed parkland. Before going to ring the bell, Maddy and I stood together on the lawn, looking toward the distant domes and towers of London. The tower bells of St. Paul's chimed, and a yellow fog moved across the buildings of our city, seeming to dissolve spires and cupolas in its wake. "Do you think he's really in that maze somewhere?" Maddy asked. "Is it possible that, at this moment, we're looking at the place where he's concealed?"

"I don't feel him there," I said, honestly.

"Nor do I," she said. "But if not London, then where?"

I looped my arm through hers, careful not to touch her skin. I didn't want her to hear the way Ashe High House wept behind us. "Let's go inside, dear," I said, and she allowed me to lead her to the bell rope.

Lord Ashe had retreated to his offices at Parliament, so we found Mary-Thomas alone, a shadow of her former self, sitting in her stiff parlor chair. Her hair, normally an architectural masterpiece, hung loose around her gaunt shoulders. Her skin was sallow, and her hand trembled when she lifted it in greeting.

The tea table was set with egg and cress sandwiches; a variety of fruit scones with clotted cream; and a coral-colored tea set Lady Ashe's cousin Manfred had brought back from China. The head girl, whose name I'd forgotten, poured tea and seemed unsteady, glancing from time to time at Lady Ashe, as if to check that her mistress was not about to have an outburst.

"Every morning, I expect to see poor Nathan in the foyer," Lady Ashe said, "carrying his bags as when he came back from war. At the very least, I thought I'd have a vision. Even if he looked dreadful, I'd know his soul persists. But there's been nothing. I've tried to make contact with my spirit guide, the Golden Cloud, thinking perhaps it could help us with our search, but even the Cloud will not speak to me. I feel as though I've been made blind."

I knew far too much about Mary-Thomas's supposed spirit guide, the Golden Cloud. Nathan loved to regale us with her stories of their correspondence. The Cloud was not a person but an incorporeal field of bright dust that spoke to Mary-Thomas through the aether. "Do you realize Mother's spirit guide has visited both Jupiter and Mars?" he asked once. "The Cloud apparently prefers Mars because the landscape there is more inviting—beautiful red hills and all that." At this, Nathan broke down, nearly crying from the hilarity of it.

Maddy expressed her sympathy to Mary-Thomas while I studied the parlor, looking for remnants of Nathan. I was simultaneously excited and filled with dread at the prospect of touching another of his possessions and what I would see next.

In one corner of the parlor hung a painting Nathan had done as a child, showing the Malebolge, the eighth circle of Dante's Hell. It was an endearing piece of work despite its macabre subject matter. Poorly drawn sinners flailed in the oval-shaped ditches of the Malebolge, waving their clawlike hands in an attempt to get the attention of the viewer. The drawing emitted a low frequency, nothing terribly urgent, and I wondered, for a moment, if perhaps the objects had already shown me all they needed of the painted forest.

"I'm afraid my invitation wasn't extended entirely for social reasons," Mary-Thomas said, confirming my suspicions. "I was hoping you girls might help me do a summoning here. If the three of us call out to Nathan together, perhaps he will respond."

"A séance, Lady Ashe? You're not saying you think he's—" Maddy asked, sounding honestly frightened.

"Oh, no," she replied. "Even the spirits of the living can be summoned under the right circumstance. Lord Ashe doesn't approve of these irregular habits of mine, of course, but I've learned from my years of summoning that such practices are valuable. The human mind can conjure such a wide variety of useful communicants."

We were compelled to agree to her experiment, though I was fairly sure a séance or summoning would not help our cause. Mary-Thomas asked the maid, whom she called Vicky, to draw the heavy parlor drapes, and we were left in what seemed at first complete darkness. Then slowly my eyes adjusted, and the gray shapes of Maddy and Mary-Thomas appeared. Mary-Thomas produced a knitted scarf and wound it tightly around her hand. I recognized the scarf as one that Nathan often wore at Christmastime.

"We'll focus on this scarf," Mary-Thomas said. "Think of pleasant times with dear Nathan. Such thoughts will act as sweet honey to draw his spirit."

She closed her eyes and breathed deeply and audibly. The clock ticked on the mantel, and somewhere in Ashe High House, a dog barked. We joined hands around the tea set. I touched Mary-Thomas gingerly, attempting to dampen the transference, as I often had with Nathan. But she obviously possessed some element of authentic psychic strength. I could feel my talent being pulled out of me and examined. A brief frown darkened her face, but soon enough she was speaking in a low monotone, asking Nathan to respond.

"We who love you need to understand," she said. "Come to us, Nathan. Tell us what's become of you."

As she spoke these words, I felt movement—a sort of churning pressure—in my stomach. At first, I attributed the feeling to indigestion, but the movement continued and became more persistent. It nearly felt as though something was trying to force itself out of my body. I was glad when Mary-Thomas released my hand and opened her eyes.

"It isn't working," she said. "I don't feel anything. The scarf isn't strong enough to draw him. Do either of you have anything belonging to Nathan—something more dear to him? He loved you girls so. You might carry an object strong enough to draw his attention."

I told her I had nothing, and then we both turned to Maddy, who seemed unsure whether she should speak. Finally, she said, "I have this." She pulled on a silver chain that hung around her neck, and from beneath her blouse she produced the silver childhood spoon that I'd asked to experiment with at La Dometa. I wondered if it had ever been locked in her treasure box at all. The shamed look on her face told me it had likely been hanging around her neck the entire time.

Mary-Thomas stared at the spoon, and tears brimmed in her eyes. "Nathan gave that to you, Madeline?" she asked.

"I cherish it," Maddy said.

"He must love you so," Mary-Thomas said. "Hand it to me, Jane. I'll take it only for a moment."

Maddy unfastened the clasp and without thinking passed the spoon to me so that I could pass it on to Mary-Thomas. As soon as I touched the metal that had been warmed by Maddy's skin, I couldn't control my reaction. My body was flung back into the chair, and with a thunderclap I was back on the stage in the painted forest, only this time, something was terribly wrong. The whole scene was tilted. Trees, like bony hands, reached up from the stonework of the floor, and the stars stared down like red, rheumatic eyes. I heard inhuman cries, and then a braying scream. In the clearing, the great stag was on its knees. The Red Goddess was on top of the animal, straddling it, and her mouth was fastened on its muscular neck. The stag screamed louder still. Blood ran down its pelt as the Red Goddess drank hungrily. I wanted to run to the creature's aid, to fight the Red Goddess back. But when I moved, she rose up to look at me, and I saw her face clearly for the first time. Her mouth and chin were soaked in gore. But the face—I knew the face, and I stood awestruck. It was my mother's own. Her eyes were full of red starlight.

The Mother-Goddess opened her mouth and howled at me in warning.

I cried out in the forest, and I awoke, screaming in Lady Ashe's parlor. My stomach convulsed again. The smell of Nathan was everywhere; I was drowning in it. Dropping the spoon, I stood up and rushed to the foyer, through the front door, and fell onto the grass of the hill, retching and fearing I would vomit. My stomach calmed just as quickly as it had spasmed, and then Maddy was at my side.

"My God, are you all right, Jane?" she said. "What happened?"

"A vision," I whispered, breathlessly.

Mary-Thomas appeared at the doorway. "Was it Nathan? Did he contact you?"

Maddy answered for me. "Jane's ill. She's not been feeling well all morning."

"Oh, my dear," said Mary-Thomas. "You ought to have told me. Should I send for the doctor?"

"I'm fine," I said feebly, allowing Maddy to help me stand.

"I'm so sorry, Jane," Mary-Thomas said. "I should have known none of us were ready for this. I'm not feeling myself either. Please come in and rest, at any rate. Take some tea. It will calm you. I'm going to lay down for a bit."

"Are you strong enough to go back inside?" Maddy whispered.

I nodded, and she helped me back to the parlor.

Before leaving us there, Mary-Thomas paused and said she'd been thinking of Michelangelo's *Pietà*, which she'd seen during her travels in Rome with Lord Ashe. I could only half-listen to her story. My mind was still filled with the image of the red and screaming woman who wore my mother's face. I could see the blood of the stag dripping down her chin and neck.

"The sculpture was there in the basilica," Mary-Thomas said, "as big as life itself—the Virgin with Jesus in her arms. And I cannot help but think that at least the Virgin had a final moment with the body of her son. What happened to him later was a mystery, but at least she was able to hold him when they took him down off the cross. She felt the weight of his body. She looked at his face. But what am I to do? I cannot hold Nathan. We don't know if he is alive or dead. Everyone tells me I must be strong. But how am I to gather strength if there is never any force that will close this open door?"

"Vidocq will close it," I assured her.

"Vidocq is my husband's solution, not mine," she said, turning to leave. "I'm afraid my headache is getting worse, girls. My thoughts are scraping against the insides of my skull." She passed down the hall, leaving us alone.

Maddy turned to look at me. "What was the vision that made you so ill?" she asked me.

I shook my head. The mad image of my mother hovered before me, and I realized I had to lie to Maddy. "It wasn't so much a vision as an ache in my stomach," I said.

"Provoked by my necklace?"

"Nathan's possessions have been particularly agitated recently. I thought that meant something initially, but I've realized it doesn't. You know how my talent is, Maddy. It doesn't make much sense. I saw colors when I touched the spoon and heard a loud thundering, then my stomach tensed."

"That's all?" she asked.

"That's all," I replied.

She studied my face carefully. I could feel the trust between us breaking.

"You know what we have to do now," Maddy said, "if you're feeling well enough."

"What would that be?"

"We have to investigate Nathan's room."

"Maddy, *no*," I said. "I'm sure Vidocq has already made that investigation."

"Yes, but he didn't know what to look for or *where* to look, did he?"

"And apparently we do?"

"Vidocq said it himself. We knew Nathan best," Maddy replied, "and yet not even *we* know everything. His room might provide a clue about what he was up to before he disappeared. And there is the fact of the secret compartment, Jane. You know the one. I'm sure Vidocq didn't find it."

"What if Lady Ashe returns?"

"She'll think we've merely taken our leave. Nathan's rooms are on the other side of the house. That's the downfall of expansive living— one's house is no longer entirely one's own."

I agreed to go, but on the condition that our "investigation" would be brief and that we would alter nothing. Maddy and I left the parlor together, making our way deeper into the mansion.

CHAPTER 14

———◆———

Nathan's rooms created a powerful confluence of sensation. The objects there were all so personal to him, and they called out to me. I felt faint in the presence of their chorus. I didn't want to see the monstrous woman who wore my mother's face again or feel the horrible pain churning in my stomach—as if something was inside of me that demanded release. I raised the feverfew to my throat and held it there, allowing the silence of it to calm me. But it wasn't enough. The objects moaned for me, summoning me. They seemed to know their master was in absence, and they mourned him.

"Are you all right here, Jane?" Maddy asked, looking once again concerned.

I nodded. "We passed a vase in the hall," I said. "Could you go and gather some flowers from it?"

Maddy did as I asked, returning with a bouquet of dripping white lilies. I held them to my chest, finally able to breathe and to see the room as merely a room—more spacious than my own, with wainscoting and low-light gas lamps embedded in the wall. Alongside the lamps were the familiar pen-and-ink drawings that illustrated stories from Arthurian legend, one of Nathan's boyhood interests. My attention was drawn to a particular piece of art that showed Lancelot in partial armor kneeling in a wood near Glastonbury, apparently

praying to a tree. The expression on the knight's face was one of reverence. Both his elegance and his long hair reminded me of Nathan.
Then, of course, there was the tree, a sturdy oak, of the kind my
mother said had given birth to me. Thinking of my recent vision, and
then of her holding me as she told me that story, made me feel uneasy.

Maddy and I had visited Nathan's room many times before,
though, of course, we were not actually permitted to do so by the
rules of the house. Nathan snuck us in during evenings when his
parents were in the city and showed us his collections, which were
largely composed of objects and talismans of the supernatural. He
was especially proud of a stringed lute that once belonged to Percy
Shelley, the poet. Shelley had reportedly played the lute on the deck
of his boat, the *Ariel,* as the schooner drifted off the coast of Italy.
After the wreck of the *Ariel,* which killed Shelley and his fellow sailors, the lute was discovered on the shore by a fisherman. It made its
way onto the black market and finally into Nathan's hands. Though
not a poet, Nathan considered himself a kind of outsider along the
lines of Shelley and Lord Byron, and the lute became an emblem
of that connection. "You know, girls," he said on the day he showed
us the lute for the first time, "it's said that when they dragged poor
Shelley's body from the ocean, he had no flesh on any part of him. He
was a skeleton dressed in poet's clothes."

"That's macabre," Maddy said.

"Sometimes I sit and think of those dead hands strumming these
strings," he continued. "Here, Jane, touch the lute, and tell me if you
can feel the presence of Shelley's hands."

I sighed and put my hand on the instrument. There was neither
music nor death in its soul. What I heard was water, a great abun-
dance of it, moving and crashing through its wooden body. I took my
hand away.

"Well?" Nathan asked.

"The lute is cursed," I replied. "Its owner will meet the same fate
as Shelley unless said owner stops acting like such a fool."

Nathan lowered his gaze, putting his fingers on the strings. "I
thought you were serious."

"Only you would be excited about a curse," Maddy said. "One day when you stop being so morbid, perhaps you'll find that people finally enjoy your company."

More than we cared for curses or his occult collections, Maddy and I were in awe of Nathan's personal space—particularly his bed and his grooming items. The dolls his mother had made for him in childhood, all in a little line on the windowpane, caused us to coo, and we even liked the smell of the room, a mixture of talc and shaving liniment.

It was during one such adventure in his bedroom that Nathan showed us the piece of paneling above his headboard that could be removed. Behind the panel was a secret compartment that he said not even Lord Ashe knew about. "I made it myself," he said, "by carving out the wall."

In the hollow, Nathan kept a wallet of money in case he found he should ever run into an emergency, a picture of both Madeline and I (fully clothed) taken using Adolphus Lee's daguerreotype machine, a bottle of bourbon, and a pistol.

"Dear God," Maddy said, "it's as though we're looking into the storehouse of an outlaw."

This pleased Nathan to no end, as it was the exact persona he was going for. We'd each taken a drink from the bottle of bourbon and felt quite wicked because of it.

It was painful then to now return to Nathan's inner sanctum under such a somber circumstance. The titillation that had occurred in this room prior was driven out by the dark spirit of his absence. The draperies were drawn, and the room was full of silence.

"I can smell him still," Maddy said quietly.

She went to remove the panel from above the headboard, careful not to make a sound, laying it on Nathan's pillow. Everything was in its place, even the pistol. But something had been added, something neither of us had seen before—a small leather journal, bound with a piece of rope. It was filthy, nearly ruined.

Maddy took it out carefully, unbound the pages and read the first line.

April 19, 18—Arrival at Malta

"It's a war journal," she said. "I didn't even know he kept one."

"Nor did I."

Nathan had written us few letters during his station on Malta. The letters were sparse of actual occurrences and were instead filled with facts about the island. During his tour, Nathan had not seen the front. Through some bureaucratic error, he had not been sent on to Sevastopol in the Black Sea, where his brigade was intended. Instead, he and his brigade had resided on the island of Malta, off the coast of Italy, for months.

He wrote to us that the island fascinated him because it was a wellspring of myth. "Do you realize that the preserved hand of Saint John the Baptist is said to be hidden here? Malta was purportedly where Saint Paul shipwrecked after his missionary journey and began writing his epistles."

Nathan's letters became increasingly morose due to his lack of physical activity and general psychological stagnation. His one remaining interest seemed to be the cloister of monks who inhabited the island, known as the Brotherhood of Saint John. "The brothers are all quite Romantic and enlightened," he wrote, "and I believe they know things that other men do not. They even seem to be involved in some secret task, and it's my aim to understand it."

I'd dismissed the notion of the brotherhood's hidden purpose as just another demonstration of Nathan's imagination, left to its devices in his boredom.

I'd come to know well that he believed many people possessed secret knowledge, not due to any infirmity on his part but because he'd been raised in a wealthy and stable household with kind parents and had little else to do than allow his thought-life to expand. As a younger man he'd come up with dozens of instances concerning individuals (the Lord Mayor, Lady Maul of Islington, and the bizarre-looking fellow who organized the human curiosities at St. Bartholomew's Fair, to name a few) who were concealing arcane arts just beneath their modern facades.

I'd argued that people simply weren't as interesting as all that. The common man worried about his bank account, ate his dinner, and took himself off to bed by nine. The closest this man came to ancient sorcery was the prayers he mumbled under his bedcovers.

My guess was that Nathan's journal of the war was filled with more of his ponderings about the Brotherhood of Saint John and their secret knowledge, and I didn't think that would make for useful reading. Maddy, however, thought differently. She wrapped the journal in her handkerchief and handed it to me. "Don't touch it directly," she said. "It might produce more stomach pains."

"We can't just *take* it," I said.

"Why not, Jane?"

"Because it might be a useful piece of evidence," I replied.

"And that's precisely why we *should* take it," she said. "Likely it contains facts that we don't want Vidocq to know and might be beneficial to our own investigation. Put it in your dress pocket."

I did as she asked. She was impossible to argue with.

"We'll take this too," she said, reaching for the pistol.

"Whatever for?"

Maddy shoved the pistol into the pocket of her own dress. "Protection." She resumed staring into the hollow above the bed. "There's something else in here, Jane, all the way at the back. Some sort of pouch." Maddy reached her entire arm into the hollow. What she withdrew was indeed a red silk pouch with a drawstring. She stood holding it for a moment, and then without consulting me, loosened the drawstring and let the contents of the pouch fall into her hand.

Immediately, she started to scream, allowing whatever had come from the pouch to drop to the floor. I hurried to close the bedroom door, begging her to be silent. "You're going to rouse the entire house," I said, returning to her. She'd stuffed most of her fist into her mouth and was biting down in such a way, I was afraid she might draw blood.

"What was it?" I asked. "What was in the bag?"

She pointed toward the place on the floor where the thing had fallen, and at first, I thought it might actually be a human finger.

I crept forward carefully and realized that it was simian in nature, likely from an ape. The finger was covered in hair and was an unnatural white color. Its fingernail was woody and yellow, and the whorls in the flesh were exaggerated due to the finger's desiccated state. It appeared to have been severed at the knuckle, and bone protruded from the ragged end.

"Looks like some sort of talisman," I said.

"Where would Nathan have gotten such a disgusting thing?"

"Perhaps he purchased it on Malta," I said. "Are there any white apes on Malta?"

"Even if there are, why would he bring it here?"

Knowing Nathan, I thought the finger was meant as an addition to his occult collection, which already boasted a dried Japanese sea horse that was said to promote virility and the eye of a large ocean fish, which purportedly granted second sight. This finger had garnered a place of honor and been housed with Nathan's most secret trove of objects.

"We have to put it back in the wall," I said.

Maddy made a horrible choking sound in her throat, and I worried that she might scream again. In fact, I worried that all of the household staff might be on their way to Nathan's rooms that minute. I acted quickly, grabbing the silk bag from Maddy and stooping over the finger. The finger would not go into the bag easily. I attempted to use the journal to guide it inside, and when that didn't work, I picked the finger up in my own hand.

This was a mistake, for as soon as I touched the thing, it no longer seemed dead and desiccated. I imagined that it moved in my hand, flexing slightly. I threw back my head and clenched my teeth. Forcing myself not to scream, I pushed the awful white finger into its bag and threw it into the hollow of the wall.

Just as I was sealing the panel off, the door opened and I turned to see Mr. Fanning, the Ashes' head servant, looking quite perplexed.

"Miss Silverlake?" he said in a whispered voice. "Miss Lee?"

Despite her state of crisis, Maddy was able to cover, saying, "Oh, Fanning, don't tell the Ashes we were here. We just miss Nathan terribly. We wanted to look at his things. That's all. We wanted to remember." And then she rushed forward and flung her arms around Fanning's neck. The old servant was so caught off guard, the last thing on his mind would be reporting our indiscretion to Lord Ashe.

Seeing Mr. Fanning again caused me to recall the morning he'd arrived at Stoke Morrow in a rain-wet carriage, horses steaming, his own dark cloak drenched, to ask if I'd heard from Nathan. Nathan hadn't come back from the theater in Southwark the previous evening, and Lady Ashe was terribly worried.

"I've been craving news myself, girls," Fanning said as he stood in the doorway of Nathan's bedroom. "There are times when I simply go out to the barn to sit with Nathan's riding things, just to remember him as he was. I thought the war would have taken him, if anything. I never imagined this."

"I know," Maddy said, wiping crocodile tears from her eyes. "But you won't bother Lady Ashe with this intrusion, will you, Fanning?"

"Of course not, my dears," he said. "Of course not. Your secrets are always safe with me."

CHAPTER 15

I left Maddy at her carriage and made my way through the southern woods alone, as it was closer for me to walk home than take the road. I'd told her that Father owned some illustrated books of zoology, which I would page through when I arrived at Stoke Morrow, specifically searching for white primates in the area around Malta, though I suspected not to find such a creature. The way the finger moved when I touched it made me feel as though it was something more than natural.

Nathan's journal of the war weighed heavily in my dress pocket. I wondered if he'd written about the ape finger and how he came to be in possession of it. Moreover, I began to wonder if he'd written anything about me. It occurred to me again that Nathan himself might be sending me the visions of the painted forest and his final night. What did he understand about the Red Goddess—and might I find some of that knowledge in the pages of his journal?

I was glad Maddy hadn't asked to keep the book. She was happy enough to have the pistol, saying she'd sleep with it near her bed in case the white ape came looking for its finger. Before we parted, she asked again about my outburst in Lady Ashe's parlor. "Are you sure you're quite all right, Jane?"

"I'm fine," I said. "More than fine. There were just too many boisterous objects in there. Mary-Thomas's Chinese tea set was likely upset due to the poor quality of the Darjeeling. It exacted its revenge upon me."

"Your reaction in the parlor had nothing to do with Nathan's spoon?"

"As I said before, Nathan's possessions have been agitated as of late. It was nothing."

"We'll have to be more careful in the future," Maddy said. She spoke kindly enough, but there was hesitancy in her voice. I could feel her gaze linger on me as I walked away from the carriage. Maddy was not a fool. My outburst had provoked her interest. If I became a suspect in her investigation, I knew that wouldn't be healthy for either of us.

The trees around me had a doomed and blasted look, and the forest became blacker by shades until I was nearly walking in almost full dark. No amount of gazing could draw images up from the gloom, and so I was left with the images in my own head—the ape's finger and the terrible blood-spattered face that looked, for all the world, like my mother's own.

So many pieces, but what was the puzzle? If Nathan was at my side, I'd have asked him what to do. What research could be done? But without him, I was adrift. Walking toward Stoke Morrow, I tried to imagine Nathan alone on the Heath, sure of himself in his dark suit and high jackboots, winding his way through the grass. His hair was parted in a careful line, and the rest of him seemed equally well made. I wanted to put myself inside his thoughts—to know what he knew. I saw him pause at the women's bathing pond in the southern clearing. The copper tip of his cane did not touch the ground. His own image was reflected in the water, and he was re-minded of something his mother once told him. When she was a girl, there was a popular technique of divination known as "hydromancy" or "reading of the water." The future could be seen on the surface of a still pool. Nathan looked carefully at his own angular reflection. A breeze stirred the water, and his face was pulled apart, becoming something new and monstrous.

Before I could fall too deeply into my reverie, a rustling in the forest drew my attention. At the base of a large oak sat what I first took to be an animal, but I quickly realized it was Pascal Paget wearing some kind of bulky fur overcoat, one of his odd French fashions, no doubt. He was huddled in the coat as if it were midwinter rather than late spring.

"Pascal?" I said. "What are you doing out here?"

"I was waiting for you, Saint Jane," he said.

When I'd once protested Pascal's nickname for me, saying I wasn't particularly good or saintly, he told me that achieving sainthood wasn't necessarily about being good. "The old priest at my parents' church said the saints exist beyond the everyday," he said. "You walk one step ahead, Jane. Alexander and I can both see it. When you're with Miss Lee and Master Nathan, it's so clear you're not like them. They're a product of London and you're . . . it's as though I'm squinting at a mirage. At any moment, you might just ascend to your rightful Heaven."

I approached Pascal at the oak, wondering if Maddy had decided to render him homeless by ejecting him from La Dometa. I felt as though I should offer to take him to Stoke Morrow and give him some of Miss Anne's black Ceylon. "You look like something terrible has befallen you," I said.

"I'm being harassed," he replied, "by Vidocq. I'm afraid he's going to harm me. That's what I wanted to speak with you about."

"Pascal, I'm sure that's not the case. The inspector is simply—"

"In France, Vidocq is known as a ruffian, Jane," Pascal said. "He was a common criminal before becoming a detective, you know. And he retains his criminal mind. He believes I'm withholding necessary information. He told me he expects the same sense of fraternity that Robespierre preached during the Revolution."

"I don't think Robespierre is much of a model for human conduct," I said. "But why is it that you wanted to talk to me about this?"

He looked at me plainly, dark eyes wide and perhaps a bit naive. "I thought your father could protect me in some legal manner, or that even *you* could protect me, Jane."

"Me? I have no power in the courts."

"Not the courts." He shook his head. "Never mind, then."

But his request resonated. Was this his way of praying for protection? Did he take my sainthood more literally than he let on? I wasn't sure I was comfortable assuming the role of holy protector.

"I promise you won't be harmed," I said. "I'll speak to my father on your behalf."

"Should I tell Vidocq what Nathan said about the Empyrean?" Pascal asked. "I feel that it might satisfy him."

My skin prickled at the idea of this. "Under no circumstance is Vidocq to hear the mention of that word," I said. "Do you understand?"

He nodded. "But you know what it is, don't you?"

"I do," I said.

"Will you explain it to me?"

"If the time comes when you must know, I'll explain."

Pascal seemed to accept this answer. He trusted me. He was perhaps the only person who fully trusted me anymore, and I loved him for that.

"I have to ask you a question now," I said. "In Nathan's belongings, we found what appeared to be the index finger of a white ape. Would you know anything about such a strange treasure?"

The blood drained from his cheeks. "You found that in his house?" he asked.

"Maddy and I, yes."

"You must leave it where you found it, Jane."

"Then you know what it is? Where it comes from?"

"Nathan brought it from Malta," he said. "Ariston Day took an interest in it. That's one of the reasons Nathan became such a favored Fetch. You don't want to have any part in what interests Mr. Day. He is not a good man, Jane. Did you leave it where you found it?"

"Yes," I replied.

He closed his eyes and rested the back of his head against the tree. "At least there's that," he said.

"Does Ariston Day know what happened to Nathan?" I asked.

"As I told you, I was escorted from the theater before the provocation began," he said. "But if I had to guess, I'd say yes, Ariston Day knows. He knows so many awful things."

At that, I said good-bye and turned to leave, but Pascal called out to me, "Jane, it's possible that Ariston Day is going to ask to speak with you soon."

I paused, unsure if I should share the story of the letter with him. Finally I decided against it, saying only, "Is he?"

"Yes, and when he does, you mustn't go to him, no matter what anyone says. Do you understand? You must stay away from the Temple of the Lamb. If you go, there won't be anything left of you." Pascal seemed to shrink inside his fur.

I thought back to Vidocq's record of Day's previous exploits, the mysterious disasters that surrounded his cults. What exactly did Ariston Day's have planned for me?

"Jane, did you see Alexander at the Silver Horne?" Pascal asked.

"I did."

"And how did he appear?"

I thought of lying, but what good would that do? "He looked burdened," I said. "And terribly adult."

"I don't believe the world will ever be as it was."

"Nor do I," I said, moving off into the southern woods, wondering if perhaps I should purchase Pascal a ticket on a steamer back to France.

Nathan's journal began to feel as though it was writhing in the pocket of my dress. Even wrapped in Maddy's handkerchief, it irritated me. It made me think of the war and how both Maddy and I believed the hardship of it would ruin our dear Nathan.

The Crimean Conflict was referred to by our countrymen as

"The Eastern Question," as if the whole of Britain was uncertain about our participation. Victoria aligned herself with Napoleon III, who was attempting to gain control over the Ottoman Empire— holy and strange—collapsing under its own golden weight. Napoleon had recognized the significance of the Ottomans after having a prophetic dream of a great tree that spread its roots to cover the earth. The tree was full of nightingales and bright parrots, all singing, and every leaf of the tree was shaped like a scimitar, pointing toward a milk-white moon. Louis-Napoleon's interpreter of dreams instructed that the vision of the tree referred to the Holy East—to Byzantium—and Napoleon must acquire that land in order for his own empire to prosper.

Maddy and I detested the war, not only because it seemed built on flimsy circumstance, but also because seeing Nathan in his red uniform and buckler sword tore our hearts. She and I discussed our concerns privately in my father's garden one placid afternoon, though the conversation quickly turned to other matters.

"Isn't there something Lord Ashe could do?" Maddy asked. "There are plenty of men who'd make better soldiers than Nathan, I'm sure."

"Lord Ashe won't prevent Nathan's leaving," I said. "It's an honor to serve in the Duke of Wellington's regiment. Nathan *requested* to serve in it."

She pretended to glance over lines of Byron in the book she held. Tall clouds glided above us, casting shadows like passing ships. "I don't necessarily think Nathan should be allowed to make requests," she said. "He hasn't had his own well-being in mind as of late."

"Are you referring to our experiments again?" I asked.

"Don't you think it's possible that you're hurting him in some irreversible way, Jane?"

"Yes, Maddy, I think I'm giving him my disease."

"That isn't funny. You don't know what your talent is. For all you know, it might even *be* a disease."

I'd considered this, of course—the numbness Nathan was feeling, the way he thought his body was not his own. Perhaps pushing my mind into his was too much for him. Or worse, perhaps the objects were finding a way to do something to him that they could not do to me.

"Do you want me to stop?" I asked.

"I do," she said, though without any real conviction. She knew well enough that if I tried to pull away, Nathan would be more upset than if Lord Ashe tried to yank him out of the Duke of Wellington's brigade.

"Nathan's chosen his own path," I said. "His time in the Crimea will have at least one positive effect—it will separate him from my talent. And when he's there we'll write him letters like—"

"Like what?" Maddy asked, glaring. "Good wives? We can't both very well be his wives, Jane."

"Like the Sisters of Mercy," I said. "We'll raise his spirits."

"But I don't want to be a nun," she continued. "That sounds more like the kind of thing you'd enjoy. Pascal calls you Saint Jane, and I don't know that I'd take that entirely as flattery, dear."

We tried not to show our concern in front of Nathan himself; instead, Maddy and I teased him about his uniform. It was such a costume after all—that bright red wool and ridiculous sash. These were not the sort of clothes that any man could die in. We ran our fingers through the fringes on his epaulettes. I put my palm against his neck, letting him listen to the sound the epaulettes made—something like rain trickling into stone gutters.

But we secretly feared his blood pouring out onto the queen's red. Even Nathan himself might have feared this. His grin wouldn't save him, no one cared about loveliness in war. I could almost picture the holes in his chest—Nathan lying in some foreign field, unable to move or help himself.

I had a single conversation with Nathan about my fear of losing him to the war. We were in my father's study, making experiments on an idol Father had purchased from a man who'd traveled in Africa. The idol was called the Baboon of Thoth—a seated figure of a baboon, meant to represent the scribe of the underworld. The baboon was Thoth's assistant who catalogued the dead and placed their hearts on a scale for weighing.

Sitting there across from Nathan, I felt my own heart being weighed, and its contents were heavy indeed.

The baboon was one of those uncommon objects that seemed to erupt with language when I touched it, and though I could not understand its words, Nathan became excited and claimed they *were* words, complete with pauses and inflections. He was wild about this discovery, cheeks flushed, eyes hectic with excitement. I asked him if his head ached or if his hand was numb.

"I'm fine, Jane. I think we should try to write down some of the words the monkey says—or at least copy down the sounds, and then we can see if anyone else can provide translation."

"It's nonsensical," I said. "Dismal thunder."

"But it doesn't *sound* like dismal thunder. It sounds like the baboon is *chanting*." Nathan studied the features of the little creature, its bulbous eyes and flaring nostrils. "How can we be sure it's not trying to communicate—that all of them aren't trying to communicate in their own fashion?"

I sighed. "I have been working this out in my own head far longer than you. Remember that. The talk is nothing more than babble."

"I imagine it will be something like that in war," he muttered. "Sound that never ceases. I've read that a man can go mad in the trenches just from the sound. And even when the explosions cease, there is still the sound of other men, packed tight in their ditches and praying."

"Oh, Nathan."

"It's all right, Jane. My mind simply drifts to my future from time to time."

"Do you fear the war?"

"I fear its effects."

"I dread it," I said. "If you don't come back—"

"If I don't come back, you and Maddy will carry on, and you'll ensure she does carry on, Jane. She pretends to be the strong one, but *you* are stronger. No one could endure life the way you do—experiencing the things that you experience. So you will care for her. You will help her back into the world. Give me your word."

"Of course," I said. "She's like my sister." And then I noticed him looking strangely at his own hand, the hand that he'd been using to touch the idol.

"Have you lost sensation again?" I asked.

"It isn't loss," he said. "As I said before, it's as though the hand has been taken up by someone else. It belongs to someone else to use. Perhaps Victoria is exercising her power over her new soldier." He laughed.

I looked again at the little stone animal between us. Perhaps the queen, but more likely the baboon itself. The objects had found their newest servant in Nathan.

CHAPTER 16

Upon returning to Stoke Morrow, I intended to immediately make my way to the library where I would read from Nathan's journal, but as I was removing my shawl in the foyer, I discovered a rather soiled-looking letter on the hall table. It appeared to have been dragged through a puddle of mud prior to delivery and was addressed in an unsure and crooked hand to one, "Jane S." I rang for Miss Anne, but when she did not answer my summons, I realized that this was her day for shopping. She would likely not return for another hour. I dusted off the letter and opened it carefully, knowing already from the handwriting and the cheap paper that it was not from Ariston Day.

The letter read:

To Jane of Stoke Morrow,

I have come to understand that you and your dirty notch of a friend came to solicit from my own sister as she practiced her arrows in the park. I will have you know that my Judith is to be left out of this affair. She has nothing to do with any of your reeking secrets, and I'll not have a person like you drag my girl down. Lord Nathan told us what sorceries you showed him at the witch's house on

Hampstead Heath. I know full and well that this demonstration
means you practice black arts and are of no good. Master Day tells
us you are not a witch. But I still believe differently. And you must
know what happens to witches, Jane of Stoke Morrow.

The letter was signed, *Corydon Ulster, Fetch,* and the pure incivil-
ity of Judith's brother's comments made me ill. I could hardly believe
that Nathan had betrayed my trust so by telling those rough boys
about what had happened at the witch's cottage. The experience
there had occurred before Nathan had gone off to war and wasn't
anything to be trifled with it. The event had fundamentally changed
us both, and not for the better.

Nathan had asked for a private meeting in the garden of Stoke
Morrow, and because it wasn't often that he and I found ourselves
alone, I immediately agreed. Maddy was occupied making a round of
home visits with her mother, Eusapia. Being alone with him made me
feel as though I'd discovered a new hour. In my heart, I begged the
clocks of England to stop and leave us there together. Nathan was
dressed in a tan summer suit with a violet pierced through the but-
tonhole, and I wore a ribboned gathering of feverfew at my wrist, lest
any objects might attempt to interrupt. I held his arm as we walked
the flagstone pathway and listened to him talk about his training for
the Queen's Guard, an endeavor that had consumed him in recent
months. It seemed a perfect evening, and I wondered if something
new might transpire between us. Maybe we'd even find a fresh
chance at romantic involvement. My hopeful heart or my wistfulness
over Nathan's imminent departure made me more pliable. I could see
his manipulations, and yet I was powerless against them as he skill-
fully turned the conversation toward an idea that had occurred to
him—a final experiment before the war.

"We must put your talent to the test, Jane. Something more substantial than observing your father's collections."

"Can't we stop calling it talent?" I said, trying to shift the conversation slightly. "It isn't really that. It came upon me without warning."

"As does talent," he said, stopping to admire the stone canopy covered in lichen at the center of the garden. The old thing interested me not a bit. It was Nathan who held my attention. His training for the guard had matured him, and he looked powerful standing next to me. "But talent also has to be honed, Jane. I know you're not interested in Crooke's psychical society, but you must allow me to make my own final experiment. If I should die in the war—"

"Don't talk like that. You'll come back to us."

"Of course I will. It's just, I don't want to imagine my soul forced to remain eternally curious about you."

"What sort of experiment?" I asked. "I thought you understood by now that the ability doesn't have an application. I've already shown you all it will do."

"But you've never put yourself in any situation of particular extremity so as to know if that were true or not," he said. "I think we should have a small adventure, just you and I, to a place that might help you focus your abilities."

I was suspect. Nathan was known for his "small adventures" to places where no son of a lord should go.

"What place? Name it," I said to Nathan.

"The ruin on the Heath," he replied.

I withdrew my hand from his arm. "We are not children, Nathan. We needn't look for adventure in haunted houses."

The house to which he referred was well known to many of us in Hampstead. It had belonged to one of the city's most infamous witches, known as Mother Damnable. Entering her house was the kind of thing that children dared one another to do. In fact, I believe Nathan had dared Maddy to do just that when we were younger, and she smartly refused. I didn't believe in hauntings, but I *did* believe in bad places, or low places, as they were known. And the cottage on the Heath was just such a place of ill omen.

"I'm not going there for one of your larks, Nathan. It's dangerous—physically dangerous. I mean, the whole roof looks as though it could collapse at the next strong wind. And you and I both know the place also seems to harbor some force that may be dangerous to the spirit."

"It's precisely that force which is necessary to boost your senses," he said. "Look, I've been there myself, and even I, who have no sort of heightened perception, no *talent*, felt something. The very timbers of the house seem possessed. If you go there—and I shall go with you, of course, and protect you at every turn—if you go there, you may discover some new illumination. I've been reading essays by Mr. Crookes—"

"Oh, Nathan, please stop with Crookes."

"Mr. Crookes says that if a certain gifted individual can be brought into a gifted place, the combination of the two will result in explosive revelation."

"But I don't know that I want an explosion."

"Jane, you must have shared your ability with us for some reason, otherwise you would have kept the whole thing to yourself. Isn't that right?"

I was quiet. In coming out, had I been looking for mere attention? Or was I asking for action?

"But how shall we go without Maddy knowing?"

"She has another tour of homes scheduled next week. We'll go that afternoon, in the light of day. What's the worst that could come of it, Jane?" He put his hand on mine, stroked my fingers in such a way that I could no longer be sure I was standing firmly on the ground. How could I say no to him—his clear eyes and his beautiful mouth, begging me?

I can see the two of us on the day we journeyed toward Mother Damnable's cottage. We were like figures in an oil painting, nearly devoured by the blackish greens and golds of the Heath. The rolling landscape fell away toward the south where a smoky brown fog hung over London. I held my wrap against the chill breeze, following Nathan's sharp and sturdy figure along the sandy path through the fallows. The Heath was rife with brake ferns, furze, and ugly dwarf trees. Neither Hampstead Town nor St. Pancras was visible, and I felt adrift in the silence of nature. There were no objects—no clamor. Such absence should have provided solace, but instead I found it disturbing. I wished I'd brought my father's pocket watch or perhaps a tumbler of salt from the kitchen. I was in need of a familiar amulet against the day.

As a child, I'd believed the Heath marked an end to civilization. One could get lost, not just physically lost, but spiritually. To venture onto it was to pass outside the boundaries of conventional reality. It was a liminal space where an encounter with a highwayman or fairy or even a brown bear seemed probable, though the bears I'd pictured were equally fantastic as any nymph. They stood on two hairy legs, wore sly human grins, lived in houses, and talked all sorts of terrible lies.

Mother Damnable's cottage lay on the outskirts of the dark hamlet known as Hatchett's Bottom, which was nothing more than a crooked gathering of narrow houses and shops that had sprung up during the late Middle Ages and remained largely unchanged by time. Hatchett's Bottom was surrounded by the Heath and stood as a bastion of humanity in the parkland. Wooden buildings leaned precariously against one another, nearly toppling their soot-blackened chimneys onto the tattered walks. The place smelled of ash and horses. Shops were designated not by name, but by picture—a white bull for the butchery; a shoeing hammer for the livery; and a red peacock, the significance of which I could not guess.

A few citizens moved along the cobblestone streets, weighted down by peasant wool and other freight, leaving me glad that we did not have to enter the hamlet in order to find the cottage. These were an impoverished people, gaunt and broken. I considered how terrible Mother Damnable's crimes must have been to be driven to the outskirts of such an awful place. The reasons for her excommunication were a mystery lost to time. The good mother herself was long dead. Only house and rumor remained. We who lived near the Heath heard tales of her at Christmastime, when all the best legends were brought out along with holly and mistletoe.

Mother Damnable bore no children, and two of her three husbands died from falls on the precarious hills of the Heath, skulls broken on protruding stones. Her third husband caught fire during a mummers' dance. His long robe got too close to the bonfire and burst into flame, almost as though it had been dipped in alcohol. The stag mask he wore for disguise fused to the very flesh of his face, and he had to be buried wearing it.

Mother Damnable was also said to have predicted the Devil's three visits to Hampstead Town, ringing a bell on the streets of Hatchett's Bottom and calling on everyone to bolt their doors. On the third visit, it was said she had tea with the Devil himself. Many people attested to passing by her cottage that day and witnessing Mother Damnable and a gaunt gentleman with long whiskers sitting at her table. They appeared to laugh over some old joke. He stayed late into the afternoon, and when he left, it was said that Mother Damnable looked at her fellow men with a superior and knowing air.

She was, at times, called a witch and, at other times, rumored not to be a witch at all but some kind of creature born from another place. It was said that Mother Damnable could pass between two worlds. And it was this claim that troubled me most. "'Tis a blighted place where the old Mother goes," wrote one minister of Hatchett's Bottom. "Children are known to kneel at her window and watch as the hag cuts open the very flesh of the air and steps through into another realm. My own son saw this act and sat upon my knee with tears in his eyes, telling me of the unholy scene. She makes worship with devils in that other place. All of them dance in a hectic circle. And in the end, the old Mother removes her skin and stands in the wastes like a tongue of fire and the devils bow down to her and call her their queen."

Damnable's cottage was set in a sort of eddy hidden by ragged elms, making it visible neither from the Heath proper nor from the grim village of Hatchett's Bottom. Nathan and I had to stumble upon the place rather than walk to it directly. The cottage was a primitive sort of dwelling, an assemblage of timber and stone that looked like it had been born from the forest. Around the house was a low, broken wall, and we entered through the remnants of a garden gate. The yard was empty but for tall grass and a tilted wishing well to the north. There was no sort of front door, which meant the animals of the Heath had been allowed to come and go as they pleased, and also that most of the objects in the house had been removed by villagers. The floor was littered with dirty grass and rushes where small animals made their homes. A rusted bacon rack hung from the single remaining roof beam like some disused instrument of torture.

"I don't like this, Nathan," I whispered, as if we were at church.

"Just allow yourself the experience," he said. "Keep me apprised of what you feel. I'll protect you."

I knew very well he could not protect me from anything in this house. No amount of physical strength would have an effect here. The cottage was only two rooms, the first serving as the common area, with a hearth and a wooden surface for the preparation of food; the second room, the smaller of the two, was for sleep. It was this room that disturbed me, for here I knew the witch had dreamed. The ceiling had fallen though and sunlight streamed through a gaping hole. There was a murmur in the house—not from any of the remaining furnishings, but seemingly from the air itself. It reminded me of my trip to the coast as a girl, the ebb and flow of the waves.

Nathan paused to look at me, and I smiled faintly. "There's nothing to the place, really," I said.

"You don't feel any particular presence?"

"I don't," I said, deciding not to mention the ebb and flow of sound. If I did, Nathan would want to experience it, and I thought I'd better make sure of what it was before I connected him to it.

He walked ahead of me, picking his way over scraps on the floor. Weeds were growing up in the golden light, as if nature was working to furnish Mother Damnable's home anew. I was thankful for those few plants. They created a baffle of sorts. If the undertow of the invisible sea became too strong, I could clutch onto the weeds and save myself from being pulled away. In the bedroom, Nathan took off his jacket, handed it to me, and began looking through the rubble. "Seems as though something burned in here."

He bent over, trying to dig what was apparently a blackened meat fork from where it was trapped between two floorboards. "If I can pry this loose," he said, "perhaps you'll be able to experience something from it."

I barely listened to him. Instead, I was distracted by the cool of the breeze. The ebb and flow of sensations was not entirely unpleasant. Light streamed through the opening in the thatched roof and shadows played across one ruined wall. The shadows shifted and turned until they looked something like the moving grass and plants of an overgrown garden. I walked toward the shadows, becoming lost in their undulations, and gradually it seemed as though the wall itself was growing transparent. I was looking not at the wall but *through* it. And there I perceived the pale forest and the white stream of what Nathan called the Empyrean. I realized that in Mother Damnable's cottage, only a thin membrane separated me from that place. I could see the surface of the membrane glistening in the half-light, inviting me to break through. The proposition excited me, made my flesh hot. I pressed my hand against the membrane, feeling its slipperiness. Pushing harder, I could feel a pressure building in my own chest. As I attempted to force my hand through the membrane, thinking I could perhaps find an entrance to the Empyrean here in the witch's house, the pressure in my chest became a kind of pain. It felt as though I was trying to put a hole through myself. And it was then that Nathan put his hand on me. I was so startled by his touch that I jumped back, and the wall became nothing more than a wall once again.

"What was that?" Nathan asked. "I saw some sort of transparent gauze."

"I don't know what it was," I said, irritated. "I didn't have time to find out."

"Why didn't you tell me you'd discovered something?"

"I wasn't sure—"

"Was it permeable?" he asked. "Could we pass through the gauze?"

"I don't know, Nathan. I was only beginning to touch it when you startled me."

"Bring it back," he said.

"I can't just bring it back. I don't even know how I brought it to begin with. I told you, I wasn't ready to show you."

"Not ready?" he asked, his tone growing sharp. "I thought we were here to look at this place *together*."

"You're making me feel as though you're using me, Nathan. As if I am a tool."

I could feel the witch's house surging around me. Its timbers developed something like a voice, and they were calling to me, not with language, but with music. Theirs was a terribly persuasive song. The timbers wanted me to lay Nathan low—to bring him down. A part of me wanted the same. He thought he could take what was not his.

"Make your own exploration," he said. "See how far you get." Nathan turned and left the bedroom.

"You said you wouldn't leave me here alone," I called after him.

He did not look back as he spoke to me again, saying, "I've realized you're the sort of thing that wants to be alone, Jane Silverlake." He abandoned me there—leaving for the war shortly after, still angry with me. Still feeling as though I would not let him in.

I fell to my knees that day in the witch's house. I was alone and I longed for Maddy. I'd been foolish to go off without her. I began to weep so hard that I became confused. I experienced a waking dream in which an old woman in a red cloak came to my side and put her arms around me. She wore a filthy lace ruff around her neck, and her face was like that of the shriveled monkey that I now found in Father's book. She told me they were all like that—those who came to take from me. "You mustn't worry too much, child," she whispered. "The young man will finish himself. Those like him always do." And I allowed her to hold me, putting my face in her hair. She smelled of wildflowers and musk and had a drowsy warmth about her like summertime. She rocked me for what seemed like hours.

*   *   *

I didn't realize how much I'd been affected by the events at the cottage until I tried to leave it and found I could not bear the sunlight outside. Dizzy, I lay down in the shade of an oak tree, far enough from the house that I could no longer hear the ebb and flow. And I remained there for an hour, unable to move, trying to let the silence of nature heal me. The vision in red had been Mother Damnable; I was quite sure of it. The witch loved me and wished to protect me, though I was not sure why.

Nathan was absent after the events at the cottage, preparing himself for the long journey to Malta. And despite my attempt to hide what we'd done, Maddy was all too aware of our trip to the Heath. She sat with me as I recovered, refusing to allow Miss Anne near me and instead keeping a cool towel pressed to my brow in an attempt to reduce the fever that invaded my body.

I was laid out on the couch in the Clock Parlor, as I didn't like being in my bedroom when I was ill. The bed, with all its pillows and fluff, could feel too much like a coffin. Father appeared from time to time at the door, saying something disjointed about how I shouldn't have gone out in the summer heat. "It's far too easy to exhaust oneself out there, Jane. That scoundrel Nathan Ashe should have known better. Your mother, after all—your poor mother."

"I'm fine, Father," I said. "It's only a spell. Nothing like what happened to Mother."

Maddy read to me from a new translation of Ovid's *Metamorphoses* that her own mother had deemed "disturbing filth" and put on a high shelf. Maddy spent a great deal of time reading the rape of Daphne, in which a girl sprite was transformed into a tree by her father so that she might avoid defilement from the god Apollo. The scene of transformation was particularly hideous, even by Ovidian standards, telling of the bark crawling up the poor girl's legs and thighs while Apollo tried to violate her. Bark encased her stomach and breasts until finally her upraised arms became leafy branches and her screams were nothing more than the creaking of the bowers. Even then the god did not relent. He tried to penetrate her still but found the girl to be entirely made of wood.

"You see, Jane," she said, "a tree girl—just like your mother used to call you."

"Is this supposed to be helpful?" I asked.

Maddy lowered the book. "Would you prefer something else, dear?"

"I'd think you might try reading something more peaceful. The state I'm in begs for that."

Here she did look a bit apologetic. She assessed me with her violet-colored eyes and bit her lower lip. "Are you actually ill, Jane? Or are you acting this way because of something that happened on the Heath with Nathan? Between the two of you, I mean."

I looked toward a pool of sunlight on the rug. "It wasn't physical," I said. "Or at least not in the way you're thinking of it. He—Nathan— wanted to try another experiment. He was desperate for it." I explained the events as clearly as I could remember them. It was wrong to have kept any of it from her. Maddy was like my shadow-self, and to hide information in such a manner was like walling off a part of my own consciousness. I even told her about the vision of the red woman that I'd taken to be Mother Damnable, making it clear I'd been hallucinating under duress (though I wasn't entirely sure that was true).

"My mother actually met Mother Damnable when she was just a girl," Maddy said. Her tone was light, as if the story mattered little, but my interest was quickly drawn. "The old witch apparently showed her something."

"Showed her what?" I asked, feeling strong enough to actually sit up comfortably for the first time in three days.

"Oh," she said, "I don't know. Some kind of trick, I think. Mother never told exactly—or maybe she did, but I didn't care enough to listen."

I rested my head against the arm of the sofa and thought of the old woman's arms around me and the lovely smell of her hair. I wondered if her tricks were anything like my own.

CHAPTER 17

Late afternoon sunlight spilled through the tall windows of the library, and as I was putting Corydon Ulster's letter in the fire, Miss Anne came to the door, fresh from shopping. She looked somewhat dissatisfied at the sight of me. "Would you like a cup of tea now, Jane?" she asked.

"No tea," I said, "but come closer for a moment, Anne." I was still feeling off balance from my memory of Mother Damnable's cottage.

After my experience there that fateful day, I'd gone to Mother's dressing room, opened the wardrobe, and knelt before the oval portrait of the Lady of Flowers. For the first time in my life, I prayed—not to the Christian God, but to the woman in the painting who looked so much like my mother. I asked her to never let me see the Empyrean again. It had marred my relationship with Nathan, perhaps even set him against me. And it would likely do the same to my relationship with Maddy. The Empyrean had been poisoning me since I was a child, I knew this now. It was the emptiness that Mother had left in me, the emptiness that infected everyone around me. I prayed harder still, knowing the worst thing about the Empyrean was that even though I could see it was a void—a terrible white blankness that could ruin all my carefully built relationships—I secretly wanted more of it. Seeing the white forest so close at hand in

Mother Damnable's cottage had been almost too much. I wanted to feel the Empyrean consume me, to erase my name and my sex, erase my very identity and leave me a magnificent and shining absence.

As I prayed before the wardrobe, the Lady of Flowers stared back at me, her dark eyes so superior. She seemed to condemn me for my weakness. She wanted me to grow strong, so I didn't fail her. So I didn't fail everyone. The way she looked at me, like she knew everything and I knew nothing, enraged me. I stood and pulled the portrait from the back of the wardrobe, letting it fall to the floor. I leaned over it and pushed my hand through the Lady's chest. I tore at the flowers on the canvas until all of it was in ruins. And then I lay there next to the broken frame, holding handfuls of the Lady and feeling the Empyrean slip away.

After that day, I did not see the white forest again for a time. My talent once gained became a kind of low hum in the background of life. But when Nathan disappeared, I could sense the forest's return. The Empyrean was coming back, calling to me. It was there, just under the surface of things, and I wondered if I could access it once again.

"Closer, Miss Anne," I said, as she was still some five feet from the fireplace in the library. The request seemed to frighten her, but she did as I asked, coming to stand directly before me.

"Hold out your arm," I said to her, "and pull back the sleeve of your blouse."

"Oh no, Jane. I don't want—"

"Do it now, Anne, or I'll tell Father you've been stealing silver-ware."

She did as she was told, as I had long ago established myself as dominant in our relationship. I placed my hand on her bare skin. The library rang out around us. Books produced a particularly agonized tone.

"What do you feel?" I asked her.

"The demons, Jane," she said breathlessly. "You know I feel them when you touch me."

"There are no demons. How many times do I need to tell you that for you to understand?" She tried to pull away, but I wouldn't allow it. I focused all my attentions on the objects, letting the great moaning of the room fill her like water fills a basin. Miss Anne began to cough, and flecks of spit appeared on her lips.

"Now what do you feel?" I asked.

"I feel everything," she said. "The whole room is inside me."

"And do you see a pale forest," I said, "with an unmoving stream?"

"It's there," she replied, nearly hypnotized by her own fear. "It's there behind the objects. A white forest. And there are demons in the trees. White demons making awful sounds and watching."

"Can you step into the forest?" I asked.

"It's a painted picture," she said. "Thank God and Christ it's only a painted picture."

I released her, and she nearly fell in her rush to get away from me. "What was it, Jane? Was it Hell that I saw?"

"Most certainly it was Hell, Anne, and it's waiting for you, gates thrown wide," I said. "Now get out of my sight."

Because Miss Anne had treated me like I was a devil throughout my childhood, I felt little remorse for making my experiment with her. The result, at least, was clear. The Empyrean had returned, getting stronger and stronger, and this time, it would not be sent away so easily.

Carefully I unwound Maddy's handkerchief from Nathan's journal and used the silk to turn the pages. It pained me to see the low crawl of his script. Things were so conflicted between us near the end. Yet I cared for Nathan Ashe, and he'd helped me learn much about myself. I felt more than a little guilt at the idea I'd led him astray. With my heart pained, I read:

April 19, 18—Arrival at Malta

Closely following the Queen's Dragoon Guard, we arrived at the island of Malta, 7:00 in the evening. Dark clouds hung above the high white rocks of the barren island. Never have I been so overjoyed to see so dismal a place. It was land, after all—a surface that did not shift and sway at the wind's every whim. The ship we traveled on was a French steamer, the Golden Fleece, a name which I found increasingly ironic over the course of our travels. Unlike the mythological Jason and the original sailors of the ship which sought that fleece, Lord Wellington's brigade was decidedly not a band of ready heroes. Rather, we were a frightened bunch of seasick English and Frenchmen who appeared to have no hope of winning any kind of war. As for the singing piece of timber contained in the prow of the mythic ship, we had no such fanciful thing. If only Jane were here to remedy that.

Stepping onto the rocky shore of Malta, my thoughts went to my secret purpose. It's true that I became a soldier to serve my queen, but I've another motive too—something I won't readily share with my fellows. I joined Lord Wellington's brigade because I knew it would make camp on this island before moving on to Sevastopol in the Black Sea. My connection to this place is, of course, Theodore de Baras, the monk who wrote so prolifically about notions of the Empyrean. De Baras lived here on the island during the thirteenth century as a member of the Brotherhood of Saint John. He indicates in his writings that he was not the only member of the Brotherhood interested in the highest Heaven. It's my hope that the monks on this island will retain the knowledge of their forbearers, and that because of my status as a member of the Queen's Guard, they will help me find the answers I seek.

If I cannot help Jane understand who she is or what she is—I think we'll all come to ruin soon enough. And so I am here for answers.

I paused in my reading, face burning. Nathan had gone to war to help me, and his experiences had torn him apart. I realized that if it

hadn't been for me, he might never have gone to war at all. I felt sad-
dened by this. Even after all that had happened, I still cared for my
old friend.

*Bunking—I don't have it in me to describe the wretched bunking
houses, though suffice it to say that we are thankfully not camping
out of doors, as some of the other posts are. We have, instead, a
series of small overcrowded rooms complete with braziers that burn
black coal and make the atmosphere quite unbreathable. I have taken
up pen again to make a note about how it feels to be away from my
people. Not my family, per se, for I grew used to being away from
them when boarded at school in my early years, but rather being
away from Jane and Madeline. When embarking on this journey,
I thought the change might do me good, and certainly, the idea of
investigating the Brotherhood excited me. But now living with
the war so close, it makes one realize how fragile and brief our
relationships are—how significant it is to keep hold of them. There
is no room for separation when it comes to love. I wonder which of
the two I'll miss more. This is an experiment of the heart. Maddy
would lose her scruples if she thought that it was not her, and it
could very well be, but still—*

*Città Vecchia (the Old City) on Malta has a sun-blasted, timeworn
look. The dirt and cobble streets seem often to lead nowhere, and
icons of the various religious sects that have held sway over the
island since the Phoenicians crouch and caper at every turn. I am
fascinated by the idea that so many of our ancestors had monsters
for gods. Touring the city with a few of the other soldiers, I made
note of a statue of particular interest. It was repeated frequently on
the island; I counted nearly twenty some statues, effigies of a tall
veiled woman holding a stalk of lilies in the crook of her arm. Her
face was downcast, and she had such a countenance of melancholy.
A local man told me in broken English that she is called the Lady of
Flowers. He said she was a mystic who lived on Malta during the
time of Christ. Her spirit apparently still watches over the island. I*

recognized the name from the writings of Theodore de Baras. Jane had reacted strongly to a drawing of this figure when I showed it to her back home, so I knew she must be significant.

I squinted up at her stone face, washed in sunlight, and tipped the good man. The English money seemed to please him, and I was on my way, catching up with the rest of the boys who were busy attempting to charm a young female fortune-teller.

22nd—We've been driven from our bunking houses in the night by vermin. Some of the men awoke, friends of mine whose sanity I can attest to, saying that there were creatures in the room, crawling things. Rats maybe. Enough to make the entire floor a writhing mat of fur.

Because of the infestation, our brigade was split up and moved to new quarters. The captain made the assignments, and as luck would have it, I was to bunk at the ancient auberge on Malta. The auberge is the place where Frankish and Saxon knights once lived together and that currently belongs to the convent of Carmelite friars known as the Brotherhood of Saint John, the very men I've come here to meet. I wonder if this is not simple luck. Perhaps the Lady of Flowers is smiling down on me?

23rd—The friars are a good and cheerful lot—not the traditional grim beasts one expects from monks. At dinner last night, they proved to be as hearty as any Englishman. We dined on boar, an animal which apparently roams wild on the island. The brothers make Christian sport of hunting the creature with bows and arrows. These good men offered to take me on a tour of their vaults after dinner, and this tour afforded me the opportunity to confess that I am quite interested in their order. My interest seemed to please them greatly.

I was not prepared for the fantastic sights I would see beneath the auberge. Apparently, the monks bury their dead in the subterranean vaults in a most uncommon way. It appears that they are first dried in great heat. One could even say they are baked. Once dried, the *corpses are put into niches in the walls in a standing position with their arms crossed, and they are left exposed for all to see.*

The dried skin of the corpses is reddish brown in color, pulled tightly across the bone of the skull. As the joints have disintegrated, the bodies have dropped into all sorts of positions. Thankfully there's no smell, aside from a faint sweetness that reminds me absurdly of black licorice. It's not the sort of grotesque display I want to be living in proximity of. But the gregarious brothers seem to have no trouble with the dead in their basement. Theirs is not a Gothic existence of mystery and horror. They lead simple lives, and I think one day I should like to live like them, alone on a beautiful island with nothing but old myth surrounding and supporting me.

While in the subterranean chamber, I spotted a stone hallway leading to a circular room that contained a Byzantine-looking gold cabinet. "What's down there?" I asked my guide out of curiosity.

"A reliquary," he said. "It's not to be disturbed."

I made note of the reliquary. Jane says it is my singular goal in life to disturb that which should not be. She might be right about that.

Aside from the crypt, the auberge is a pleasure. Walls covered in arabesque silk in nearly perfect condition showing verdant ferns and exotic animals—a veritable Eden within the old hotel. Carvings have been done on coral. Filigrees of silver line doorways.

We were served pale brandy at night by the laughing friars who want to know of England, as it seems to them another world. They ask us to describe again and again St. Dunstan's Day, Bartholomew's Fair, Buckingham and the Tower.

After the evening of storytelling, I took up conversation with one of the friars, a fellow who seems to be in charge, called Romegas. He was a wizened man with a trim white beard and the most astonishingly clear eyes. I asked him about the macabre display in the lower regions of the auberge, and at first he tried to evade my questions with humor, but as I pressed him, he become more circumspect. "Have you an interest in the soul, Signore Ashe?"

I said that I did.

He nodded solemnly. "One day I promise to teach you more about it. The quality of the human soul is a difficult subject, but here on Malta, there are ways of coming to some understanding of it."

"And what of the reliquary in the catacomb," I asked. "Do you have a piece of the one true cross or the jawbone of Augustine hidden there?"

Romegas raised his white brow. "Reliquary, Signore Ashe? There is no reliquary in the auberge."

25th—Storms all day on the Mediterranean. The sky above Malta is black and alive. Rolling swells break upon the rocks. Still, fishermen can be seen perched out there in the hollows. There is no news of Lord Raglan's vessel, and we cannot move from Malta without his order. So we wait. I am glad for the waiting, as it gives me more time to investigate.

I lit a long taper and took it down into the crypt to examine the so-called reliquary that Romegas denied. At the end of the hall, in the circular room, I found not only the Byzantine cabinet but, astonishingly, another statue of the Lady of Flowers—the very same that I'd seen repeated in the streets of Città Vecchia. This statue was nearly six feet in height, draped in red linens, a stalk of stone flowers held in the crook of her arm. Dead flowers were heaped dramatically around her feet. Certainly she was a pagan idol, and not fit for the Catholic auberge, and yet it was clear she had been decorated and paid alms quite recently.

I was confused as to why a pagan idol would be lauded in the crypt by Catholic monks, and I turned to the golden cabinet, hoping for answers. Like a traditional reliquary, the cabinet had a variety of drawers, many of which I found to be empty. But in one, I made a rather grotesque discovery—the finger of what appeared to be a white ape. I took the finger from the drawer and studied it. I couldn't imagine anything more heretical than putting an ape's finger in a reliquary. How was it possible that Romegas and his brothers had done such a thing?

I don't know what came over me in the next moment, but I

couldn't stop myself from slipping the severed finger in the pocket of
my military jacket. It was wrong of me to take the brothers' relic,
and perhaps later after I've studied it a bit more, I shall put it back.

I paused again in my reading. Nathan had not returned the ape's finger to the reliquary, but had instead found reason to bring it back with him to England. I wondered what the meaning of this might be. And here again was the Lady of Flowers—the figure my mother had invoked as she lay dying in the Clock Parlor. The Lady who came back to me again and again.

Rather than turning to the next page, I closed the book and left it on the desk. Reading Nathan's words made me feel as though I no longer could bear being alone. I would go to see Maddy, and tell her what I'd learned.

CHAPTER 18

I decided to walk across the Heath to reach La Dometa, hoping the great expanse would put my mind at ease and allow me to better contemplate Nathan's journal and the new facts I'd learned. I had a hunch that it wasn't the war itself that made Nathan seem so ill upon his return; it had something to do with the auberge and those rambling catacombs where the Lady of Flowers was worshipped.

As I pondered Nathan's experience, breathing great lungfuls of bright air and listening to the rustle of yellow gorse, I caught sight of a figure sitting on a craggy rock near the path. The young man's dirty red uniform jacket made my heart skip, and I wanted to veer off into the cover of the trees. But he'd already spotted me. There was nowhere to hide from him. He was a broad boy, sandy-haired, with a deep and jagged scar running across his right cheek. He bore an uncanny resemblance to our confidante, Judith Ulster, and I knew that I must be looking at the Fetch, Corydon Ulster, who'd delivered the awful letter to Stoke Morrow. I wasn't the least bit pleased at the prospect of an encounter with him.

Corydon was peeling the white bark off a birchwood branch with his fingernails, letting the thin, curled pieces fall to the ground. He seemed in a state of contemplation, looking first at the bark and then at me, as if comparing me to the wood.

"So there you are," he said, furrowing his brow.

"You've been waiting for me?" I asked.

He looked terribly grim. "You know who I am, miss?"

"I believe you're Corydon Ulster," I said.

He shook his head. "I used to be Corydon Ulster. I'm a Fetch now. Did you receive my letter?"

"I'm sorry to say I did," I replied.

He tossed the half-peeled branch to the ground. "You've been meddling where you oughtn't."

"We're trying to find Nathan Ashe."

Corydon laughed harshly. "I've heard all about that. You girls fancy yourselves detectives."

"We don't fancy ourselves anything," I said.

"You made her cry, you know that?" he asked, tension building in his voice. "My sister, Judith, is a strong girl. She never cries. But that day, after she talked to you, she walked home in tears. I follow her sometimes. She doesn't know I watch, of course. The other Fetches watch too."

"I'm sorry we made your sister cry, but it isn't we who made her unhappy, Corydon," I said. "You took care of that yourself when you abandoned your family for a *cult.*"

"Brave words for a girl alone," he sneered. "A *witch* alone."

"I'm not afraid of you or any Fetch," I said. Even as I heard the words coming out of my mouth, I wasn't sure if they were true.

"Course you're not," Corydon said. "Things in this world don't bother you."

"I'm afraid I don't know your meaning."

"Master Day told us you'd play dumb," he said.

"What does Day claim to understand about me?" I asked.

"Master Day doesn't *claim* anything. He states it as fact."

"And what does he say?"

Again, Corydon laughed, and it was clear he didn't intend to be forthcoming.

"I'm on my way to see someone. You'll excuse me," I said.

But Corydon was off his rock and standing in front of me before

I could even take three steps. His face was an ugly mask, desperate and angry. He was big in the shoulders, and I feared he could bring me to the ground. "Let me feel it," he said. "Let me feel what Nathan Ashe felt. I want to see the Doorway."

Corydon's hands were on me, one gripping my arm and the other groping for my breast. I reacted without thinking—or perhaps some unconscious part of me took over and did the thinking. My own hand was suddenly at Corydon's throat. I did not squeeze the throat but rather allowed my ability to fill him. My power flowed like cold water through my arm. I could feel his pulse against my palm, and I pushed my talent against that pulse. I imagined it flowing up the column of his throat toward his brain and down his throat toward his heart. Ulster slowly loosened his grip and stood staring at me with what might have been awe. I kept my hand at his throat, and his body began to shake, as if in seizure. One of his gray eyes trailed off to the left, and his jaw went tight, causing him to bite his own tongue. Blood ran from the corners of his mouth.

I wondered, in that moment, if I could kill Corydon Ulster with my talent. And was he *worth* killing?

This last thought startled me into letting go of his neck, and he crumpled to the ground. I regarded him quietly, wanting to hurt him again. There'd been a kind of pleasure in such release. I found I was still angry, but I could not stop myself from thinking of Judith Ulster's tears.

I leaned close to him. Corydon seemed barely conscious, his left eye still lazy. "Don't you ever come after me or any of my friends again," I said. "Learn some manners, Mr. Ulster, or you might not fare so well next time."

I left him there, walking off into the woods, shocked by what I'd done. I looked down at my own hands. I'd never permitted the transference to overtake another person so completely. Had there been such power in me all along?

By the time I reached La Dometa, I'd steadied myself. I'd considered whether I should tell Maddy about my encounter with Corydon and decided against doing so. The story would only upset her and make her fear for my safety. The newly hired servant who met me at the door informed me that Maddy wasn't feeling well herself, and I didn't give much thought to the illness, attributing it to her continued anxiety over Nathan. Eusapia Lee instead greeted me in the parlor, wearing a black veil and sitting on a straight-back chair. A vase of marigolds and an untouched cup of tea sat on a table next to her. I knew from previous conversations with Eusapia that marigolds represented the Virgin Mary's sorrow and joy—losing a son but gaining a god. Adolphus Lee's photographs of naked women covered the walls of the parlor, and it was once again difficult for me to believe that Eusapia did not find such images distasteful, though she'd always acted as though her dead husband's work was beyond reproach.

"My dear," I said to Eusapia. "Why are you wearing that veil?"

"Is that you, Jane Silverlake?" she asked, peering through the dark gauze. "The light hurts my eyes," she said. "And the air hurts my skin."

"Have you seen a doctor?" I asked.

"No doctors can cure me," she said. "But bring one for Madeline if you like. My girl is ailing. The last of our clan—sick, so very sick. Go and see her, Jane. Go and see as she withers away."

"What is her sickness?" I asked.

Eusapia looked toward her marigolds. "Her symptoms are a sign of horrors to come," she said more to herself than to me. "Horrors to come."

I ascended the stairs, glancing at pictures of Melchior Lee, which Eusapia kept as a type of shrine to her son after he died in the Opium Wars. I found Maddy in her bedroom, dressed in a gown more voluminous than her traditional fare. The air smelled sour, as though she'd vomited. It was clear she'd been crying too. "What is it, Maddy?" I asked. "What's wrong?"

She shook her head. "Jane, it's an awful feeling. I haven't been able to hold anything down."

"Your mother said I should bring the doctor."

"He's already come," she said. "Mother has forgotten. She forgets so much. I wonder if my brain will one day be as broken down as hers." There was a drowsiness to her voice that I was not accustomed to. Perhaps the doctor had given her something for her nerves.

"And what did your physician say, Maddy?"

"I don't want to talk about it."

"What do you mean?"

"I need to sleep, Jane," she said. "I'll feel better if I sleep. Is there any news of Nathan?"

"No news," I said. "But I've read a portion of his journal. He apparently found the white ape finger on the island of Malta. He stole it from a group of monks. I think it may well have some connection to the trouble he's gotten himself into."

Maddy closed her eyes. "What else did you learn?"

"He went to Malta not only to join the war effort but also to continue his investigation into the occult phenomenon that he believes surround my abilities."

"He was truly obsessed," Maddy said.

"But he wrote about me in a kind way," I said. "As if I wasn't an experiment, but someone he loved."

Maddy opened her eyes to study me. "He loved you as a sister, yes," she said. "I always knew that. Does he say anything about his love for me?"

"I don't recall anything, no. We're mentioned rarely, only in passing."

"But if you had to guess," Maddy said, "would you say he loved me as a man would love a wife?"

I was startled by this question. "I think he *cared* for us both, Maddy."

She attempted to rouse herself. Red blotches appeared high on each cheek; her lips looked bloodless. "But do you think he *loved* me romantically?"

"I don't know. You need to rest. We'll talk about this later."

"It's always later," she said. "And we never say what we mean."

"What are you getting at?"

"I think Nathan was in love with me, Jane. I think he was in love with me, but he didn't know how to say it plainly. Or perhaps—*your* presence prevented him from doing so."

My dress suddenly felt too tight and my skin was hot. I couldn't bear her jealous wrath after what had happened with Corydon Ulster in the woods. Was it possible that no matter how strong I grew, I would never be stronger than Madeline Lee?

At that moment, I knew if I stayed in her bedroom any longer, I wouldn't be able to hold back my feelings. I excused myself and rushed down the hall.

Descending the stairs, I felt myself dropping through layers of memory, desperate for something better than the present moment. I loved Maddy. She'd made me feel almost normal for so long. How could she act as though I'd been an intruder in her relationship with Nathan?

I remembered a time when she and I were in my dressing room at Stoke Morrow taking turns at the gilded mirror, her fox fur cape tossed over one corner of it. The head of the fox, still attached, had yellow glass eyes that watched us with care.

"You know Nathan loved how we fixed you up last night," Maddy said. She was running a brush through her black hair methodically. The brush was Limoges and of good weight. The city scene painted on its back was all spires and cathedrals bedecked with light. Maddy had made me what I was, and on certain days I think she believed she invented me whole-cloth, using the strength of her fantasies to drape my bones in flesh.

"Did he?" I asked.

"He said you looked like a countess walking down a grand palazzo in Florence."

I tried to thank her, but she said I need not. "I'm happy to make you a countess any day, Jane. And yet, there should be something more for us both. I think we'll both have families one day. Can you imagine our children playing together, Jane?"

I realized I could not.

"Do you recall the famous line that the Lady of Shalott said in Tennyson's poem?" Maddy asked.

" 'I am half-sick of shadows,' " I say.

"You have a perfect memory for poetry."

I attempted a smile.

"I *feel* as the Lady feels," she said. "All these recent happenings with Nathan—our walks and our conversations—are but shadows, and I'd like my life to finally begin. Wouldn't you?"

I didn't know how to answer. What did she mean by "life"? Marriage and children? The processes of aging?

Instead I took a moment to envision the second birth of the Lady of Shalott, her gasp of air in a noisy outer barony. For the Lady, release from her cloistered tower meant death. She knew the consequence of going into the world, but the Lady could not bear mere glimpses of her beloved Lancelot in the magic mirror. Instead, she wanted to touch him—"his broad clear brow . . . his coal-black curls"—and so she left her cloister and died for love. By the time Lancelot discovered her, she was dead, drifting in a boat at the river's edge not so far from the tower where she'd spent her days. I was generally disgusted by Lancelot's final musing: "She has a lovely face." As if his judgment was what mattered. As if the lady was no more than a surface for a man to look upon.

"I want to *thrive*, Jane," Maddy was saying. "I want both of us to thrive."

I gathered the strength to take the brush from her and stood behind her at the mirror, not a magic mirror of Shalott, but my own dressing glass. Maddy looked hopeful and beautiful in that moment. What would it feel like, I wondered, to crack the brush against her skull? An awful notion. She was mine, and I was hers. And yet she had a lovely face—*I could not stop myself from thinking this*—certainly lovelier than my own. But what did Nathan think? A horrid question. If Nathan ever chose one of us, the fantasy would be broken. Floodwaters would rise.

CHAPTER 19

In the weeks that followed my last visit to La Dometa, I saw nothing of Maddy. She did not call upon me at Stoke Morrow or even write, and I was left to while away the hours, paging through books and sitting at my mirror glass, wondering what she was thinking of me. It seemed that she and I kept a city of grief buried between the two of us. Discussing Nathan's feelings for us was the beginning of an excavation, and such archaeology was proving too much to bear.

Long shadows crept over my father's house, threatening to pull me down into a life of solitude again. Miss Anne watched me carefully from doorways, body poised, as though she might flee at any moment. Father finally came to sit by my side in the Clock Parlor one evening and said, "Tell me what bothers you so, Jane. Is it the Ashe boy?"

"It's not," I replied. "I'm all right, really."

For a moment, he looked as he had before Mother died—full of quiet strength. "I've been lost in my own sorrows for so long that we barely know how to speak to one another," he said. "But I can tell when my own daughter is in pain. Please don't shut me out entirely."

"It's Maddy," I said. "She doesn't want to talk to me. She thinks I've taken something from her. And I worry that perhaps she's right."

He leaned close, putting his hand gently on the shoulder of my linen dress. "You have your mother's heart. She thought her whole world was going to fall apart more than once, I'll tell you. But the world never broke. She was always strong enough to keep it whole. You are too."

"I don't feel like I am," I said.

"You are, my darling. You just don't know it. Rest assured that Madeline Lee will come back to you. She wouldn't dare stay away."

I decided that my best hope for recovering Maddy was the coming Festival of Saint Dunstan. Its arrival would make her miss Nathan even more, as we traditionally attended the event at his side. She would believe that if he was somewhere in London, he'd try to make his way to Parliament Hill Fields for the celebration. I sent letters to La Dometa, imploring Maddy to come to Stoke Morrow so we could make our plans for attendance. A costume was traditionally required, as the festival also served as a spring masque for the citizens of the Heath. Pascal visited me twice in one week, assuring me that Maddy's absence was largely due to the illness that still plagued her—a nausea which came in the morning but abated by early afternoon.

"Does she talk about me, Pascal?"

"Of course, Saint Jane. Often."

"And what does she say?"

"She misses you but she needs time to make sense of her own thoughts," he said. "She'll come back when she's ready, and I'm sure she'll be ready soon."

It was during this period of isolation that I took up Nathan's journal of the war again and forced myself back to Malta and the auberge. I found it comforting, at first, to read his words, but as the tone of the journal changed and the events became distorted, that comfort faded and finally disappeared entirely.

May 1—Prince Louis Napoleon reached Malta this afternoon on a ship called the Orinoco. I glimpsed the man from afar. He looks

*much like the paintings I've seen, though heavier. Still no sign of
Lord Raglan, whose brigade we are meant to join, and we have
been told to hold the course in waiting. I'm coming up empty-
handed in my search of the auberge as well. None of the texts in the
library refer to either the Empyrean or the Lady of Flowers, and I
can find no record of Theodore de Baras. I am also worried that the
Brothers may know I have taken their ape finger. They look at me
with concern when I pass them in the halls, and it seems that even
Romegas is more guarded in my presence.*

*The best piece of evidence I've gathered is nothing concrete, but
an odd story that Romegas himself told me—a myth really. I got up
the courage one evening after dinner to ask him about the various
idols on the island, saying I was particularly interested in the
statues popular around Città Vecchia that represented the Lady of
Flowers. I, of course, did not acknowledge I'd seen a similar statue
hidden in his own catacomb.*

*"Ah yes, the mysterious Lady," Romegas said. "May I pour you a
drink, Signore Ashe? Our own Brother Bianchi makes a pleasant
digestive from grapes gathered in the northern countryside."*

*I accepted the wine, and we settled ourselves by the fire. I was
reminded again what a wonderful and comforting place the
auberge could be. Perhaps I'd been wrong to think the monks
suspected anything of me. Romegas seemed entirely himself that
evening—open and congenial.*

*"The Lady of Flowers lived here on Malta at the time of Christ,
and during her lifetime she gathered a cult that persisted even after
her death," he said. "She was a mystic who claimed to be a sort of
avatar. Are you familiar with that word?"*

I told him I was not.

*"It's common enough in the Hindu religions. In English, you
might say incarnation—the physical manifestation of a god on the
earth."*

"So the Lady of Flowers believed she was a goddess?" I asked.

*"Not precisely," Romegas said, taking a sip of his dark wine
and looking toward the fire. "She claimed to be a projection of the*

unnamed goddess—a piece of her. You must understand that all of this is nothing more than a fairy story, signore. Our pope would be disappointed in me for telling it at all. I'm simply relaying what I've heard. In part, this fiction about the goddess was perpetrated by the Lady herself, but it has been embellished over the years. The Lady's goddess has accrued many names. Some would say that she is Sophia or the Sapientia Dei—the eternal female who is the embodiment of God's wisdom. She is said to have lived with God before creation, not as wife but as partner and equal. Others would argue that she is not a part of God's system at all, that she existed before him and became his inspiration, a primal archetype. She is the idea for everything, and yet she herself is nothingness, the magnificent void that existed before the universe. Her eternal body takes the form of the void, just as the Greeks gave name and personality to the ocean and the sky."

I tried to behave casually as Romegas spoke, in order that he should feel at ease enough to continue. But his story fascinated me, and my excitement continued to mount.

"When the universe was created, the unnamed goddess did not disappear. She sat alone and watched creation from her high aerie. Some would say the Lord eventually relegated her to Hell along with the rest of the monsters who existed before creation, but I don't think that's right. She continued to exist on her own terms in a fragment of the original void."

"I thought you said she was the void," I said.

"It's mythos, signore. There's nothing logical about it. She is the void and lives inside the void."

"And the avatar?" I said. "The Lady of Flowers?"

Romegas smiled at my eagerness. "That's quite another story. The unnamed goddess saw our world as a place of suffering and confusion. She took pity on humanity because Creation was corrupt and growing more so. Not only was the world populated by the inventions of God, but soon Man himself began to make his own vain inventions. And these inventions possessed such troubled souls."

Here I thought to myself about the souls of objects and how Jane could make them sing. I wondered what she would make of this story.

"In her great compassion," Romegas continued, "the goddess is said to have dressed a piece of herself in flesh and sent that incarnation into the stream of time. The avatar was to be a protector of mankind. You'll hear the fisherman on the island, those who remain half-pagan despite our best efforts, talking about how the Lady of Flowers keeps them and upholds them. But the Lady was also saddled with another task. It is said that if the world became too terrible, if man made too many creations, too many broken and clamoring souls, the Lady would rise up and bring back the void. She would unmake what has been made by the Lord and therefore bring solace to the earth."

"She would destroy the world?" I said.

"Not destruction precisely. The unmaking would provide a solution—a new kind of Paradise."

Perhaps I was feeling my drink, or I was merely intoxicated by Romegas's amiable manner, but I suddenly had the fortitude to ask him whether he'd heard of Theodore de Baras.

A faint look of surprise passed over the old monk's features, and I wondered too if I detected a momentary expression of anger there as well.

"I haven't heard that name in many years, Signore Ashe."

"It's only that I read some of his writings in England and wondered if there might be more at the auberge."

Romegas sighed deeply. "The work of de Baras is kept in a private library that I'm afraid only the Brothers have access to. He is not particularly well regarded here because of his bizarre theories."

"Is he buried in the vault below?" I asked.

"He is not," Romegas said. "Brother de Baras disappeared when he was thirty-nine years of age. His body was never found."

I sat with that information, staring into the depths of my digestive, and wondering what had happened to the monk.

I closed the journal, still using Maddy's handkerchief to handle it, and stared blankly at the worn leather cover and then at the wall in Father's study. Romegas's story of the unnamed goddess and the Lady had resonated with me. They too had heard the suffering of objects that I had heard all my life. Nathan had clearly come close to understanding all of it. Yet something had happened that made him return to England, not full of knowledge, but utterly disoriented and weak enough to become a follower of Ariston Day. I wanted to continue reading, to finish the journal entirely, but there was something I felt I should do first, something I'd been considering for a long time but never found the courage for. Questions of my own history seemed pressing once again.

I went to the kitchen, where Miss Anne was preparing what smelled like lamb in a copper kettle over the fire. She was startled by my appearance, and I stood very close to her, as if I might touch her at any moment.

"Do you still keep in contact with Miss Herron-Cross?" I asked.

"Oh, Miss Herron-Cross," Anne said, nervously. She was sweating from the heat of the fire, and she used a rag to wipe her brow. "Those were the days, weren't they, Jane?"

"I suppose they were. Do you hear from her at all?"

"We used to write letters," Miss Anne said. "Such lovely letters. I kept her apprised of the goings-on at Stoke Morrow."

"So you know where she is currently?"

"Only a few years back, she was acting as head maid at Saint Hilda's School. Hilda's isn't so far from here—just to the south, you know."

"Go and fetch my heavy walking cape and boots," I said.

Miss Anne stopped stirring her kettle abruptly. "Jane, you're not thinking of bothering Miss Herron-Cross, are you? We should all let the past be the past, I think."

"I'll ask for your advice when it's required," I said firmly. "My walking cape and boots, Anne."

*   *   *

Saint Hilda's School was a rambling gray manor house set on a wide acre of grass and elm. I'd seen it before on trips into London, but I never imagined Miss Herron-Cross might be inside. A school for girls was a rarity in London, and from what I understood Saint Hilda's was more a place for cultivating manners than it was an institution of science or the arts. I often wondered why Father, in his depression, hadn't simply packed me off to such a place. Perhaps he'd felt too ashamed, knowing Mother would never have done so. He kept me at Stoke Morrow out of some duty to her.

Girls in dark uniforms, which looked almost like habits, idled in the yard and watched as I made my way up the long stone path. Their ages ranged from quite young to nearly eighteen, and they all seemed uncertain of me. I looked neither like a servant nor like the kind of woman their tutors were grooming them to become. My walking boots and cape were almost mannish, and I knew the expression on my face was not one of sweetness or charity. I was, in many ways, not like a woman at all. Nor was I really like a man. I was a third type, gray-eyed and unnatural. I thought about brushing my hand against each of these girls' cheeks, allowing them to see that the very brick and timber of quiet Saint Hilda's was filled with life and pain. The shingles on the roof blazed like doomed stars and the doorframes howled with useless life. I wanted these girls to know the world was not as simple as what they'd been taught. Manners meant nothing when there were horrors and wonders waiting at every turn.

But in the end, I left them alone with their beliefs. I was nervous about seeing Miss Herron-Cross after all these years. She'd said such awful things about me before her departure. She believed me truly depraved.

A young woman in a maid's uniform met me in the stone foyer of the school and informed me that Miss Herron-Cross was indeed still at Saint Hilda's, though she was no longer employed as head maid. She'd suffered a series of episodes nearly a year before, falling twice, and she'd been bedridden ever since.

"May I speak with her?" I asked. "She was my caretaker when I was very young."

The maid became suddenly warm. "Oh, that might be just the thing to lift poor Susana's spirits," she said. "Follow me, dear."

I was ushered into a small room with a high window, which provided the only source of light. Miss Herron-Cross appeared nothing like the staunch matron I remembered. A white sheet was pulled up to her chin, and she stared at me absently with liquid blue eyes. The years had shrunk her, made her insubstantial. The young woman who'd escorted me said, "I expect you both have some catching up to do. I'll leave you to it."

"Do you recognize me?" I asked Miss Herron-Cross when the maid was gone.

She swallowed dryly. "I do not."

I put my hand lightly on her hand, allowing the transference to occur.

She tried to push away but was too weak to do so. "Jane Silverlake," she said. "What in the name of God are you doing here?"

"I've come to ask you about your last days at Stoke Morrow," I said. "I've wanted to speak with you for some time but haven't had the courage. Though as of late, it seems I'm building fortitude."

She made no response and continued merely regarding me.

"When you left your post, you told my father that my mother had a troubling nature. That she was somehow unnatural. Do you remember?"

She cleared her throat. "Evelyn Silverlake was as singular a woman as I have ever known."

"Careful not to blaspheme," I said softly, "or I shall touch your hand again."

She huddled beneath her sheet. I remembered how Heron-Cross would lock me in my room near the end of her tenure at Stoke Morrow, so she would not have to look at me or feel what I felt.

"Tell me what you remember of my mother then," I said.

"Evelyn wasn't like you if that's what you're asking," she replied. "She couldn't make the house moan or the walls spit fire. Your father first met her when she was wandering in the southern woods. She was walking there among the trees in her tattered frock, and she didn't claim to have any sort of home or people. I don't know if anyone ever told you that. Your father inexplicably asked for her hand in marriage soon after their meeting, and if you think she was a good mother to you, Jane, I don't know that you're remembering correctly. She was scarcely present. She kept venturing back into the woods and then onto the Heath, as if she was searching for something, but she never told any of us what it was she was looking for. My own mother used to tell me of spirits that walked the southern woods and waited there to ensnare men. They wanted a house to grow whatever plot they were brewing. I always thought Evelyn was something like that—some desperate spirit who needed shelter for a time. When she died, none of us were particularly surprised because, quite frankly, she didn't seem to know how to live."

I shook off Miss Herron-Cross's disturbing words—keeping my mind focused on the issue at hand. "Did she ever mention someone called the Lady of Flowers?" I asked.

"Never," she said. "Most of the time Evelyn didn't speak at all. When your father first brought her to Stoke Morrow we all thought she was mute." Miss Herron-Cross paused for a moment. "But there was the church she grew interested in—the one in Spitalfields. They didn't worship God or Christ. What they worshipped did have something to do with flowers if I'm remembering correctly."

"Spitalfields," I said.

"That's right. Not an area most of us would ever go to, but Evelyn Silverlake went there like the world couldn't harm her. As if it didn't truly exist."

"And do you know why she died?" I asked, feeling like a child again in Miss Herron-Cross's presence and disgusted with myself because of it. "Do you know what made her so sick out in the field of shale?"

She coughed and then spat phlegm into a handkerchief. "Evelyn Silverlake's death was unnatural, to be sure. It was as though she . . . faltered. Like she could no longer hold her place in the world. And so she closed her eyes and looked at us no longer. She gazed instead at that place she was meant for."

"What place?" I said.

"I already told you I don't know that. I didn't understand your mother, and I don't understand you. Why can't you just leave me alone?"

I did not thank Miss Herron-Cross as I took my leave, and I did not wish her peace. Instead, I thought of Mother, all alone on the Heath, closing her eyes and gazing on that other place.

CHAPTER 20

I returned to Stoke Morrow, and though Father had recently come home from his law offices I didn't go to greet him. I couldn't bear it. I had too many questions, and I knew that they would hurt him. He'd buried the past, endeavored to make as stable and normal a life for me as he could muster. I thought about Miss Herron-Cross's comment about Mother's absence during my childhood. She was right, of course, yet I also had many memories of Mother sitting at my bedside and whispering her stories to me. The more I thought about these memories, the more I realized the instances of storytelling had happened in the dead of night after Mother had returned from walking and everyone else was in bed. These were private moments between us. It was difficult now to remember the precise nature of her stories, other than the one about the pregnant oak, and the more I tried to conjure those narratives, the more tangled my memories became until it seemed Mother had spoken to me in an altogether foreign tongue. Or that she had not spoken at all but merely hovered over my bed, somehow imparting the stories through silence. I took Nathan's journal to my bedroom and opened it, hoping to find answers there or, at the very least, distraction.

5th—Have had an uncommon time of it since my last writing, which I see has been days. Romegas recommended that I take a walk down a long country road to look at the ruins of a civilization called Crendi. The ruin is said to be Phoenician in origin, though, according to Romegas, it is perhaps much older. "Crendi was a favorite place of meditation for your own Theodore de Baras," Romegas said. "It was, in fact, the last place he was ever seen," Romegas said. "There is a temple in the ruin where the ancients made worship to the Lady of Flowers. You'll find it intriguing, no doubt."

I told him I would certainly make the walk, for sport if nothing else.

As I traversed the road from the auberge to the ruin, the Mediterranean sparkled like a gem to the east. Wildflowers grew alongside the road, and the sweet smell of those flowers combined with the scent of the sea to make the air into an elixir of life and death. The ruins of Crendi revealed themselves slowly. Large pieces of white rock appeared and, at first, seemed to be natural formations of the landscape. Then a post and lintel came into view, like our own Stonehenge. Finally came the remnants of buildings, most of which had collapsed. There was a flat-roofed circular structure which fit the description of Romegas's temple, and I sat on a rock to take my lunch (a sandwich made with cured meat that was foreign to me—venison perhaps).

I'd forgotten my hat, and my skull was baking. To escape the punishing heat, I finally entered the temple though I was hesitant to do so. The place filled me with a sense of foreboding and made me think again of the disappearance of Theodore de Baras. To be sure, the bright sun had altered my perceptions. Mirages danced before me in the shadows of the temple, and I felt suddenly dizzy, barely able to stand. I went to the stone altar and sat down, searching for my canteen. Our captain had warned us of symptoms that could arise from heat exhaustion, and I feared I was suffering such an attack. It was when I began to drink that I had what I believed to be another hallucination—this one far more concrete and distressing. Looking over my raised canteen, I saw a figure appear in the doorway. I understood immediately the figure was not a man, though it stood upright on two legs and swayed from right to left. It was simian in nature—apelike. Because it was backlit by the harsh sun, its features were cast in shadow, and I could not see its face. From what I could discern in the half-light, it was covered in long white fur, the same sort of fur that sprouted from the finger I'd found in the reliquary.

I lowered the canteen from my lips, and the creature was gone, as if it had never been there. I assured myself the vision was a product of sun-sickness and that I merely needed to get myself back to the auberge.

7th—I have not been able to put the vision of the creature out of my mind. On top of that, my sun-sickness is still with me. No food will stay in my stomach. The Brothers seem concerned, talking of dementia. Romegas himself visited my bedside, and I asked him if there was some species of white ape living on the island.

He raised his brow. "I suppose it's possible. Some animal might have been brought over from the Africas. There was once a large cat that threatened an outlying village. But an ape is not likely, signore. Why do you ask?"

"It's nothing," I said. "A symptom, very likely."

9th—Rumors are circulating among the men that a council of war was held last night to determine whether our battalions should be moved on into Stamboul and then toward Crimea. I am in no state to go to war. My remaining symptoms are as follows: extreme fatigue and dizziness, dryness of the mouth and eyes, and perhaps worst of all, night terrors. I awake nearly every night, drenched in sweat, and see the creature standing in my quarters—often hovering over my bed to examine me. I remain very still, and it puts its face close to mine. Such a face it is—not like an ape at all, but somehow more human. Like some hybrid or missing link. But the eyes are the worst. Empty sockets. Sometimes after I've stared into them for a long while, I can see my own face reflected back from the depths of the holes. As if I am trapped down there, deep inside the white ape.

I've gotten it in my head that I do not suffer from sun-sicknesses, but rather the vision of the white ape at the temple infected me in some way—perhaps the air of that place put some disease in me. I feel that if I could only find the papers of Theodore de Baras, all would be made clear. I'd make sense of the ruin and what befell me there. But there seems no space in the auberge I have not searched which could contain the private library that Romegas mentioned.

I decided to walk the sunbaked streets of Città Vecchia, among black-hatted priests and clerical students. I stopped villagers nearly at random to ask if they knew of a white ape which inhabited the island. People began to treat me as if I was mad and finally, an old woman spoke to me in a voice barely audible above the din of the street. "You have been to Crendi?" she asked.

I told her I had.

"You went to pay homage to our Lady?"

"No," I said. "I paid no homage."

"Then you must make a sacrifice."

"What kind of sacrifice?" I said. "What's required?"

"You must decide that for yourself, Englishman," she said, moving off into the crowd before I could ask another question.

By evening light, I made my way toward the ruins once again. It seems the wildflowers have all perished in this intolerable, baking sun. All that remains are blackish weeds that cover even the most modest patches of soil. The weeds have nearly obliterated a stone wall that runs alongside the path. The plants looked like a disease, spreading out from the central infection of the ruin.

I brought with me the severed finger from the reliquary, doing so almost on instinct, as one might bring a rosary to church. When I stepped into the shade of the temple, I took the finger from my pocket and studied it in the dim light. It looked just as it had in the auberge, desiccated and timeworn.

Just then, the temple walls appeared to swell and contract around me, as if I was inside a great stone lung. I placed the ape finger on the altar. "Is this what you want?" I asked the darkness. "Will this suffice?"

There was no answer, of course, and I felt foolish and even sicker than before. I took the finger from the altar, thinking I would still return it to the reliquary. It was when I turned to leave the temple that I saw the creature once again, crouched alongside one of the broken walls. The beast was digging in the dirt, making a small mound of soil. When it looked up, I felt a cold fear. I'd interrupted its business. It rose to full height, and I stared into the pits it used for eyes. They were the color of the space between the stars.

I attempted to make my escape, but the beast blocked my path. I stumbled back and fell against the altar. The beast came at me, putting its rough hands around my throat. It brought its face so close, and I was there inside of it once again, staring out from those terrible eye sockets. And worse yet, I felt it was now also inside of me.

How I made it back to the auberge, I do not know. But writing this, I feel that I am no longer alone. The creature has joined itself to me—like a rider on my soul. Is it possible that my experiments with Jane made me susceptible to such an experience? Did she open me to these alien elements of the universe?

I felt a flood of guilt reading this and wanted to stop. I had opened Nathan to this world, after all. And it was one that he could not possibly hope to control. I read on:

—I've grown sick of my silent searching. I feel full of the beast. At the auberge, I cornered one of the Brothers, a small man who could not defend himself, and told him I'd bring him harm if he didn't take me to the private library, the one that held the papers of Theodore de Baras. I showed him my knife, and he complied. The library was located behind a tapestry in the burial vault. Of course it was. Why hadn't I searched the vault more carefully?

The dead Brothers in the walls watched as I entered their sacred storehouse. Candlelight played off my blade as I asked the weak monk why Romegas had sent me to the ruin at Crendi in the first place. "Was I meant to be some sort of sacrifice?" I asked. "Or was it merely a means of disposing of me?"

The monk shook his head, cowering.

I showed him the finger I'd stolen, no longer afraid of being found out, no longer caring. "And this?" I said. "What does this mean?"

He seemed stricken by the sight of the ape finger and would not speak.

I told him to give me the papers of Theodore de Baras and leave me. I sat in the stone library and read the papers slowly by candlelight, translating the Italian. In de Baras's words, I discovered not more of the same philosophical musings I'd come across in London, but a detailed description of a series of horrors that he'd enacted in order to explore what he called the Empyrean. His words changed my entire understanding of my current situation and of Jane's. I intend to take the papers to her. I'll show them as proof. And I'll hope to God she will believe what they say and take action.

The narrative ended abruptly here. Nathan left the rest of the journal blank, except for a few symbols he'd drawn near the end and then scratched out. What horrors had he read of in de Baras's papers, and why hadn't he shown the papers to me upon his return to England as he intended? Who or what had prevented him from doing so? I was left to sit and wonder.

CHAPTER 21

By the time Maddy finally returned to me, St. Dunstan's Day was
nearly upon us. She arrived at Stoke Morrow in one of her more
boyish ensembles—a pair of plum-colored bloomers and a dark vest.
She'd pinned her black hair and tucked it under a bicycle hat, and I
wondered if this clothing was meant to provide some kind of protection against the day.

The afternoon sky was cloudless, and we walked together in the
garden toward the Roman ruin. I wanted to take her arm and talk to
her about everything I'd learned from Nathan's journal, but she still
had such an air of coldness about her. I didn't want to drive her away
again.

"We shouldn't have argued," I said.

"I'm not here to talk about that, Jane," she replied, stiffly, adjusting her cap. "I'm here to discuss how St. Dunstan's might prove useful to our search."

"Are you feeling better then?" I asked. "Physically, I mean."

"There's still nausea in the morning," Maddy said. "But the doctor
tells me I'm fine."

"Any idea what's the matter?"

"I don't—" she said, trailing off. "I'm not ready to talk about it."

And because she seemed much improved, both physically and men-

tally, I accepted this. I wanted nothing more than for both of us to feel
at peace. We left the garden and went to my dressing room to look
for clothing that might be used for costumes at the festival's masque.
I spoke carefully, keeping things cheerful, though I could not help but
ask the question that had been nagging me all morning. "Maddy, did
Nathan ever show you any papers he brought back from the war?"

"Papers?"

"Yes, perhaps a manuscript in Italian? They would likely have
been the writings of the monk Theodore de Baras."

"No, Jane, nothing of that sort," she said. "Are you finished reading his journal yet by the way? I'd like to have a look."

"Not quite finished," I lied.

"You are the *slowest* reader, Jane."

"I know, Maddy. I know."

The festival was held at twilight on the southern edge of the Heath,
close enough to Stoke Morrow that Maddy and I could walk and
did not need a carriage. Torches flickered hotly on the festival
grounds, casting living shadows in the oak groves. Silver bells rang
out, and the air smelled of the burning tapers that were carried in
honor of the saint's canonization. A series of tableaus were enacted
on a wooden stage draped in aubergine tapestry to portray seminal
events in the life of the saint—his birth, his near death during an
affliction of boils, his near marriage to Lady Ephesia, and of course
his numerous duels with the Devil, which culminated in Dunstan's
catching the Devil by the nose with a pair of fire tongs and nailing a
horseshoe to one of the creature's black hooves.

Men and women of Hampstead Town had come dressed as figures from allegory and myth. The whole event had quite a pagan
feel. It seemed impossible that the festival should happen without
Nathan Ashe, who had once dressed as Artegal, the knight of justice,
and drunk so much wine that he began to believe he *was* Artegal,
going around and challenging everyone to a sword fight.

Saint Dunstan's story reminded me of Mother Damnable's, though he was lauded and she was loathed. Such was the way with men and women. He was a Benedictine monk who'd temporarily made his home in a hovel near Parliament Hill during the eighth century after being expelled from the archbishopric in Canterbury on the grounds of being a magician. Further charges against him were particularly curious, as he was said to have possessed a harp that played the anthem "Gaudent in Celis Animæ Sanctorum" of its own volition whenever the Devil came near. Apparently the Devil came often to Dunstan, as the harp was said to be heard over the Heath both day and night. The notion of the automatic harp, of course, reminded me of my own unnatural association with objects, and so I sympathized with Dunstan. His harp seemed not wicked at all, but rather a useful tool. He was exonerated during his own lifetime, and when he died, his body, interred at Glastonbury, did not decompose but remained incorrupt, smelling of sweet flowers. At times it was even said to weep.

A rumor circulated that a relic of Saint Dunstan was to be produced at this year's tableau, and everyone conjectured as to exactly what that relic might be. A jawbone seemed likely, as that sort of relic was in fashion. Others believed it would be the tongs that Dunstan once used to grab the nose of the Devil. I knew that whatever was produced would be some form of counterfeit and couldn't bother myself to care. Maddy and I had other business to attend to.

We walked the grounds together, closely studying the revelers dressed in their medieval garments, knowing that Nathan might be tempted to appear. He claimed to like the festival more than Christmas, after all. Others must have had the same idea. I saw a somber Lord and Lady Ashe in the crowd as well as Inspector Vidocq, who wore a golden mask that was meant as a representation of the sun god, Helios. He was followed by two agents of the police in black hoods. Their costumes made me think of night following day.

Maddy leaned close to my ear and spoke in a hushed voice. "I've brought Nathan's pistol," she said, patting the purse she carried on her belt. She wore a brass breastplate and a pair of her father's pants, claiming to be Britomart, a female knight who represented chastity.

"You did no such *thing*," I said. I'd decided not to wear a costume at the last minute, wanting to be no one but myself.

"Of course I brought it," she replied, taking a candle from a tow-headed child who was distributing them through the crowd. "What if we run into difficulty?"

"What difficulty would we find at the Festival of Saint Dunstan? We've been coming here since we were girls."

"The world has changed," was Maddy's only response.

We did not run into difficulty per se, or at least not difficulty in its traditional guise. But it was during the festival that we came across Pascal Paget and Alexander Hartford. I was surprised to see them together, as Pascal had earlier expressed reticence about even being in the presence of Alexander. The two came up out of the southern woods. Pascal was chasing Alexander, who moved with some determination. Alexander was meant to be Hypnos, god of sleep, and wore a loose black shirt with ribbons on the sleeves and a pair of dark riding pants. A red poppy was pinned above his heart. He'd pushed up his silver mask so it rested on his forehead, and his entire face was revealed. Pascal was Thanatos, daemon god of death. He wore gold face paint around his eyes, carried a replica of a broadsword, and had a pair of black wings tied to his back with what looked like bailing wire. Remembering the story of their love affair, I was moved by these costumes, and I wondered if they'd chosen them independently, mourning their past.

I overheard enough of their argument to understand that Pascal was pleading with Alexander to stop whatever it was he intended to do, and Alexander was telling our French comrade to simply turn around and walk back into the woods—that the matter was none of Pascal's concern.

Pascal's face was flushed, and there were tears in his eyes, streaking the gold paint. When he saw us, he nearly succumbed to some sort of swoon. Alexander, on the other hand, brightened. His ruddy American face lit like a lamp. "Jane Silverlake," he said, "just the girl I've been looking for."

"Whatever for?" I asked, already on guard.

"You certainly wanted nothing to do with us at the Silver Horne," Maddy said.

Alexander produced an envelope from inside his tunic. I recognized the fine paper and the dark wax seal. "I've brought you this message from Master Day," he said. "Not many receive word from him. It's quite an honor." Clearly, Ariston Day had not made his prior letter to me public to his Fetches.

"You don't have to accept this *honor*," Pascal countered.

Alexander held onto his smile, but barely.

I took the letter and broke the wax seal, reading quickly. It was written in the same elegant script as the previous missive—hard lines of ink plunging and rising—but the tone and content of the message was quite different.

Miss Silverlake,

I was clearly not direct enough in my previous invitation. Allow me to rectify that. You should know that I am aware of what you did on the night of Nathan Ashe's disappearance. Moreover, I'm aware of what you are. Come to the Temple of the Lamb, and we will speak frankly.

The letter was signed simply: *A.D.*

A chill traveled from the letter, up my arm, and toward my heart. *He was aware of what I'd done that night and of what I* was? I thought again of myself at the stone fissures, waiting for something—or someone—to rise. The pieces of shale lay around me like so many broken teeth.

A complicated feeling of disgust and hope washed over me as I creased Day's letter and put it in the pocket of my dress. I wondered if he could really tell me something about what had happened that night.

"Well, what did it say?" Maddy asked.

"Ariston Day wants me to see him in Southwark."

"She's not going into that pit," Maddy said to Alexander, "and if you know what's good for you, you wouldn't go back either." Her tone made me concerned that she might take out the pistol and begin waving it about.

Alexander was not thwarted. "Miss Lee, I wouldn't expect you to understand. And Master Day doesn't expect you to understand. He wishes only to speak with Miss Silverlake. *She* understands."

I looked into Alexander's emotionless eyes and realized he'd been completely taken over by Day. The vessel of his body had been compromised, emptied of its essence and filled instead with Day's will. Like Corydon Ulster, Alexander was no longer the boy he'd once been. He'd become a Fetch.

"I'll see him tomorrow," I said.

Pascal looked horrified. "Jane, you don't know what you're saying."

Maddy made as if to touch my arm, but I pulled away.

"She does," Alexander countered. "Master Day said she would understand, and she does. She understands perfectly." Looking at Pascal, he said, "You aren't at all who I thought you were. Not at all."

"Don't mistake me," I said. "It's not because I understand Ariston Day. But I want to find out what he knows about Nathan's disappearance. Even if he lies, and I'm sure he will, his stories will at least provide direction."

Alexander's grin broadened at this. "Yes, I suppose that's the case."

After the boys departed, moving off in separate directions, Maddy and I made our way to the torchlit field where the traditional tableau of Saint Dunstan's life was taking place. A crowd had amassed, and it appeared the show had already begun.

"Tell me why you're being so foolish," Maddy said. "You can't imagine that traveling into Southwark to see the Devil himself is a wise choice."

"What if Ariston Day is the only person who knows what happened to Nathan?" I said.

She paused at this. "Well, you're not going alone," she said. "Pascal and I will accompany you."

"Absolutely not," I responded. "Day has asked to see me, and I'll go. I don't want to endanger anyone else."

She gave me one of her knowing looks. "Stoke Morrow only boasts one carriage, Jane. Your father will have it with him. Will you ride a horse into London to see Mr. Day? I wasn't aware you had a saddle."

I glared at her. "You're so utterly manipulative, Maddy. Remind me again why I remain friends with you."

"Because you have no other choice," she said, not unkindly.

"If you must come," I said, "you'll stay in the carriage and wait for me."

"Whatever pleases you, Jane," she said. She enjoyed the fact that she was gaining the upper hand, but I knew that being in control would not be to her advantage. She did not know everything that I knew—nor the full reason for my visit.

Light from tapers turned faces in the crowd eerie in the purple dusk. The character of Dunstan was played, as usual, by a priest from Gravesend who cultivated his long mealy beard all year in preparation for the role. Onstage, Dunstan was having a vision of the harrowing of Hell. Demons, both fat and thin, gathered in a circle around the old priest and were in the process of prodding him with various metal instruments that looked like they'd been taken from the local tannery.

"I thought that old priest died last winter," Maddy whispered.

"Possibly he did," I said. "His body looks fairly corrupt."

Dunstan moved downstage, making room for his vision to appear at the center. The demons were a group of hairy blacksmiths from Paddington, and they'd paused their torment long enough to move some pieces of scenery and reveal the craggy mouth of Hell, which looked like a papier-mâché cave draped in black crinoline. I knew the story well enough, having watched it every year since I was a child. After the crucifixion, Christ was said to have descended into Hell to gather the worthy and bring them up with him to their rightful place in Heaven—and during a particularly trying period in his life, Dunstan apparently had a vision of this tremendous event.

The mouth of Hell was surrounded by flame light. And from the mouth came the face of a great dragon with a jaw that swung open on a brass hinge. The dragon howled taunts at Christ, fire pouring from its throat, acrid smoke drifting from its nostrils. But, of course, Christ was not afraid. He raised his hand to the dragon, and screams issued from its leathery insides.

"Who's playing Christ this year?" I whispered to Maddy. "He's new, isn't he?"

"How should I know?" she asked. "Maybe it's the actual Christ, and he'll come down and talk some sense into you."

Then the great dragon's mouth fell open and remained so. In the dragon's throat was a wide hallway on which painted screens showed the ruddy cliffs and precipices of the Hell.

Proserpine, the queen of the underworld, was brought forward, writhing on a catafalque. She was dressed all in white with flowers in her red hair, and she moaned as if in ecstasy. I'd heard that the young woman who played Proserpine was actually quite a prude in life and intended this moment as some sort of statement against bodily pleasures.

"Dear God, I hate that girl," Maddy said.

Proserpine was a pagan goddess—righteous in her beauty, but Christ rebuked her, raising his right hand. The queen bowed her head, embarrassed at her lasciviousness.

Bouquets of black moths fluttered up from beneath the stage. A woman in the audience screamed when some of the moths alighted on her face. Christ took a moment to look at her, breaking character. Or perhaps his concern was the concern of Christ.

I knew what was to happen next. The Devil was supposed to come from the mouth of Hell, not to offer temptation, as he did in the desert, but to mock the son of God for even trying to enter. But Satan did not appear. The mouth remained empty, as if something had gone wrong with the play.

Jesus glanced again at the audience, distracted.

And then an odd wistful music rose from the mouth of Hell— a high-pitched song I thought I recognized. A demon appeared, dressed in a black domino. His face was covered by a mask of black muslin. The demon spoke two words to the audience.

The words were: "She approaches."

At that moment, a shifting shape appeared in the mouth of Hell— a character I'd not seen in previous renditions. Before I had a chance to get a good look at the figure, the new relic of Saint Dunstan was brought forth as promised, carried by two boys wearing cherub wings.

The relic was a harp, without any of its strings, its wooden body rotten. This was Dunstan's harp, which had warned him of the Devil. And seeing it, I knew it was dangerous for me to be in the proximity of such a gifted object. There was suddenly a ringing in my ears and the curtains fell at the edges of my vision.

The stage was no longer a stage.

It had become a surface of fiery brightness.

I wanted to turn to Maddy and ask if she'd witnessed the trans-formation of the stage, but I could not. I was transfixed, for the figure that came forth from the mouth of Hell was draped in sheer red gauze and her body was wrapped in flowered garlands. I could see that the skin beneath the gauze was of a bluish tint, as if she'd drowned. She stood before Christ, a silent glowering goddess.

And then Christ himself bowed before her.

This could not be right, I thought.

Christ would not bow.

The doorway behind them was no longer the mouth of Hell. It was a shimmering gateway, and I could see the white forest beyond and the still stream. Flowers glowed like weird lamps in the under-growth. It was the Empyrean, that cold pure place, and I knew that neither the white forest nor the figure of the goddess were part of the performance. This show was meant only for me.

The goddess was looking directly at me, extending one flower-decked arm and pulling it back slowly, as if moving water. She wanted me to come to her. She wanted me to join her. *She's there, blooming in the darkness, silent and waiting.* I realized this was both the Lady of Flowers and the Red Goddess who felled the stag. They were one in the same. Her face was obscured by red gauze, and I longed to see her more clearly. I wanted to know if she once again wore the face of my mother.

I began to walk toward the edge of the stage as if in a trance. The woman wanted me, and more than anything, I wanted to go to her. As if to entice me, she reached up and began to pull her veil away. I saw the braid in her dark hair exposed and then her gray eye. With a kind of ecstatic horror, I realized it was not Mother beneath the veil. No, on this night the goddess wore my own face. It was me on the stage, standing before the Empyrean, drained of my humanity and filled up with the stonelike power of another world.

I felt Maddy's hand on my arm. "Jane, where are you going?"

I tried to pull away. Maddy was nothing in that moment, a mere insect at my side. Despite my fear, I strove to walk toward the god-dess, but Maddy would not loosen her grip. And then the vision col-lapsed and was gone. Christ was again doing battle with Satan in a kind of choreographed dance.

I felt light-headed and began sinking to my knees as the awful na-ture of the vision came crashing down upon me. How could the god-dess have stolen not only my mother's face but now my own? What meaning could that have?

Maddy took me by the arm and led me to the southern woods, far from the festival grounds, and she held me there. I was shaking, and she tried to keep me warm, but her touch didn't help. Instead, it reminded me of why I'd agreed to go to the Temple of the Lamb despite Pascal's wise warning. It was for none of the reasons I'd stated. The puzzle of what I'd done that night in the forest had become too much. I believed Ariston Day might understand things, not about Nathan, but about me.

"Please tell me what you saw on the stage," Maddy was saying.

Before I could speak, we were interrupted by a sound from the trees behind us and then a voice—"Can I help in some way, mademoiselles? Is something the matter?"

It was Inspector Vidocq, dressed as gilded Helios, and I was not glad to see him. "A passing hysteria caused by memory, Inspector," Maddy called. "Our Nathan used to be such a prince of Dunstan's Day."

"What memory, in particular, concerning Mr. Ashe caused you to break down in such a way, Miss Silverlake?" Vidocq asked with interest.

"No particular memory," I said, weakly. "There are just so many here."

"But there must be one," he said. "A lady does not collapse in the forest from vague recollection, does she?"

I grasped for something and surprised myself by coming out with, "Nathan nearly kissed me here last year."

"What?" Maddy said. "You never told me that, Jane."

I immediately wished I'd made up a lie, but my vision and the pressure from Vidocq forced a truth out of me. "We were watching the reenactment of Dunstan's trials, and Maddy, you had stepped away. Nathan told me he wanted to know what it was like to touch me deeply—to be inside me."

"And why would he want to do that?" Vidocq asked.

"Because Jane is so utterly pure," Maddy said in an acidic tone. "Nathan probably thought touching her would lead to a religious experience."

I looked toward the ground, hoping Vidocq would take such an answer, but he did not seem satisfied. The fact was that Nathan had been drunk. I pushed him away, wiping my mouth and glaring, all the while feeling my anger rise. After he forced his kiss on me, I didn't want to control myself anymore. I wanted to unleash my rage. Once, I'd wished for nothing more than a kiss from Nathan, but when it finally came, I realized his kisses were not kisses at all— they were manifestations of his deranged need, not for me, but for the other world.

CHAPTER 22

When Vidocq departed, I found myself unable to speak to Maddy. I closed my eyes and lay there in the dead leaves, and images of the goddess on the stage vibrated inside my skull. I felt myself drawn back to that final evening when Nathan disappeared. The night when I'd done things I could never take back.

The three of us had convened in the Roman ruin of my father's garden with a plan of eating a light supper of apricots and cold quail in an attempt to recapture a camaraderie that had not returned with Nathan from the war. Nathan, Maddy, and I no longer slipped easily into old feelings, and the ruin seemed like the natural place to try to rekindle what was neither quite romance nor friendship. Our plan quickly dissolved as Nathan registered another complaint about his hand. Once again, he said it felt as if it was no longer his own, and he asked if I could move it for him—like he was some marionette.

"Of course I can't control your hand, Nathan," I said. "How many times do I need to say that?"

"Oh please, let's stop," Maddy said. "Nathan, you won't get any better if you keep fixating on these experiences with Jane."

"It's true," I said. "Our experiments are no longer healthy for you. Perhaps they never were."

Winter leaves, fallen from the surrounding oaks, floated on the surface of the pool, and desiccated vines navigated the statuary like the dried arteries of a riverbed. Nathan paced at the feet of Mercury, examining his right hand in the evening light.

"Let me see your hand, Nathan," Maddy said.

He brought it to her gingerly, as if carrying an over-full cup of tea.

She took his hand in both her own and squeezed his index finger. "Do you feel that?"

"No. Not a bit," he said.

"Perhaps we should have a doctor come," I suggested.

"It's a temporary discomfort, I'm sure," Maddy said. "Mother has bouts like this when she suffers from nervous distraction. Is this the hand you used when you practiced firing your rifle?"

Nathan nodded.

"Then that's the answer, isn't it?" Maddy said. "Overexertion of the nerves. Best not to think about it."

"But it's my *hand*, Madeline," Nathan said. "How am I not to think about it?"

She sighed. "Perhaps we could bind it for you, that way you won't overexert it again. Jane, do you have any scarves we could use for binding Nathan's hand? Nothing too dear. Just a bit of cloth."

"I—" But I had no time to finish. Nathan removed himself from Maddy's care and announced he was going to smoke. As soon as he was out of earshot, Maddy's demeanor changed from one of calm disinterest to something more serious. "I fear he has lost himself," she whispered to me. "We have to be careful here, Jane. He isn't behaving as our Nathan. Our boy didn't come back to us from the war."

"That's why I wanted a doctor."

"We mustn't bring a doctor into this. Father saw doctor after doctor in the last year of his life, and they did nothing. What if a doctor wanted to hospitalize Nathan? He'd be taken from us, perhaps permanently."

I wanted to argue that a doctor's job was to clarify—to interpret—and if Nathan required hospitalization to cure his instability, then so be it. His time on Malta had left him visibly less substantial.

A diet of rations etched his figure, and the sea air and sun peeled back a layer of his essence. He'd become a slate on which Ariston Day could scrawl superstitions. The more time Nathan spent with Day, the more symptoms arose—dim vision and temporary loss of voice. Nathan even had a new acrid smell about him. Maddy called it a scent of bad dreams. "It's as if he's passed through some cloud of aether," she whispered to me, "and he's come back to us with the outer reaches of the universe still clinging to him."

I went to sit by the statue of Athena, hoping for wisdom. The goddess's face was cracked down the middle. Athena, like the other gods, was little more than a restless shell. The stone from which she was made emitted a low long sequence of tones, nothing particularly divine. I drew a quiet breath. "You've read the papers, Maddy. Many soldiers are coming back from Crimea temporarily—damaged," I said. "One doesn't observe the fall of an empire and return clicking one's boot heels. Nathan's experiencing a variety of male hysteria."

"We must stick it out," Maddy said. "The only cure for him is a good dose of everyday life. Act as you always act. Nathan will come around."

"And if he does not *come around*?" I asked.

"We'll have him committed to Bethlehem Royal. How's that? We can wear black when we visit him, as if we are both widows to his madness."

"I'm making my departure now," Nathan said, appearing from behind a column, the butt of a cigarette still pinched between his fingers. He looked haggard. Maddy was right; he wasn't our Nathan anymore. "Day's hosting a provocation tonight in Southwark that I must attend."

"Don't go," Maddy said. "Stay with us."

"The provocation is important," Nathan replied, beginning to make his way down the stone steps. Maddy ran to him and clutched his arm. Perhaps it was because she startled him that Nathan pushed her. Regardless, he gave her such a shove that she fell. Nathan took two more steps before looking back, and he seemed confused as to why Maddy was on the ground.

I put my hand on her shoulders and said, "Are you all right, dear?"

"Fine, Jane. I'm fine."

I glared at Nathan. "Are you really in such a hurry? How could you?"

"How could *I*, Jane?" he said. "I think the question here is really, how could *you*."

"I haven't done anything."

He turned his back on us. "Yes, you're an innocent, aren't you? You've no control over any of this. How long will that be your story, I wonder?"

Maddy and I watched as Nathan walked into the twilight of the southern woods. This was the woods where the three of us had once played out tales of mystery and fantasy among the trees of Lebanon. She stood at my side in the Roman ruin, and I believe we both knew that life as we understood it was coming to an end. We were losing Nathan to Ariston Day. Nothing would be as it once had been. Perhaps that was even for the best. And then, before I quite knew what was happening, Maddy turned to me, cheeks flushed, and said, "Jane, I need to speak to him. I can't just let him go off like that."

"He'll come back tomorrow," I reasoned. "We can talk to him—"

Before I could finish my thought, Maddy was rushing down the steps of the ruin, holding her train so it wouldn't drag in the mud. She disappeared into the windblown shadows of the forest, the contours of her body shaded and then finally lost.

After Nathan and Maddy were gone, I found myself alone. The stones around me in the folly grew silent, as if holding their collective breath. I could hear a horse's hooves on the Hampstead road accompanied by a creak of carriage wheels. Beyond that was the churn of London itself, the distant machine that was overgrowing its boundaries.

Being in the world without my friends frightened me. It made me feel small and unfit.

I made my way down the staircase and onto the lawn. The grass pulled at the hem of my dress as I followed Nathan and Maddy's path into the trees.

I will tell you how I found them—how Paradise fell.

When I came upon them in a forest clearing, Maddy was pressed against a linden tree and Nathan was over her. I'd never noticed how much taller he was than she. His hands were on her dress and laced into her dark and tangled hair. At first I thought he was hurting her again. That makes me sound naive, but I thought he was being cruel, and I was about to step out of the bracken and call to him—to tell him to stop. And then I saw Maddy's chest rising and falling as she took short, quick breaths. He kissed her mouth so gently, and I thought of the way he'd forced himself into my own mouth and how I'd pushed him away. Unlike me, Maddy returned his kisses as he clutched the sleeves of her dress, pulling them down so the fabric began to slip from her shoulders, and the white of her flesh was exposed.

I hid in the tree line at the edge of the clearing and watched. The bark of the linden seemed a living bed where my friends lay together. Gnarled shadows moved over them, caressing them just as Nathan caressed Maddy.

I had never felt so very alone, not in all my life. Watching them, I knew I had nothing to add to their symmetry.

As Nathan tore at the clasps of his own shirt, kissing Maddy's neck, I thought of how foolish I was for pushing him away on Saint Dunstan's Day. I should have let him have me. I no longer cared that he only wanted what was inside of me. It was better than not being wanted at all.

This thought made me furious with myself and with them, and I wished we were surrounded by objects there in the forest. I wanted to raise all those wild and clattering souls. I'd make a wall of souls and sound, and then bring it crashing down on all of us. But we were in nature, and I was powerless. I was the helpless fool they imagined me to be. Quiet Jane who would never have left her rotting house if it hadn't been for their help. They were the ones who knew how to live. This scene in the woods proved it. I continued to watch as Nathan lowered Maddy to the forest floor. I watched longer still, though I will not recount their lurid movements. There were no tears in my eyes. I felt as though I'd become a tree in those woods—my feet had turned to roots, my flesh to bark.

My retreat was silent too even though the forest floor was littered with bramble. Perhaps I floated. Or perhaps the forest agreed to assist me, just that once. It was, after all, the place I'd come from—born from a tree, said my mother. And why shouldn't that be the truth? The forest knew me, and though it did not speak to me, it respected me nonetheless.

I stole away, moving through the woodland groves, and I did not return to my father's house. Maddy would likely go to find me there after she parted with Nathan, and I couldn't bear to see her. Instead I moved deeper into the Heath. I wanted the great gray fallows to swallow me. The silence of nature pressed in upon me as I stumbled toward the Kenwood pond. I would look at Daubenton's bats, which emerged each evening to crawl on the twilit rocks, searching for insects. They were monstrous animals, furred and senseless with black eyes and sharp snouts. The ugly bats were what I needed. I wanted to see them slip in and out of the crevasses. They would make me think of my own heart, how it slipped in and out of normal life, how it at times seemed as foreign and monstrous as those creatures.

But just before I reached the bathing pond, I veered off and found myself at the flat field of shale where my mother's dogs had taken her. It was the place where she'd sickened. I loathed that place, and I feared it too. This was where Mother had seen the other world, the world that had tried to swallow her. I walked along the rocks, looking down into the black fissures that led into the earth. There was no world in them, only darkness.

I lay down among the rocks, willing my body to become entirely still, attempting to forget what I'd seen in the woods.

I remember looking deep into the fissure next to me, studying the darkness. Eventually I pressed my mouth against it, and I prayed for Nathan to be taken—or not just taken but *transformed*. I wanted Maddy to lose him. I wanted him to lose himself. I pictured Nathan falling into those fissures in the shale. He would be swallowed as my mother said I should never be. He would live in the world below—in the still white forest—while Maddy and I lived in the world above. Nathan would have his Empyrean after all.

Did I lose consciousness on those rocks, listening to the echo of my curse? I think I may have, and when I awoke I no longer felt entirely myself. A red woman, the same one I'd later see on St. Dunstan's Day, came to sit with me. Seeing her on the stage had jarred something loose in me, helped me to remember. Her face was veiled. She put flowers on my body, tucking them in my bodice and weaving them in my hair. It was clear she cared for me. She loved me in her way.

I dreamed of Nathan leaving Maddy by the linden tree and going off to the Theater of Provocation for *The Royal Hunt*. He tightened his belt and adjusted his military coat as he walked the narrow path toward the road.

The red woman told me he would suffer, as she twined white flowers in my hair. She made a song of his suffering and sang it. The vibrations of her music filled me. With every step, Nathan slipped deeper and deeper into my unconscious mind, as if dropping through the cracks of the earth.

I slept and dreamed.

And where my mother had once been poisoned, I thrived.

CHAPTER 23

Blackfriars Bridge creaked beneath the weight of the jolting Lee carriage, threatening to plunge us into the rushing waters of the Thames below, and the rapid beat of horses' hooves matched a quickening of my own heart. Maddy, Pascal, and I were traveling over the bridge to Southwark for my meeting with Ariston Day, and looking through the small carriage window, I was reminded of another dark river—the River Styx. Stories were made from those rare instances when a hero successfully crossed that boundary to walk among the dead. To be sure, I didn't feel like a hero. Seeing the Red Goddess wearing my face on St. Dunstan's Day had affected me greatly. Everything I'd been trying to forget was surfacing again, and I was filled with guilt and regret. I knew that what I'd conjured from the field of shale may have destroyed lives, and I felt myself to be as low and jealous a creature as was ever made. When I looked into the faces of my friends, I became all the more determined to put right the wrongs I'd done. But in order to do so, I still needed to understand my own nature. If that meant meeting with a devil, then so be it. Even a devil as odious as Ariston Day.

I was glad when Maddy took my gloved hand and held it there in the carriage. Everything had been so confusing between the two of us as of late. I wanted nothing more than to feel close to her again. She and I shared a bench, our skirts intermingled, and Pascal sat across from us, holding a cane with a heavy brass handle he'd brought for protection. Maddy produced the pistol from the pocket in her skirt. She'd been carrying it since St. Dunstan's Day. "You'll take it with you, Jane," she said.

Pascal's eyes widened, and he leaned forward. "Where on earth did you get that?"

"None of your business," she said.

"He knows we've been in Nathan's room," I told her. "And I'm not carrying a pistol into the Temple of the Lamb."

"Give me one good reason why not," she said. "It isn't safe in Southwark, especially not for a woman. You really should have told Ariston Day to come to Hampstead—any sort of educated man would have offered that in the first place."

"He'd never come to Hampstead," Pascal replied, darkly. "And he doesn't have the sort of education any of us can imagine."

Maddy went on about the impoliteness of Ariston Day, and it was calming to be mothered by her. But when she started squeezing my hand too aggressively, I tried to distract myself by looking once again out the window. The view of the Southwark slums from Blackfriars was one of crooked houses inked on a vellum sky. Dwarf stone walls circled cinder gardens. An exhaustive tangle of streets, for which no map had ever been drawn, sprawled in all directions. The Roman soldiers had used the area to bury their dead, and in our time, it housed many of the city's stink industries (glue factories, vinegar makers, tanneries, and the like). A brown haze drifted across over the cupolas and towers, nearly obscuring the skeletal dome of the pleasure garden called the Temple of the Lamb, beneath which we would find Ariston Day's Theater of Provocation.

The Temple itself was not the Gothic behemoth I'd imagined but rather had the tarnished brassy look of those buildings built under William IV, complete with a once gleaming dome that had become a gaudy house for ravens. The streets of Southwark did not teem with activity as in central London; instead, denizens lurked about and tried to make themselves invisible to our procession.

As I stepped from the carriage, I felt the filthy air prickling my skin—so different from the air in Hampstead Town.

"How will you signal if you need our help, Jane?" Maddy asked from the open carriage window. Lines appeared on her brow, and I half expected her to dangle the pistol out the window and offer it to me once more.

"If I haven't returned in half an hour," I replied, "send Pascal after me. Certainly, he knows his way."

"And if, by then, it's too late?" she said.

I touched her arm. "You mustn't worry, Maddy. These are things which we cannot affect."

She leaned down and kissed me gently on the corner of my mouth. It felt to me like a final act, a bidding of farewell, and I worried I might never see her again.

"Be cautious, mademoiselle," Pascal said from beside her. "One can quickly become confused in his presence." He paused. "And if, by chance, you see Alexander, tell him he can call on me. Tell him I will speak to him again."

I agreed to do just that, at the same time remembering the emptiness I saw in Alexander's face. Could a Fetch even know what it meant to be in love?

As I turned from the carriage, I attempted to conjure Nathan's face. Already I was forgetting details, knowing my image of him no longer precisely matched the man himself. If I never saw him again, I would lose more and more of that face until there was nothing of him at all in what I imagined. I set my resolve against such an outcome. I would correct what I'd done on the field of shale.

As these thoughts fulminated, two young men dressed in shabby Fetch red—the very uniform that Nathan had worn—appeared at the threshold to the Temple. These were Day's foot soldiers. Both of them bowed deeply and did not stand until I spoke.

"I'm here to see Ariston Day," I said.

"Certainly, missus," said the shorter boy. "We know very well why you're here. We'll take you to him. Follow us."

I was escorted down a stone hall, away from the raucous tavern of the Temple, which I glimpsed only briefly. The tavern was garishly decorated with what appeared to be artifacts of amusement. Guarding the doorway was a metal tiger with gas flame eyes that belonged in a house of horrors.

I remembered that Inspector Vidocq said he could not find the Theater of Provocation, and I wondered how we would enter it. I followed the Fetches down a winding stone staircase that led into the earth. Torches lined the stony walls, and the three of us walked in silence, giving me time to imagine various scenes beneath the broken pleasure dome. Chambers flickered and transmuted in my imagination. I pictured everything from a debauched hold of opium eaters to a secret golden theater illuminated by candlelight.

At the bottom of the stairs was a velvet curtain.

"The theater is behind the curtain?" I asked.

"Sometimes it is," said the shorter Fetch, "and sometimes it isn't."

After following my guides behind the curtain, we paused in complete darkness while the taller Fetch lit a torch. A blaze of firelight showed me a scene that I recognized. The three of us were standing inside the vision I'd first encountered when I touched Nathan's button. This was the painted forest where the Red Goddess drank blood from the stag.

"What's the matter, missus?" asked the shorter Fetch. "Haven't you ever seen an underground forest before?"

"I have," I said, more to myself than to him. "That's the problem."

The false trees still smelled of paint, and the trunks were tightly grouped in the darkness along a gravel path. It was a forest drawn by an unschooled hand; the imperfect circle of a phosphorescent moon hung above. The forest looked even more artificial than it had in my vision. This was not a proper theater, but a childish world, the environment in which *The Royal Hunt* had played out.

Branches extended upward into battens of thunderheads made from some diaphanous fabric. The vaulted ceiling, visible through the clouds, was decorated with bits of mirror glass and polished shells, which picked up the light of our torch and flickered like strange stars. There were animals too—taxidermy pheasants and foxes peering from the underbrush with melancholy glass eyes, patches of fur worn away. Wind in the reeds, perhaps from a hidden phonograph machine, could be heard. Unlike an actual forest, this place offered no sense of tranquility—only a constant reminder of the unnatural dark—the rumble of man-made objects.

"This is what we call the inner forest," the taller boy said. He was the cleaner of the two Fetches as well, though covered in freckles and moles. I wondered if he might be the Fetch who'd sliced through Corydon Ulster's cheek while Judith looked on. "Do you like it, missus?"

"I can't say I do. Where is Ariston Day?" I demanded.

"We'll be there soon," the shorter one said. "Please don't grow angry, missus. We know you won't take us to the Paradise if you're angry."

"What is this Paradise you're talking about?" I asked.

"Watch your tongue now," the taller Fetch said to the shorter. "Mr. Day wouldn't want you talking to her like that. We're not to say anything about the Paradise."

"We never get to talk to anybody," said the shorter.

"Then speak," I said. "Tell me."

"We know you've got some *abilities*," the shorter said, "the kind Mr. Day has been looking for. We know you could make these trees talk to us if you touched us. You might even be able to make this into a *real* forest if you wanted to—a forest in the promised place."

"I can do nothing of the sort," I said. "You've been misinformed."

They laughed quietly, stone rubbing against stone.

"We're almost there," said the taller. "Mr. Day is waiting by the water's edge in the grove."

I wondered how large this inner forest could be. What were the dimensions of the subterranean chamber, and was it possible that there was really some underground lake here? I worried that this might actually be a theater of my imagination, shifting and changeable, one scene replacing the next in liquid fantasy.

"Tell me why you call yourself Fetches," I said.

"It's an old story," said the shorter. "We don't know its source—probably from Rome. Mr. Day likes all that bygone lore."

"You shouldn't tell her our story," said the taller Fetch. "It's meant only for us. A woman can't understand it."

"The missus will understand," said the shorter. "Mr. Day says she will. And anyway, she isn't so much like a woman, is she? Just look at her." He cleared his throat. "The story goes that every one of us humans has a double down in the pits of Hell. So Hell is full of people who look just like those you see on the streets of London. The rich bankers have doublers, and the poor flower ladies have doublers. Little boys and little girls have doublers that grow old down in Hell just as those little boys and girls grow old here in London. And these doublers, they're called Fetches because when it's your time—when your final hour has struck—your doubler comes up from Hell to *fetch* you. The last thing that you see is yourself standing in the doorway of your sickroom or crouching above you where you've fallen in the street."

"That's wretched," I said.

"We claim to be our own doublers," continued the shorter Fetch. "We're no longer the people that live above, you see?"

"Yes," I said. "Children of Hell. That's quite clear."

CHAPTER 24

When we emerged from the false trees, I found not a lake but a shallow limpid pool surrounded by clusters of stones. The clouds above were made from the same battens of dark fabric, hanging low in the sky over the pool. And there, by the silvery water, was a man seated in a cane chair. Ariston Day was not precisely what I'd expected—not degenerate. His face was clean-shaven, and he wore a gentleman's damask tie the color of coral with a silver tack. His arms and legs were lank, and his dark hair hung about his long face like an open curtain. I could see no part of the Irish peasant in him, nor did he appear to be the deranged messiah of a cult. He looked rather like some vestige of the previous century—a feudal lord ensconced in his stronghold. The bones of his cheeks were aristocratic and angular, and the more I studied his face, the more it seemed that it might be a mask made from a substance other than flesh. I wondered if it was possible that Day himself might be a piece of theater—a painted facade.

Day was caught up in a reverie, staring toward the bottom of the silvery pool, as tendrilous shadows cast from a lamp behind the trees caressed him. When the taller boy announced our arrival, Ariston Day glanced at us with a certain ease, and he made what was meant to be a brief, casual smile, but movement caused the mask to momentarily crack, and his mouth took on a look of malignancy. The way his lips shifted over his teeth made me feel as though I should run back into the forest.

"Jane Silverlake," he said, standing and offering his hand. "My humble welcome. I'm glad you finally decided to join me."

I'd removed my gloves and did not offer my own hand in return, knowing the transference would occur and not wanting this creature to experience any part of it. "I'm not sure I had a choice," I said. "You were persistent."

"There are always choices," Day said, dismissing his Fetches with a flutter of his hand. "So many choices, really. That's part of the problem, isn't it? Won't you join me?" He indicated the chair next to his. I did so, glancing out across the odd pool. Its water reflected the lantern light that filled the subterranean chamber. There was a stale scent here, the smell of a place that had no traffic with the outside world. Day lifted a worn leather portfolio that had been leaning against the side of his chair and carefully placed it in his lap. I wondered if he meant to show me something. "I'm sure you'd like to delve into business right away," he said. "I've heard you're a matter-of-fact sort."

"The play you were putting on here," I said. "May I ask you to explain it?"

He ran his too-dark tongue over his teeth. I did my best to pull my gaze from his mouth and look into his eyes. "I know it appears irregular," he said, "but honestly it made for an enlightening evening, an evening that would have been entirely positive had not poor Nathan gone missing."

"What was the play meant to be?" I asked, knowing the answer well enough but wanting to hear his explanation. I studied the trees, the animals, and the moon as he spoke. They seemed to quake in my presence.

"*The Royal Hunt*," he said. "My boys worked on the trees for weeks, and they tell me it's difficult to get the color of the bark just right. Do these look right to you?"

I didn't answer, as the color of his trees was the last thing on my mind.

"All of England was once covered by such trees," he said. "Clearings were sacred because they were rare. And the hunt, well, there has always been a hunt—a gathering of men who track a beast—be it mythical like the unicorn or somewhat more common, like a fox, or, in our case, a stag."

In my mind's eye, I saw the stag from my vision racing through the forest, pursued by the Red Goddess. She appeared to float through the trees, darting this way and that, finally catching the animal by its throat.

"The hunt was a hallowed act, the stag a sort of divinity," Day said. "To kill the stag was to enact a scene from the greatest of all human myths—the death of a god. And as we know, the god must die to bring about a new era on earth."

Paul Rafferty said Nathan had played the stag, and I tried to imagine my old friend in a pair of stag's horns and a pelt. I wondered what enlightenment Nathan thought he might derive from such an act. "And who killed the stag that night?" I asked.

Day chuckled. "Killed the stag? Why, no one killed the stag, my dear Jane. The hunt was theater. We only play at death." He paused. "Perhaps we should talk about the reason I've brought you here."

"The note you sent with Alexander Hartford indicates you think I've done something." I paused here, anxious but still composed enough to bait him. "It seems more likely that it's *you* who've done something. I've read of your previous misadventures."

He leaned forward, causing his chair to creak. He was no longer a feudal lord; he was an animal, leering at me. This attentive, clever creature was the Ariston Day I feared. "You are aware of the qualities that make you of interest, dear Jane. And you are aware of what you've done. Don't play at naïveté. You showed your colors to Corydon Ulster. Why not show them to me as well? Mr. Ulster approached you at my behest, after all. Fetches rarely act of their own accord."

"You sent him to harm me?" I asked.

"To *test* you. I wanted to verify the claims made by Nathan Ashe."

"I assure you that Corydon Ulster wanted to do more than test me, Mr. Day," I said, grimly.

Day leaned back in his chair and relaxed, as if we were taking part in an utterly cordial conversation. "Be honest with me, Jane. You know where Nathan Ashe has gone. In fact, it was *you* who put him there."

I felt a sudden pressure in the air, as if the entire Temple of the Lamb above us might come crashing down. How much information could Day possibly have? "I don't know what you mean," I said finally. I was not going to fall into his trap.

"You put Nathan Ashe in the Empyrean, Jane Silverlake."

Hearing the name of that secret place on his lips made my heart skip. "I did no such thing," I said, yet even as I spoke, I pictured myself pressing my mouth against the fissure in the field of shale and pleading for help.

"You banished Nathan because your emotions got the best of you," Day said.

I was quiet, having never imagined Ariston Day would bring me into his awful cave to talk about my heart.

"But it doesn't matter," he said. "Nathan's disappearance was only the beginning. Soon we'll all be reunited."

"What do you mean?"

"Occult philosophers have long conjectured that the entire natural world is but an expression of the spiritual," Day said. "But you, Miss Silverlake, you alone sense souls in the unnatural objects produced in our terrible factories. You alone see souls in industry. And you believe there is something perverse in this. Don't you? That's why you wear flowers—to prove you are still a woman. To prove you are not an *unnatural*." He gestured to the feverfew tied at my wrist. "But with your relationship to objects, Miss Silverlake, you can help us transcend this pitiful existence. Help us reach what Nathan called the Empyrean—and what I know is the final Paradise. It has been sealed off since creation's dawn. We need to break that seal, expose civilization to its cure."

"You're talking nonsense," I said.

"Am I? I think rather this is why you've come here, Jane. Because

I can help you understand. You've heard of the new science—called archaeology?"

"I've read of it."

"Then you may know one of its primary tenets—the concept of 'stratification.' A geologic time scale has been posited by our own English archaeologists working in Egypt and Greece as a way of comprehending the progression of the ages. The earth is made up of layers, and to dig into those layers is to move backward through time. Stratum lay one on top of the next, and the deeper we dig the further back we go."

"Did you bring me here for a lesson in the applied sciences?" I asked.

"Humor me a bit longer, Jane. Imagine a form of *spiritual* archaeology. If instead of digging into earth's layers, we could dig into the invisible layers of pneuma, digging all the way to the *bedrock*."

The bedrock was where Nathan wanted to live. To live upon the rock, away from the shifting soil.

Day looked at me with a kind of threatening adoration. "Until Nathan described your abilities, I believed spiritual archaeology would be impossible to achieve. I merely fiddled about with the manipulation of dreams through ancient versions of theater."

"Mr. Day, I don't know what Nathan told you, but I'm not what you think. I am especially not a tool for so-called 'spiritual archaeology.'"

"I didn't believe him either and then Nathan showed me something that was very dear to him. Something that he'd brought back from Malta."

At first, I thought Day might be talking about the ape's finger, but then he lifted the leather portfolio from his lap. When he opened it and took out an unbound sheaf of yellowed pages written in Italian, I knew almost immediately what I was looking at.

"*You* have the writings of Theodore de Baras?" I asked.

"So you know of these papers already?" Day said.

"I've read Nathan's journal," I replied, realizing the appearance of the papers had caused me to drop my defenses. I was telling Day too much, and this was precisely the reaction he wanted.

"I intercepted these pages, Jane," he said, carefully. "I'm sorry I didn't let Nathan show them to you, but I had to be sure all the pieces fit before I decided how to proceed."

"And what do they say?" I asked.

Day leaned close once again, speaking in a direct and matter-of-fact tone. "They explain your very existence, my dear. The so-called Lady of Flowers was only *one* incarnation of the unnamed goddess who controls the gates of the Empyrean. There is a line of such incarnations running down through the ages, right up to the modern day. All of these women have the power to fling open the doors if they so choose. All of them can bring about the new Paradise."

I found I could not breathe, thinking of the red vision I'd seen time and again.

"What the papers reveal," Day continued, "what excited your beloved Nathan Ashe, is that you, Jane, are the incarnation of the goddess in our current era. You can return all of us to a primitive dream, curing every ill of modern society. Rome is a disease. London is a disease. You are the cure. You can unmake what should never have been made to begin with."

His words caused an unexpected reaction in me. Beneath my anxiety, I felt a certain power begin to rise. It coursed through my limbs, and I felt as though I'd been waiting all my life to hear this. In just a few words, Day's story explained my near lifetime of suffering and isolation.

I pulled myself back, knowing I couldn't allow myself to fall under his spell. His business was to proselytize, and I did not want to become part of his religion. By himself Day was dangerous. With me at his side, he might be lethal.

"I don't think I should be here, Mr. Day. I need to collect my thoughts."

"I wouldn't leave, Jane. Not just yet."

"And why not?"

"Because I can help you reunite with Nathan," he said. "If you will, in turn, help me."

I felt my anger boil at this. "I'm not here to barter," I said. "If you think you know how to bring back Nathan, then tell me, or—" I raised my hand as if I meant to touch him.

Day extended his own hand in response. "I'd love to be hurt by you, dear Jane. To experience your power as Corydon Ulster did—even to go mad from it. It would be to know supreme bliss, to connect to something I once thought unknowable."

I lowered my hand, looking toward the pool. "If you understand what I've done to Nathan," I said quietly, "tell me how to mend it."

"You sound guilt-ridden," Day said. "A goddess feels no guilt. She merely *acts*, and her actions are a pronouncement."

"I won't get caught up in your fantasy," I said. "Just give me the information I've come here for."

"What I know is the same as what you know, Jane. You put Nathan in the Empyrean, but *how* you did it is not easily summarized. To understand that, we must first understand your very existence. Theodore de Baras says those of your kind are the intercessors. You are the gate and the bridge, as delicate a fabrication as has ever walked upon earth."

His mouth was so vile, but his words were necessary.

"In de Baras's papers," Day continued, "he writes of meeting a girl very much like you in Rome. She was a child of the streets—simple and without guile—yet she had a gift. As he describes it, she could make the ancient statues sing, and she caused bright lights to rise up from the cobblestones, like sunlight dancing on the ocean's waves. When de Baras found her, the girl was attempting to use her talents as part of a street performance in the plaza before the Pantheon, but her abilities only frightened the crowd. They wanted the simple amusements of jugglers and snake charmers. Only de Baras recognized her for what she was, having already come into contact with the cult of the Lady on his island home. He took her back with him to Malta and kept her at the ruin of Crendi, imprisoned there in a temple, unbeknownst to the Brotherhood of Saint John. The monk fed her and clothed her in exchange for access to her talents. He made experiments with her, much as Nathan once made experiments with you, only de Baras took his experiments further. When the girl began to refuse him, he took her clothes, kept her chained to the stone altar in the temple. He found that cutting her flesh was a way of opening the fabled doorway."

"Stop," I said. "I don't want to hear this."

"But you must, Jane. You *must* hear it so you understand something more of yourself and the dangers you may face. There were other ways to open the door as well. All of the methods involved fear. De Baras hints that, eventually, he was actually able to walk into the Paradise and come back again. But after that, he became increasingly paranoid, believing that some creature had followed him out of the white forests of the Empyrean and returned to the temple with him. De Baras believed the monster meant him harm because of what he'd done to the girl."

I thought of the white ape Nathan had seen in the ruin. Was it possible that this was the same guardian that de Baras had drawn out of the Empyrean? Before I could think further about this, I heard something moving above us. I looked up to see a flash of red between the illusion of thunderheads. There were Fetches crawling in the clouds on some sort of wooden latticework. "What's going on?" I asked Day.

"They only want to look at you," he said. "And who can blame them? You are to be our savior, after all. You are the great scourge. Queen of all queens. The goddess reborn."

I stood, smoothing my skirts. "I'll take my leave."

But he would not be silenced. "The world has not been good to you, Jane," he said. "It offers you nothing. Your true home is waiting—Nathan Ashe is waiting. You pulled him away. You *moved* his body because you wanted to wrestle him from Madeline Lee. And on the evening of *The Royal Hunt*, in a moment of terrible agitation, Nathan Ashe let himself go. He surrendered to you, allowed you to pull him from this world and into the next."

I'd been so full of grief while lying prostrate in the field of black shale on the Heath that I'd been capable of anything. I'd awoken hours later when the sky was black and starless, thinking madly: *What have I done? What have I done?* Not remembering any of it clearly. "Even if that were true—" I said.

"I want to restage *The Royal Hunt*, Jane, but this time, you will be the sacred beast. I want to provoke you. I believe I've discovered a means of opening the doorway and keeping it open permanently. I'll help you fulfill your destiny and reunite with Nathan. I believe that the Empyrean will transform earth, make it finally pure."

I stared down at Day in his cane chair. Flame light moved in his oil-dark eyes. "I'm sorry, Mr. Day," I said. "I don't think we can help each other."

On legs of glass, I made my way through the dark of the trees toward the faint glow of the staircase, listening, all the while, to the Fetches crawl through the clouds above me.

"This is bigger than you," Day called after me. "Look at what a filth-ridden hole our city has become. Think how overgrown it will be in one hundred years or even two hundred. So much pain and suffering. You owe this to humanity, Jane. You owe it to us all."

CHAPTER 25

On my hurried return to the carriage, which hovered in the greasy sunlight of Southwark like some black and untenable island, I barely took notice of the dim figures in the streets. I'd spent my life not believing in the savior Christ or the Christian God. As Stoke Morrow was empty of my mother's presence, the world to me felt empty of an all-knowing, all-seeing deity. The idea that I was an incarnation of some primitive goddess whose very name was lost to time went against rational thought.

In the muddied street, my arm was brushed by something soft, and I imagined it was Ariston Day or the ghost of Theodore de Baras softly caressing me, trying to steal my power. But it was neither Day nor de Baras. Rather it was something like a child, standing at my feet. I say "like" because the urchin was of an indiscernible age and sex, shrunken as my mother had been when her blood slowed. The small creature moved with the some deliberateness, lifting a bouquet of wilted daisies toward me.

"I have no money," I said, passing by the urchin, though the silence of the daisies appealed to me in all that moaning ghetto.

"Not for sale," the urchin said, peering up at me with soot-dark eyes. "I am told to give them to you, mum."

"And who gave you such instruction?"

"Mother," said the child. "Mother says you are beautiful and deserve them."

"Well, I am nothing more than plain," I said.

"Mother says you must come to our church in Spitalfields, called the Hall of the Red Star."

I paused at this. Miss Herron-Cross had also mentioned a church in Spitalfields, one that my own mother had shown interest in. "The Red Star?" I asked. "And what do they worship there?"

Tears welled in the child's eyes, glistening in the grime on its cheeks. "Please take the flowers, mum." The child got to its knees, holding out the bouquet.

I took them, looking at the nearly rotted heads of the daisies.

"And please be kind to my family," the child said. "Deliver us from the terrors that are to come."

"Terrors? What terrors?" When I realized the child wasn't going to respond and was instead mumbling more prayers to me, I moved away as quickly as I could.

I opened the door to the Lee carriage, saying we should make haste before we were all left penniless and bruised. But when I looked into the dim cab, I saw only Pascal on the velvet seat. He seemed unsure, more of an innocent boy than usual.

"Where's Maddy?" I asked.

His voice was thick with emotion. "She wouldn't listen to reason, Jane. I had to remain with the cab, so the driver didn't abandon us in this place. She went looking for you. The process was taking too long."

"Too long?" I said. "I wasn't gone half the hour, Pascal."

"As I told her. But she was concerned. She said you're naive in ways she is not."

"Follow me, Pascal," I said, tossing the daisies onto the empty bench seat across from him. "We have to find her."

"But what of the carriage, mademoiselle?"

"It will remain. I have no worry of that." I said this loudly enough so the driver would hear. "What worries me more is going back into the Temple with no one at my side."

We hurried along, and I kept my eye open for the urchin with the flowers who wanted to worship me.

"I've never been in the tavern above the theater," Pascal said, walking double-step to remain at my side. "Ariston Day says the Fetches mustn't go there because it's full of heathens who don't understand the ways of truth."

"Today is your inauguration into falsehood and lies then," I said. "I doubt that Maddy would have been able to find her way to the theater without an escort." I said this *hoping* she had not. I didn't want to picture her lost in the inner forest with Fetches crawling above her through the hideous sky.

The Temple of the Lamb above the Theater of Provocation contained a kind of alehouse cum pleasure garden that had been oddly decorated with the remains of the beastly amusements for which Southwark was once famous. Various wax figures slouched in the dim high-ceilinged room. Nothing as marvelous as those in Madame Tussauds, these were in varying states of decay. The wax had deteriorated, so that the figure of Queen Elizabeth looked like a ghoul with a stiffened ruff about its neck, and Saint Augustine had lost so many inches off his original height that his robe pooled at his feet. Rather than causing the tavern to look like a carnival, these figures made it seem the death of joy—a graveyard for oddities. They hovered inside this sphere of death, bent and malformed, unable to straighten their bodies and stand.

I didn't see Maddy in the alehouse, which caused my heart to race. Either she had wandered down the stairs toward the inner forest or she was concealed in some back room. Both options were equally undesirable.

I had no real way of communicating with the fellows in the

Temple. To me, they were throwbacks to a lost era, dressed in ill-fitting suits and wearing hazy beards about their jowls. And yet I persevered, moving through what felt like layers of the real—successively digging deeper into the unreal, toward the long, stained plank of wood that served as a bar. Just as I was beginning to ask the barkeep if he'd seen a woman of my own character in this place, I was grabbed by the wrist, quite roughly, and turned to see an old man with some palsy in half his face. His blue eye looked toward his mouth, and his lower lip on the right side drooped nearly to his chin. He held me tightly, indicating that I should move along with him. When I tried to wrest my arm away, he only fastened his grip.

"Let her go, monsieur," Pascal said, attempting to push his small frame between the man and myself.

The creature shoved him, and Pascal fell backward into the arms of a thick barmaid, who clutched him around his rather frail chest. She nearly choked with laughter as he struggled against her.

Patrons watched as the man dragged me toward the back of the Temple. We passed wax replicas of Victoria and Albert that were nearly translucent, as if their royal souls had come to ruin in this place. I realized even screaming would do no good. Everyone could see plainly what was happening; the twisted-faced man was pulling me toward a curtained doorway. Behind me, another man helped the barmaid subdue Pascal.

A thought rang inside me like a call to war—I could not pass behind the muslin curtain. I would not let the old man have me. I projected horrors onto the curtain, and felt pressure build inside my chest, as if water was pushing at some dam, surging and ready to be free. I could see shadows shifting on the curtain, coalescing to the point where they became the pale forest and the milk-white stream. And just as in Mother Damnable's house, I could feel there was a membrane that separated me from that forest. Fighting against the man, I wished with all my heart I could tear through the membrane and escape the tavern.

Then the rumbling came, faint at first. I could feel it in my chest and soon realized the whole of the Temple was beginning to vibrate.

Liquor bottles fell from shelves. Tables began to migrate across the warped wooden floor. I was connected to the entire room, and I was moving it. Controlling the objects. I sensed that I could cause the entire Temple to burst apart if I wanted to, and I knew what lay beneath the facade of common reality: the cool of the white forest, and it was waiting for me.

The fool who held me became terrified by the shaking Temple and released me. I wanted to bring the whole place down on his head, but I restrained myself. Instead, I walked back and collected Pascal from the startled barmaid and we made our way together through the tavern, down the stairs toward the Theater of Provocation. As we rushed, Pascal called out that we could not enter without an invitation.

"I just *had* an invitation," I said.

"That isn't how it works, Jane. Without a new invitation, things could be any which way."

"What does that mean?"

"It's unstable," he said. "The theater is unstable. And just what happened up there? What did you do in the Temple?"

I didn't know what to say to him. I still felt the rush of my own power. "I made the Temple obey," I answered. "I made all of it obey."

I tore back the curtain at the bottom of the stone staircase, and even before my eyes adjusted to the darkness, I could see that something was wrong. The inner forest was gone. There were no trees, no battens of clouds, no animals lurking. Pascal and I stood in the cold empty chamber of the catacomb, surrounded only by pillars and dust.

"This can't be," I said. "They can't have packed the whole thing up so quickly."

"They did," Pascal said. "I told you that. The Theater of Provocation does not behave as other places do. At any rate, Maddy isn't here."

"No," I said, peering into the empty darkness. "No one is."

*   *   *

As we left the Temple, a terrible sick feeling overtook me. First I'd lost Nathan. And now I'd lost Maddy. There were no visible police in the vicinity, and neither Pascal nor I knew the area well enough that we could find a station, even if there were such a thing in Southwark. We didn't dare stay in the streets, as the malingerers appeared to have caught on that we were in distress. Instead, we climbed into the black coach.

"It's possible she's making her way back to La Dometa," Pascal said.

"Why would she have returned alone without the carriage?" I asked. He had no logical response, which disappointed me, as I was so desperately looking for one. "We need to find Alexander," I said.

"Oh, Jane, no. Not that."

"He's the only one we know who's still in Ariston Day's fold. He might give us some hint as to what's happened. You know where he is, don't you, Pascal?"

"I suppose I can guess."

"Then take us there."

CHAPTER 26

———◦•◦••◦•◦———

Alexander Hartford was working with the London Society of Medieval Studies on an expedition of archaeology. He'd procured the job as a means of legitimizing his stay in London to his father, the shipping magnate, and I assumed in some way it must also support his work with the Theater. Otherwise Day wouldn't have allowed one of his Fetches to wander off into the real world.

According to Pascal, the Society of Medieval Studies had taken up excavation alongside the Society for Antiquities in a subcrypt of St. Michael's Cathedral after a custodian had accidentally broken through a thin layer of decorative flooring in the burial chamber of Saint Dogmaels, discovering a forgotten stairway leading into the earth. Our carriage arrived at St. Michael's, and its towering edifice put me immediately on edge. Churches, like Bibles, did not agree with me.

Pascal and I were greeted by a dark-haired clerk in a pair of wire-frame eyeglasses. He was fresh-faced, no more than twenty-five, and believed we'd been sent by the London Garden Society. Apparently the Garden Society intended to write an article on the excavation of the subcrypt for their monthly circular. We did not correct the clerk's misassumption, and he politely held the lantern for us as we descended, telling me to watch the hem of my dress. "The black dust is apt to creep up and make all kinds of mess," he said. "To be honest, I'm not sure why you gardeners want to know about the crypt. Nothing living down here—just a bit of mold."

"We have a wide variety of interests that go beyond gardening," I said, attempting to sound official.

In the burial chamber, members of the society worked carefully in shadowed alcoves, dusting stone vessels and recording details on tablets. The clerk informed us that the vessels contained burnt human bones that likely dated back to the Saxon era. "Houses of worship have been built on this site since the eighth century," he said. "There's even some conjecture about another burial chamber beneath this one. My opinion is that someday we'll discover our whole city is just a series of graveyards, one stacked upon the next."

Pascal slipped his hand around my arm and squeezed. "I don't know about this Jane. I'm feeling claustrophobic."

"That's actually heartsickness you feel," I whispered. "I'm quite familiar with it myself."

We found Alexander at the far end of the crypt, covered in black dust and rather powerful-looking in his shirtsleeves and thick trousers. He was labeling pieces of a broken stone cross, and he nodded silently to Pascal, who made a sharp intake of breath, nearly like a squeak. Alexander squinted at me as I told him a few details of what had happened with Ariston Day and asked if he knew where Madeline might be.

"You denied Master Day?" he asked.

"What did you expect?" I said. "That I'd swoon and fall into his arms as all you gentlemen seem to do?"

"You shouldn't have denied him, Jane. He'll have you regardless of your wishes."

"Stop that, Alexander," Pascal said abruptly. "Stop acting like you're one of them."

Alexander looked at his old friend in the dim crypt, still holding a piece of the stone cross in his hand. "If not one of *them*, Pascal, what am I?"

"You're one of us," Pascal said. "One of the good ones."

"*You're* good? A confirmed invert is good?"

"Don't talk to him like that," I said.

"How did I ever care for you?" Pascal asked. "Who did I think you were when we were together in France?"

Alexander scoffed. "Some delirious thing you built up in your head when you were a boy. Some fantasy."

"I'm sorry for my delusions," Pascal replied. "I'll never let that happen again."

"Madeline's safe," Alexander said, turning to me. "She's gone away of her own volition."

"So you know where she is then. Tell us," I said.

"She'll come back when she's prepared to come back. I won't say more. Talking to you is now forbidden."

"What do you mean, *forbidden*?"

"I told you Day will have you despite your wishes," Alexander said. "It's all part of his plan. I don't know the specifics, so don't bother asking."

"He can't just toy with me," I said. I considered grabbing Alexander and forcing my talent so deep inside him that it caused him to have a seizure like Corydon Ulster, but other than giving me the satisfaction of punishing him, what good would it do? Pascal would be horrified by my violence, and it was entirely possible Alexander didn't have the information we needed. I could never be sure how much information the Fetches were privy to.

"Neither of you have any idea how deep this situation goes," he said, and for a moment, Alexander appeared to be his old self, not some Fetch. "Come with me, and I'll show you what we've found down here and then you have to leave."

"Alexander, look at me," I said, firmly.

He put the section of the stone cross in a basin and gave me his full attention.

"I want you to know that if Madeline doesn't come back to me safely, I will harm you," I said. "And then I'll harm Ariston Day and all of his Fetches. I'll show you things to make you wish you had no eyes. This crypt, for instance, is not a crypt. It's a living, breathing organism, and it can cause you great pain if I instruct it to do so. Are you aware that I'm capable of this?"

He gave a single nod.

"Then you will transmit that information to your master as soon as we leave, and as for his *plan*, it won't work. I will not be controlled. Now take me to whatever bit of rubble you want to show us."

Pascal looked at me in awe as we followed Alexander deeper into the catacomb. We entered a circular room with a tall object draped in broadcloth at its center. Alexander pulled the cloth away, and standing before us was the same type of statue Nathan had described in his journal, the woman in Mother's painting—the Lady of Flowers. Her head was lowered, as if in prayer, over a stalk of stone lilies held in the crook of her arm. Her face was like a mask, nearly featureless with only the slightest indentation to indicate eyes and mouth.

"Who is this?" asked Pascal.

"We don't know," Alexander replied. "Nor do we know why it's in a Christian burial chamber, but it reminded me of the stories Nathan told us about the island of Malta. It's some goddess, but we can't ascribe her to any known religion. And watch this—" He pushed his hands against the stomach of the Lady, revealing a movable panel there. The panel slid away and the inside of the statue was hollow. I stared into her darkness.

"It's empty?" Pascal asked.

"So it would appear," Alexander replied.

"Not empty," I whispered. "Full of silence." This idol was the antidote to the storybook fables of the religions of Man, the goddess of nothingness. She had no story and did not speak. She was a never-ending hush, and I felt that silence spooling out within myself as well. But I would not believe that unmaking the world was my destiny. Ariston Day was wrong.

*   *   *

I nearly put my arm around Pascal to comfort him as we crossed broad and crowded Holborn Street outside St. Michael's. He shrank inside himself against the noise of passing carriages and omnibuses, perhaps agitated because of the occurrences in the crypt. Certainly the transference caused by my touch wouldn't help him feel better, so I merely remained close at his side as we made our way through London's mud, returning to the Lee carriage.

"Do you think Alexander was telling the truth about Madeline abandoning us of her own accord?" Pascal asked.

I didn't know how to answer. What motive could Maddy have for doing such a thing? She'd come along to Southwark to protect me. Alexander was a Fetch and part of the theater; he was, therefore, a liar by nature. It was difficult to even remember Alexander before Day had overtaken him. But there had indeed been a brief time when all of us were together and cheerful. This was after Nathan had returned from the war and before Day had sunk his barbed hooks fully into the skin of our boys. In their period of rekindling, Alexander and Pascal made for an excellent addition to our group—diffusing at least some of the tension. But those old days were past; we walked in the tatters of our own history.

"I don't know who's telling the truth these days."

"But he *was* a good man, Jane," Pascal said. "When I met him in Nimes, I was so alone, and he became my companion. He cared for me and would have done anything for me. How does a soul change so profoundly?"

I thought of Nathan and the laughing young man he'd once been. "One day, perhaps, we'll know how the world is made, Pascal, but until then, I fear we are to remain as lost as this."

I decided the only thing to do was return to Hampstead Heath and attempt to contact Vidocq. Telling Eusapia that her daughter had gone missing would cause her to drop even further into nervous illness. I could not look to her for help, and I knew neither my father nor the Ashes could assist us. "Jane, what were those threats you made to Alexander?" Pascal asked. "And what did you do in the Temple? How did you cause it to shake?"

We were hurtling north on Harley Street toward Hampstead. Our driver had been instructed to take a less frequented street to avoid the traffic on Tottenham Court.

"What I told Alexander was largely a bluff," I said. "I want the Fetches to be afraid of me. As for the shaking Temple—I don't understand that entirely. But I think we are being drawn toward some ending, for better or worse."

Black fog crept alongside our carriage, and lamplighters were busy along the streets. One would have thought it was midnight instead of four o'clock in the afternoon.

CHAPTER 27

I did not need to search for Vidocq. Vidocq, in fact, found me. Pascal went off to La Dometa to see if Maddy had returned, and I was left to meditate in my father's conservatory among the exotic plant life. The foundation beneath the greenhouse had crumbled, and the floor of the room was cracked and tilted. Several large panes of glass had fallen from their leaded frames, allowing the Heath's cool damp air to fill the room. I didn't mind this state of disrepair. Sitting in the greenhouse made me believe nature would one day consume Stoke Morrow entirely, and I would no longer be forced to suffer the house's shadows.

I tried to work out some solution to what had occurred when the old man had grabbed me in the tavern. I'd clearly manifested a vision of the Empyrean due to anxiety, as I'd done with Nathan, so perhaps Ariston Day was correct. If provoked forcefully enough, I could open a gateway to that other place, but what then?

I was so deep in my meditation that I barely heard Miss Anne knocking timidly on the doorframe. Her knock at first seemed yet another obscure sound rising from the objects around me. At her persistence, I opened my eyes and found her looking skittish, as if she'd caught me in the midst of a Satanic ritual. "What is it then?" I asked.

"You have a visitor, Miss Jane. The Inspector Vidocq is here asking to see you."

"Admit him," I said, adjusting my dress and wondering why he wanted to see me. Likely not to bring good news.

"You'll see him in the Clock Parlor?" Miss Anne asked.

"I'll see him here," I said. "The sun has a calming effect today."

"You do look vexed, miss. What's happened—something to do with Mr. Ashe?"

"It's not of your concern, Anne. See the inspector in."

"Jane," Miss Anne said in a serious tone. I turned to look at her. "I'm sorry," she said.

"Sorry for what?" I asked, but Miss Anne had already disappeared.

She returned briefly to install Vidocq in the rattan chair across from mine, cane resting between his long legs, both large hands propped on its handle. Miss Anne only glanced at me briefly as she left the room, and once again, I saw an expression of remorse—or was it pity? Vidocq himself was calm and focused. I was glad he did not decide to smoke one of his black cigarettes because it would likely harm the fragile plant life. "Please excuse the interruption, Miss Silverlake."

"It's no interruption," I said. "I need to speak with you."

Vidocq didn't act surprised. "You are wondering about Miss Lee, I suppose," he said.

"How did you know?"

"I wouldn't be a very good detective if I didn't make it my business to observe the movements of the young Mr. Ashe's boon companions."

"You were having us followed?"

"Protected is more like it. I was having you protected. But apparently my agents' vigilance had no effect, as Miss Lee is yet to be found."

"But she must be near," I said. "She was in the carriage, and then she came looking for me. Ariston Day must know her whereabouts."

"Mr. Day is also a difficult person to locate," Vidocq replied. "And yet he found you of such consequence that he brought you into his theater where only young and sullen men of money are permitted."

"Yes," I said. "I suppose that's correct."

Vidocq studied me keenly. "I know you confiscated my information regarding Ariston Day after our interview, Jane."

I sat utterly still, waiting.

"And I know you created a panic in the Temple of the Lamb. You have some gift, isn't that right? Something you didn't reveal during our interview. Madeline Lee made obscure reference to it. That's what I've come here to talk to you about."

"I thought you put no stock in the supernatural," I said, trying to retain my composure.

"Answer my question, Jane."

"It's an affliction," I said. "I've experienced it since childhood—a psychic anomaly. Ariston Day mistook it for a thing of greater significance. That's why he invited me to Southwark."

"I'm wondering if you'll allow me to experience it," Vidocq said. "You can transfer the sensation through touch, isn't that right? I had quite an interesting conversation with your maid on that very topic. Anne was hesitant to reveal anything, of course. She believes you can put her in Hell."

So that was what Miss Anne was sorry for. "There is no Hell," I said, quietly.

"But there's somewhere else. You can show me, Jane. You're the Doorway, as Nathan Ashe said."

"I'm finished letting others in."

"We need to explore your ability further," he said. "This is quite an exceptional case, and I no longer think I'll find Nathan Ashe caged in the basement of some tenement building or even dead in the Thames."

"Why is it that all men wish to *explore* me?" I asked. I started to stand, intending to excuse myself. Stoke Morrow provided plenty of places to hide. But before I could leave the room, Vidocq gave some signal to his agents who were waiting in the hall. They entered quickly, taking hold of my arms and forcing me back into my seat.

The agents were strong and wore leather gloves, as if they knew how dangerous it was to touch my skin.

"Let me go," I said. "My father will have you all deported for this."

Vidocq approached and put his hands on either side of my face. I struggled to move my head away from him, but his grip was tight. In my state of agitation, I could not control the transference. I allowed the inspector to hear the greenhouse's glass panes crying softly to themselves, and he saw the shifting pools of color produced by the cracked marble floor. Both glass and marble became telescopes, looking onto a faraway place of white trees and a still stream. The inspector's eyes grew wide, filling with the kind of fear I dreaded. "Why didn't you show me this before?" he demanded.

I glared, wanting to destroy him.

"I'm taking you to my offices for further questioning," he said.

"You're arresting me?" I asked, incredulous.

"I pray the evidence you've obscured won't prove fatal to Nathan Ashe," Vidocq said.

"My talent isn't *evidence*, and I'm not going anywhere with you."

But even as I spoke Vidocq's gloved agents were lifting me from my chair. Like it or not, I would go anywhere they pleased.

I was escorted down the crumbling steps of Stoke Morrow, an agent on either side, Miss Anne watching from the front window of the house. In a carriage separate from Vidocq's, I was taken not to a proper jail, but to an office on Bond Street. The building was an unassuming brownstone with a tailor shop in its storefront. A stoic agent sat across from me in the carriage, smoking a cigarette. Like all the agents, he wore a mustache and wooly sideburns, and I hoped he'd catch all that hair on fire.

"I am simply to be kept here?" I asked, looking out the window at the tailor's shop, "along with bolts of fabric and sewing machines?"

The agent lifted the cigarette from his mouth and said, "For a time."

"I wish to speak with my father."

"The barrister will be contacted, mademoiselle."

"I should like to speak with him immediately," I said.

The agent shifted uncomfortably in his seat. "There is no immediate here. The inspector works by his own clock."

"And I'm to be held for questioning? Is that it?"

He waved his hand to indicate he didn't know the answer.

"You can understand how irritating this is, can you not?" I asked.

"Mademoiselle must realize I am nothing more than the arm of Vidocq. I do what the inspector tells me."

"So, as the arm, do you believe Monsieur Vidocq is making any headway in the case of Nathan Ashe?"

The agent looked into my eyes, and I couldn't tell what he was searching for—my guilt or perhaps my innocence? "As the arm," he said, "I have seen no headway made in the case. But that does not mean there is none. Only Vidocq sees the entire puzzle."

"I'm beginning to think we've all put our trust in a criminal idiot," I said.

"I wouldn't let Vidocq hear you say that," the agent replied.

"I'm no longer concerned with what Vidocq does and does not hear. What's your name?"

"I'm called Karl," he said.

"Are you aware that *both* of my friends are now missing, Karl?"

"I am," he said. "And I'm sorry for it. We're looking for Miss Lee."

"Tell Vidocq that I mustn't be held here for long. Tell him if he tries to hold me, I'll find a way of escaping, and it might not be pleasant for anyone involved."

"Of course," Karl said. "You may trust that I will tell him this." He handed me a handkerchief from his pocket, and the look of kindness on his face made me feel that I *could* trust him. Karl seemed a man of his word.

*   *   *

Without another audience with Vidocq, I was taken up a narrow flight of stairs by Karl and another agent and locked in a terrible yellow room. The only furnishings in the room were a wooden chair painted green, a straw bed, and a stand with a basin and a cracked pitcher for washing. This room was, in every aspect, a cell, though one that was entirely controlled by Vidocq and not by the Crown. The objects in the room recognized my presence and shivered. I could barely hear them murmuring due to the clatter of sewing machines in the tailor's shop below. I went to the window and looked onto the walk, where Vidocq was giving orders to the other agents before once again mounting his coach and setting out. Seeing him depart in such a perfunctory way infuriated me, and I determined to demand more forcefully that I be allowed to speak to my father.

This plan did not work in the way I anticipated, as no one came to the door of the cell when I called. I pounded my fist against the door until an agent came to tell me that the inspector had given strict orders not to make contact with me until he returned. "If it so pleases you, mademoiselle, could you cease all that pounding?" he said.

"Where is Karl?" I said.

"Why would you want to speak with Karl?" the agent asked.

"Because he listened to me."

There was some conversation that I could not make out, and then the agent moved away from the cell door without reply.

There was nothing for me to do but to sit and wait for Vidocq. But he did not return, and soon the sun was setting, turning the smoke-filled London sky a shade of leathery brown. I was in a room without a lamp, and soon enough, with nothing else to occupy me, I fell asleep on the prickly straw bed, imagining it to be full of burrowing insects.

That night, I dreamed of a stag that stood atop a hill and looked over an infinite forest. It was the same stag I'd seen in my vision of Nathan's final evening. When the great animal began to run, I moved along with it, hovering somehow between its horns as it crashed through the forest. The oaks shuttled by with such speed I thought we'd surely smash into one. Finally, we stopped in a clearing. There in the center was a great tree, and I approached the tree reverently. My dress was a dark red, and its fabric moved as water might. I saw the knot in the tree that had burst long ago and knew it to be the place from whence I'd issued. The hole inside the tree, covered in dried sap, was the womb where I'd incubated. I knelt beside the tree and finally lay on the forest floor, staring up into the branches at the light spilling through. I thought how good it was to be with the entity that had born me, even if the entity was alien. In that moment alongside the tree, I knew the measure of my own power.

I fell asleep in the dream, and in doing so, awoke in the darkness of reality. I wasn't sure where I was at first, but soon enough the knowledge of the cell came back to me, along with the notion that there was someone else in the room. A presence sat on the edge of the straw bed—a dark body that seemed to swell and contract. There was no moonlight, and the gas lamp outside the window had gone out, so it was impossible to ascertain the identity of the figure. I listened for the noise of objects—clothing or jewelry—and it was then that I realized I could hear the twittering of the spyglass that Madeline sometimes wore around her neck. In that same moment, I smelled her perfume.

"Maddy?" I asked.

"It's me, Jane." Her voice was hushed, and there was a distinct note of coldness there.

I began to sit up.

"Don't move," she said. "Just listen."

"Where did you disappear to?" I asked, still half-asleep and wondering if this might be a continuation of my dream. "I was so worried."

"I've been working on a plan to find Nathan," she said. "We have to find him soon. Time is running out."

"I understand that, Maddy."

"You *don't*," she said. "You've never understood. When I left the carriage yesterday, I didn't follow you into the Temple of the Lamb. I went to the Thames, to look down into its murk. I've feared this entire time that Nathan simply fell into the river and drowned. But when I saw the bulwarks, I knew that Nathan was not in that black water. The embankments were too high. It would have been impossible to simply fall in. On top of that, I did not *feel* him there. Then joining me at my side was a man I did not recognize—a man with black hair and a silver tie pin."

"You met Ariston Day?"

"The same. And he told me how we could find Nathan. He told me exactly what we had to do."

"But he lies, Maddy. Don't be swayed. He's serving his own purposes and doesn't care about Nathan at all. There are things I never told you. He's a charlatan—"

"Quiet," she said. "I'm finished listening to you. Day is attempting to help me. We have to try his way."

"Maddy, what's happened?"

"Do you want to know why Nathan came to us in the first place?" she asked. "Do you want to know why Nathan was with us at all?" The tone of her voice had turned so bitter, it frightened me.

"Tell me," I said.

"I met him on the Heath one day when I was walking with Mother, and I knew him for Lord Ashe's son. I told him there was a girl at the house called Stoke Morrow—a girl who didn't know anything about the world. She'd been shut up in her father's moldy environs for so long that she might have gone a little mad. I asked him if he'd be willing to come along with me and take you out, Jane. I told him we could all go walking, and I asked him to think of you as *charity*."

"Are you trying to be cruel?" I asked.

"I'm trying to be honest for once," she said. "It was all a lark for him at first. For both of us, really. We tried to make you a civilized person, but it didn't work. And then you showed Nathan your abilities and everything went wrong. There have been so many times I've wished we'd never let you out at all."

I felt my heart folding in upon itself. "Rest assured I would have found the door myself eventually."

"Jane, I have been ill every morning for the past week. I've seen the doctor, and do you know what he said is causing my ailment?"

"Tell me."

"He believes me to be with child. Nathan's own."

This information struck me squarely in the chest with such force that I blurted, "I saw you together in the woods—you and Nathan."

Maddy was silent, her shadow expanding. "He was wild that evening, utterly unlike himself. I was as confused about what we were doing as you must have been. But these are the results of that. These are the results."

"Maddy, I—"

"You'll come tomorrow to the Crystal Palace at three o'clock," she said. "In a hall at the palace there is to be an exhibition called the Great Illumination. You'll meet me there behind the red curtain. Do you understand?"

Fear crept into my throat at the prospect of finally being forced to enter the Crystal Palace in Hyde Park. "But why?" I said. "And how am I supposed to get out of this cell?"

"You'll meet me there at three o'clock. Tell me you understand."

"Yes, Maddy, I understand, but couldn't we choose another meeting place?"

Her shadow stood. The room was still too dark for me to see her face. I could see only the outline of her corseted dress. The door opened, and instead of one of Vidocq's guards standing there, I saw a red-coated Fetch holding a dripping candle and waiting to escort Maddy away. The chalky whiteness of her face flared in the candlelight. She looked like a girl asleep.

The door closed behind her, and I ran to it, banging my fist against its surface. "Give her back to me, you vermin," I called. "Give her back."

"Who are you talking to, mademoiselle?" asked a Frenchman's voice from the other side of the door half a minute later. It was one of Vidocq's guards.

"Where were you?" I called to him.

"I was sleeping, mademoiselle," he answered. "And I'll return to doing so if you'll only be silent."

I lay down again and could not sleep. Maddy was traveling with a Fetch? Doing Day's bidding? I knew I had to save her. Despite everything, I still believed in her goodness. She'd been my connection to humanity for so long. She and Nathan both. I'd risk anything to save them.

CHAPTER 28

My prison door opened early the next morning, and I found not Inspector Vidocq as I'd expected, but Pascal Paget, wearing a black traveling suit, looking terribly nervous and standing next to the good agent, Karl. Shards of sunlight fell across my yellow cell, and the young men looked to me like twin Seraphim, descended. "You're free to go, mademoiselle," Karl said, and there was a certain satisfaction in his voice.

"Free? Vidocq has not even spoken to me. Have I been detained all night for no reason at all then?"

"It's been decided your presence is unnecessary at the present moment," Karl said. "Last night the inspector discovered the entrance to the Theater of Provocation. Ariston Day is in custody."

"Arrested?" I said, disbelieving.

Karl nodded. "Day and some of his Fetches."

"We don't know if Alexander was among them," Pascal said. Taking a look around the room, he added, "Let's be gone from here, Jane."

"The inspector believes questioning Day will take several days," Karl said, "and your father has put a great deal of pressure on us for your temporary release."

I thought of Father. He was good to me though he didn't understand me.

"I have a message for Vidocq before I go," I said to Karl. "Tell him there may be serious trouble on its way. I believe Ariston Day to be planning something, and even if he is incarcerated, you men should be put on point."

"Is there any direction mademoiselle thinks we should point?" Karl asked.

"Toward the Crystal Palace in Hyde Park," I said. "That's my guess. Today at three o'clock."

Bond Street was crowded with a tumult of shoppers—mostly women in elaborate hats and crinoline—and I leaned close to Pascal as we walked to hear further explanation of my release. Father had threatened to report the whole affair to the minister of the interior, and Vidocq admitted he could not provide grounds for holding me. The truth of the matter was, of course, too far-fetched to hold water, and the inspector was already pleased with the arrest of Ariston Day, believing Day was the key he needed to solve the case.

"I apologize that this didn't happen yesterday," Pascal said. "We've been trying to procure your release since Miss Anne told me you were taken. She *is* sorry, Jane. She didn't know how the inspector was going to react. Your father would have come himself, but—"

"You don't have to make excuses for him, Pascal. Father hasn't truly involved himself in my life for some time. He tries—but thank you for your help." I went on to tell him that Maddy visited me in the night and what she'd instructed me to do.

"Are we going to the Crystal Palace then?" he said.

"I don't know that we have much of a choice."

"But you believe this has something to do with Ariston Day?"

"I believe she's been influenced by him, yes. Maddy was not herself when she came to see me. I'd like to go somewhere else before we venture on to Hyde Park, though."

"The Lee carriage is yours, Saint Jane," Pascal said. "Where are we off to?"

"There's a church in Spitalfields," I said, "called the Hall of the Red Star."

Pascal shook his head. "There's a cholera outbreak in Spitalfields. I don't think the driver will take us there."

"I'll be persuasive," I said. "I must see it before three o'clock."

"Why is the church so important to you?"

"It's a link between my mother and me," I said. "I hope to come to some understanding about my relationship to the Empyrean there as well." It was good to say the word *Empyrean* freely without fear of discovery. "Pascal, I need to know more than Ariston Day if I'm to keep us all safe from him."

Spitalfields was a vast wasteland in London's East End. It had once been home to prosperous silk factories, but when the industry moved on, the factories had been turned into tenements, and the workers were left wageless and destitute. The buildings sagged and looked as though they might collapse at any moment, and as the Lee carriage passed these black and broken hovels, downtrodden faces stared out at us from the glassless windows. Spitalfields was worse off than Southwark it seemed, and every piece of brick and mortar cried out to me. I thought of how Ariston Day said that the unnamed goddess must rise up and put an end to the suffering of Man. She must unmake that which should have never been made. These poor faces, watching from the wreckage, made me wonder, for a moment, if he was right and such a time had come.

The church lay in the remnants of an ancient Roman cemetery and was not much more than a shanty house with the cryptic name painted over the door: The Hall of the Red Star. The moment I saw the church, my heart sank. The pinewood door had been torn off its hinges and tossed into the side yard, and several pews had been thrown into the yard as well.

"It looks as though someone made it here before us," Pascal said.

I stepped from the carriage and into the shadow of the doorway.

"Careful, Jane," Pascal said. He did not advance into the church with me, as if he knew this was something I needed to do alone.

The inside of the church was more damaged than the outside, and it was clear that some catastrophe had befallen this place. Pews were overturned, and a large hole had been punched through the front of the makeshift altar. The smell of smoke lingered in the air, and resting in the nave was what appeared to be a defaced statue of the Virgin. This was not the work of the vandals, though. Mary had been transformed with care, and I recognized her new persona immediately. Her face was covered with white paint and a bushel of dead flowers was fixed to her arm with baling wire. The final touch was a bit of red textile, draped around her shoulders. *She's there, blooming in the darkness, silent and waiting.* It appeared as though the statue was the only thing in the church left untouched.

"If you're looking for worship, you won't find much opportunity here," said a woman's voice. "The bishop's gone. Everyone's been frightened away."

I turned, and saw a woman of some fifty years standing in the shadows. She was dressed plainly in a gray matron's gown, marred by dirt and ash. Her face was kind yet weathered. Perhaps she'd been attempting to bring some order to the wreckage before we arrived.

"What's happened here?" I asked.

"Boys in red coats, night before last," she said. "They demanded information about our worship. Said they'd been sent by a man in Southwark who aims to comprehend our ways. The bishop told them such things as our beliefs couldn't be expressed in words. One has to *live* the meaning. The boys grew angry at this and made their threats. They would have killed the bishop, I think, if it hadn't been for Mr. Bayard, the butcher, who came and drove them out."

"That's terrible," I said, imagining the Fetches ransacking this place.

"Aye." She squinted at me. "And what is it you've come for? You don't look like you belong in Spitalfields yourself."

"I'm from Hampstead Town. And I've come for the same reason as the boys, I suppose. For information. Though I don't intend violence. My name is Jane Silverlake."

The woman paused only a moment at this, long enough for me to see a flash of what might have been understanding in her eyes.

"My mother—" I began.

"Evelyn Silverlake," the woman said.

"You knew her, then?"

She shook her head. "None of us knew her—not well. Such a thing wasn't possible. Evelyn Silverlake came here a few times to speak to the bishop directly. She was confused. She didn't understand the things that were happening to her, the sensations she was feeling. I tried to speak with her myself. Tried to tell her about the Old Mother of the Heath."

"The Old Mother?" I asked. "You mean Mother Damnable?"

"Aye, but we don't call her that down here. That's what people called her out of spite."

"Are you telling me that Mother Damnable and my mother were alike in some way? They both experienced *sensations*?"

"Difficult to draw such comparisons," the woman said. "Old Mother knew what she was. She knew how to use her gifts. That's why everyone called her a witch. But even Old Mother didn't know exactly what she needed to *do* with these gifts. The bishop says one day someone will come who knows."

"You mean a person who knows how to bring about the unmaking?" I asked quietly, as if to speak these words too loudly would grant them authority, "To bring the Paradise?"

The woman frowned. "Now you *do* sound like those boys from Southwark. We aren't looking for any Paradise, my girl. There is no making or unmaking. That line of thinking is a fool's game. Over the years, there've been plenty of men who've tried to purify the world, to return it to an innocence they believe it's lost. But all of that is just an attempt at gaining power—a grab for the sword, as our bishop would say. Such men want to be a kind of king. The role of the gifted one has nothing to do with power or with kings. She's meant to keep a *balance* between earth and aether."

"Aether?" I asked.

"Just a word," she said. "Call it what you like: the Upper Sky, the Unmade, even the Empyrean. Men have given it so many names over the course of history. But those names don't really matter, in the end. It's the unchanging matter. A place without qualities. Neither hot nor cold, wet nor dry. The aether remains while all else shifts and fades."

"I still don't think I understand your meaning," I said.

She gave me half a smile and said, "Everything has an opposite, Miss Silverlake. The aether is the opposite of creation. It's always there, invisible but burning bright. It's the pale web that holds the universe together. The idea that this man in Southwark believes he should dissolve the boundary between two realms—it's a terrible thought. We could never live in that rarefied environment, not for long. The gifted one is the keeper of the beautiful Unmade and she's our keeper too. She doesn't seek to destroy creation or even wash it clean. "

"Then what is she supposed to do?" I asked. "How is she to prevent someone from harming the balance?"

The woman shook her head. "Not even the bishop knows such things. I believe the Old Mother knew some of it, though. If you could speak to someone who knew her, then you might learn a bit more. But then again there were few brave enough to make her acquaintance."

"Thank you," I said. "And perhaps I could ask my father to help gather funds for repairs on your church."

"That won't be necessary," the woman said. "But there is something you could do." She extended her hand.

I was taken aback only momentarily. I put my hand on hers, and she closed her eyes, listening to the room around her, which did not weep but sang. She saw her church was not a ruin but a place of brightness and wonder. This unfettered place was just beyond the ruined surface.

"What happened in there?" Pascal asked as we left the Hall of the Red Star.

"I'm not sure," I said. "But I think it was what I needed. I'd like to go to La Dometa now."

"But Maddy isn't there," Pascal said.

"It isn't Maddy I want to speak to," I replied.

CHAPTER 29

Eusapia Lee saw me in her parlor among Adolphus's decorations, which buzzed around us like a hive of insects. She was in a greater state of disarray than usual, eyes hollow and tendrils of hair creeping out from beneath her black house bonnet. I approached her carefully. There were times when Eusapia seemed to entirely forget who I was even though she'd known me since I was a girl. But I needed her at this moment, needed her to remember everything.

"London is a black mill bent upon the destruction of youth and innocence," she lamented, waving a hand, as if to indicate that the black mill was about to materialize in the parlor.

I worked to shut out the clamoring souls of the room so I could listen to Eusapia, who informed me that she believed Madeline was not abducted but may very well have taken her own life.

"That seems too much of a leap," I said, not wanting to tell her that I'd spoken with Maddy the previous night. There would be far too much to explain, and such explanations would likely only disturb her further.

"The black mill took my poor Melchior at such a young age," she said. "I thought you girls were the lucky ones. You were protected from the mill here in the northern heights, watching the churnings and tremulations of London from afar. But you see what has happened to my Madeline. We are still a part of the mill—even here in Hampstead Town."

I looked at the clock on the mantel and saw the hour was growing late. I was due at the Crystal Palace soon enough. "Eusapia, there's something I have to ask you. Maddy told me that you met Mother Damnable when you were very young—that you had some *experience* with her. She showed you something."

"Why ever is Madeline telling my private stories?" Eusapia asked.

I started to apologize but was cut off.

"She has no stories of her own, I suppose. The poor girl lives in her mirrors and her fantasies of young Mr. Ashe. I've protected her too dearly, watched over her like a doting hen. When I was coming up, Jane, there were too many of us. My mother had a whole litter of children with which to contend. At every chance, we attempted to squirm loose from the pile. From time to time, we *did* escape, and we experienced reality without the filter of our parentage."

"Eusapia, I need to know what Mother Damnable showed you. It's very important."

Maddy's mother gave me a curious look and then said, "I was only five, you know. A soft little duckling, lost in the brambles. Mother Damnable was the strangest thing I'd ever seen that had thought to call itself a human being."

"She was terrible, then?"

"Not terrible, Jane. Stupendous. She was filthy and she wore— God, I will never forget—she wore an Elizabethan ruff around her neck. She was dressed as though she was some fine woman, and perhaps she believed she was. Her red cloak even hung all the way to her feet."

"Did she speak to you?"

"Oh yes. Yes, she did."

I waited, thinking Eusapia would go on. When she did not, I prompted, "And what did Mother Damnable say?"

"No one has ever asked what the witch said to me. It's better not to repeat a witch's words, isn't it? Everything a witch speaks is an incantation."

"I haven't heard that."

She pressed her tongue against her front teeth, thinking. "Mother Damnable spoke in such an odd dialect; I barely made out what she said. She babbled it, really. She told me something about how all things would soon be as they should be. She was going to see to it."

"Did you run from her?" I asked.

"Oh no, my dear. I was no fool. Mother Damnable, when alive, was only slightly less renowned than now that she is dead. To run from her would garner her wrath. Instead of running, I smiled at her and told her she was as fine a woman—a very fine woman indeed. Perhaps she took a liking to me because of this. Even Mother Damnable had her vanities. She grasped my hand, and suddenly we were *moving*, though I did not use my legs. Eventually, she put me on her back, and I rode her like I rode the goats at Papa's farm. Mother Damnable was older than I am now, and yet there I was with my arms around her neck, pressing my face against her ruff and feeling the shifting of her red robe. I allowed myself to be propelled by her through the woods, going so far and deep I was sure I'd never find my way home. Finally, we stopped at the edge of a clearing—a beautiful clearing that I've never found again despite my attempts. And it was there that Mother Damnable indicated to me a tree—a great and brooding oak."

"A tree?" I said with interest.

Eusapia nodded solemnly.

"What then?" I asked.

Maddy's mother looked off into the distance, eyes reddish and damp. "Other children told their parents that Mother Damnable could split open the air and walk into Hell. But that wasn't right. They mixed up their stories because what they saw didn't respect any logic. I know what Mother Damnable could really do because she showed me: she knelt in the woods before the great oak. She bowed to the tree, and made signs with her hands. Then she parted her red robe, and I saw her pale and sickly flesh beneath. Running from her navel to her breastbone was a deep cut, a sort of incision. She pressed her fingers into the cut and slowly pulled back her skin,

stretching it, opening herself up. And there within her body lay another place. It was not Hell, as the children claimed. There was no
fire and no devils."

I felt light in the head as Eusapia spoke. "The other place was *inside* her, you say?"

"The white forest," Eusapia said. "And the white river that wasn't
made of water. And the creatures that crawled there."

"Creatures," I whispered.

All of the objects in the room were howling. I could no longer
block their sound. I pressed my fingers against my own chest, remembering the churning pain I'd felt when I'd touched Nathan's
objects and the feeling that traveled through my body when pressing
on the membrane in Mother Damnable's own cottage. I thought of
what the woman in the Hall of the Red Star had said to me: *the gifted
one is the keeper of the beautiful Unmade.* Was this how she kept it,
then? It was all inside of her?

"The old witch didn't die, you know," Eusapia said in a conspirato-
rial tone. "She simply disappeared. People in Hatchett's Bottom said
she walked into Hell when she grew tired of our world. But I know
different, Jane. The hole in her chest—she must have stretched it too
big. It finally swallowed her up."

CHAPTER 30

In the darkness of the carriage speeding toward the Crystal Palace, Pascal would not give me a quiet moment. He was seated on the bench across from me, speaking quickly, half in French, saying something about Alexander and Ariston Day. I found I couldn't attend to his topic, as the image of Mother Damnable pulling open her own chest was fixed in my mind. I pictured the white forest inside her. Was she keeping balance? Was that the way it was done?

"Are you listening to me, Jane?" Pascal said sharply, tapping my arm.

His touch was enough to draw my attention. "I'm sorry, Pascal. Tell me again."

"Ariston Day has escaped."

"Escaped?" The carriage momentarily dimmed, and I found it difficult to believe I'd grown so fractured as to not have heard this information before. But how could I really be surprised? Of course Ariston Day had escaped. Such a creature couldn't really be imprisoned. "How?" I said.

Pascal produced an evening issue of the *Magnet*, the publication that was often first with news but lacking in accuracy. Above the fold was an ink drawing of Day in one of his trim suits, standing on a wooden box in Speakers' Corner at Hyde Park. Day's eyes looked nearly as animalistic as they had when I'd spoken to him at the Temple, and he was shouting something to a crowd of onlookers.

"Alexander sent this article along with a terse letter of farewell," Pascal said. "I wish I could speak to him, Jane. I know my Alexander is still there, Jane, inside of the thing that Ariston Day has made."

"Farewell?" I said. "Is he going back to America, then?"

Pascal shook his head. "Read and you'll see. I don't think you're going to like it much."

The article described how Day—who the *Magnet* reported was being held in connection with the disappearance of Nathan Ashe— had made a bizarre escape from a makeshift prison on Oxford Street. Inspector Vidocq himself was not present at the time of the escape, though a number of his men were keeping watch. Apparently, boys dressed in the uniform of the Queen's Guard had entered the building and used wooden cudgels to subdue the French agents. A smoke bomb was detonated, and Ariston Day simply walked free from the room where he was being held, like some spirit that could walk through walls. Unable to return to his captured theater, Day was bold enough to appear hours later and mount a box at Speakers' Corner to deliver a speech in which he detailed a vision of what was apparently the apocalypse.

To me, this rather public demonstration was troubling. Day had a history of being so careful and secretive. I worried that his boldness implied he thought he no longer had anything to fear because his goal was already within reach. In his speech, Day heralded the end of time and the beginning of a Paradise unlike any earth had ever known. Industry and experience would be replaced by a great white innocence. He said that the Paradise would be brought on by the incarnation of a powerful goddess who'd been living unnoticed among the thoughtless men and women of London. And then Day had done the unthinkable. He'd spoken my name to the crowd gathered in Hyde Park. "Jane Silverlake" was printed there clearly in black-and-white type.

I lowered the newspaper to my side. "He named me?" I said, horrified. "But what purpose does that serve?"

Pascal shook his head, looking pale. "This must have something to do with what's to happen today at the Crystal Palace, don't you think?"

"Yes," I replied, still finding it difficult to believe Day had gone so far.

"Are you really a goddess, Jane?" Pascal asked.

"That doesn't even sound like a reasonable question," I replied.

"But *are* you?"

"Pascal, I'm only beginning to understand what I am. 'Goddess' isn't quite the word. It's possible there is no word. But believe me, Ariston Day doesn't have a clue as to what I truly am."

"We must be wary of him," Pascal said. "We don't know what he intends."

"I'm through with being wary," I said. "Day has gone too far. Every half-witted mystic and self-proclaimed man of science will soon be knocking at the door of Stoke Morrow. We can no longer hide. It's time for us to move ahead with this, I think. But first we must find Maddy at the Crystal Palace and get her away from him."

"How are we to do that?" Pascal said. "Day has his army."

"Trust me when I say I'm stronger than he is, Pascal. I believe I always have been. I've just been afraid to show it—even to myself."

When the street became congested near Grosvenor Square, Pascal and I disembarked from the carriage and made our way through the city's passages that Nathan had once shown me. These makeshift habitats for the poor were filled with tokens of daily life: bits of altar cloth and damask decorating broken tables, birdcages with no birds to inhabit them, and blackened iron heating stoves. From the outdoor sitting parlors, we moved into darker alcoves, places mad with stolen tea trays, tiny tables, and the like. At times these passages were the width of a traditional alley, yet at other times the walls grew terribly close, no more than two feet apart. Too narrow to bring a coffin through, Nathan used to say, though it was customary to hold open-air funerals in the passages. He once told me there were even areas designated as holy places where the passage dwellers made worship.

I stopped dead in one such chapel when I saw a shrine to what had once been the Virgin but was now transformed into something quite new. Mary's face was painted white, making a mask of her features. She was draped in a mantle of red and lauded with wildflowers. Someone had used baling wire to attach a stalk of wilted lilies to her hand, as with the statue in the Spitalfields church.

"The same desecration we saw at the Hall of the Red Star," Pascal said.

"It isn't a desecration," I said. "It's the transformation of myth."

"But who would make such a thing?"

"Word is spreading," I said, almost to myself.

Pascal stepped forward, took a daisy from the altar, and presented it to me. "For your continued benevolence," he said.

His humor made me nervous; still, I accepted the flower.

The Crystal Palace floated over the lush grasslands of Hyde Park, and Pascal and I hurried through groups of wealthy picnickers who lounged on the great lawn. Reflected sunlight blazed in the thousand glass panels that made up the surface of the palace, making the building difficult to look at directly. Red and gold flags fluttered from the glass parapets, and the transept was inhabited by a full-grown oak tree, enclosed in glass.

Pascal paid our entrance fee, and I followed him into the transept, where the great oak stood in its prison. Men and women moved around the towering tree, marveling at it. I gazed beyond the transept toward the wide pavilion that opened onto the various halls of history and science. "We must be careful to avoid the new inventions," I said. "I don't know how my body will react to them."

Pascal, ever the kind boy, took my arm and led me on.

We passed through chambers, various and extravagant, looking for some sign of Madeline, Ariston Day, or the Great Illumination, which was to be our meeting place. We found ourselves in a room that housed scenes from the New World. Large taxidermic cats and serpents lurked in a silken jungle. In one scene, a puma was about to spring upon a brocket deer, and we were told by the small placard nearby that the cat intended to pull the deer's neck back until it snapped.

"So that's what it's like to be in America," Pascal said. "No wonder Alexander can be such a bastard."

"We have to keep moving, Pascal," I said, glancing at a tower clock mounted near the glass ceiling. "It's almost three."

We followed the hall through the volcanic ruins of Pompeii, where a sign warned us to BEWARE OF THE DOG, which we later found petrified in ash—a poor little terrier curled into a fetal stone ball. From Pompeii, we passed through the courts of Byzantium, then a Greek palace and a room that was entirely devoted to a collection of various artifacts of Araby. A golden monkey leered down at us from its pedestal.

All the objects were singing quite loudly in what nearly sounded like a chorus. It worried me that perhaps these objects understood I had arrived, and they were, in some sense, rejoicing. The ages of man were glad that I had come.

We continued on through the musical court where the head of Apollo rested on a central pillar and around him danced an array of fauns, playing instruments. Nowhere did we find any announcement regarding the Great Illumination. The palace was so vast that finally I resorted to asking a tour guide—a stodgy man in a shabby brown suit. "You'll find it beyond the Egyptian Gallery, mum, and there'll be no greater marvel in all of London this year. You'd better hurry. The show's about to begin."

Pascal and I raced through the Egyptian Gallery, where the animal-headed gods watched silently and waited. I thought of the white ape Nathan had met on Malta and wondered again what the creature had done to him. My head was filled with visions of that primitive monster, and I wondered if Ariston Day was correct that I could be something equally primitive and terrible. I'd brought harm to Nathan, brought harm to Maddy. I forced myself to brush these thoughts away.

Beyond the Egyptian Gallery, we found neither Maddy nor Ariston Day, only a hall with hundreds of glass bulbs dangling from wires, crisscrossing the high arched ceiling. A crowd of some two hundred people had amassed, men and women dressed in their finest, all staring up at the little glass balls on black wires, waiting.

"What is the Great Illumination meant to be?" I asked.

"They intend to show everyone electric light," Pascal said. "I read about it in the *Times*. Electricity is conducted along those wires and brings fire to the filaments inside the glass bulbs. It's man's newest invention."

"Harnessed fire," I said softly, fearful of what such an invention would do to my senses. Despite my growing sense of strength, I knew I must not underestimate Day. Each of the bulbs was already ringing, making a shrill, otherworldly noise, and just as I was about to tell Pascal we should leave, two things occurred simultaneously.

A mustachioed barker mounted the stage and began announcing to the onlookers that they should prepare themselves, as the Great Illumination was about to begin. "The god Prometheus will descend upon London-town to give us fire," he said, "and none of you will ever be able to look away." Then directly, I saw a flash of red uniform in the crowd—the queen's own red, streaked with grime and soot. It was, most certainly, a Fetch.

"They're here," I said.

"Where?" Pascal asked, craning.

"Keep an eye out for Maddy," I replied. "She's confused. I think it would be better if we all got out of here and met Ariston Day on some other terms."

"But, Jane—" I didn't let him finish. I made my way through the crowd toward the red curtain where the barker stood. It was behind the red curtain that Maddy said I should meet her. In the darkness there, I found neither Ariston Day nor any Fetches nor Madeline Lee. There was only a large glass box, standing on end, nearly six feet in height. It reminded me of an Egyptian sarcophagus and had a brass perimeter decorated with various animals of England—a pheasant and a fox, a grouse and a stag. Wires from the Great Illumination ran along either side of the box, and glass bulbs had been screwed into the box itself. I was wondering at the purpose of the box when I heard the scuff of a boot behind me and turned to see Maddy—looking worn down in her violet dress, as if she hadn't even thought of sleeping.

"Here you are, finally," she said. "I didn't think you'd come, Jane."

"You asked me to. Of course I've come. But Maddy, we must leave. The electric lights—I don't know what they'll do to me."

"Ariston Day knows what they'll do," she said. "Step inside the box now."

"Maddy, I—"

"None of your arguments. I won't hear them."

I looked again at the gleaming coffin. "What purpose does it serve?" I asked, feeling strangely frightened by the box.

Maddy took Nathan's pistol from the pocket of her skirt. The gun made a blunt statement in her hand, a kind of ending, and I wondered if one of the Fetches had shown her how to use it. I wished that I'd taken the pistol from her when she offered it at the Temple of the Lamb. I should have known it would be safer under my command.

She trained the pistol on me. "You've left me no choice, Jane. I know what you did. He *told* me what you did. You have to get into the box so we can help Nathan. There isn't much time."

"Day told you?"

"That's right." She put her thumb on the hammer and cocked the pistol.

"Maddy, please don't do this. Ariston Day isn't even his name. The man is nothing but a fabric of lies. I should have explained before. I read the entire report written by Vidocq. If I did something to Nathan, I'm sorry. I can't tell you how sorry I am. Yet there are other ways to bring him back, there must be."

Without warning, Maddy fired the pistol. The sound of it rang out so loudly I could hear nothing for a moment. I waited to feel pain, but there was none. Looking to my left, I saw a hole in the red curtain. A woman on the other side was screaming, and I could hear shouts from the crowd as people scrambled to escape the hall.

"You would shoot me?" I asked. "Have you lost your mind entirely?"

"I wasn't aiming at you," Maddy replied, and her eyes betrayed her utter desperation. "It was a warning." She cocked the pistol again. "You took Nathan away because of your jealousy, Jane, because you couldn't stand the idea of him choosing me. But I'll have him back. You'll show me where he is. Now do as I say, and get in the box."

My hand was shaking as I found the box's latch among the brass animals carved on its side. I feared that Maddy was wild enough to actually shoot me, and I knew I had to play her game long enough so I could figure out what to do—how to stop her without harming her. When the door swung open, stale air wafted out, and I wondered if there was any ventilation in the crystal coffin. I had no time to consider this further, as Maddy had pressed the pistol into my back. It sang to me softly, a kind of lullaby.

"How could you?" I said, my voice nearly breaking.

"You'll see, Jane," she replied grimly. "This is necessary."

"Maddy, you're my closest friend. We've nearly shared the same heart for—"

"No more poetry, Jane," she said, gesturing toward the box once more.

I stepped inside the glass coffin, and Maddy closed the door, locking it from the outside. I turned to look at her. Her dark doll's eyes, the delicacy of her nose and cheeks, all of it was the same, yet this must have been some other Madeline Lee, one who could be this terrible.

The sounds of glass and metal roared around me as soon as I was inside the box. It was a violent noise, as if a dark storm was building. I began calling to Maddy, asking why she would do this. Why didn't she trust me?

"Trust you?" she said, eyes hard and face chalky. "I saw it even before Ariston Day explained. You poisoned Nathan and then put him in that awful place."

"I didn't mean—"

"The only possible way to get Nathan back is to open the Empyrean, Jane," she said, "and the only way to open the Empyrean is to force you to do so. You haven't cooperated with any of this. You've been hiding your deeds all along."

"Day doesn't care for Nathan," I said. "He wants the Empyrean open for his own purposes—and those purposes are darker than you imagine."

She did not soften.

"Open the door," I begged, putting my hand on the glass, an action that made the screaming grow louder in my head. The sound tore through my skull as if it could split me in two. "But please don't put yourself and Pascal in danger. We can leave if we all go now. We'll find another way to get Nathan back, I promise."

But as she backed away, I suddenly understood Ariston Day's plot—his provocation. He hadn't actually needed to talk to me in Southwark at all. He'd summoned me there, knowing I would bring Maddy, and it was she he wanted to talk to. Only she could complete the provocation. I was helpless against her because I wanted so badly to protect her.

The roar was still building at the back of my head. I could feel the blue of the sky beyond the palace walls, and I longed for the green silence of the parkland. The glass of the coffin wanted dissolution. All of the objects in the palace wanted their release. And I would be the one to give it to them.

I pressed against the barrier that separated me from my friend. "Maddy, whatever Ariston Day has planned, I swear to you, it's not going to bring back Nathan. It's only going to draw us deeper into—" But my own voice was drowned out by the sound in my head, and my thoughts fell to pieces under the strain of it.

As I was trying to gather myself, to control the environment around me in some way, the curtain had fallen and I saw the great crowd had departed from the hall, frightened off by the gunshot. They had fled, and only some twenty Fetches remained. The white slice of Ariston Day's face appeared among the sea of their red coats, his black featherish hair, his salmon-colored tie and the glint of silver tie pin upon it like a captured star. He was smiling up at me, adoring.

I turned to look for Maddy, but she was gone. I was alone on the stage, caged like an animal for everyone to see. And I watched help-lessly as the Fetch with the ugly grin who'd brought Day's initial message to Stoke Morrow pulled the black switch at the side of the stage attached to an electrical box.

Suddenly the bulbs ignited, each filled with electric light, and it was as if the tip of a drill had been applied to my skull. The ringing was no longer ringing; it was the sound of a great brass church bell in a tower. I fell to my knees. Too late, I understood why Day had brought me here. These lights—this focusing of electricity—was not *an* inven-tion of man, it was *the* invention of man. And when I looked up, I saw that each individual bulb was surrounded by a halo. It seemed to me that bright flowers were strung across the glass ceiling of the Crystal Palace, creating an ethereal domain. I could feel the palace slipping away. The field of bright, screaming flowers was drawing me toward it. Somewhere in the distance, a pane of glass shattered and then more glass was breaking. The entire structure of the Palace was shaking, and I felt I might bring it down at any moment.

Pascal was suddenly outside the box, calling to me and fumbling for the latch. A vortex of energy churned about the hall. And I soon was not *in* the vortex—I was the vortex. I could feel it pushing its way out of my chest. I could not respond to Pascal or even look at him any longer because I was wholly other than him. We were not the same kind of creature. I was blooming in the darkness. Maddy had long ago put a surface on me, a facade of normality. And now she'd helped to tear it away. I could feel that surface sloughing off into the aether, and I tried my best to hold the doorway closed. I didn't know what would happen if it opened. Who would I hurt? The buzzing electric lights were too much. I felt the fullness of my power burst forth from my chest. The box exploded around me, and I was falling up toward the ceiling and the field of glass flowers.

The sky became the ground. I was going to strike it. No time to brace my body. I was going to hit.

CHAPTER 31

I felt that I was everywhere at once; my essence had moved beyond the boundaries of my own flesh into stillness and silence. Without opening my eyes, I listened for the murmur of objects, and impossibly, I heard nothing. I extended tendrils of myself into the far distance, attempting to experience even the presence of one soul. But there was nothing. In the open air of Hampstead Heath, I could at least hear my own clothing or the dull hum of faraway London bricks. But it was as if every object in the world, every clamoring soul that I'd perceived since the death of my mother, had simply ceased to exist.

I opened my eyes and was greeted by stark white light. The Crystal Palace was gone, and it appeared I was floating in some eternally bright and empty space, a world washed clean. Then slowly, trees materialized—sturdy oaks with white bark and pale toothy leaves. Flowers appeared soon after, burning like lanterns in the underbrush. I lay on a bed of white grass, mere inches from one of the oversize blossoms, and it seemed as though the light inside the petals fluctuated, growing brighter and then dimmer. There were fine veins in the petals too, like those that can be seen beneath the surface of a fair woman's skin. I felt the glow of light in my own body, growing brighter and dimmer, responding to the light of the alien flowers. I was part of them, and they were part of me.

Finally, I was here in the forest of my dreams—Nathan's Empyrean and Ariston Day's Paradise. Being swallowed wasn't the end. This was a beautiful new beginning in a place with no sorrow or pain. I lay on my back and ran my fingers through the white grass, finding it cool. There was no breeze or movement in the forest, and stranger still, no *smell*. It was as if nothing here had ever lived. This was the aether. Such lack of life made the forest magnificent, just as the gods themselves who'd never lived were magnificent.

I heard a woman moaning some distance away. The moan was confusing—a dark stain upon this place. And then I remembered Maddy firing Nathan's pistol and forcing me into the glass sarcophagus surrounded by electric light. I remembered feeling agony when she betrayed me. Such emotion should not have tainted the Empyrean, and yet it was here.

The woman was still moaning, and I recognized her voice. Maddy, who'd put everyone in danger, was close at hand.

I rose from my place in the white grass, checking myself for injury. My dress was torn around the neck and shoulders and I'd suffered cuts from broken glass. Blood leaked onto the fabric of my dress, making red flowers on the silk. I caught a glimpse of a purple gown beyond a patch of bright flowers. It was Maddy, trying to stand, and looking at her, I felt a rage rise up in me unlike any I'd ever know.

"Madeline," I called in a voice that was loud and hard. The sound of it seemed to echo off the white sky.

She looked startled and before I could speak another word, she was moving toward the cover of the white trees.

"Don't you dare," I called to her.

She did not stop. If anything, she ran faster.

I stood and followed her into the woods, watching as her purple dress flickered among the white trunks. I found I could move more easily in the Empyrean, as if I *owned* the space. I called Maddy's name again, but still she did not slow. I wove among the trees that were not trees at all. They were like bones. The Empyrean was some vast body.

I caught Maddy by a ribbon trailing from her purple gown, and she fell, face-first, into one of the white trees. She screamed, clutching at the bark and then turning to claw at me. I took both her wrists and held them. There was no transference in the white forest, for there was nothing to transfer. But I drew strength from the trees themselves and held her down.

"This was so foolish," I said. "I worked so hard to protect you."

"Where is Nathan?" she spat.

"Nathan?" I said, outraged at the ridiculousness of her question. This had all gone well beyond Nathan. "Let me look, Maddy. Let me see if I can find him." I turned my head from side to side and called out his name. "It looks as though Nathan's not here," I said caustically. "Is it possible that Ariston Day *misguided* you?"

"Let me go, Jane," she screamed.

With all my force, I shook her against the white tree, knocking the back of her skull against the bark. "Do you know what I am?" I said.

"I do," she said. "He told me."

"Then you should be bowing your head."

She did not bow. She looked at me defiantly. "Where is the Crystal Palace? Where is London? What have you done with everything?"

"*I* did this?" I asked, incredulous. "Maddy, are you going to listen to me or do I have to thrash you against this tree again?"

She grew quiet, ceasing her struggle. "Just tell me where everyone has gone," she said. "Is London no more?"

"You assume I know more than I actually do," I said. "I've been trying to tell you that." I gazed into the white forest. The space among the trees was eerie, as if pregnant with some unseen force. "London exists. But I certainly don't know how to get back there. What did Ariston Day tell you would happen?"

She drew a breath. "He said the electricity from the Great Illumination would augment your talent. He said it would keep the door open long enough so all of us could pass through and look for Nathan."

"And how did he know such a thing?"

"He's had meetings with William Crookes of the queen's Society for Psychical Research. Mr. Crookes used electricity with his mediums to great effect. One woman was said to be able to produce a full-bodied apparition when she was augmented with electricity."

"More human experiments," I said. "That's charming, Maddy."

"What are we going to do, Jane?"

"We're going to clean up the mess that you and Ariston Day have made," I said. "But I'm in charge here. You'll do everything I say. Do you understand?"

She nodded. "Will we find Nathan?"

"If you ask me that again, I will strangle you."

"Yes, Jane."

"We're going to walk," I said. "Go quietly. I believe I know what things live in these woods, and you wouldn't want to meet them."

We made our way through the white trees; Maddy went first because I no longer trusted her to walk behind me. My rage had subsided, but I felt the connection between us was torn. She was no longer a sister. I had no sisters. Nathan was right. I was the kind of thing that walked alone.

Maddy glanced back nervously, perhaps checking whether I was about to transform into a blazing goddess and take my rightful seat in this weird atmosphere. But I remained myself, still tattered and bleeding. Unlike walking on the Heath, there were no paths by which to travel, and edging through the trees made our traversing slow. Though there was a great deal of flora in the Empyrean, we saw literally no fauna. No insects or birds. Everything was terribly pristine. Untouched and impossible.

"What pollinates the flowers?" Maddy asked. "There must be some sort of insect here at least. It can't all just be plants."

"They only look like plants," I said.

She bent over to smell one of the glowing oversize flowers. "You're right. There is no scent," she said. "And it's as though I'm not seeing any of them clearly. I can't quite focus my eyes."

I could see the Empyrean clearly enough. In fact, the more time I spent there, the more its images resolved in front of me. Every piece of foliage was becoming articulated.

"You shouldn't have brought us here, Maddy," I said, calmly now. "I don't really know what any of it means. And we're no closer to finding Nathan now than we were in London. In fact, we may be further away." I turned to look at her. "Why didn't you simply tell me you were carrying Nathan's child?"

She paused for a moment and then said, "Because this was *my* problem, Jane. For once, something was my very own, and it had nothing to do with your godforsaken talent. Finally, there was something between just Nathan and me—something normal. A child."

"Yes," I said agreeing. "And I am so far from normal."

"You're like a tidal wave," she said, "that picks up everything in its path and drags it along. We're all at the mercy of your currents. Ariston Day says that no part of you is even *human*."

This pierced me. "Do you believe him, Maddy? You, of all people."

She turned to look at me, remorseful yet determined. "You said it yourself. These plants, which look so very much like plants, are in fact not. You look so much like a girl, but—"

"Yes," I said grimly. "I am not."

"I'm sorry, Jane."

"Don't say that when you don't mean it. I'm tired of talking in circles with you."

"But you must understand why I used the gun," she said. "For once, I wanted to be in control of my own fate."

"And look where that's gotten you," I said. "You're in the false forest—perhaps for eternity."

"No," she said, hastening her step.

"It's not going to help you to run away," I called. "Haven't you learned that yet?"

When she stopped short, I knew she'd discovered something—even before I saw the red coat spread beneath the tree.

The Fetch was bleeding from an ugly wound in his neck, turning the red of his coat an even darker shade. The skin around the wound looked as though it had been torn by a dull blade, splaying the flesh. Maddy recognized him before I did—his rough American face was badly bruised. "Alexander," she said, kneeling at his side. "What's happened to you?"

His lips were chapped and white, and his eyes searched the sunless sky. "Ariston Day," he whispered.

"Where is he?" I asked.

Alexander made a gurgling cough. "Things weren't going according to plan and he became—violent."

"Did he do this to you, Alexander?"

"Jane," he said, as if seeing me for the first time. There was blood on his teeth when he smiled. "The Great Doorway. Bringer of the Paradise."

"You can see well enough Day was wrong about all that," I said. "He didn't understand what it meant to open the door."

"He still doesn't," Alexander said, "and now it seems the door wasn't enough. He needs to bring the wall down."

"The wall?" I asked.

Alexander took a wheezing breath. "The wall . . . the membrane . . . the skin. I don't know what to call it. It's what encloses this place, holds it away from earth. Day is making sacrifices in the woods. He says we've displeased the gods of the Empyrean and the only thing that's left is blood sacrifice. That's what these coats were meant to represent all along. We Fetches wear our blood on the outside, and he's bleeding every one of us he finds."

"Can you stand?" Maddy asked. "Can you come with us?"

"I think I'd better lie here," Alexander said. He coughed again. "Pascal isn't with you?"

"He isn't," I said. "We've found only you."

"I was terrible to him," Alexander said. "I treated him so badly, and for what? Feeble transcendence?"

"Pascal wants to talk to you," I said, "He believes you aren't lost, and I hope he's right."

Alexander grimaced. "If you see him, tell him I cared for him. Tell him I forgot myself when I pushed him away. I'm Sleep and he's Death. He knew his purpose all along."

I bent down and squeezed his hand. "You'll tell him, Alexander, when you see him again. Now, can you explain to us exactly what Ariston Day is attempting?"

"There's a wall," Alexander said. "The wall that separates the Empyrean from our world. Day believes he can bring the wall down now that he's inside. Believes he can unite the two halves and bring about the unmaking. He doesn't want a doorway anymore, you see. He wants it all to be of one piece. He intends to let this Paradise spill out into London like a disease. We thought we might live in something beautiful. But now that I've seen it, I know the Empyrean will bring blight. It will undo everything I love."

"How will he bring down the wall?" I asked.

Alexander shifted in the white grass. "He thinks the gods will do his bidding if they're sated. And there's something inside the wall—a mechanism that will help him bring it down, a machine."

"Where is it?" Maddy asked. "Where is the wall, Alexander?"

"Keep walking," he said. "The wall surrounds everything. You'll run into it eventually. That's how we found it."

Maddy put her shawl over him. Though it was not cold in the Empyrean, I was glad for her gesture. It didn't seem right to just leave him there to die.

"We have to move quickly," I said to her. "Whatever work Day is doing, he can't be allowed to finish."

Maddy and I made our way through the trees, trying to keep our skirts from catching on roots and bracken. No matter how far we walked, we seemed to make no progress. The landscape of the Empyrean was all the same—white trees and the odd glowing flowers. We didn't reach the wall. There seemed to *be* no wall.

Evening came, making me realize that the sky wasn't so much a sky as some kind of membrane that emitted light like the tulips. The membrane shifted its color to a dull painted dusk.

"Look there," Maddy said, pointing to a red coat in the underbrush.

We approached and found a Fetch who hadn't been as lucky as Alexander. The boy was nearly beheaded—a grisly piece of his spine protruded from his neck. There was another boy some ten yards away, hanging upside down from a tree over a pool of his own blood. He'd been drained like a slain deer.

Maddy turned her head. "Jane, how could Ariston Day do these things? These were his followers."

I thought of ancient priests and the rituals of sacrifice—the things men would do in an attempt to please their gods. Yet Ariston Day did not comprehend the gods of the Empyrean. He was slaughtering blindly, hoping for an answer to his prayer.

Maddy was the first to slow, one hand on the trunk of a tree, peering ahead into the dim forest. "Jane, I . . . how far have we traveled?"

"It seems like miles," I said. "But there's no true way of knowing. Space in the Empyrean feels different."

"How large can it be—this *forest*?"

I sensed that question was unanswerable, and I think Maddy knew this herself, as she did not press a second time. We rested at the base of a tree with thick roots that spread over the ground. There was the same absence of smell even when we were so close to the tree's bark.

"Go to sleep," I said. "I'll keep watch."

"Jane, when I told you I didn't think you were human, I didn't mean—"

"You meant it," I said. "We should speak the truth to each other here. And I don't even know if I *want* to be human anymore after all that's happened."

"Don't say that," she said. "We'll make our way back to London, find a way to carry on."

"Do you really believe that, Maddy?" I stared into the forest around us. "I've feared coming to this place all my life. I suppose because I knew that when I arrived, there would be no way to go back." I turned my attention to her again. "I'll find a way for you to return. You and Pascal, if he's here."

"You'll come with us," she said, taking my hand. "We'll find Nathan and we'll all go together."

I pulled my hand gently away and said, "When you took me from my hiding place at Stoke Morrow so many years ago, I thought I'd fallen into some dream. I didn't believe life could be so good. Now I realize I was right all along. I'm awake, Maddy. Now I'm awake."

She looked at me, searching, and I wondered how my face looked to her at that moment. It felt like an impenetrable surface. I was an idol and my skin was all of stone.

"Go to sleep," I said. "Dream of London."

CHAPTER 32

After Maddy closed her eyes, I watched the sky, wondering whether false stars would appear as night descended. But soon enough, I realized there would be no stars in the Empyrean. No painted moon. This was not some storied forest or sacred grove. It was neither a Heaven nor a Hell. We'd fallen into a secret place that was not earth or anything like it. As the woman in the Hall of the Red Star had said, this was the beautiful Unmade, the opposite of creation. In terms of Ariston Day's spiritual archaeology, this place (if it could be called a place at all) predated man and his religions. It was the pale beginning, a sprawling hush.

The evening sky, like the flowers, pulsed with a gentle and electric light, allowing me to see the spaces among the white trees. Ariston Day was out there somewhere, scrambling like a rat in the wall—the skin which surrounded and contained this place. He was an intruder who did not belong in this secret domain. I knew I had to find him before he could finish his work, before he could destroy the boundary between earth and Empyrean.

*   *   *

I was careful not to wake Maddy as I stood. I left her there in the heart of the white forest, turning back only once to look at her. The woman who'd been my friend for so many years was like a discarded doll, curled there among the roots of the tree. She was exhausted, having fought so hard to win Nathan back. My guilt and my anger were gone. After everything we'd done to each other, I knew her life would be better without me. I only hoped that I could get her safely back to London. She was still young. Years would pass, and this place would begin to seem as though she'd dreamed it. Even I might seem a vision from a dream—a shade dressed in red that appeared from time to time on the ridge of the Heath to stare down at her.

It was as I walked into the phosphorescent dark and pondered Maddy's future that I began to hear movement among the trees. Perhaps the presence of my old friend had been preventing me from truly opening my senses to the Empyrean. Maddy was the physical reminder of the girl I'd been.

Leaves rustled, and I saw the shadows of tall, long-limbed creatures appear. Like the forest, the creatures came into focus slowly, and I found I was not afraid. These were the white apes—the same that Nathan had seen on Malta, the ones I'd dreamed of after the death of my mother. Father said the gods were like animals, and he could not have known how correct he was. These were the old gods that had disappeared long ago, perhaps before even man had learned to write his history down, but they still hovered at the edge of human memory like the Red Goddess herself. They were striding creatures, some six feet in height with rough, whitish fur and pale orblike eyes that seemed electric—the color of the evening.

The white apes did not seem to notice me—or perhaps I simply did not surprise them. Was it possible they were already accustomed to my presence? I counted fifteen such creatures in my proximity alone, and I wondered how many more populated the forest. The tall god-apes continued their striding, restless perhaps because their home had been infiltrated. I found that I could sense their thoughts, just as I'd once sensed the souls of objects. I extended my talent toward them, and it felt as though I was running my hands over smooth marble.

The apes paused in their striding. They shuddered as I used my talent to stroke their thoughts, as if the act gave them pleasure. They knew me, and they called me by a name—speaking it in unison. I understood that the word they used could be loosely translated to mean "silence." But it was part of a lost vocabulary, some ancient tongue, and the translation was imprecise. The word meant more than "silence." It was also "home" and "peace" and "eternity." It was both the name of the apes' deity and the name for the place that surrounded them now. And in the music of this ineffable sound I saw the lineage of the goddess—all the avatars who spanned the course of history. These dark-eyed women ranged beyond number, and they were bathed in the deep glow of red starlight. The women were poised, waiting. They watched me with interest, wondering how I might proceed. I understood them to be my predecessors, echoes of the original goddess—each a piece of the Unnamed's primordial soul. And I was the next in their line.

Beyond these female figures, I saw a churning chaos—a sea of light that was both the beginning and the ending of all things. The music of the spheres rang out from this fiery realm, calling to me, charging every atom in my body. I allowed myself to be drawn toward that place of burning light, gliding over the avatars, who raised their faces to watch my passage.

It was in the glow of that great primordium that I saw something astonishing—a final vision: a vast and wild image of myself. Yet this image was not a mirror. What I saw in the chaos was Jane, the Goddess. Jane, the Queen. She was perhaps my future, an Über-Jane, as magnificent a woman as I had ever looked upon. I floated closer to her, and when her gaze fell upon me, I saw that her eyes were entirely white, like the bleached stone of an ancient ruin.

The goddess hovered there in amniotic suspension. Concentric rings rippled out from her body. She wore a mantle of crimson that expanded and contracted like a living organism, and woven in her hair were white lilies and oak blossoms. When she spread her arms, the mantle opened, and I saw that she was not made of flesh. Her skin was something finer—a substance that could neither wither nor die. Her body was composed of the same imperishable material as the trees of the Empyrean.

Somehow she *was* the Empyrean. Her body was the trees and the pale river and the flowers that burned. She was the silencing of souls, the pure one. The aether. And like this place, the goddess was eternal.

She extended her hand toward me.

I felt grateful and blessed. I reached out, feeling a thrill of excitement, wanting nothing more than to touch her perfect form. If I did, I knew I could forget all of my earthly sorrows, all of my pain. Everything that had happened with Maddy and Nathan would be swept away.

And just as the tips of our fingers were about to brush, I heard someone crying in the distance—a boy who was hurt. It was likely one of the Fetches, calling out for help as he was dying. Ariston Day was still murdering his followers in hopes of finding a spot in his so-called Paradise. I thought of Maddy alone in the forest. I thought of Pascal and even of Alexander. This wasn't a place for any of them—for any human being. I had to send them all away. To save them and save London.

The goddess did not care for any of them. She was alone in her aerie forever.

I drew my hand back, and the goddess closed, like a great eye, folding in upon herself, as visions do when they are ignored. And I felt such horror when I saw her go. I'd given up everything—lost my future to save the past.

I returned my attention to the god-apes, hoping to draw some further secret from them or even to bring the goddess back. I continued to touch their smooth thoughts, trying to access further memories, trying to find an edge to grab hold of. But there were no edges. The smooth interior of the apes went on forever. The more questions I posed, the more impenetrable the surfaces seemed. It was then I realized that not only was the smoothness *inside* of the apes, but it was outside too. I looked around, and there through the trees, I saw the wall that Alexander had described. I was stunned by its sudden manifestation. If it was made of stone, it was a single stone, unbroken by seam or mortar. I could not see the height of it because the trees blocked my view, but my sense was that the wall was a looming edifice that nearly scraped the false sky.

I pushed my way through the edge of the white forest and stood with my body touching the wall, feeling its cool surface with my hands. Like the trees and flowers, the wall did not seem quite real and was made of no substance that I recognized. I thought of how Alexander had called it a membrane or a skin, and I began to make my way along the perimeter, pressing myself against the smooth surface. At times, the space between trees and wall was so narrow I could hardly fit. All the while, the god-apes watched me with their strange and luminous eyes. Nathan had written that the white ape he encountered on Malta had eyes like dark holes bored into its skull, but here in the Empyrean, all the creatures' eyes were bright hollows filled with the same electric light that pulsed in the flowers and the sky.

I searched for some difference or seam in the surface of the wall—a door or a gate, some entry. And yet, I could not find that difference. I could only feel the wall ahead and the trees at my back. The sensation of being pressed against the wall drew me to a moment in my history, when Nathan, Maddy, and I lay on the stone floor of the ruin in my father's Roman folly. Our arms and legs were spread, as if making snow angels. We did not speak; instead, we closed our eyes, and in that moment we were a single soul, falling through time. We could not be separated from one another. None of us would ever be lost. Nothing came to an end.

Thinking of that impossible and long-ago time, I closed my eyes and guided myself along the wall only by touch, and after a few minutes of doing so, my palm tracked through something wet.

Instead of being pleased by this discovery of a change in texture, I was disgusted. The wall had been violated. Nothing was meant to remain here. And yet, I felt the substance left behind—tacky and wet. I wiped my hand on my dress. In the luminescent darkness of the Empyrean night, there was no true color, but from its smell, I knew the stuff. The smell was of a butcher shop. Blood had been spilled on the wall.

The blood ran in a smeary line, as if someone had been dragged, leaving this trail behind. And then I found the body crumpled on the ground. It was the tall freckled boy who'd given me the tour of the inner forest, the one who'd likely cut open Corydon Ulster's face. His red coat was torn, and there was an ugly wound in his chest. Unlike Alexander, this boy was dead, eyes rolled up in his skull, mouth open in final pain. Another of Day's sacrifices. The wound appeared fresh, and the body was still warm. I wondered if this was the boy I'd heard screaming while I was communing with the goddess. If so, Ariston Day had to be close at hand.

The white apes in the trees shuddered at the presence of the dead boy. I searched him, trying to find some sign of what had happened or what was happening within the wall. In his pocket was a miniature painting of a girl. She was dressed in colorless chiffon—a foolish child of nobility like this Fetch. There was nothing else. He was an empty boy, a vessel shattered.

It was near the discarded body that I finally found an indentation in the wall—a faint lip, which might indicate a doorway. I thrilled at the feeling of it. It was the opening I needed, and I'd already begun working my fingers around the indentation when someone whispered my name.

I nearly fell against the door and turned to see Pascal emerging from the tree line. He stood between two of the god-apes, oblivious to them. Pascal looked so small and fragile. He didn't belong in this cold place. He could not see the creatures, and that was all the better. I did not want him to have to suffer such distortions.

"Pascal," I said, so glad to know he was alive.

"Jane, I saw him," he replied, voice thick with emotion. I thought he meant he'd seen Alexander, lying brutalized and wounded. But continuing, he said, "Nathan Ashe, Jane. I've seen Nathan Ashe in the forest."

For a moment, the world around me collapsed to a single point. "Tell me," I said. "Where did you see him? How is he?"

"I awoke among the trees," he said. "I didn't know where I was and there was no one with me. I began calling for you because I thought you must be near, but there was no answer. I began to walk, thinking I would find someone, and then I saw a man ahead in the distance. He was shambling along through the forest, and at first I thought he was a Fetch, as he wore a tattered red coat. His hair was unkempt, and he looked terribly thin—a near skeleton. Then I saw the fur mantle, the one Alexander said they'd placed upon Nathan's shoulders when he'd played a stag in the provocation. I knew it had to be Nathan, yet I didn't call to him. His figure frightened me, Jane. It was as though I was looking not at my friend, but at a thin specter, a remnant. I followed, trying to remain as quiet as I could.

"Nathan walked until he reached a wide river, and I must say it was the most curious river I've ever seen. The whitish water did not flow. In fact, it was not water at all but some solid matter that only looked like water from a distance. Nathan knelt beside the river and tried to dip one frail cupped hand into the water to no avail. The river had a hard surface, just as I suspected. He grew angry at the stream, banging a fist against it. Then he stood to walk along the river and I followed. At a parting of the trees, Nathan entered the forest again. I did not have to walk far before I saw where he was going."

"And where was that?" I asked, barely able to breathe. It was difficult to think of our Nathan walking in this tomb of a place alone for nearly two months. What had he eaten? Surely he must have known enough about the strange hard water in the stream by this time to avoid it. Or had he fallen further into madness? Did he walk about and perpetually repeat these same activities in this pure place? I felt a terrible guilt again hearing what a wreck he was, and I remembered the pain I'd experienced at Mary-Thomas's séance—pain in my own stomach when she'd called to her son. There were the visions of the stag being devoured by the Red Goddess too. What happened on the night of Nathan's disappearance was now clear to me. It should have been clear all along. I was the Red Goddess and Nathan Ashe was the stag. Ariston Day said I'd pulled Nathan into the Empyrean, but in actuality, it was more like I'd devoured him. The soul of the Red Goddess had eaten the soul of the stag. Nathan had been the one to transmit the images of the goddess and the stag to me. For he had been concealed inside my own body all along.

"I can barely describe what happened next," Pascal said. "It was so awful. I'm having some difficulty *seeing* in this place, Jane. It's as if nothing here has substance. Things waver before my eyes like this is the ghost of a world."

"What do you believe you saw?" I asked.

"Nathan had built a sort of shelter among the trees, using the shirt he'd been wearing when he disappeared and the belt from his trousers. It was no sort of protection really, but one wouldn't need shelter here. Nathan sat in his tent and took out his pocket watch, opened it, and stared down at the clock face, as if the watch was some inscrutable puzzle to him. I must have shifted my weight, making a noise, because Nathan looked up—and Jane, his face was nearly unrecognizable. Nathan was deformed. His skin was partly white, and his brow was covered in white hair. He showed his teeth like some animal. I think he *was* part animal. Thank God he didn't see me. I ran from there as fast as I could, knowing I had to find you, knowing you would know what to do."

During Pascal's telling, I'd clenched my hands so tightly that I had to consciously work to unfasten my fingers from my palms. In the Empyrean, Nathan had started to become the white ape that inhabited him on Malta—the rider on his soul that had once punished Theodore de Baras. I had opened Nathan to such an experience, made such a horror possible. I wondered what widespread infection would come to earth if Day was able to complete his plan.

"Do you want me to take you to Nathan?" Pascal asked.

"I want you to stand back," I said, resolved. "I have something to take care of first."

Pascal did so without further question, and I put my hands against the smooth surface of the wall, feeling for the indentation and finding it again. I heard the white apes rustle behind me as I touched the outline of the door. The creatures willed me forward, as the objects in Mother's dressing room had once willed me to open her wardrobe. I wondered for a moment if the apes were excited or if they sought to warn me. Perhaps, on some level, Pascal heard them too because he said, "Jane, is it growing colder here? Is there a wind?"

I slid my hands along the edges of the door, looking for a latch. But there was nothing. And it was then that I realized I shouldn't be searching with my hands. I'd used my talent to find the wall; I needed to use it again to open the door. I closed my eyes, allowing my senses to slide along the surface. And then, yes, there was a handle on the door, as invisible to the naked eye as the god-apes in the forest were invisible to Pascal. I grasped the handle and turned it.

A passage opened, and Pascal moaned behind me. I tensed, fearing that Ariston Day might spring out, but there was only the cool dark ahead.

"What is it, Jane? Where does it lead?" Pascal asked.

"I don't know," I said. "But there's something I have to do in here."

Pascal followed me into the wall—good friend that he was—and I thought of Maddy in the forest, hoping she was still asleep and that she would not attempt to find me.

We found ourselves in what appeared to be a long hallway, so high that no ceiling was visible. It was an eerie place, filled with wooden machines from another time. Hand-twined rope connected the hulking contraptions to one another. Dust was thick on the machines, as if they had not been used in ages.

"Machines?" Pascal said. "But who put them here, Jane?"

"If I had to guess, I'd say these are no more machines than the forest out there is actually a forest. We're in the belly of a goddess," I said, not adding that I believed it to be my own belly. "I can't even begin to comprehend what they might mean."

The dark machines ran the length of the hall, falling away into shadow. To move around them, one had to skirt the perimeter, trying not to catch one's clothing on the odd edges. As we made our way deeper into the catacomb, I heard a subtle hissing, a quiet sound of pain.

"Where is that noise coming from?" I asked.

Pascal pointed toward a rather frightening machine covered in glistening hooks, and lying inside the contraption was a body in a red coat, chin against his breast. It looked like Nathan himself at first, crushed. The youth had a similar nose and long poet's hair, streaked with gore. The boy stared at me, still half-alive.

It wasn't Nathan, of course. It was the cruel-looking Fetch who'd brought the initial letter from Ariston Day to Stoke Morrow. He'd become another of Day's blood sacrifices. Looking at his body, mangled in the machine, I knew that this boy *was* Nathan as much as we were all Nathan. All of us had disappeared under the thrall of Day's will and been transformed by it.

The Fetch's blood had run into the gears of the machine, greasing them. Pascal and I watched as he closed his eyes and breathed his last breath.

"You won't be able to stop Ariston Day," Pascal said. "If he's committed such atrocities as this, he's so obviously mad. He'll harm you, Jane. I know he will."

"Go back into the woods, Pascal," I said firmly. "Find Maddy. She's sleeping beneath a tree not far from here. Keep her safe. And don't tell her about Nathan, not yet. I need to see what state he's in first."

"But what about you—in here all alone?"

"You don't need to worry about me," I said. "I'm the Doorway, remember?"

"No you're not," he said. "You're Jane Silverlake, a good friend of mine."

I hugged him to me. "Thank you, Pascal." But even as I said this, I could feel my power spinning outward, caressing the machines. I was so much more than the Doorway. I was all of this—the Empyrean itself. I was the cold goddess. If my friends hadn't come into my life, perhaps I would have remained that melancholy creature who walked in shadows, keeping balance between earth and aether merely by existing. But being drawn out of Stoke Morrow had changed me. The flesh and blood part of me had grown strong. I'd learned to love the world, to love the people around me. I'd become almost human for a time.

"Pascal," I called out. "I want you to do something more."

He turned back.

"When you find yourself in London again, you'll go to Stoke Morrow and tell my father that all is well. His daughter had to go, but she's fine."

"But, Jane—"

"You'll tell him I love him and that his house isn't haunted any-more. He won't ask questions. He'll understand."

Pascal bowed his head. "Of course, Saint Jane."

"Go to Maddy now. Help her find her way home and take care of her. She's going to need you."

As he left me, I gathered my strength, looking at the complex system of machines and thinking of the Psychomatic Dispensary in Piccadilly. I'd broken that dispensary and ended the show. Maybe I could break these machines too before it was too late.

CHAPTER 33

I walked on alone inside the wall and finally found Ariston Day there in a bleak alcove, fine suit wet with blood, hands stained with gore. He'd wiped his brow, smearing himself with the stuff, as he hovered over one of the wet machines. The body of the last Fetch lay at his feet, and I saw that it was Rafferty, poor Rafferty who'd been kind to me, who'd kissed me gently and asked to take me to dinner. Day had cut him open at the neck. The yellow-white of his clavicle was laid bare.

Day made a terrible keening sound as he worked at the machine, trying to move its frozen parts. He didn't notice me until I was nearly upon him. Perhaps it was my shadow that drew his attention, a moving image cast by the torches that he'd lit. Day looked up, and there was confusion on his long face, as if I could not possibly have come before he was finished with his work.

"Jane, my dear," he said—a ridiculous greeting considering he was covered in the blood of his minions. His ugly lips looked wet in the torchlight. Had he been drinking the blood? Did he imagine that such an act would satisfy the gods? He stepped away from the machine, resting his back against the smooth wall and sliding down into a kind of squat, hands held limp before him. His boot tip touched the head of dead Rafferty.

"What have you done?" I asked.

His expression was curious, a clenching of the jaw that tried to be a smile. "Failed," he said, "I suppose I have failed, and now I shall never give the world a Paradise."

"Can you really call this Paradise, even now that you can see it?" I said. "It certainly can't be the place you imagined. There might be a Paradise, Ariston, but it is elsewhere. This is a place of silence, never meant to be touched."

"It's a good place," he said. "It's the Garden."

"It only looks like a garden," I replied. "It's full of things that, should they come into contact with London, would destroy it."

He furrowed his brow. "I never meant to destroy anything. I meant to heal it."

"There's no return to the Garden," I said. "And there's something you've been too foolish to realize in all your research and experiments. Something I've known for a long time but could not quite articulate. I am the Red Goddess, Ariston. You were right about that. But what I know now is that the Red Goddess and the Empyrean are not distinct from one another. I am not the Doorway to this place. I am one with it. I am the Empyrean, and we are all inside of me, in the silent landscape of my heart."

Day watched me carefully as I spoke, calculating.

"What could you hope to achieve here?" I asked. "How could you hope to control this place when it so clearly belongs to me entirely? The only way to dissolve the walls would be—" I stopped myself, realizing what I was about to reveal. The only way to dissolve the Empyrean was to dissolve the goddess. My own flesh was the membrane—the wall.

But Day was already standing, the tool he'd used to murder the boys—a long crude piece of sharp metal that might have once been used to gut animals—gripped in his hand. He looked like some obscene and ridiculous priest, mouth open with longing.

I lowered my arms and let him come because I saw there was no other way. In my heart, I saw the stag—massive and horned—a dark creature running toward the forest deep, crashing through the bracken. Then it was gone.

Day shoved the tool into my stomach. The pain felt as though he was breaking me in half. I pictured my friends, my father, and the beautiful Heath where the trees were lush and true. I thought of myself walking with Maddy and Nathan, and as we slipped deeper into the lovely wilds, I pushed my body forward against the blade, driving it deeper.

Black stars opened across my field of vision, and I felt as if I was emptying like a pitcher. I could hear Day speaking some litany about the emergence of a new creation story. He said it began with the sacrifice of a god. "I should have known all along," he said. "I couldn't bring down the wall myself. I had to wait for you, Jane. The death of a god is necessary. And of course you came. You wanted to save your friends. Your heart has always gotten in the way of your power. And now we'll have the Paradise, you'll see."

I reached down and caught Day's hand, which still gripped the blade that was lodged inside me. With all my remaining strength, I forced the knife upward, making a long deep cut in my own skin. Black stars exploded around me, momentarily obscuring the interior of the wall. Pain seared through the very center of me, and I could taste blood in my mouth, could feel it rolling down my chin. I willed myself to remain conscious. To finish this.

"You think you know my secrets," I said to Day. "You think you understand the Empyrean. But you know nothing." I pulled the blade away from him and threw it aside. The jagged metal had left a wide cut in me, beginning near my navel and moving up toward my breasts.

I pressed my fingers into the cut and with great effort pulled back my flesh. Day stared into me. His was the horror of a priest who realized all his sermons were mistaken. Every word he'd spoken was proven untrue. I looked down into the cavity that I'd opened, and there I saw no organs or bones. I did not even see the white trees that had filled Mother Damnable. I was instead filled up with the universe itself, a bright and turning sphere of countless planets and stars. And beyond the universe was the beautiful Unmade where everything began and would end. I was the sum of all of this. The balance existed inside of me. And I saw that such a sense of the infinite was driving Ariston Day toward his own oblivion. He was so small compared to it.

The ape-gods were around us then. They'd filed in through the open door, and at that moment, they surpassed me to fall upon Ariston Day. He did not struggle. He only continued to stare at the center of me in the shifting void that surrounded the planets and the stars. I watched as the creatures pulled at Day's arms, forcing them backward until the joints in his shoulders popped. He howled in pain, begging for their mercy and then for my mercy. One of the white apes tore off Day's lower jaw and left him making a terrible airy moan, unable to form words. Another scooped out his eyes, one by one. By the time they were finished, Ariston Day's body looked like a pile of meat and bone lying before the machines.

And then the gods came to me, lifting me up just as I was no longer able to stand. They lifted my body with their bloodied white hands and carried me in silent procession out of the wall and into the quiet forest. They made no sound, but their soundlessness became a kind of song. The gods set my body on the wide white river that Pascal had described, and I found it was no longer still. The warm water carried me swiftly in its currents, and the folds of my skirts expanded in the white water. The warmth of it caressed the hole in me, soothing my pain.

Time moved differently on the river. Morning came to the Empyrean, and I saw Maddy and Pascal, walking together on the shore. They carried Alexander between them; his arms were slung around their shoulders. They did not see my body. Perhaps by that time I was already beneath the white waves, or perhaps like the gods, I was invisible to them. Around my friends, the Empyrean was dissolving—floating away like so much smoke. I could see the Crystal Palace reappearing. They would make it back to London. They would go home, and I found myself longing momentarily for their companionship, for my father, and even for the dark halls of Stoke Morrow, but the river bore me on.

Farther along, at a bend in the river, I saw Nathan Ashe crouched by the water. His flesh was withered and white, sprouting thick patches of hair. He looked at me when I passed like he understood the mystery of my procession better than he understood his own timepiece. He was one of them, the god-apes. Nature and supernature had collapsed within him. He knelt by the water's edge, dipped his hand into the white water, and drank a communion from it.

Like me, Nathan would stay.

There were others too on that pale shore—Mother Damnable dressed in red with a wide lace ruff around her neck. She'd been the witch of the Heath, but in the Empyrean she was resplendent. There too was the girl from Rome who'd suffered at the hands of Theodore de Baras. I could still see marks on her wrists from where he'd chained her, but here she was free. And then farther on was the Lady of Flowers, beautiful in red linen, holding out her hand in a sign of love. There were others too, so many, women whose names I did not know, but whom I understood entirely.

And finally when I reached the mouth of the great white river, I saw a lone woman, dark haired and pale. She wore a mantle of red starlight at her shoulders, and she gathered me from the waters and dried me with that garment. The woman held me in her arms, and I looked up into her face and saw it was the face that I'd known long ago.

Mother did not speak, for there at the edge of the river, we had no need for words.

Everything was known between us, then and always.

CHAPTER 34

I can see them all—the ones I loved. I watch their years spool out.
The case of the disappearance of Nathan Ashe was put to rest
by Inspector Vidocq, who made the unsubstantiated claim in his final
report that Ariston Day had murdered all of his Fetches, beginning
with Nathan. How Day disposed of the bodies was yet unknown. But
they were gone, all of them except for two—Corydon Ulster and Alexander Hartford. Ulster had been convalescing in the sick ward of
Bethlehem Royal after an accident on Hampstead Heath and claimed
that an angel dressed in red starlight had saved him from the fate
suffered by his compatriots. Vidocq reported that Ariston Day himself had simply disappeared, as he had in each of his previous incarnations—in County Sligo and Suffolk. The inspector warned that if
authorities were not vigilant, the madman would resurface under a
different name in a different city to gather the sons of wealthy men
and expose them to exploit and horror.

An empty plot was made for Nathan Ashe at Highgate Cemetery.
There was a marble bench beside the beautiful white monument
where Lady Ashe could sit and contemplate his life. The epitaph read
simply: LOVING SON, BELOVED FRIEND. My own father went to sit with
her on certain afternoons. She would ask if he intended to make a
memorial for his daughter, Jane, who'd disappeared along with the

poor misguided followers of Ariston Day. Father told her softly that there would be no piece of stone for Jane. She was everywhere around him and inside of him, his precious girl. No stone could hold her essence. And yet Father did take pause at the statues that were cropping up all over London—statues of a woman with her head bowed low who held a gathering of flowers in her hands.

Maddy gave birth to a daughter and called her Jane Ashford Lee. Although Nathan isn't with her, she keeps a picture of him, taken with her Father's daguerreotype machine, on the mantel above her fire. In the picture, he looks young and strong, as though he'll never die.

From time to time, Nathan comes to sit with me in a glen of the white forest. I spread out over him like a red sky, now more an essence than a girl. He no longer looks like the young man he once was—the boy in the daguerreotype. He's the same as all the other white creatures who walk the Empyrean, except there is something different in his eyes. Something that gives him away every time.

We watched the christening of Maddy's child together. There were so many flowers at the baptismal font in the small chapel (maiden pink and feverfew, harebell and yarrow), and Maddy could find no one who might tell her where they'd all come from. The flowers had simply appeared. *As if sent from the Lord himself,* said the sweet-faced girl who kept the chapel clean.

Maddy knew it was not God who'd sent them, at least no sort of god anyone imagined. She looked toward the statue of the Virgin that stood near the altar, studying its eyes, perhaps waiting for them to move. When the statue proved to be nothing more than a piece of stone, Maddy glanced away, returning her attention to the child and her friends. Gathered at the chapel for the christening were Pascal and Alexander, Eusapia Lee and my own father, and even Lord and Lady Ashe. All of them watched with joy as Jane Ashford Lee reached for the flowers that surrounded her. She cried out until the priest put a daffodil in her hand, and she gripped it as if she'd never let go. All of London, every building and every object within that city of wonders, shuddered at the force of her grip. Even the Empyrean shook for a time. Yet the child herself was silent and lovely upon the earth.

AUTHOR'S NOTE

The Crystal Palace was originally erected in Hyde Park as part of London's Great Exhibition. Subsequently, the structure was moved to Sydenham Hill. For the purposes of this novel, I have retained the Hyde Park location.

ACKNOWLEDGMENTS

My gratitude to Sally Kim, whose thoughtful editing helped bring this book to life, and to my agent, Eleanor Jackson, who believed in me and provided invaluable guidance at every turn. I'd also like to thank the entire team at Touchstone who worked tirelessly on this book. For thoughts on the manuscript and general encouragement, I'd like to thank Brian Leung, Scott Blindauer, David Lazar, Colin Meldrum, Ryan Hamlin, Garnett Kilberg Cohen, Jennie Fauls, Gabriel Blackwell, Chrissy Kolaya, Christine Sneed, and Cora Jacobs. Thank you to my family for all their love and support, especially to my mother, Denise, and my father, Michael. And finally, thank you to Chris Breier for listening, commenting, and providing affection.

ABOUT THE AUTHOR

Adam McOmber is the author of a collection of short stories, *This New & Poisonous Air*. He teaches literature and creative writing at Columbia College Chicago.